MW00748754

Seeing the Light

a Marie Jenner
mystery

E. C. Bell

Seeing the Light

a Marie Jenner
mystery

E. C. Bell

TYCHE BOOKS LTD.

Seeing the Light

Published by Tyche Books Ltd.
www.TycheBooks.com

Copyright © 2014 Eileen Bell
First Tyche Books Ltd Edition 2014

Print ISBN: 978-1-928025-08-5
Ebook ISBN: 978-1-928025-13-9

Cover Art by Guillem Mari
Cover Layout by Lucia Starkey
Interior Layout by Ryah Deines
Editorial by M. L. D. Curelas

Author photograph by Shelby Deep Photography

All rights reserved. No part of this book may be reproduced or transmitted in any form or by any means, electronic or mechanical, including photocopying, recording or by any information storage & retrieval system, without written permission from the copyright holder, except for the inclusion of brief quotations in a review.

The publisher does not have any control over and does not assume any responsibility for author or third party websites or their content.

This is a work of fiction. All of the characters, organizations and events portrayed in this story are either the product of the author's imagination or are used fictitiously.

Any resemblance to persons living or dead would be really cool, but is purely coincidental.

Contents

Dedication

This book is dedicated to my husband, Harold—who believed in me even when I didn't.

Farley:
My Death and What Came After

That "walking into the white light" thing is crap. The only light I saw was the electricity arcing around me as I jerked to the floor like I was doing the funky chicken.

Then everything went black.

Not white. Black.

I woke up and thought I'd been tossed clear until I saw my body by the electrical panel, still doing its death dance as the last of the current rattled through it.

Tendrils of smoke curled up from the hair, and that's when I went crazy. Crying and trying to crawl back to myself, I did all that as I watched my body disconnect and ooze to the floor like a half-cooked chicken. A half-cooked funky chicken.

I'm hilarious.

When I pulled myself together, I went over to see if I could figure out what had happened. My free hand was in my pocket, though, so the current hadn't used that route, and for a while I couldn't see anything out of place. Other than the fact I was dead, of course, I really thought I hadn't done anything wrong. Then I saw my sock.

Okay, so I'm supposed to wear work boots, but it was as hot as the hubs of hell down in that basement in the summer, so I was wearing sandals and socks. And there was water. Why hadn't I noticed the water? It looked like I'd been standing in a river, for Christ's sake.

My sock had wicked the water up to my foot. Obviously, when I touched the hot wire, the electricity searched for the quickest way to ground. That had been through me, to my wet foot, and out. The result had been fireworks and me getting tossed out of my body like a sack of potatoes off the back of a truck.

Son of a bitch. If I could have, I would have moved the body, so nobody else could see the mistake I'd made. I couldn't. I could only stand and glare at the water that soaked into my clothes and put out my hair with a hiss and a small sigh. Or maybe the sigh came from me. Who the hell knew for sure.

The cops came and I made an ass of myself trying to get their attention, but by then it was beginning to sink in. I wasn't getting back into the old skin sack again. And beneath the crying and wailing and gnashing of teeth, I was relieved. This life was finally done, and I could get on with whatever came next.

Here's the kicker, though. When the paramedics wheeled my body out, I couldn't follow. I hit that open doorway like it was a thick pane of glass and bounced back about a foot. All I could do was watch as they loaded my body into the ambulance and drove away.

There were no sirens. They don't use sirens for the dead.

Stage One
Getting to Why

Marie:
The Interview

Here's the way it was supposed to work. I was supposed to put on my second best dress and the one pair of pantyhose that didn't have a hole and go to the Palais Office Building, a five story red brick holdover from the 1920s hidden away on a nice side street in downtown Edmonton, for a job interview. I was supposed to wow my potential new boss, Mr. Don Latterson, and I was supposed to get that secretary slash receptionist job. And then my life was supposed to get better.

It didn't go that way. Of course.

There was only one other interviewee waiting in the small reception area in the office of Don Latterson's import export business, called, not too imaginatively, Latterson's Import Export.

"Wish me luck," she said, when Mr. Latterson silently hooked his finger at her, calling her into his office.

"Good luck," I said. I didn't mean it. I wanted the job for myself, after all.

When she ran out, sobbing, three minutes into her interview, I felt guilty, like I'd somehow jinxed her. I also felt relief. Maybe I had a real shot at the job.

It wasn't a lock, of course, because sometimes my big mouth gets me into trouble, but things were looking up.

Don Latterson stepped out of his office. He was in his forties and starting to run to fat. His hair, what little that was left if you don't count the absolutely atrocious comb-over, was brown streaked with gray, and his blue eyes looked parboiled, like he'd drunk his lunch instead of eating it.

"Marie Jenner?" he asked.

I nodded.

He hooked his finger at me, and I followed him into the office, shutting the door behind me. Then I waited for him to offer me a seat so that the interview could begin.

He did not do that. He sat down himself and stared at me until I felt acutely uncomfortable, and then pointed at an electric typewriter sitting on a small table by his desk.

"Do you know what that is?" he asked.

I wondered if there was some trick to the question. "An electric typewriter?" I finally asked.

"It is not just an electric typewriter." He ran his fingers over the plastic cover lovingly. "It is the Selectric II, the best electric typewriter ever made. Do you know how to use it?"

I was sure I'd seen a computer on the desk out in the reception area. Did he actually expect me to type stuff on one of these?

Whatever. He's the potential boss.

"Yes, I do," I said. "Absolutely."

It was at that moment that I felt cold air wash over me. I turned around, thinking I hadn't latched the door properly. That's when I saw the ghost.

He stood half in and half out the closed door, staring at me. Stupid me, I stared back.

I knew better than to make eye contact. Dead's dead and better left alone, but he caught me off guard.

"Can you see me?" the ghost asked, looking just about as shocked as I felt.

"Oh no," I whispered. He wasn't just dead. He was aware that he was dead. Good grief, why had I made eye contact?

"Holy shit, you can see me!" the ghost cried.

I shook my head, a completely useless thing to do, because it just proved beyond a shadow of a doubt that I could, in fact, see him. Then Mr. Latterson spoke up. He didn't sound happy.

"What did you say?" he barked. "Turn around and answer me this instant."

Oh lord. I needed to regroup, and I couldn't do it in front of my potential boss.

"Can you excuse me for just one moment?" I asked. Without waiting for his answer, I left his office, shutting the door in his very surprised face.

I heard the ghost follow me, and in the reception area he actually started dancing. I closed my eyes for a second, in a vain attempt to compose myself. He couldn't have picked a worse time to make his appearance, and here he was, dancing around like an idiot or something. I had to get hold of the situation, and I had about two seconds to do it.

"You have to go away," I said.

He stared at me, caught in mid-caper. "What?"

"You have to go away!" I yelled, and then turned toward Mr. Latterson's closed door, wondering whether he'd heard me. He probably had. He was probably in the process of tearing up my resume.

My throat thickened with quick tears. This would have been a good job. A really good job.

"You won't get the job if you cry," the ghost said.

"Like I want it now," I muttered.

I walked to the door leading to the hallway, intending to leave, when I thought about my crappy job at the Yellowhead Cab Company. I had to get away from my boss, Gerald the Tyrant and paycheques that never quite paid all the bills. Not all in the same month, anyhow.

I thought about my mom. She was sick, and she was counting on me.

I needed this job. Even with a ghost.

"How long?" I asked.

The dead guy looked confused. "What do you mean?"

"How long have you been dead?"

If it was just a couple of days, there was a good chance he'd move on all by himself. I wouldn't have to do a thing.

"Oh." He took a deep breath, even though he didn't need to do that anymore, and I could see he'd been holding in his stomach. I tried not to roll my eyes. Men.

"Six—no, seven days. I think."

My heart sank. Seven days. That was almost too long. He might be stuck.

"How is it you can see me?" he asked. "Nobody else can."

"I've been able to see all of you since I was little." I shook my head. There was no time for small talk. "Listen—"

"Farley," he said, and smiled at me, looking pathetically happy. "My name is Farley Hewitt. And you are?"

"Marie," I said quickly, knowing this was wrong too. I felt like I was in a car crash I couldn't stop. "Farley, I can't finish the interview with you in the room. You're distracting, know what I mean?"

He nodded eagerly. It was getting pathetic. Almost as pathetic as me acting like I still had a chance at this job.

"So, leave. Please. If I get the job, I'll be here tomorrow." I wasn't getting the job. I already knew that, and felt the sigh come up from the bottom of my soul. "We can talk then."

"All right. Sounds good. Great."

As he headed for the door that led to the hallway, I realized I had no idea what I was going to say to the living man standing on the other side of the door. I must have made a noise—probably a sob, I was feeling that desperate—and the ghost turned back to me.

"What's wrong?"

"I can't think of one thing to say to Mr. Latterson that would explain why I ran out of his office in the middle of my interview." My throat tightened again, dangerously. "I'm never going to get this job."

Farley pointed at the desk behind us. "Tell him you thought you heard the phone ringing out here. He just got this system and tried to set it up himself. It won't ring in his office. He screwed it up."

I recognized the phone system sitting on the desk. It was the little brother version of the one I used at the Yellowhead Cab Company, the job I was desperate to leave. I knew what Mr. Latterson had done wrong—what everybody did wrong when they tried to set these things up on their own. I touched a few buttons and my heart quit beating so trip hammer hard. It might work.

I nodded at the ghost, to thank him for the help. Then I threw my shoulders back, slapped the smile on my face, and opened the door to Mr. Latterson's office.

Fixing that phone saved my interview. Mr. Latterson was so

impressed when I made it ring that he hired me on the spot.

"Welcome on board," he said. "You start tomorrow morning. Eight sharp."

Then he pointed at the door and said, "Get out."

So, I left.

I had the job of my dreams. I also had a ghost. And the ghost got me the job. What was I going to do?

I didn't want another ghost in my life. They are trouble. Just ask my mom.

She sees ghosts, too. In fact, she does more than see them. She helps them move through the three phases of acceptance to the next plane of existence. She seems to think that I could do the same, if I just tried.

I wasn't interested in any of that. I'd seen what it did to my mom. I'd seen what it had done to her life—and to mine. I didn't want to have a life like hers.

I wanted to be normal.

I stood outside the Latterson Import Export office, trying to decide whether or not to walk back in and turn down the job, when Farley oozed through the door, grinning like a Cheshire cat.

"Did you get it?" he asked.

"You were spying on me, weren't you?"

"Well, yeah," he said, sheepishly. "Just wanted to stick around, make sure you didn't need any more help. The phone trick—it worked, didn't it?"

"Yes," I sighed. "It did."

"So, now you owe me. Get me out so I can prove my death wasn't an accident," he said. "I have to prove the idiot cops wrong."

It took all my control to keep from running out of the building, screaming. Farley's death was an accident. An accident!

Even Mom hated working with the dead who die accidentally. They seem to hang on to this plane harder than any other spirit. They don't want to believe that something stupid they did led to their own demise.

"Well?" Farley asked. "You gonna help me or what?"

I stood staring at him, my mouth gaping as I tried desperately to think of something, anything that would get me out of this situation. I couldn't help a ghost who'd died accidentally. Heck, I couldn't help a ghost at all. My mom could. Not me.

Walk out, a little voice in my head cried. *Before you get in too deep. Walk out and never come back.*

I took a deep breath, ready to tell Farley I couldn't help him, when the cutest guy I'd ever seen in my life walked right through Farley and up to me.

Farley screamed as he exploded in fragments of mist and ecto goo. My nerves were so shot from the interview that I screamed too.

"Are you all right?" the cute guy asked, his face concerned. "I thought you saw me."

"You son of a bitch!" Farley yelled. He pulled himself together and took several hugely ineffectual punches at the cute guy's head. "How dare you walk through me like I'm not even here!"

"I'm fine," I said, trying desperately to ignore Farley, who looked like he was ready to blow a gasket. "You just surprised me."

"So, what are you doing here?" the cute guy asked. He smiled, but it didn't quite touch his eyes.

He was cute in that tall, dark and handsome, way that I always found too attractive. He was six foot four, at least, and his hair wasn't just dark brown, it was nearly black. Same with his eye lashes, which were unbelievably long and thick. And his eyes. So blue, I couldn't look away.

See? Tall, dark, and handsome.

I tried to smile nonchalantly, wishing Farley would shut up for a second so I could think. "I was here for an interview. Mr. Latterson hired me. I'm supposed to start tomorrow."

His smile disappeared. "Don Latterson?" he asked. "What are you doing for him?"

"What are you, a cop?" I snapped. Cute's cute, but I didn't need the third degree.

"No," he said, and had the good grace to look embarrassed. "Sorry."

"That's okay," I replied, embarrassed myself for overreacting. "I'm Mr. Latterson's new receptionist." I stuck out my hand. "Marie Jenner."

He smiled. "I'm James," he said, and shook my hand. "James Lavall."

A hand shake should be perfunctory. Three shakes, no more. Ours went on a lot longer than that. And I was back staring into his blue eyes. They were mesmerizing.

Farley picked that moment to start sobbing, his hands over his face.

"I'm not here," he cried. "Someone killed me, I'm not here anymore, and that son of a bitch took my job." He looked at me, pain and grief etched into his face. "Help me prove it. Please. You're my only hope."

I pulled my hand from James', with difficulty. "I should get going," I said. "Places to be, and all that."

Then I half-turned, so I was facing Farley. "I'll see you tomorrow," I said. He nodded, still sobbing, and I took a giant step sideways, so I wouldn't have to step into him. Of course, this put me really close to James. Of course, James smelled as good as he looked.

Once I was finally away from them, I ran around the corner to the stairs. As the exit door sighed shut, I heard both of them say, "I'll be waiting for you."

Good grief.

Marie:
So Now What?

I had to hurry to get to the Yellowhead Cab Company job on time. I made it with two minutes to spare, and sat down at the desk I shared with Jasmine, the day dispatcher and one of my best friends.

"Did you get the job?" she whispered, glancing over her shoulder for our boss, Gerald the Tyrant.

"Yes," I sighed, and pulled the headset on.

"Excellent." She smiled. "So are you quitting tonight? Maybe I should stay, just to watch."

"I'm not going to quit." I sighed again and sat down.

"Why not?" Even though her three kids were already on the bus heading for home, she put her purse on the desk top and stared at me. "What's wrong?"

"I don't know if I can handle the job," I said. "I think I should hang on to this one until I'm sure."

It had nothing to do with handling the job. It had to do with Farley, the ghost. However, Jasmine didn't know about my problems with ghosts. She knew about Arnie Stillwell, my stupid stalkery ex-boyfriend, and she knew about my mother being sick. But the ghost issue—nope.

She frowned, and I knew my weak excuse wasn't convincing her. It wouldn't have convinced me.

"That's too bad," she finally said. What she meant was, "Tell me exactly what you mean by that."

For a second I wished I could, but I didn't open my mouth. Seeing ghosts made me too weird, and I didn't have so many friends that I could scare the good ones off with the truth.

"You're going to be late," I finally said. "Say hi to the kids for me."

She looked at her watch, gasped, and scooped up her purse. "We are going to talk soon," she said. "I want details." And then she was gone.

I sighed again, knowing I was being too dramatic and not having the strength to stop. I sat down, hitting the first lit button on the phone as I did so.

"Yellowhead Cabs." I rang the words out in that sing song voice every dispatcher in every office in the world affects. "How can I help you?"

My replacement was late, of course, so I didn't get home until nearly 4 a.m.. I made sure I opened the door to my apartment very slowly, because sometimes the difference in air pressure made Sally—the drug addict who died in my apartment a month before I rented it, and who I did NOT see before I signed the stupid lease—hysterical. I wanted no part of her histrionics. I just wanted sleep.

I pulled my cell phone from my pocket, so I could charge it. I had to charge the stupid thing every night because it was ready to die. I knew I needed to get a new one. I couldn't afford it. Just one more thing I couldn't afford.

The red light blinked as I put in the charger. A voice mail message. At first, my stomach clenched. It couldn't be Arnie. He didn't have my cell phone number—at least I was pretty sure he didn't. Hoped he didn't. Prayed quite regularly that he didn't. It couldn't be him.

Maybe it was another job offer. I crossed my fingers. Maybe I could just let the receptionist job—and Farley—go. When I looked down at the number, I saw it was from my mother.

"Oh Mom, what do you want?"

I pressed the button and heard Mom's breathless, "Marie, are you there, girl?" followed by the sharp hacking cough that sounded so horrible—so final—that I pulled the phone away from my ear.

I didn't want to listen anymore. Really, all I wanted to do was stop the message. I was sure I didn't want to hear what she had to say.

The coughing seemed to take forever, until finally, Mom was able to speak. I was right. I didn't want to hear that message.

She needed money. She didn't want to say it, and she knew I wouldn't want to hear it, but that was the gist of her message. Apparently, Ramona, my oldest sister, wasn't able to help out as much as she'd said she would, and if I could help, just a little, Mom would be eternally grateful.

The message finally ended, and I thought about the thirteen dollars in my bank account. I'd be paid in two days from my cab job, but I had to cover rent, plus some of my bills. If I was going to help Mom, I'd have to keep this new job, at least for a while.

After that, sleep eluded me.

It wasn't Mom's money problem keeping me awake, though. It was the interview. The interview, and meeting Farley. Interacting with him. Watching him go from happy as heck to crying like a baby, and begging me to help him.

After an hour of flipping and flopping, I got out of bed and went to my front closet. I pulled the big pile of newspapers I had stacked inside it onto the floor and plunked down beside them, preparing to go through them, one by one. Usually I looked for jobs, checked the obits, and read the comics. This time I was looking for an article about Farley's death.

He said he'd died six or seven days before, so I started with the ones published the week prior, perusing them as quickly and thoroughly as I could.

"He said he was killed, so it has to be in here somewhere," I muttered, pulling out another paper from the pile and flipping through the pages. "There has to be something."

There was nothing about him on the front page, or even on the front page of the local section. I finally found an article, three brief paragraphs, two pages from the end and way below the fold, entitled "Local Man Accidentally Electrocutes Self". A small photo of Farley, either a passport or booking photo, accompanied the article.

"Dammit," I muttered, and ripped out the article, ramming it into my purse. Why hadn't I seen it before the interview? If I had,

I never would have gone. Never in a million years.

As I settled back into bed, Sally wandered in through the wall of the closet and sat down on the living room floor, aiming an invisible remote control at an equally invisible television set. I ignored her, because she was unaware that I was even there. She was reliving the last hours of her life, as she did every morning. I had two more hours before she started screaming.

The dead are everywhere, I thought as I pulled my blankets closer to my chin, and closed my eyes. Sometimes it feels like there's no way to get away from them. No way at all.

Sally, sitting approximately where she'd died, moaned gently, like the wind through leafless branches, lulling me to sleep.

Farley:
Death's Good When You
Have Someone to Talk to

What a fucking relief! Cute little Marie Jenner had seen me, talked to me. I wasn't alone, anymore.

She seemed bright. She figured out the telephone snafu quick enough to win that job, anyhow. I bet she'll be able to help me figure out what the hell happened to me. Because, for the life of me, I can't remember how I died.

I needed to remember. In fact, it was vital that I remember.

So, as happy as I was to have someone to talk to, I really needed to have her help me figure out how I died. Just as long as it wasn't an accident.

That would not stand.

And if she couldn't do that, I hoped she'd at least be able to figure out how I could get out of the building. I mean, I love the old girl, but even a ghost needs a day off from work.

Right?

Marie:
First Day of Work Exceeding Expectations. Almost.

I called my mom first thing in the morning, and managed to pick a fight with her about Ramona and her money issues. Nice, huh? No, not really. Worse, fighting with her about money meant there was no way in the world I was talking to her about another ghost, and on top of everything else, I almost missed the last bus to work.

I hoped this wasn't setting the stage for the rest of the day, but when I arrived at the Palais, Farley wasn't waiting for me at the front entrance. I was as surprised as I was pleased. I would have bet a rather large amount of money that he would have been.

He'll be waiting in Mr. Latterson's office, I thought, and trudged up the stairs. He wasn't.

That's when the day started to brighten appreciably. Maybe he'd moved on during the night.

I settled my purse under my new desk, and took off my sweater, hanging it over the back of my new chair. They weren't just new to me. Both the desk and the chair looked like they'd never been used before. I caressed the top of the desk. It felt like satin compared to the sticky plastic topped one I shared with Jasmine at Yellowhead Cab. If the ghost had actually moved on,

I could get used to this.

I jumped as Mr. Latterson's office door swung open and he walked into the reception area. He looked pointedly at his watch and frowned, even though I was ten minutes early.

"Good morning," I said, and smiled. "I want to thank you again for hiring me."

He pointed at the coffee machine. "Coffee. Black with three sugars. First appointment in fifteen minutes. Let me know when he arrives."

He stared at me, as though waiting for me to say anything that would give him the opportunity to yell. I kept my mouth shut until he wheeled back into his office, slamming the door shut behind him.

Wow. Nasty. Almost as bad as Gerald the Tyrant. I hoped the coffee was going to help.

I opened a cupboard or two, searching for and finding the coffee and filters. It only took a moment for me to get the Bunn started and as the coffee brewed, I found the cups. The machine was fast, and in a couple of minutes I had two cups of steaming coffee sitting on the counter.

I spooned sugar liberally into one, then picked it up and walked to Mr. Latterson's door. I knocked, entering when he bellowed something I could not understand.

He was on the phone. "Yes," he said. "Yes, Mr. Carruthers, I'm all set up."

As I walked his coffee to him, he glowered and covered the receiver. I could still hear Mr. Carruthers, whoever he was, yakking into Mr. Latterson's ear. I set the cup on the desk.

"Do you need anything else?" I asked.

He shook his head, but after he sipped the coffee, he half-smiled and mouthed thanks.

"You're welcome," I whispered, and backed out of his office, quietly closing the door behind me.

That was much nicer than Gerald had ever been to me. That I could definitely get used to.

Mr. Latterson's appointment showed up, fifteen minutes late. He was a guy about my age, and good looking, in that greasy snake way that can make your skin crawl if you get too close to him. He leaned over my desk, as if hoping to catch a glimpse of my breasts. His aftershave wafted over me in waves so thick I wished it was possible to open the window a crack.

"So, what do we have here?" he asked.

"Are you here to see Mr. Latterson?" I pulled away from his eyes and his overwhelming aftershave, trying to keep a smile on my face.

"Yep. Tell him Raymond is here."

"Last name?"

He smiled. "He knows who I am."

I wanted to snap, "Just tell me your last name so I don't have to hurt you," but I smiled, instead. "The problem is I don't know you," I said, voice like honey. I'm not kidding, positively like honey. "So, please, just tell me your last name."

"All right," he replied, as though he was doing me the biggest favour in the world. "The name's Raymond Jackson."

"Thanks, Raymond Jackson," I said, and smiled at him, hoping it looked at least half-real. "Please have a seat." I pointed to the far wall where three chairs and a small coffee table were nestled. "I'll let him know."

"I'm good here," he said, and parked his left butt cheek on the edge of my brand new desk. Trying to keep the smile on my face, I picked up the receiver and let Mr. Latterson know Raymond had arrived.

It didn't take him long to burst out of his office, looking as angry as he had before I'd given him his coffee.

"You're late," he growled at Raymond, who shriveled before my eyes. "You know how important this meeting is."

"Sorry," Raymond said, and hung his head.

"Sorry's not good enough, boy," Latterson pointed at the door. "Let's go."

"What would you like me to do while you're out, Mr. Latterson?" I asked.

He stared at me like he couldn't quite remember who I was or why I was there.

"Get the mail," he finally said. "Don't open it. And stay out of my office. Going in there when I'm not here is verboten. Verboten. You got that?"

"Yes," I said. "Verboten. Got it."

The door slammed shut, and I was alone. Or I thought I was, for about a second.

"Macho Don's a real dick, isn't he?"

Farley's voice preceded him through the door of the small closet next to the front door of the office. He'd obviously been hiding in there until I was alone.

"Hi Farley," I said, hoping I didn't sound as disappointed as I felt.

He didn't answer, he didn't smile, and he wasn't dancing any more. In fact, he looked kind of horrible.

"Did you have a bad night?" I asked.

"You know what I miss?" He walked to the front of my desk and leaned into it as though he couldn't stand upright any more. "I really miss beer. Especially the first one of the night. And televised poker games. They're pretty entertaining—or they were, when I had enough beer." He sighed, deeply and melodramatically.

Oh.

"That sounds nice," I said, even though it didn't.

"And taking a crap," he said. "I miss that, too."

"Farley!" I giggled and gasped at the same time, sounding like I was twelve years old. Not the best way to handle a ghost having a crisis. Luckily he was still ignoring me.

"It was the most satisfying bodily function I had left." He sighed again. "I cried like a baby for two days when I realized I wasn't going to be able to take a crap ever again."

"Farley—" I said again, trying to sound more adult. Then I stopped. I had no idea whether what he was doing was normal or not. Maybe I needed to let him talk this kind of stuff out.

But really? Drinking beer and going to the bathroom were the two things he missed? Really?

He glanced at me. "Ever again sounds like a hell of a long time, doesn't it?"

"Yes, it does," I replied.

"When my wife took our kid and left, my life became this blur of sameness, know what I mean? I worked, I ate take out, I drank beer and watched TV. When I drank enough beer, I'd fall asleep until I could go to work the next day. Taking a crap was the high point of my day." He grinned, without one drop of humor in it. "No wonder I miss it."

"Farley," I said, determined to get control of the conversation this time, for sure. "We need to talk about how to move you—"

"Move me out?" he said, his smile back, frantic, and a teeny bit scary. "Oh man, that would be great—"

"Out of what?" I asked, then shook my head. He was not hijacking this conversation again. "No, I mean moving you on."

"On?" A frown formed between his eyebrows and leaked to his mouth, pulling the corners down so that he looked angry and bitter and old. Definitely old. "On? What the hell does that mean?"

"It means moving you from this plane of existence to the next," I said, my voice going high and tight. I took a breath and blew it out to calm myself. "That's what you need to do. And I should be able to help you."

I hoped.

The frown deepened. "Are you talking about heaven and hell?"

"No. Yes." I sighed impatiently. "Sort of. It all depends on what you believe."

His mouth worked. "Well, forget it. I'm not doing that."

"But you have to," I said.

"Why?"

I stared at him, flummoxed. I couldn't exactly tell him he needed to move on so I could enjoy my new job, now could I? No, I couldn't. And I really didn't have a better reason at the moment. I was pretty sure Mom had mentioned the "why" of moving on to me at some point, but mostly what I remembered were the fights.

"Just because," I finally said. "All will be revealed."

All will be revealed? Holy crow, now I was sounding like a fake gypsy soothsayer at a carnival or something.

He stared at me for a long moment as though he was thinking exactly the same thing, and then shook his head. "I don't care if all will be revealed," he said. "I told you I just want to find a way through the barrier thing holding me in this building."

"A barrier?"

"Yeah."

"Wow."

I didn't remember him saying anything about a barrier holding him in the building. But then, I'd kind of freaked out about the whole "accidental death" thing, so maybe I'd blocked it.

What I did know was, my mother had never mentioned dealing with anything like that. She'd talked about ghosts, those who were aware, preferring—or feeling compelled—to stay close to their place of death. They could leave, but if they lost focus (Mom's words) they snapped back to the place where they died. Sometimes they attached to a person rather than a place. That happened to Mom a lot, and it was messy. Ghosts ended up following her everywhere. Even the bathroom. However, I was certain she'd never talked about any of them being held in a place by a barrier.

I decided to be up front with Farley about this, because, honestly, I couldn't even figure out how to fake it.

"I'm not sure how to do that."

"Oh." His features tightened. "So, I'm stuck in here."

"I guess so."

I desperately tried to remember what else Mom had told me, hoping for something that would calm him down. Nothing came. What was I going to do?

"Okay, so you can't get me out," Farley said. "Good enough. Can you help me figure out who killed me, then?" His eyes brightened and he leaned forward. "You could do that, right?"

Oh. My answer to this particular question wasn't going to calm him down. Probably the exact opposite.

"I don't think anyone killed you, Farley." I reached into my purse and pulled out the newspaper article I'd found. "It says here the police think your death was an accident."

"I know," he barked. "I told you that. I also told you they're wrong!" He shoved at the paper on the desk, growling when his hand skidded through it without moving one sheet. "That would have meant me screwing up somehow, and I didn't screw up . . . at least I don't think I did. I really don't remember too much about the actual event. But I was always careful—"

"You can't remember your death?" I felt my heart drop into my shoes. Literally. I could feel it, beating away, in my stupid shoes. This was so much worse than him being trapped in the building.

He shook his head and snuffled, still perched on the edge of my desk. "All I get is dead air when I try to remember the accident, and two whole days before. There's something—I'm sure there is—but I can't for the life of me remember what."

He had to remember what happened to him. Mom had been very clear on that.

24

"It's up to us to help them work through the fog to the light," she'd said. "To the light and through."

Memory loss meant Farley was stuck in the fog. It explained why he hadn't yet moved on. It also meant I was going to spend a bunch more time dealing with him, doing this.

"Do you think I can't remember because I was electrocuted?" he asked.

"Maybe. I don't know." I felt like crying. He was stuck. And I was stuck with him.

"Well, what about me being dead? Does that screw with memory?"

"No." I shook my head. "Not usually."

"Well, there has to be a reason I can't remember. Right?"

Right. Probably something traumatic. Something he really didn't want to remember.

"You said someone killed you." My voice sounded desperate, but I couldn't stop it. "Why did you say that if you can't remember your death?"

"Because the cops did a really crappy job investigating," he said. "That I do remember." His voice sounded hollow. "Carruthers pushed them so he could get the crime scene tape down quicker. Told them I was depressed. A drunk. That it was probably my fault . . . And they bought it."

Carruthers. The name of the man Mr. Latterson had been talking to. "Who is that?"

"Owner of the building," Farley said shortly. He looked at me. "Did you know this place is nearly 100 years old?"

I had no idea what he was talking about, but decided to let him rattle on while I tried to figure out what to do. Electrocution was fairly traumatic. Maybe Farley was right. Maybe the electricity had knocked out his memories.

"Before I—died—Carruthers was getting me to do some work around here," Farley continued. "Painting and buffing and adding greenery to the main foyer. Crap like that. He said he was trying to get renters back."

"Well, that's good, isn't it?"

"No. The old girl is falling apart. The roof is ready to go, and that furnace." He shuddered and shook his head. "I tried talking to him about the furnace after I shut it down this spring. That's when the yelling started. 'Just make everything look okay on the outside, and shut your mouth,' he says. So I did. Invisible became my middle name.

"It bothered me though, you know? Not doing the job right. And then, after, the cops deciding I had been an accident. That bothered me too. I even tried to figure out what the cops missed. I didn't find anything. Just the black spot on the cement where my body landed. Talk about depressing."

Not half as depressing as being told that the ghost I had promised to help was stuck in the building where he worked, and couldn't remember his death.

"I imagine," I said, trying for an upbeat tone and managing to sound hysterical. "I need to do a little research to figure out why you're being held here. So how about if you go wander around. Try to remember as much as you can, or something. I'll find you when I have information for you."

Farley looked hurt. "I just told you, I can't remember."

"Well, keep trying. It's important for the process."

"Are you talking about that moving me on thing?" He scowled. "I told you, I'm not doing that."

That's when I hit the wall.

"If you don't want to move on, then why are you even here, bothering me?" I snapped.

Farley stared at me as though I'd slapped him across the face. Hard.

"Because I can talk to you!" he finally cried. "I'm lonely, for Christ's sake."

He stormed to the entrance of the office, and didn't turn around when I said I was sorry. Just oozed through the door and out of my space.

I felt like dirt.

I should have realized he was lonely. Good grief, I'd be lonely if I was trapped in a building and had no-one to talk to for a week. All I'd done was think about myself. That was not fair. Not fair at all.

I needed to help him, that much was certain. Since I had no idea what I should be doing, I needed to call my mom for advice, fight or no fight.

I glanced at the clock on the wall above the door, and decided I'd call her over lunch. However, I had a couple of hours to kill before that.

The mail came, and I flipped through the envelopes. I'd been instructed not to open them, but decided that organizing them wasn't against the rules.

I put the bills in one pile, and the bank statements in another. One of them, from a bank I'd never heard of, had the name Rochelle Martin on it. I was about to write "Return to Sender" across the front, but stopped, deciding not to make any assumptions on my first day. Maybe Mr. Latterson was letting this Rochelle Martin woman use his address or something. I put it in a separate pile. That left three letters from a lawyer's office.

Letters from lawyers were always a bad thing when I lived at home with Mom. I hoped they were better news at an import export office, and put them in their own separate pile.

And then, my work was done.

"Good grief," I muttered, glancing at the time. It was only ten o'clock. Was it too early to go for lunch? How long was lunch, anyhow? "This is ridiculous."

I straightened my desk, even though it didn't need it, and then grabbed my purse. Almost pulled out my cell phone, then didn't. No cheating. I could wait until noon, which I assumed was the time I could go for lunch. Mr. Latterson hadn't told me much of anything before he left, but I didn't want him to return and find me away from my post. Or whatever.

I would wait.

I tried using the computer, but Mr. Latterson had it password protected. Now, I was willing to bet that he had the password written on a sticky note on his desk—he looked the type—but he'd told me not to go into his office. Verboten, I believe he said. If he came back while I was using a password protected computer— well, I couldn't see that going well at all. So I sat and suffered in silence, until noon.

Then, I left.

I found a park bench located between some trees at the front of the Palais, and sat down. The sun shone through the leaves of the willow arching over the bench, and a tiny breeze brushed my hair from my forehead, cooling me as I unpacked my ham and cheese sandwich. I was starving and grabbed half the sandwich, ramming it into my mouth and taking a huge bite.

"That looks good."

I turned, my cheeks bulging like a chipmunk's. James Lavall, the good looking guy from the lobby the afternoon before, had appeared beside one of the evergreen trees next to the building. He was wearing a pair of jeans and a white wife beater undershirt and looked all sweaty. That actually wasn't bad, because he had great muscles. Also, he was nicely tanned. I hadn't noticed either the tan or the muscles the day before. He looked great.

He put down the rake he held and took off his gloves. God, even his hands looked good. Well formed, with long, strong, fingers. They looked like he'd always touch me gently with them. At the thought, my cheeks grew hot.

"Hmm?" I mumbled.

"The sandwich," he said. "It looks delicious."

I couldn't say anything, because my mouth was still chock-full of the sandwich he was admiring. However, I could smile, so I did, keeping my lips locked tight, so he wouldn't be able to see any ham or cheese caught in my teeth.

"I'm glad I found you," he said, and looked down at his beat up work boots. "I owe you an apology."

An apology? For what? I still couldn't talk, but chewed as fast as I could. Swallowed, chewed some more, finally managing to say, "Why?" around the wad of bread and meat that was left.

"For giving you the third degree yesterday." He smiled apologetically. "I used to work for a private investigator, back in the day. It looks like I haven't dropped the 'act like a cop' attitude."

"That's all right," I said. And then I surprised myself by saying, "To be honest, I was thinking about turning down the job."

"Oh," he said. His face was blank as he thought. "Why?"

"Cold feet," I said shortly. That was close enough to the truth. "It didn't help me when you got that look when I mentioned Mr. Latterson's name."

"Sorry about that," he replied. "My uncle told me to watch out for him."

"Your uncle?"

"The P.I."

"Oh. Why?" I asked. My mood darkened. Now it wasn't just a ghost. Now there was something not right about my new boss.

"I didn't ask and he didn't tell me," he replied. "He just said watch myself around him." He shrugged. "He might be wrong. Latterson could be perfectly fine."

"Is your uncle the P.I. wrong a lot?" I asked, hopefully.

"No." He shook his head. "Hardly ever."

"Heh," I said, though I didn't feel like laughing. "Maybe I shouldn't have taken the job."

My appetite was absolutely gone, so I impulsively held out the other half of my sandwich to James. "Want this?"

"I can't take your lunch," he said.

"Please. I'm full."

He shrugged, took the sandwich, and sat next to me. Suddenly, the park bench didn't feel large enough for both of us. I squished closer to the left armrest.

He took a bite—smaller than the one I took, I noticed—and chewed. Swallowed.

"This is great," he gushed.

"It's just ham and cheese."

"Well, you definitely have a way with ham and cheese," he said. Sucker that I am, I blushed again.

"Thanks," I whispered.

He ate his half of my sandwich and then pulled a chocolate bar from a pocket, and offered to share it with me. It was a Coffee Crisp, my personal favourite, so I accepted, gladly.

While we enjoyed the Coffee Crispy goodness, we talked. I told him about my old job and Gerald "The Tyrant" Turner, my boss from hell. He told me about his uncle, the private investigator. How he'd worked with him every summer while he was in high school and full time after, and how his uncle had talked about James taking over the business when he retired.

"So how come you're working here?" I asked. "It sounds like you had a good set up with your uncle."

"I know it sounds like that," he said. "But sometimes the paycheques were few and far between. I needed more stability. You know—"

"A living wage and benefits. I understand."

Our eyes locked. I mean, literally. I couldn't have looked away if my life depended on it. I felt like I was drowning, but in that good way. Which meant I had to look away. I couldn't.

"Exactly," he whispered. Then he looked down at his hands, and when our eyelock broke, I felt as though I'd been given a reprieve I didn't really want. "I really hurt him, the day I told him I wasn't going to go into the business with him. I feel bad about that."

I wondered if it had been as bad as it had been for me with my mom.

Oh God. My mom. I was supposed to call her about Farley.

I pulled my cell phone from my bag and looked at the time. I only had a few more minutes before my lunch hour was over.

"Expecting a phone call?" James asked.

"No. Actually, I need to make one."

He leaped up. "I'll get out of your way."

"I wish you could stay," I said, then felt my face heat. Good grief, I was acting like a lovesick teenager. "It's just—"

"You have to make a phone call." He smiled. "Boyfriend?"

I laughed. "No. My mother."

"Oh," he said, and his eyebrows rose. "Your mother?"

"Yep," I replied. "My mother."

He hovered, and I knew he wanted to know why I was calling my mom in the middle of the day, but sharing time was definitely over.

He took the hint and moved off, picking up his abandoned rake. "Next time I'll bring the sandwich," he said.

"It's a—" Good heavens, I'd almost said, "it's a date."

"That sounds good," I said. And then I pointedly turned away from him, and began to punch the numbers in to connect with my mother.

I heard him move to the other side of the evergreen tree, and then the *skritch skritch* of his rake started. I knew if I could hear him, he was going to be able to hear me.

He wasn't trying to listen to my phone call, was he?

I walked away from the bench, and James, and only when I could no longer hear his rake did I push "enter." I realized I was probably being paranoid. However, sometimes being paranoid is a good thing.

The phone rang once, and then I nearly jumped out of my skin when I heard Mr. Latterson's voice behind me.

"Jenner," he said. "Shouldn't you be working?"

I turned and he was standing by the front door. He tapped his wrist, like he was pointing at a wrist watch. When I mouthed the words "Lunch hour," he frowned.

"It's over," he said, and disappeared inside the Palais.

The phone rang in my ear a second time, so I quickly

disconnected and ran for the door. Even though I'd managed to make myself late back from lunch, and Mr. Latterson had caught me at it, I felt nothing but relief. I hadn't had to talk to Mom about Farley. I'd tried, and it hadn't worked out.

Telling myself I'd figure it out on my own, I hit the stairs running.

Farley:
Marie Learns Something

I left Marie alone for a couple of days after that. I wanted to give her time to figure out what was going on with me. Not that I didn't want to help, but I figured I'd leave it to a professional. Besides, all that crap she said about moving me on hadn't made me feel too great.

I enjoying hanging around, watching everybody. It was like living my life, without all the aggravation. When I wasn't on one of my bloody crying jags, that is. Those, I could do without.

Here's the thing. I knew where I'd be going, if I let Marie move me on. No way in the world there would be the wings and clouds and shit for me. I'd been an asshole most of my life, and I knew I wasn't sidestepping hell. However, if I just hung around, there was no sidestepping involved.

The fact that people actually believed my death was an accident really bugged me, though. I couldn't stand anyone thinking I'd screwed up. I wanted to clear my name. So, I tried to come up with a way to talk Marie into helping me do that, without all the "moving on" business.

The owner of the building, George Carruthers, had hired someone else to do my work, so I spent some time following him around. I could tell from the moment I saw him that he was an idiot. A young, good looking idiot.

He spent a lot of time making to-do lists and things like that. And he nosed around in my stuff. Arranging my tools. Throwing out my magazines. Cleaning up my piles of perfectly good wood and putting it all in a corner. Saying—out loud—that he was going to throw it all away. I spent some of my time cursing a blue streak and trying to figure out how to get rid of him.

Mostly, I stared at the furnace, and the black streak on the cement in front of it, as if I was somehow going to understand everything that had happened to me.

Marie:
Researching Farley's Death

Farley did as I asked, and left me alone. So, for the next couple of days, I did what I could to find out if there really was anything odd about his death. I started by interviewing people who had offices in the Palais. I hoped that something I found would jog his memory. Luckily, Mr. Latterson went out every morning with Raymond, so I had time.

Too much time, if I was going to be honest about it. I was definitely not working hard for all the money he was paying me. Hey, whatever. It's his money. He could give me as much as he wanted.

Everyone I chatted with from the building seemed to have an opinion about Farley's death, but all I really learned was, none of them—except the miserable blonde from 310 who called him a lech and was certain he drank at work—remembered anything else about him at all. Pretty sad.

Mr. Latterson finally gave me the password to my computer, warning me that the computer was just for business. Nothing personal. Ever.

Bosses always say that, so I decided that I just wouldn't let him catch me. After I'd talked to most of the people from the building, I tried a little online research the next time he left with Raymond.

I actually Googled "ghost trapped in a building." Of course I found nothing but hours of mind numbing garbage. After I read as much as I could stand, I shut my computer down and stepped out for a breath of fresh air.

I was only gone five minutes, I swear. When I came back, Mr. Latterson was sitting at my desk, staring at my computer screen.

"You don't actually believe in this crap, do you, Jenner?" he asked. I recognized one of the websites I'd checked out earlier that day.

"No sir." Why hadn't I cleared the computer's history cache? Why why why?

"I catch you wasting my time again and you're gone," he said, conversationally. He closed the offending website and pulled himself out of my chair.

"I understand," I whispered.

"Clear this off. Now."

"Yes sir."

I kept my head down for the rest of the day, promising myself I'd never do anything that stupid again.

I would have to continue to do research at work, because I don't own a computer. The way my finances were, I didn't think I'd ever get one. However, I'd make darn sure that I remembered to clear the history, after I researched. Every time.

As I was leaving the Palais that evening, I realized I hadn't seen James, the cute caretaker. I decided I'd find him and talk to him the next day. For research, of course.

After all, he had taken over Farley's position, so maybe he'd seen something when he was cleaning up the furnace room where Farley had died.

All right, so maybe that's not the only reason I wanted to see him.

Mostly, I wanted to share another sandwich with him. He was funny, and had given me the bigger half of his chocolate bar, which quite possibly meant he was a nice guy. There was nothing wrong with wanting to hang around with a nice guy, was there?

Of course there was. I knew that better than anyone. But, I could dream.

The next day, after Mr. Latterson left, I found James cleaning some gunk off the third floor stairs. He was whistling tunelessly as he scraped the goop into a dustpan and tapped it into a garbage bin.

"What is that?" I asked.

"No clue," he said, attacking whatever it was with vigour. "I try not to think about it."

"Probably your best bet," I said. And then I stood there like an idiot while he continued to clean.

"Is everything all right?" he finally asked.

"All right?" I stammered, confused and then embarrassed. Here I was, standing and staring like a love struck teenager. "Oh yeah, everything's fine. I wanted to ask you about Farley Hewitt."

"Farley who?"

"Hewitt. The guy who did this job before you. You know, the one who—died."

"Oh. Oh. Yeah." He wiped up the last of the mess with a cloth, and dumped everything into the dust bin. "I don't know anything about him."

"What about the way he died? Do you know anything about that?"

He stared at me. "Why do you want to know about that?" he finally asked.

"I heard he might have been murdered," I said. "Just wondered if you saw anything—I don't know—suspicious down in the furnace room. That's where it happened, you know. In the furnace room." I realized I was babbling and snapped my mouth shut.

James didn't look amused. "I heard it was an accident," he said shortly. "I didn't find anything 'suspicious' down there." He frowned. "Who told you he was murdered?"

There was no way in the world I was telling him a ghost told me.

"Just the talk around the building," I said. "You know."

"I don't think there's anything to it," he said. His smile returned. "If you want to come down and check it out, be my guest."

"Thanks. Maybe I will." I smiled back, feeling way too much relief. I turned, ready to head up the stairs to my office, when he spoke again.

"Maybe after, we can have lunch."

"Yeah," I said. "Maybe."

And then, I escaped. Yes, that's exactly the way it felt. Like I was escaping.

I can have dreams, and I can pretend that I can eat lunch and laugh and do all that normal stuff, but I knew I couldn't. There were no dates in my future, no matter how nice James was. Not until Farley moved on.

Even though James hadn't given me anything to work with, I hoped the rumours I'd gathered from the other Palais renters would be enough to jog Farley's memory and give him the push he needed to move on. I quickly typed up everything everyone had said to me—except for the "lech" comment from the blonde in 310—and after I saved it on a small flash drive, I headed out to see if I could find Farley.

Obviously, he was in the building somewhere, but where? On the roof, enjoying the sunshine? I doubted that. Spying on people in their offices? Maybe. I headed down to the basement, deciding I would start with the furnace room. Farley had spent a lot of time in that room while he was alive. With any luck, he'd continued the habit.

I tried the door to the furnace room, expecting it to be locked. It wasn't, and I slowly turned the handle, feeling like I was breaking and entering, which I guess I was.

A reddish light from somewhere below let me see the stairs. I grabbed the handrail and tiptoed down into the furnace room proper.

I was right. Farley was there, staring at the furnace as though mesmerized by the gun metal grey of it all.

"Farley?" I called. "Whatcha doing?"

"Jesus!" He grabbed his chest, feigning a heart attack. Well, maybe not really feigning. He wrapped his arms around his chest, as though he was trying to hold himself together.

"You look like you've seen a ghost," I said, then laughed, nervously, when all he did was stare at me. "Are you all right?"

"Yeah," he said. "What are you doing here?"

"Looking for you."

His eyebrows raised. "I'd half-expected you to take off. I mean, dealing with Macho Don and me. Doesn't make for the best work environment in the world."

"The pay's good," I said. "What can I say? Besides, you're beginning to intrigue me."

He smiled at that. "How do you find me intriguing?"

"Well, the fact that you can't remember much about your death intrigues me," I said. That was more or less the truth. "And the fact that you got miffed with me—"

"Miffed? What kind of word is ..."

"Don't get pissy, let me finish."

"PISSY! What are you trying to do, girl, cut the heart right out of my chest?"

"Good grief, relax!" I said. "I'll try to use better words to describe your moods. More manly words. Would that help?"

"I was mad," he sniffed. "Not miffed or pissy. I was *mad*. Different thing entirely."

"Yes, of course it is. Now, do you want to hear why I came looking for you?"

"Okay." He tried to act like I hadn't stung him with the "miffed" thing, but couldn't pull it off. "Tell me."

"Well, I've been talking to people in the building. Just to see if anyone had heard anything about your death. You know?"

"And?"

"Everybody has a theory," I said. "Some of them think the cops got it right and it was an accident." He snorted derisively. I ignored him. "And there was an old lady who was convinced you were a spy."

"Matilda Jamison, from the second floor." Farley shook his head. "She's on her computer all the time, checking out conspiracy theory sites. She told me once it was for research. She said she was going to write a book. I don't think she ever will. Personally, I think she believes everything she reads."

"So we're agreed," I said. "Seemed kind of far-fetched. Besides, you don't look like a spy."

"Oh?" He laughed. "Not Double O Seven enough for you?"

"Not really."

There was something wrong with the way he looked, and it had nothing to do with him not looking like a spy. He seemed thinner, somehow. Like if I tried hard enough, I'd be able to see through him. And his colour wasn't good—meaning he didn't have as much of it. He looked faded, like an old photograph left too long in the sun.

"How do you feel?" I asked.

"What do you mean, how do I feel?" he snapped. "I'm dead, for Christ's sake. How should I feel?"

He regained some colour and density as he spoke. Maybe I was seeing things.

"Never mind," I said. "I also talked to a woman from 310—"

"Blonde?"

"That's the one."

"That's Andrea," he said, and smiled. "She's sure a looker."

"Yes, she is," I said. Men.

"And that boss of hers treats her like dirt," he continued. "I feel real sorry for her."

Why do they always feel sorry for the beautiful blondes?

"She said she thought you were a drunk," I said, nastily, then wished I could take back my words at the look on his face.

"I never drank at work," he said, softly. "Ever."

"I'm sorry, Farley."

"She's entitled to her opinion, of course, but why—"

"I don't know." I stared down at my shoes for a moment, then looked back at him. He'd faded again. I could definitely see a difference this time. "Don't let it get to you."

"But there's nothing I can do about it now," he whispered. "No way to tell her she was wrong about me."

"I know," I said.

He wiped at his face, and then sighed. "Was that all?"

"No, there was one more. A guy, creepy salesman type. He said he heard that there was something wrong with the electrical panel."

"What?"

"The electrical panel—Farley! What's wrong?"

He had wrapped his arms around himself, quaking with cold, or maybe fear. He closed his eyes, and then jerked them open, looking terrified.

"Oh," he said. It sounded more like wind through tree boughs in winter than an actual word. He sank to the floor beside the furnace. "Thanks for the information."

"Are you all right?" It was a stupid thing for me to say. He wasn't. But I couldn't think of anything else.

"No." He stared down at his hands and legs, and I gasped. He was translucent, nearly transparent. I could see the furnace through him, but there was no light. That was bad.

"I saw something," he whispered. "Only a flash. My hand on something that didn't belong . . ."

His voice faded, and then he reached over and touched his sandaled foot.

"Look at that," he muttered. "The toe of my sock is gone. Must have been the current going to ground. I'm glad I can't feel that. It should hurt like hell."

I looked at his foot, gasped and turned away. It looked like half-cooked hamburger.

"Farley," I said. "Tell me what you saw."

My voice was shaking, and it wasn't just because of his foot. I'd never seen a ghost fade away like Farley was doing. Something was very, very wrong.

"I don't know what it was. I can't remember," he said.

"Do you know where you were?" I asked.

He pointed. "The electrical panel," he muttered.

"So, you saw something in the electrical panel that didn't belong?"

"Yeah." His eyes wandered back to his blown out toe, until I snapped my fingers in his face, bringing his attention back to me. "At least I think so."

"Show me," I said, leaping up and running to the burnt, blackened panel. "What shouldn't be here?"

He squinted. "I don't see anything," he finally said.

Dammit. "Are you sure?"

"Yeah." He sighed. "Maybe the frigging cops took it with them."

That made sense.

"Or maybe I imagined it."

Damn. So did that.

'Let's say for a moment that there was something rammed in there," I said. "Why would someone do that? Seems kind of dangerous. Doesn't it?"

"And stupid," he replied. "Unless you were trying to short out the electricity to the whole building—or kill somebody."

That got my attention.

"Who else comes down here?" I asked.

"No-one but me," he said.

My God, maybe somebody *had* killed him. "Who would want you dead?"

"I don't know. I don't want to talk about this anymore." He slipped down the side of the furnace until he was almost lying flat on the cement.

"Please focus, Farley," I said, desperately. I could barely see him. Just a smudge on the cement at the base of the furnace. When I realized he was lying almost where he died, I freaked.

"You have to stay with me, Farley!" I yelled. "You're remembering what happened, but you have to remember it all. Don't go!"

He sighed, dead tree limbs rattling. "Why not?"

"Because maybe you *were* murdered."

He chuckled, and came back a bit. Just a teeny bit, no doubt, but at least it was something.

"I told you it wasn't an accident," he said. "I wouldn't have done anything that stupid."

"Just promise me you'll hang on while I dig around some more. I'll see if I can find out if the cops took anything. And I'll keep talking to the people in the offices. There has to be something, some reason—"

"Start with this place." He tried to pull himself up to sitting. I wished I could help him, because it was like watching a bug on its back. Of course I couldn't. "It hasn't been brought up to code since it was built."

"Okay, sounds good, I'll check that out," I said. "And while I'm doing that, what are you going to do?"

I was going to suggest that he check offices, to see if there were big piles of drugs, or weapons of mass destruction or something. After all, he was the spook. The words dried up when Farley finally pulled himself to sitting and all the colour drained from him. Every bit.

"I'm going to lie down for a while," he whispered. "I don't feel that good."

I opened my mouth to say something, anything that could keep him with me, but I was too late.

Blink, and he was gone.

Marie:
Why Would a Ghost Feel Sick?

I stared at the spot where Farley had been, and knew that my mouth was hanging open, but couldn't pull myself together enough to shut it. I'd never, ever, seen a ghost disappear like that. Ever.

What was going on?

I searched around as though he'd stepped outside my field of vision, stopping before I looked behind the furnace.

"Maybe he moved on."

Even as I said the words, I knew they were not the truth. Spirits that move on are bright. Imbued with light. Farley looked like a smudge of shadow before he disappeared.

Sometimes spirits fade, losing so much inner essence that they aren't visible anymore, even to people like me. He hadn't done that, either. He'd just—blinked out.

"He said he felt unwell. They never feel unwell." I tried to think, feeling a little unwell myself. *Why would a ghost feel sick?*

I glanced at my watch, and gasped. Mr. Latterson was going to be back any moment. I had to go.

I skittered up the stairs and carefully opened the door, checking to see if anyone was in the lobby. Luckily, it was empty, and I ran to the stairs that led to the upper floors, and managed to get into the office and to my desk before Mr. Latterson showed up.

"Did you get that paperwork done?"

I opened my mouth to say yes, but he didn't give me time to actually answer.

"It absolutely has to be in the mail before the end of business today. You know that."

"Yes, and—" I said.

"Get it done. I'll be back at 3:30." He turned on his heel and marched back out of the office, slamming the door shut before I could tell him everything was complete and waiting for his signature in the "out" box, just like he'd ordered.

It looked like I had the afternoon to myself, too.

I stared down at the computer, wishing that Googling "ghosts, moving on to the next plane of existence," would help me. I didn't waste my time. There was no help out there for me online. I knew that.

The only one I could really count on for information was my mom, and I wasn't ready to talk to her, yet. It didn't have to do with the fight I'd had with her. Well, not really.

The truth was, I did not want to let her know I had another ghost problem. I'd made the mistake of telling her about Sally. The only good advice she gave me was to get noise canceling headphones for the screaming. The rest of the time, all she would was say, "I told you so," and "You should have listened to me." She was convinced that because I could see ghosts, they were somehow drawn to me.

They weren't drawn to me. I was just having a string of bad luck.

Anyhow, calling my mom was out.

I decided to assume Farley would be back. One thing I could do was get information for him about some aspects of his life. That had sometimes worked for Mom when she dealt with a "recalcitrant spirit." Her words, definitely not mine. Then, maybe, Farley would move on the right way, and I'd be free. I set my fingers on the computer keyboard, and thought, hard. What did Farley need?

I tried to remember what Mom did when she first encountered a ghost with awareness, but couldn't grab onto any one thing. She'd talked to them about their lives, their work, the way they died, everything associated with them. No true starting place.

I decided to fake it, and Googled the Palais. Maybe it was the place itself. Maybe that's why he couldn't leave.

I thought I'd lose it when the search engine ground out thirteen million hits. I pulled my hair back in a quick ponytail, punched in "Edmonton" with Palais, and was rewarded with a much more manageable number. "Let's see what you can tell me," I whispered as I opened the first page.

Four hours later, I'd gone through most of the information I could find online about the office building, carefully cleared the history cache file on my computer, typed two more letters for Mr. Latterson, calculated my monthly budget, had a small cry, and tried a new hairstyle using pencils to hold my hair in a catastrophic attempt at an up-do.

I shook out the last pencil and stared down at the small pad of paper on which I'd scribbled information about the office building and its history. I hoped I hadn't wasted my time, because Farley had still not returned. I glanced at the clock above the door, and started to tidy up. It was nearly time to head to my other job.

Mr. Latterson came back just as I was emptying the coffee carafe, which I had decided was my last job of the day.

"I need you to stay," he said. "I have a call coming in, and I want you to handle it."

I looked at the clock. If it was only five minutes, I'd be fine.

"Who's calling?"

I swear I heard Mr. Latterson's teeth grind as he said, "My ex-wife. I'll tell you what to say. Just write it all down."

I wrote down everything he told me on a scrap of paper, and then sat, purse in hand, as he floated in and out of the office, nervously, sweat staining his off-white shirt in large damp patches.

"Would you rather take it yourself?" I asked, laughing inwardly. I knew, without a doubt, that no-one voluntarily talks to an ex-wife. No-one.

"No, I have work to do," he replied, wringing his hands and brushing back his bad comb over until it stood at attention on the top of his head. "Say exactly what I told you to. Got it?"

"Yes."

I glanced at the clock again, feeling a nervous flutter in my stomach when I saw seven minutes had passed. I was going to be late if I didn't leave very soon.

"You're certain this call is coming in?"

"Yes, absolutely, without a doubt."

He nodded, his hair dancing in a fuzzy greying halo on the top of his head. Laughter fought nervousness until I felt hysterical. I did a little deep breathing, to calm down.

We both squawked when the phone beeped, and Mr. Latterson retreated to his office as I picked up the receiver.

It took me fifteen minutes to get his furious wife—I was certain she was not yet an ex, no matter what he said—off the phone, and by that time he had snuck out, leaving me to lock up. I was definitely late for my cab job, and the one thing my boss Gerald the Tyrant could not abide was my being late.

The same rule didn't seem to apply to the others, I thought as I half-ran down the crowded sidewalk to the dank office building I'd inhabit for the next eight hours of my life.

I was lucky. Gerald wasn't at his desk. Jasmine was, though, and looked pissed, because I'd made her late getting home to her kids.

"I'm sorry, I'm sorry," I said, throwing my purse under our desk and taking the headphone from her hand. "Any way I can make it up?"

Jasmine smiled, in spite of herself. "You come to my house for a meal and some TV," she said. "We haven't done that in a while, and my show has gone right off the deep end! You have to catch up."

"That sounds nice," I said. And it did. It really did. Going to her house with all her kids and noise and laughter was always nice. Kind of like going home, without the fights.

"Then you can tell me all about your new job and why you're still here," she continued.

I nodded. She headed for the door, and then turned.

"And you bring the dessert," she said. "Got it?"

"Got it," I replied, and then she was gone, and I was alone with the headset for the rest of the night.

Not counting the beginning, the shift ran surprisingly smoothly. I was standing in my apartment at 1:57 in the morning, looking forward to a full five hours of sleep, when Sally wandered into the kitchen.

She examined the counter tops with fascination, something I'd never seen her do before. I felt a touch of dread. New was never good. Not with ghosts.

I tiptoed around her and into the bathroom to splash warm water on my face and wash the day away. Sally followed me, and stood next to me, staring at our reflections in the mirror. She'd never done that before, either. She glanced down at her hands, then back up at the mirror.

"What's going on?" she asked, staring right into the reflection of my bloodshot eyes. "What're you doing here? And why do I keep sinking into the floor?"

As if to push home her last question, she oozed a few inches into the cheap lino of the bathroom floor. She didn't pull herself up to floor height, just walked through it as though through the surf on the beach.

"Feels odd," she said. "It should hurt, but it doesn't." She frowned. "Did you tell me your name?"

"No." I sighed as I watched my chance for a good night's sleep disappear. "No, I didn't. My name's Marie."

"Why are you in my apartment?"

"It's my apartment, now."

Sally looked surprised and stepped up out of the floor to look me in the eye.

"Did I forget to pay the rent?"

"No. Nothing like that."

I dried my face slowly, carefully refolding the towel before facing Sally. This next bit was tricky. I remembered what it was like for Mom when ghosts became aware, but didn't realize they were actually dead. For some reason, more often than not, this happened to drug addicts. Mom had never figured that out. I had some theories, but wasn't going to test them now. I wanted some sleep, and I wouldn't get it if Sally became hysterical. "Come into the kitchen. We need to talk."

The ghost started to shake as she followed me out of the bathroom. Then she frowned, and pointed. "Where's my TV?"

"This isn't your apartment."

"Oh. Right." Sally glanced around the fairly empty room, and her frown deepened. "Where's your TV?"

"I don't have one."

She snorted. "You gotta be kidding. What do you do? You know, for entertainment?"

"I don't have much time for entertainment."

I shook my head, impatient with myself. This wasn't helping Sally, and it sure wasn't getting me any closer to sleep. "We have to talk."

"Okay." Sally would not focus on me. She wandered around the small kitchen, running her hands—which were getting brighter by the moment—over the counter tops.

"I loved this place," she whispered. "It was the best place I ever had. In my whole life." She smiled wistfully. "That's kinda sad, isn't it?"

"It's a nice place, Sally. You picked a very nice place." I watched the woman fade, and tried to match the tone Mom had used. This wasn't going to be hard. Sally was very close. I could feel it. "There are people who would never have had such a nice place."

"Yeah. That's true. And I paid the rent. Every month." Sally touched the faucet, and ran her hand into the sink. "So I guess that's the best I could have hoped for. I did all right, I guess."

"Sally—"

Sally held up her hand, stopping my words. "I died, didn't I?" She glowered. "Was it an overdose?"

"Yes."

"Son of a bitch! I knew that shit was bad." She shook her head. "Well, you get what you pay for, I guess." She glanced at me, a quizzical look on her face. "You some kind of an angel? You know, like that TV show?"

I had no idea what she was talking about, and shook my head. "No. I'm not an angel."

"I gotta repent my sins, all that stuff—" Then she frowned. "Man, I'm too late for that, aren't I?" She put her hand to her mouth and groaned. "I'm too late for all that. I thought I had time."

Sally began to glow. It was weak, no doubt about it, and just around the edges of her torso and the hair on her head, making her look like she was standing in front of a high powered spotlight. She wasn't standing in front of any light, though. The light was coming from her.

"Sally, look at me. Focus on me." I stood in front of the ghost and stared into her eyes. "What you do next is up to you. Entirely up to you."

I remembered Mom speaking those words. Sally was so close to the end. So close. I felt my strength running to her through the connection our eyes made. Oddly, it made me feel stronger, more alive.

"What do you mean?" she asked.

"What would you like to do? If you could choose anything, what would you like to do?"

I half-expected her to say, "Get high." Lots of drug overdoses said that, at first. She didn't.

"I would like to stop." Her eyes closed briefly, and tears, glowing eerily in the half-light of the room, hung on her lashes. "I've had enough. It's enough." Her eyes opened, and I was surprised at their startling green. I'd never noticed the colour before. "Is that okay? If I just—stop being?"

"Yes. If that's what you want."

"I wish you could hold my hand. I'm scared."

So was I, but I didn't let her know that. I stepped closer, so she could feel my heart. I remembered Mom doing that. I could see it calmed the ghost. She was glowing brilliantly. She was almost ready.

"Don't be afraid," I said. "It's nearly over. Can you see the light?"

"Get outta here!" Sally grinned at me, briefly regaining some substance. Her glow was bright white, flecked through with red and black. "I'm actually going to walk toward a white light?"

"No, that's not the way it works. The light comes from you. Can you see it?"

Sally glanced down at her hands, then held them up in wonder. "Yes, I can." She smiled. "I look kinda pretty. What are the flecks? The black and the red?"

"It's your life—what you've experienced. You take it with you wherever you go."

"And if I stop being?"

"Then this light stops too."

"That's probably for the best." Sally began to cry, gently. "I'm really tired, you know?"

"I know." Her weariness hit me in waves, and I tried to stay strong for her. She needed it, and I gave as much as I could.

Sally's glow cast my run down furniture in a stark, flat light. The only place the light took on life was within Sally. It began to swirl around her, through her, and the red and black flecks slowly drowned in the white. Her eyes glowed, ever brighter, as she made her final decision.

The white light, which glowed through her translucent skin, brightened until all I could see were her eyes, brilliant green. Then the green drowned in the white, and the light folded in on itself, until it finally was one point, tiny, floating in front of me until it too disappeared. With it went her fear, her weariness, everything that had been Sally. I was finally, truly alone in my apartment.

"Good-bye," I whispered. Then I tottered to the phone, carefully staying away from the last place Sally had inhabited, and dialed Mom's number. I felt about 100 years old.

"Hi Mom," I said, and burst into tears. "I moved Sally on." I couldn't stop crying. Didn't want to. "What do I do now?"

Mom explained what would happen to me in the next few hours. Sleep was not in the mix. I listened carefully to her, and promised I'd do everything exactly as she said.

But I didn't tell her about Farley. Not a word.

Farley:
What Nightmares Are Like When You're Dead

I don't know what happened, but it was horrible.

I was having a nightmare, like nothing I'd ever had before. I was used to the snake dream, and the falling from a high place dream, and that nasty series of screamers I had when the wife left me and I was really alone for the first time in my life.

It wasn't anything like that. This felt like reality. Reality through hand blown glass. You know the stuff. Crappy glass with bubbles and shit in it, to make it seem genuine or something, distorting what you see through it until it's hard to say what it is you're looking at. I couldn't make sense of anything, and wondered if this was what Hell was like.

Was I in Hell?

After what felt like an eternity, I blinked back into Marie's darkened office. How long had I been gone?

I stumbled into the hallway. It was dark there, too. Jesus, how long *had* I been out? I started to run, then stopped that foolishness and dropped through to the main foyer with the nice furniture and fake-but-so-good-you'd-swear-it-was-real greenery, and pressed my face up to the ornate glass and steel door.

I could see the sun touching the trees across the street from the building and people trudging to work, sipping their coffee in their to-go cups and acting like they wished they were anywhere else.

I wasn't in Hell. I was back in the Palais.

"Thank God." I leaned my head against the glass of the door, wondering if it felt cool or warm to the touch. Of course, I wasn't really pressing my head against the door. I was pressing it against that barrier that was holding me in the building.

I lost it again for a while, banging my fists and screaming until my throat was raw and my voice was nothing but a harsh whisper. Then I slid down the door, leaning against it and crying. And I couldn't seem to stop.

Marie:
Post "Moving on my First Ghost" Blues

I was tired—read exhausted—after my no-sleep-and-moving-Sally-on night, but I also felt exhilarated. I'd moved a ghost on. Well, she'd done most of the work, but I'd helped. As I grabbed a coffee on my way to the Palais, I thought that maybe, just maybe, I was going to be able to pull off moving Farley on to the next plane of existence. Then I'd have my office to myself, and would be able to live my life the way I wanted. Ghost free.

One thing that surprised me, though. My apartment felt really empty without Sally. Almost creepy.

The coffee helped. By the time I walked up the front step of the Palais, I was feeling energized and ready. Ready for Farley, if and when he came back.

Even though I hadn't asked my mother about Farley specifically, she'd talked my ear off about what can happen to a ghost who doesn't move on.

Most do. Move on, I mean. They understand, they are prepared, and they take the next step, whatever that is. However, some don't. They could be like Sally, and not even realize they are dead. Or they could be like Farley, and decide they aren't going to move on.

This resistance usually comes from fear, or so Mom says. They don't want to face judgment, or whatever. If they can be convinced that the only one doing the judging is them—and that judging is wrong—all is good, and on they move.

Sometimes, they feel like they didn't live a real life, and decide to stay and live vicariously through the people around them. Those usually get bored, really quickly. Hanging around with the living can do that. As much as we living like to think we're fascinating and all that, most humans spend a lot of time sleeping, and eating, and watching television. Not really the high octane lifestyle these ghosts are craving. So, they eventually make the move, with a little help from someone like my mom.

Some of them stay for other reasons. Revenge is the top of the list, with hubris running a close second. Unfortunately, trying to "get the guy who got me" is as detrimental to a spirit as "nothing as small as a germ could have killed me, so I'm sticking around to find out what it really was." These ones slowly lose all connection to this world. Mom calls it "losing the light." They darken and fade until there isn't enough essence left to attract anyone. This includes people like my mom and me. Then, they truly are stuck, forever.

She didn't mention a ghost blinking out, though. Not once.

I should have asked her about it. I know that. But she just would have started in on the "You know this is your calling, Marie," and I would have said something stupid like, "I don't want a calling that leaves you alone and dying in your fifties," or something. I didn't want to fight, so I didn't mention it to her.

I was pretty sure that the blinking out wasn't another form of fading away. Mom had said that the first thing all spirits had to come to terms with was the manner of their death, and Farley couldn't remember how he'd died. Maybe blinking out had to do with his memory loss. If he could just remember how he died, then the blinking would stop. I was almost sure of it.

So, I was feeling energized and sympathetic and hopeful. Until I saw Farley, that is. Then all those feelings took a back seat to feeling dread. Lots and lots of dread.

He was leaning near the inside of the front door of the Palais, and he was crying. No. He was sobbing like a kid would, open mouthed, with tears streaming down his face, leaving a trail of light, like phosphorescence, from his eyes, down his cheeks, to the floor. Those trails of light were the brightest thing about him. That was not good.

When he saw me, he scrubbed his face with his hand and then pointed at me. I could tell he was yelling angrily, even though I couldn't hear him yet. Great. Fear and anger, rolling off of him in waves. First thing in the morning. Just what I needed.

"What the fuck happened to me, Marie?" he cried, when I pushed open the door. "Why didn't you warn me about this?"

I couldn't talk to him in front of all the other people straggling in to work. "Come to my office," I said, ignoring the guy from 215 who had followed me into the building and who thought I had been speaking to him. He looked confused for a moment, then wandered to the stairs, glancing back over his shoulder at me before he disappeared. He looked afraid.

I decided to take the elevator, even though it was old and clunky and scared me, and rammed myself in it with ten other people. Farley didn't join, so I was able to try to pull myself together just a little bit before I got to the third floor and stepped out.

"So what happened to me?" I had barely walked around the corner when Farley appeared, still yelling. "I want to know, now."

I held up my hand for silence, and unlocked the door. He followed me, and had the decency to keep his mouth shut until we were inside the office and the door was once again closed.

"Tell me, right now," he barked. "Did you send me to Hell or something?"

All right, so I admit, I snapped a bit.

"I didn't 'send' you anywhere!" I cried. "I couldn't, even if I wanted to. Tell me what happened to you yesterday. I need details—"

"How am I supposed to know?" he snapped back. "I tell you, girl, I have about one nerve left, and you have figured out how to rub it exactly the wrong way. I don't know what happened!"

I took a deep breath and tried again. "Can you remember anything?"

He stopped ranting. "Yeah," he said. "I can."

"Well, tell me. Please."

He paced back and forth in front of my desk. "One second I'm talking to you, and the next, Poof! It was like I was having a nightmare, only ten times worse. I saw a wire in my hand. Then the lights went out. And then I was back looking at the wire and the lights went out. Over and over and over. I could hear a voice, like someone was talking underwater or something, talking about me. Then lights out. Until it started again." He stopped and stared at me. "What the hell is going on with me?"

"No idea," I said.

All right, I could have handled it better, but wow. On top of blinking out, he had a nightmare? I needed to think.

Luckily, Mr. Latterson walked in, scowling because the coffee wasn't on. As I started the Bunn, he walked to his office without saying a word, and shut his door.

That's when it hit me. Sally had lived the last hours of her life and her death, over and over, before she became aware. What if, even though he was aware, Farley was doing something similar when he blinked away?

"I think you're reliving your death," I said. "In your dream."

"Nightmare," he said.

"Okay. Nightmare." I poured a coffee for Mr. Latterson, and added sugar. "You do know that's weird, right? Ghosts don't usually have nightmares."

"That ain't my fault," he said.

"No, it's not. But for some reason you're doing it."

"Some reason? You don't know why?"

"No," I said. "Not yet."

I held up my hand before he said anything more. "Now you said you grabbed a wire that didn't belong, and then darkness. Where was the wire?"

"In the electrical panel, downstairs," he said. He blinked. "You think that's what I thought I saw, before?"

"Could be. Do you have any idea who would have put a wire in the electrical panel?" I looked at him hopefully. Maybe he was saving that bit of information for a big ta-da. I didn't get that.

"No," he said, shaking his head.

"You're sure?"

"I told you!" he yelled. "I don't know!"

I shouldn't have pressed him. I could see he was on the verge of freaking out, and I really truly didn't want any more of that. He needed to remain calm, which meant I needed to be calm. Not my best trick, but I'd give it a shot.

"We'll figure it out, Farley," I said. "I think learning this is part of the passage for you."

"Passage?" he asked, then shook his head. "Forget it, sounds like more of that mumbo-jumbo life after death crap. I don't wanna hear it."

That made me laugh.

"What's so funny?" he asked, snippily.

"It feels just a little bit odd having a ghost tell me that he doesn't want to hear any mumbo-jumbo life after death crap." I laughed again, and I could hear the tinge of hysteria in my voice before Farley started laughing with me.

It felt good to laugh. Even if I was hysterical.

I took the cup of coffee into Mr. Latterson, who was huddled over his phone speaking urgently to someone on the other end. He didn't acknowledge me and I heard Farley snort as I quietly closed the door, poured myself a cup, and sat down.

"What a dick," Farley said. "Does he always treat you that way?"

"Usually," I said. "It's all right."

"No, it's not," he replied. "He should be polite. Know what I mean?" He shook his head. "Nobody's polite anymore. It's— uncivilized."

"Maybe I'll get him a book on etiquette, when I get my first paycheque," I said. Farley snorted something close to laughter. "However, I found out something about this building. It might be—I don't know—a clue or something. Want to hear it?"

"Hell yes!" He parked himself on the edge of my desk. "Spill."

"'The Friends of the Fort,' a historical society, found out that the main beams in this building—I think they are the main beams of the main floor, but I could be wrong, things got pretty confusing when I tried to find original blueprints for the building—anyhow, the Friends of the Fort think the main beams of this building were taken from a fort built around here in the 1800s.

"Apparently, the big fence around the fort was called a palisade, so when the original owner used some of the posts in the foundation, he decided to call the building the Palisade. His wife hated the name and made him change it to the Palais. She liked the French sound, I think she was a social climber . . . Sorry. On a tangent. I didn't get much sleep last night." I took a sip of coffee. "The society is pushing to have the building designated as a historical site. Do you think this could have anything to do with what happened to you?"

"Well, maybe," he said. "Would it do Carruthers any good?"

"Carruthers? The owner, right?"

"Right. Figure out if this historical designation deal could make him any money. Or, lose him money. Because he's all about the money, and he hasn't been close to breaking even on this place in a while."

"All right, I will. I'll also check out more people who are renting offices here. Anybody you pissed off?"

"Not overly." He sounded afraid. "But check out Ian Henderson up in 310. He's an asshole from way back."

"All right." I started writing his name and room number on a pad of paper beside the phone, then stopped. "310. Why do I know that office number?"

"That's where Andrea works," Farley said.

The blonde who thought Farley was a lech. Oh. "Are you sure?"

"Yeah. Please. Just check him out."

"Will do."

"Thanks."

He didn't look thankful. He looked distracted.

"Are you all right?" I asked. He smiled.

"That's nice," he said. "You being concerned. I haven't seen that in a long time, Rose—" He stopped, and blinked.

"Who is Rose?" I asked. He wouldn't answer.

"Come on, tell me," I pushed. He shook his head, aggravated, then sighed.

"Rose is my daughter," he said. "She's all grown up, has her own life, and thinks I'm a jerk."

"Oh," I said. "Your daughter."

"Don't read anything into that," he replied. "Just because I think about my little girl—"

He stopped speaking again and cocked his head, as though he heard something. I heard nothing, and suspected he was trying to get me to quit talking about his daughter. Which made me think she was exactly who we should be talking about.

"Tell me more about her," I said.

"Hush." His head was still cocked. "Can't you hear that?"

"Hear what?" I asked. "I can't hear anything. Farley, we have to talk about your daughter—"

"Oh, for heaven's sake," he snapped. "Give it a rest. There's something wrong. Are you sure you can't hear anything?"

"No," I replied. My voice sounded angry tight, so I took a quick breath to relax. "What do you think you're hearing?"

"It sounds like water," he said. "Running water."

"Like the water in your nightmare?" I asked.

"No," he said. "This sounds real."

Oh.

"Farley," I said, keeping my voice as calm as I could, "whatever thoughts you're having, let them come. It's all natural. All part of the—"

"Passage, yeah whatever," he said. "There's something wrong. I gotta go."

When he disappeared through the closed front door, I really wanted to throw something and yell at him, but I didn't. For one thing, I knew he'd be back. For another, Mr. Latterson was in the next room, and wouldn't appreciate me yelling obscenities and breaking coffee cups.

That didn't let Farley off the hook, though. "You can run, but you can't hide," I whispered as I rolled a fresh sheet of paper into Mr. Latterson's Selectric II. "You are going to move on, like it or not."

I'd only typed half of Mr. Latterson's letter when Farley came back, wild-eyed.

"Go down and help the idiot! He's got a flood going in the basement, and he can't stop it!"

He was talking about James. James was in trouble! I flew out of the office and down the stairs before I even had time to think. When I hit the big steel door for the basement, I stopped. "What should he do?"

"The shut-off valve," Farley said. "Behind the furnace, right by the water meters."

I threw open the door and ran down the stairs into pandemonium. Farley hadn't been kidding. There was a flood, and James was leaping through and over the water like a demented gazelle trying to escape from a crocodile.

"James!" I cried.

He stopped for about a second, and stared at me. "It's dangerous!" he cried. "You should leave!"

"Use the shut-off valve!" I yelled back. I couldn't believe how much water there was. God, a person could drown in that much water. "Behind the furnace, next to the water meter!"

"I know where the shut-off valve is," he said, and disappeared behind the furnace. The water slowed, and stopped. He sloshed back, smiling. "Thanks," he said.

"Idiot," Farley growled. I could almost hear his teeth grinding. I ignored him.

"Are you all right?" I took another step down, stopping just before the waterline. "Did you cut yourself? You're bleeding."

James looked down at his hand, and flinched. "I am bleeding—oh God, I'm really bleeding . . ."

He staggered, so I stepped down into the knee-high water and took him firmly by the arm. I pulled him over to the steps, sat him down and, grabbing a cloth that was floating by, wrapped his hand to stop the blood.

"Thank you." He smiled, and I couldn't help myself. I smiled back. "How did you know I had a problem down here?"

"Let's say I had a feeling," I said.

"He's an idiot, Marie! A fucking idiot!" Farley cried.

I ignored him, concentrating on stopping the flow of blood from James' ever so nice looking hand.

"Fuck me," Farley said. "Fuck me all to hell."

Marie:
Saving James

James was so good looking, even with the water and the blood and everything, it was hard for me to think. All I knew for sure was, he needed help.

"You have to go to the hospital," I said. "Can you walk?"

"Yeah. I think so." He looked at the cloth covering his wet hand and blanched when he saw blood blossom through it. "Maybe not."

"Should I call an ambulance?"

"No, I'll be all right." James took a deep breath, and pulled himself off the step. "Maybe a band aid or something—"

"It's worse than that. You're going to need stitches." He swayed and I grabbed his arm. "Do you need to sit down?"

"No. I'm all right." He reached for the hand rail resolutely. "It's just—they use a needle to put in stitches, don't they?"

"Yeah, they do."

He glanced down at his hand, blanched, and looked away. "It's not going to scar, is it?"

And then I said something truly stupid. I said, "Some women think scars are sexy." I was just trying to take his mind off the blood and everything, but he looked up at me hopefully. Even more stupidly, I looked back, into his eyes.

"Really?" he said. "Do you think they're sexy?" He took a step up and his work boot slipped as water squelched from it in a small river. He clutched my shoulder frantically, and I grabbed him, to help him stay upright.

"Not really," I replied, wishing I'd just kept my mouth shut. "But some women do. I've heard."

I tried not to feel the heat of his body through his thin tee-shirt. I couldn't help but notice how lean he was, flat slabs of muscle and bone working together in a fine way. I pushed myself away from him so our hips were not rubbing together, so that his hand did not cup my shoulder so intimately, but he pulled me closer, and curled his hurt hand up to his chest.

"I don't have many scars," he mumbled. "Not too many."

We finally made it to the doorway at the top of the stairs, where we swayed as one. I saw a UPS driver standing by the outer doors, staring at us.

"Help me," I snapped. The driver dropped his package and grabbed James by the other arm. I could see he was trying not to get blood on his uniform. We scurried out into the warm sunshine, and stopped.

"Where's your car?" the helpful driver asked. I shook my head, trying to think. It was hard with James' hand on my shoulder.

"I don't have a car. Can you give us a ride over to the Royal Alex? It's only a couple of blocks." I tried to smile over the driver's suddenly nervous head shake but stopped when James slumped forward, mumbling about "black dots," and, "I can barely hear you."

"Please help," I begged. "It'll only take a minute."

"It's against the rules, and I have deliveries to make." The driver looked as though he sorely wished he hadn't been taken in by my smile. So, I smiled harder and placed a hand on the driver's arm.

"Be a pal, okay? I really need a ride."

The driver stared at me for a long moment, then ruefully nodded. "All right, but you can't tell anyone I did this." He threw the door open and pushed the junk strewn on the floor out of the way. There was no seat on the passenger side. "Don't let him bleed anywhere."

"No problem." I grabbed James more securely by the shirt, and half-dragged him to the open door of the van. "One more step and you can rest."

He smiled at me, then tried to take that one step into the van, and nearly brought us both crashing to the ground.

"Help me!" I fought to keep James from falling down completely, and the driver rolled his eyes, gingerly grabbing the back of James' shirt.

"Don't let him get any blood on me." He muscled James in to the van. "You'll have to sit on the floor beside him."

I surveyed the situation as he went and belatedly retrieved the package he had dropped in the Palais front foyer. By the time he came back, I was squished against James, trying to keep him upright.

"You could sit here." The driver gestured to the area beside his seat, covered in paperwork and old coffee cups. "Closer to me."

"No, I'm fine right here. Let's get going. He really doesn't look so good."

"No he doesn't." The driver snorted. "That's a lot of blood. Are you sure he only cut his hand?"

"I think so."

"Hmm." He pulled out into traffic. "You're not going out with this guy or anything, are you?"

"No." I shook my head vehemently. "He works in the same building I do. That's all."

"Well, good." The driver smiled at me, and leaned my way. "How about you and me going out for a coffee after we get this guy stitched up?"

"Touch her and die."

The driver stared, shocked, at James, as he struggled to consciousness. I must admit, I did some shocked staring myself.

"Are you sure you're not dating?" The driver looked nervous, and quit leaning my way. "He kinda acts like—"

"We're not dating," I snapped, slapping James' hand away from my waist. "Thanks for the offer, but I can't go out for coffee." Then I pointedly ignored them both. I didn't need one bit of this.

When we pulled into the Royal Alex Emergency a few minutes later, the driver threw the vehicle into park and sat, staring out the windshield.

"Aren't you going to help me?" I asked, knowing the answer as he pointedly ignored me, but having to try anyway. James mumbled something, and put his head on my chest. I tried to push him away, and he grinned up at me.

"Nice perfume."

"Thanks." I wasn't wearing perfume. There was no way in the world I was telling him that. "Can you walk?"

He tried to focus his eyes. Deep rich, blue eyes, beautiful, really, until one wandered off, appearing to investigate the bridge of his own nose. I tried not to watch, but it was like a traffic accident. You can't turn away. "Prob'ly."

"Good."

I didn't really think it was good. In fact, I was certain both of us would end up in a heap outside the UPS truck, but I had run out of options. The driver was revving the engine and huffing impatiently. "Let's go, then."

"Sounds good." James closed his eyes, then opened them again. "Did I move?"

"No." I tried to decide whether to laugh or cry, and couldn't come up with a definitive answer. "You didn't."

"Hmm. This is going to be tougher than I thought," James said.

The UPS driver revved the motor again, redlining it. James swung his head in the driver's direction. "That's not good for the engine."

The driver growled something I didn't catch and gestured grandly for both of us to get the hell out of his truck, his goodwill evidently spent.

I maneuvered my way over James, got out of the van, and reached up for him. "Just one step, and we're out."

"All righty."

James appeared to muster every bit of strength he had left and hoisted himself out of the van. He stumbled a step or two, and I grabbed his shirt to stop him. He stood, compliantly enough, as I slammed the door of the van shut, and waved a thank you to the driver, who did not acknowledge us, driving off with a small squeal and a blast of black smoke as something in the engine let go. I didn't bother watching after the van limped to the street and died blocking two lanes of traffic. I had enough to worry about.

We staggered into Emergency. There, the blood on James caused a flutter and I hoped we were going to get in quickly, until the staff realized it was simply a cut to his hand and we were directed to the waiting area. We sat for a long time, watching the chairs empty around us.

"Thanks for coming with me," James said.

"You're welcome." I glanced over at him. Some of his colour had come back. "Will you be all right alone for a minute? I have to call Mr. Latterson and tell him where I am."

He looked concerned. "I hope I don't get you into trouble."

"It's all right." I stood. "You needed my help."

"If he gives you a hard time—"

"Don't worry about it." I walked away from him, and to a bank of phones. I called the office and was immediately directed to voicemail, so I left a detailed message, hoping that he was out at one of his all day lunches and wouldn't notice I was gone.

"Everything all right?" James asked when I came back.

"Everything's fine," I replied, hoping it would be.

"Good." James shifted in his seat, glancing at the injured and ill littering the plastic chairs in the waiting room. "I don't like hospitals," he finally said.

"I don't either."

"I hate the smell. And the needles." He shuddered. "What about you?"

"What about me, what?" I didn't know whether I wanted to talk about this to him, though I'd started it.

"How come you don't like hospitals?"

A ghost wandered out from the bathroom and sat beside me, putting his head on my shoulder. I tried to shrug him away, but he didn't move. I realized he'd fallen asleep.

"God." I jerked my shoulder up once more, to dislodge him, only managing to work his head into my shoulder. I hate that feeling. They are so cold. I stood and walked a few steps away.

"I'm sorry. I shouldn't have asked." James looked like he thought my reaction was his fault—which, if I was in a particularly bitchy mood, I could say it was, because he was the reason I was in the hospital in the first place. Because he was injured, I decided to cut him a tiny bit of slack.

"It's all right."

The ghost snorted himself awake and moved on to another woman, a grandmotherly type who was waiting for her husband to get his ear reattached. The ghost sighed and settled his head onto her shoulder, falling back to sleep almost immediately.

"I don't like hospitals because my mom has cancer, and I spent a lot of time in places like this before I moved to Edmonton." This surprised me. I don't like to talk about my family.

"Is she going to be okay?"

"She was in remission for a while. Now, it's not looking good."

"You said you moved here—isn't she in town?"

"She lives in Fort McMurray." I tried to smile, but it was hard. "When I left, she was in remission. Now she's not."

"Are you going to go back?"

"Probably not."

"It must be hard, being away from her."

"It is." I couldn't look at him. "But the rest of the family's there. She has people around her."

"I meant, it must be hard on you."

"I know what you meant." I was finished confessing. This place was making it hard for me to think.

"James Lavall?" A steely-eyed nurse peered out at the waiting room. "Is there a James Lavall here?"

"Here," James replied, and pulled himself upright. I tried to help him stand, but he shook his head, then walked toward the nurse. She frowned.

"James Lavall?" she asked again.

"Yes. That's me."

"Are you sure?" she asked, frowning mightily.

"Is this a test to see if I'm coherent?" James asked, reaching in his back pocket with his good hand for his sodden wallet. "I'm James Lavall."

"Oh." The nurse glanced at James' ID, and nodded, as if finally satisfied. "I know a Jimmy Lavall. Guess I was expecting him."

"Jimmy Lavall's my uncle."

"Oh." The nurse touched his arm and led him a little farther away from me. I leaned and listened as hard as I could, intrigued by the odd conversation they were having. "He helped me out once. Got me a heck of a settlement. Thank him for me, will you? When you see him."

"What's your name?"

"Stella. Stella Stevens." She smiled again. "I bet you look like Jimmy did when he was young. He's a handsome man, given his age."

"I'll tell him that, too," James said.

"Now let's get you into room three, shall we, and see what

you've done to yourself?" She guided him through the big double doors that led to the examination rooms, and I lost sight of them both.

The ghost sleeping on the grandmother's shoulder shifted, snorting, and I held my breath. I didn't want to attract his attention again. All he did was drop back to sleep, snuggling in to the crook of the woman's neck like a child sleeping in his mother's arms.

Twenty-five minutes later, James burst through the double swinging doors on the arm of the nurse, laughing uproariously, his hand swathed in white bandages. He clutched Stella's elbow with his good hand, and steered her over to stand in front of me. I was surprised that it ticked me off a bit, him clutching Stella's elbow like that, but chalked it up to some sort of Florence Nightingale syndrome. After all, I'd practically saved the guy's life. All she'd done was stitch his hand. I tried to smile.

"Marie, I'd like you to meet Stella Stevens. Stella, this is the woman who saved my life, Marie Jenner."

"I don't think I saved his life, exactly." I laughed way too heartily as I shook the nurse's hand.

"It was a nasty cut. It was a good thing you brought him in." The nurse twinkled a smile at James. "I should get back to work. Good to meet you, James. Remember to say hi to your uncle for me."

"Will do." James waved at her as she hurried off through the grumbling, hurt throng still waiting for her ministrations. "Shall we get back to work?" I realized he was talking to me, and quit glaring at the nurse.

"Do you think you should? Maybe you should take the rest of the day off or something."

"No, I'll be fine. Just have to keep it dry." He snorted. "Might be tough, the way the basement is, but I'll do my best."

"Should we take a bus?" It was either the bus or walking, and I didn't feel like walking twelve blocks. Inadequate footwear.

"Nah, let's grab a cab. The least I can do is get you back to work in style." He walked to the courtesy phones, and in short order a cab was waiting for us.

"I should have thought of that," I muttered. "I have connections."

"So do I." James smiled, and held the door for me. "Milady."

I got in, scooting over as far as I could so there was room between the two of us in the back seat. No more shoulder holding for me. James gave the driver the address for the Palais, and leaned back in the seat next to me. I swore I could feel heat radiating from the man, and leaned away from him, so I could think.

"How does your hand feel?" I asked. I thought it was a safe question.

"Not bad. Stella gave me a shot. Took the edge right off." He grinned and held his bandaged hand up for me to see. All the fingers seemed to be in the right places, which was a good sign.

"Are you sure you should go back to work?"

"Yes. I want to figure out what happened down there. A water spigot shouldn't blow apart like that." He shook his head, then glanced over at me. "Thanks, again. That was fast thinking on your part."

"If I'd thought a little bit faster, I could've convinced someone in the building to give us a ride there—and back." I tried to laugh, and almost succeeded. "But any UPS van in a storm, I guess."

"I guess." James stared out the side window, then glanced over at me again. "Listen, I'd like to thank you properly. How about supper? Tonight, maybe?"

All right, so he was cute, and I liked sharing a sandwich with him out in front of the building and all that, but there was no way in the world I was dating the guy. There was no dating in my future. I slapped my "let's be friends" smile on my face. "No can do. Sorry."

"Oh." James looked disappointed. "Tomorrow night?"

"Nope."

"The weekend?"

He wasn't taking the hint, so I decided to put him out of his misery, quickly. "I think it'd be better if we don't go out on a date."

"Oh." James looked positively wretched. "I wanted to thank you. What if we didn't call it a date? Just a supper? Two colleagues out for—"

He was making this very difficult, and I sighed. "Maybe. Sometime. Not this week, though."

"All right." The smile was back on his face, and I felt like kicking myself. I'm supposed to be strong about stuff like this. Then, I really thought about what he'd said about the spigot.

"James, do you think I could see the spigot? The one that cut you?"

"Sure. Why?"

"Oh, I'm interested. Remember Farley Hewitt, the guy who died down there? Maybe the spigot had something to do with his death."

"Doing a little sleuthing?" He grinned.

"Maybe a little." I grinned back. I couldn't help it. His smile was infectious. "So, what do you think?"

"I'll get it for you when we get back."

The silence between us was comfortable. I glanced over at his handsome profile and wished, for a small moment, that I could bend the no dating rule. It could have been fun—but I wasn't willing to take the chance.

The cab pulled up to the Palais and we got out, walking into the main foyer.

"Give me a minute," he said, and disappeared through the door to the furnace room. He was back in moments, his good arm wet to the elbow. He held a shard of the spigot in his hand.

"Watch it. It's sharp."

"Thanks." I carefully took the piece of metal, and tucked it in my sweater pocket. "Are you going to be all right?"

"Yes." He looked embarrassed. "It was the blood."

"I know how it is. I lose it over spiders." I grinned at the look of relief that flooded his face.

"Really?"

"Yeah, really. I act like a real girl, screaming, the whole bit."

"I have trouble seeing that."

"Well, it's the truth." I pointed to the elevator. "I have to get back to work. Thanks for the cab ride."

"You're welcome. When we can talk about that supper?"

"Next week." As I turned away, I tried not to sigh. I'd deal with it when Farley had moved on, and I felt stronger.

"Good."

Marie:
The Hero, Back at the Office

Mr. Latterson and Farley were both waiting for me when I walked into the office.

"You *do* know you only have a half hour for lunch," Latterson started.

"Just tell me you left the idiot at the hospital," Farley growled at the same time.

I didn't know who to look at. Decided to deal with the living first, and turned to Mr. Latterson. "There was an accident, in the furnace room," I said. "James—you know James?"

He shrugged, but didn't stop me.

"James Lavall, the caretaker for the building. He cut his hand, and the furnace room flooded."

Mr. Latterson reacted to this news, strongly. "What happened in the furnace room? A flood? How the hell—"

"I don't know," I said, deciding for the moment not to mention the spigot. I had no idea why it had blown apart, but I wanted the chance to discuss it with Farley, alone. I hoped that talking about it would spark something in his memory. I hoped.

"James hurt himself, so I helped him. Then I had to take him to the hospital." I pointed at the phone sitting on my desk. At the red flashing light, indicating a voicemail message. "I called."

Mr. Latterson stared at the phone. It was obvious he hadn't

71

seen the light. "Oh," he finally said. "Oh, well, that's good." He patted me on the back, called me a hero, and then disappeared into his office.

Then Farley and I were alone.

"Somebody messed with the spigot, Farley," I said.

"Your face is flushed," Farley said acidly. "What, are you falling for that guy?"

I stared at him for a second, then sat down and stared at the top of my desk. "No, I'm not. Give it a rest."

"Well, quit looking like that, then." He frowned ferociously, then blinked. "What did you say?"

"I said I'm not—" I started. Farley shook his head impatiently.

"Not that," he said. "You said something about a spigot. What about it?"

"Oh. Somebody screwed with it. That's how James cut his hand. He went to turn it on, to run water, you know, and it blew apart." I pulled the piece of twisted metal out of my sweater pocket and put it on the desk.

Farley stared at it for a long time. "Did the idiot—"

"His name is James. James Lavall. Don't call him an idiot." I felt warmth as I blushed. God, now I'm standing up for him. What was wrong with me?

"Did he use a hacksaw on this?" Farley asked, pointing at the spigot.

"No. He said he found it this way. He was trying to change it, when it blew." I really looked at the metal piece, and understood why Farley had asked the question. It did look like it had been cut. I touched one of the edges, gingerly, then pulled my finger back. No wonder James hurt himself on it.

"Why would someone do this?" I asked.

"The bigger question is, who did it," Farley replied.

"I don't have a clue."

"Maybe Carruthers," Farley mumbled. "Maybe him."

"Carruthers? The owner of the building? Why would he do something like this?"

"I don't know," Farley said. "Just a thought." He leaned in, getting as close as he could to the spigot. The piece of metal had cut the varnish, leaving a small white scar.

"Is it ever sharp," Farley said. "No wonder the kid—James— cut himself. Those edges look like so much razor wire."

And then, he faded. Most of his light left him. He looked like a smoky smudge curling over my desk, staring at the sharp edges of the broken spigot.

"Farley!" I cried.

"What's wrong with your voice?" Farley asked, his eyes never leaving the spigot. "You sound like you got cotton in your mouth."

He faded even more, and when he looked up at me, his eyes looked like two burnt coals, dead black in the grey of his face.

"It's funny," he said. "Razor wire that close doesn't look dangerous at all."

Razor wire? What was he talking about? Why was he fading so quickly? This was bad. Even worse than the time before. He was like a black hole, sucking all the light and colour from everything around him. He just kept staring at the spigot as though his eyes were glued to the thing.

"Farley!" I cried. "I can barely see you, what's going on . . . Farley, don't go!"

Then Mr. Latterson stuck his head in the room, demanding to know what all the yelling was about. And blink. Farley was gone.

Farley:
To Hell, Again

My hand on the wire, the sound of the hacksaw, the voice, like hearing it through a tube, and then white. Then it would start again. Thirty-five to forty seconds, tops. Over and over and over again. Not being able to hear what the voice was saying past "that would sell on eBay" or some shit. All I could tell for sure was that it was my hand on the wire, and I knew the voice from somewhere.

Jesus, Marie, help me. Please.

Marie:
Again with the Blinking

I didn't check to see if Farley was hiding somewhere in the office, because I had to concentrate on Mr. Latterson, who was yelling at me because I was being entirely too loud. He said, "Stop wasting my time and money and get back to work."

"I will, Mr. Latterson."

When his door shut, I clicked the computer mouse. The only name Farley had mentioned before he disappeared was the owner of the building, George Carruthers. It was time to find out as much as I could about him.

What I found was a big fat zero, zilch, nada. Well, close to it, anyway. George Carruthers owned a bunch of buildings besides the Palais in Edmonton, and he'd recently moved from the Palais to an office in a much more fashionable part of downtown Edmonton.

Other than that, he managed to stay right off the grid. I'd have to figure out another way to get information about him. However, that would have to wait, because Mr. Latterson's afternoon appointment walked in.

It was Raymond Jackson, aftershave wafting from every pore, as usual.

"So, is he here?"

The drinks he'd had with lunch—or for lunch—were barely disguised by the spearmint candy in his mouth. I noticed the new diamond chip imbedded in his right incisor, and tried not to roll my eyes. I could only imagine what this bad boy wannabe's car looked like.

"He's in his office. One moment and I'll get him for you." I walked to Mr. Latterson's door, though I could've pressed the intercom button. I had to get out of the aftershave.

"Mr. Latterson." I knocked and entered, frightening him so badly papers flew from his hands in a small avalanche. "Your two p.m. is here."

"Good." Latterson tried to act like he was cool and together, but only managed to rub the sweat from his face into the thinning hair on his scalp. It was not a good look for him. "Send him in."

Raymond sauntered by me, his hand touching my back and sliding around to cop a quick feel as he stepped to the door. I sidestepped him, and his hand hung, groping in the air like a squid pulled from the ocean.

"Thanks, Sweetie," he said, the diamond chip glittering. "We'll talk later."

"You're welcome." I held the smile as long as I could, which was until the door clicked shut, then staggered over to the entry door and opened and closed it several times, trying to clear the air so I could breathe. I glowered at the controls for the furnace and air conditioner. Why couldn't I move air in this office?

James, even though he was injured and all that, was the handyman. He needed to do something about my situation. I put the phone to voice mail, and stalked out to find him.

I wasn't mad at James about the air conditioner. Not really. I was worried about Farley, and about my mother, and about my money problems, and every other stupid thing that seemed to have landed in my lap since I took this job.

Luckily, I realized there was a very good chance I was going to take it out on James, injured or not, so, I turned right instead of left, and walked out the ornate front doors. I'd walk around the block, get some air and some perspective, then go back in and figure out Farley's problem. If I could.

The big problem was, the further I walked, the less perspective I got. Meaning I had no idea in the world what I was going to do about Farley.

So, I decided to call my mother, for real this time. I was ready to put my own crap aside for the moment to get to the bottom of Farley's situation. Something really weird was going on with him. I needed help.

That's when I realized I'd left my stupid cell phone in my purse, which was under my stupid desk. I wasn't going back there. Not yet. I needed a phone, but couldn't remember if there was a phone booth on the block. It's something you don't look for, when you have a cell phone in your pocket.

I had to walk three blocks before I found one. Luckily, it looked like it was still in working order, so I picked up the sticky receiver, trying not to think about who had used it, and what was making it feel so tacky.

I had to do the collect call thing, because, of course, I didn't have any change on me either. Then, I hung up before my mother answered.

It wasn't because I'd jammed again about talking to her about Farley, or because she couldn't really afford to accept the call, because I knew I'd be paying for it. No, I hung up the phone because I couldn't think of any way to have a decent conversation with my mother when a ghost was crammed in the phone booth with me.

The ghost materialized beside me, and she was glowing. I'd seen her on the streets the past few weeks, screaming at passersby. At first I'd thought she was one of the unaware dead, but I soon realized she was very much aware of her situation. I also realized she was furious about it. That made her dangerous. So, I kept my distance from her, until that moment. At that moment, she was right in my face.

"So, how we gonna do this?" she rasped.

She had been old when she died. That was about all I could tell. Living on the street for much of her life didn't help me figure her age with any accuracy at all, past old. She still had a white straw hat on her head, with plastic flowers of various sorts pinned all over the brim. I guessed she'd done the decorating herself. It was not attractive.

I hung up the phone and tried to step away from her. She was cold. Much colder than Sally had been. There was a craziness to her aura that set my nerves on edge. Phlegmy yellowish curds floated through her glow. It wasn't pretty, the way some of the dead my mother had helped had been. And it wasn't sadly striking, the way Sally's had been. No, this was ugly, and crazy, and I wanted out of the phone booth more than I could say. However, she was standing in the door. I would have to go through her to get out, and I didn't think I'd be able to handle what I found when I did.

"Well, Girlie, looks to me like you think you own this here place, but, as you can see, it's mine." She pointed to a series of scratches in the plexiglass next to the phone that meant nothing to me. "That's my name. That means—"

"This phone booth is yours."

"Yep. That about says it all." Orange mixed with the yellow, whirling in a sickening whirlpool around her. I couldn't keep my eyes from it.

"Please let me out. I don't want any trouble." I tried closing my eyes, but she leaned closer and her aura invaded me in a frightening whirl that looked sick and smelled smoky, burnt, like rubber tires set aflame. I felt ill.

"You got trouble, Girlie. More than you can handle, I wager."

I opened my eyes in time to see her walk into me.

It should have been quiet and cold, but it wasn't. It was screaming madness in there, and I felt my heart slow dangerously as I tried to fight my way through her. She was gluey, and smelled more and more like burning tires until I wanted to scream.

I didn't though. I pushed my way through her and the open door, landing at the feet of two Business Types who'd been walking together, each talking on his own cell phone. They stopped as one and stared at me as I scrabbled around on the sidewalk, trying to pull myself together.

In my head, the ghost cackled crazily, and so loudly I could barely hear the younger BT ask me if I was all right. I dragged myself from the phone booth, and the cackling lessened, taking on the sound of cellophane being crinkled in someone's frantic hands. I kicked away a little further between the two men, both of whom jumped aside, obviously not wanting to let someone who was insane touch them. Then I turned and watched the ghost move on.

It was bad. She wasn't ready. Not the way I'd seen the ones who moved on with my mother. Not the way Sally had moved on. And I'd never seen one choose to go to their form of hell, before.

I cowered behind the younger of the two guys as they tried to decide whether to call the police, and watched the spirit's aura swallow her whole, blackening as it did. First the faint bits of white that had been left in her aura were gone, then the yellow curds, and then the orange, all swallowed by the black. It whirled into the centre and disappeared. Through the crinkling of the cellophane, I could hear her scream. It stayed with me a few seconds after the extinguishment of her aura.

I shakily pulled myself upright, first using the back of the younger man's rather expensive pants, and then his jacket for purchase. He was now alone with me, because his friend had made a dash for freedom.

"Please let me go," the younger man said. Begged, really.

I could see more fear in his eyes than I had in mine. So, I let him go.

"I'm sorry," I gasped, still trying to shake the screaming out of my head as I brushed at the dirt I'd obviously transferred from the sidewalk to his jacket. "I'm so sorry."

He pushed my hands away, because I was grinding the dirt into the jacket a lot more than I was rubbing it off. "Are you all right?"

"Spider," I said. "I saw a spider. In the phone booth."

"Oh." The fear on his face disappeared, replaced by a patronizing smile. "So, you're all right?"

"Yes." I took a deep breath and let it out, slowly. "It was a big spider."

"Well, as long as you're all right." He stepped away from me, and pushed the cell phone back to his ear when it beeped. I could see the other man, who had run away when I did my lunatic dash for freedom from the phone booth, standing at the end of the block with his cell phone glued to his ear. The man who had stayed waved and walked toward him. The other man saw that I had seen him, and skittered around the corner, out of sight. The braver of the two followed, and finally, I was alone.

I searched for a place to sit down, because that had taken more out of me than I liked to admit. There was no place other than the phone booth, so I tottered back to the Palais.

James was cleaning up another goopy looking mess in the front foyer when I came through the doors. He waved at me with his bandaged hand, then looked absolutely horrified. He dropped his bucket and mop, and ran over to me. I must have looked worse than I felt, and I felt horrible. I was glad when he took my arm and led me to a chair.

"What happened?" he asked, as he helped me sit down. My legs were shaking so badly, I honestly don't know if I would have made it under my own steam. "You look like you've seen a ghost."

Well, that didn't help. I stared at him for a moment, then started laughing. Then I couldn't stop alternating between braying gusts of hysterical laughter, and sobbing. I tried to get hold of myself, really I did, but it was like I was standing way over at the other side of the foyer, watching myself completely lose it, and there was nothing I could do.

James actually carried a handkerchief, which he lent me as I tried to get myself under control. It smelled nice. Freshly washed. Just like him. That thought brought on another round of laughter and crying, and then, as suddenly as it started, it was over. I felt drained, and had no idea how I was going to handle the rest of my day. Then I looked into James' anxious eyes, and had no idea how I'd handle the next five minutes. I decided the spider gambit was a good one, and worth another try.

"I saw a spider," I whispered as I handed the damp handkerchief back to him. "A really big one."

"Boy, you weren't kidding about those things getting to you, were you?" I could see that he wasn't buying what I was selling, but I was too tired to try anything else. I nodded, hiccupping once.

"It was really big."

He nodded again, absently, as though he'd already dismissed my inordinate fear of spiders. "Do you know Helen Latterson?"

"Mr. Latterson's wife?" I shook my head. "Only talked to her on the phone once. Why?"

"Well, she called me a little while ago. She has a job for me."

"Mr. Latterson's wife has a job for you?"

"Yeah. But not as a handyman." He smiled, sheepishly. "Remember, I used to work for my uncle?"

"Your uncle the private investigator, right?"

"Right. He's out of town and I told him I'd take his calls until he got back."

"And she called?"

"Yes."

82

"What does she want?"

"Information about Don Latterson." He looked at me, and seemed embarrassed. "He's getting ready to divorce her, she thinks, and she wants to find out all his assets—and where they are—before he cuts her loose. She says she needs the information right away." James looked miserable. "Normally, Uncle would handle this kind of thing, but—"

"He's on vacation," I said.

"And I can't get hold of him." He looked even more miserable. "There usually aren't any phone calls when he's out of town."

"So, you need to find out how much Mr. Latterson has and where he's hidden it."

"That's about it, yeah." He glanced at me, and for the merest second, I saw someone else hidden behind mild-mannered James Lavall. That person looked sharp and smart—and cold. Cold as ice. Then he was gone, and James' good-natured befuddlement came back, so quickly I almost didn't believe I'd seen what I'd seen. "Do you think you can help me?"

"You want me to go through Mr. Latterson's stuff? To see what I can find?" I laughed at the look of horror on his face.

"It sounds so bad when you say it out loud," he said. "Never mind. I'll figure out another way to do this." He pushed his hair back with his bandaged hand. "There has to be another way."

I thought for about a second. "Mr. Latterson's probably going to go out again. If he does, I'll see what I can find. If I see anything interesting, I'll let you know about it, and then you can figure out how to get it yourself."

I wasn't sure why I said that to him. Maybe because he carried a clean handkerchief, and shared. Maybe because I saw someone else hiding behind James' façade, and that intrigued me. Maybe because Mr. Don Latterson really was a dick. Maybe a combination. Whatever it was, the look of relief on his face was nice to see.

"Oh, that'd be great! Just a hint, to set me in the right direction." He grinned and took my hand, and I felt his heat warming me. "I definitely will take you out somewhere really nice. I owe you huge."

"We can talk about that later." I put my hands on the arms of the chair, and considered standing up. My legs had stopped shaking, and I thought maybe I could do it. "I should get back to the office."

"Maybe you should sit a couple minutes more." His worried face was back, and I wished I had a mirror. How bad did I look?

"No, I can get up." I tried to smile at him, hoping it looked reasonably natural. "Really. I'm fine."

He smiled back, so I must've done all right. "Want me to walk you to the elevator?"

"No. You go back to your mess." I pointed at the goop. "Any idea what it is, this time?"

"No idea." He grimaced, then laughed. "Whatever it is, it's part of the devil-may-care world of the caretaker." He stood, giving me a chance to admire the way he was put together.

I felt my face heat when he caught me staring, so I turned away and walked purposefully toward the elevator.

"Talk to you later," I called, as the elevator door opened. I didn't look back at him. No way. I stepped into the elevator like a queen or something, and didn't collapse in a hugely embarrassed ball until the doors slowly slid shut.

Mr. Latterson was still in his office with Raymond. That wasn't good. I needed them to leave if I was going to get into his office, and look at his bank statements. However, I could go online and see what I could find out about him. So I sat down and hacked into Mr. Latterson's life.

I felt a little bit twitchy as I did so, because I had my back to his office door, and I really did not want to let him catch me. He'd lost his mind on me for looking at websites about ghosts. How would he react to me checking out his online life?

Luckily, it didn't take long because I didn't find much. A pathetic looking website that hadn't been updated in forever, and that was about all. Talk about flying under the radar.

I had a couple of his bank account statements sitting on my desk, but they were still in their envelopes, so I couldn't check them out. I needed to, though, if I was going to find any information for James.

I glanced at the clock above the door. Mr. Latterson usually left before this time. What would happen if he stayed until the end of the day? I wouldn't have enough time to go through his office, and still get to my cab job on time. I couldn't afford that.

Gerald the Tyrant would pink slip me as soon as look at me if

I was late again, and I wasn't ready to let that job go, yet. In fact, I was starting to think it was important that I keep that job, because something didn't feel right with this one. If a man hides money from his soon-to be-ex-wife, there's a good chance that a newly hired receptionist could get ripped off, too.

Darn it, anyhow.

I heard raised voices in the next room, and quickly shut down Mr. Latterson's website, clearing the history moments before Mr. Latterson threw open the door and stormed into the reception area.

"Don't know when I'll be back," he said, anger and sweat steaming off him in a nasty mist. "Lock up."

Ray followed on his heels, avoiding my eyes, and then the door slammed shut. I waited until I heard the elevator go down, carrying them away. This was the break I needed.

I was lucky. The lock on his door was old enough that my old credit card actually popped it open. I quickly checked his office, but found no bank statements. I glanced at my watch. I had an hour before I had to leave.

There was a closet in the back corner of the office. I checked the door, and it was unlocked. Inside was a bunch of stuff, including a lock box. I picked it up, and saw a hair stuck across the spot where the top and bottom of the lock box met. It was Mr. Latterson's. I could see where the hair dye stopped on it, and everything.

"Oh my God," I muttered. "A hair? He's watched too many movies."

I carefully removed the hair and opened the box. Inside sat all the bank statements, including several for Rochelle Martin. They had all been opened, and were in their own file folders and everything.

What they told me was, Mr. Latterson had money. Lots of it. Just none of it was in his regular accounts. Most was offshore. Across the top of each of the offshore statements, he had obligingly written the access numbers.

There was also the Rochelle Martin account. It held nearly one hundred thousand dollars. What I found in Mr. Latterson's business and personal accounts? A couple of thousand in each, and that was all.

I wondered what was going to happen when I gave all this information to James. He'd give them to Mrs. Latterson, and then she'd clean Mr. Latterson out the way he was trying to do to her. Probably.

Ain't love grand?

All James really needed were the names of the banks and the account numbers, but I took out every statement and made photocopies of them, including Rochelle Martin's.

Then, I carefully returned the statements to the file folder, and put it back into the lock box. I locked it, and reached for the hair, which I'd placed nearby.

I couldn't find it and nearly choked on my tongue. It looked like it had floated away.

Why there would be a draft in that closet when I couldn't get one tiny bit of air movement in the front reception area was beyond me, and I tried not to think about that as I flailed around, my heart pounding in my chest. Then I saw it—at least I hoped it was the same hair—floating gently next to a pile of papers under the box.

I grabbed it and stuck it back on the lock, my hands shaking so badly I almost lost it again. When I was certain that everything was as he'd left it, I carefully relocked Mr. Latterson's office. I hid the photocopied documents in the bottom of my purse, my hands still quivering. It looked like I had palsy or something. Then, I locked up the office for the night.

I'd stolen documents from my boss, for the cute caretaker, for Heaven's sake. What was I trying to prove?

I was trying to make things right for his soon to be ex-wife and kids. That's what I was trying to prove. No one should walk out on his wife and kids and leave them destitute. No one.

Farley:
The Nightmare Continues

"That'll sell on EBay," flash. "That'll sell on EBay," flash. "That'll sell on EBay," flash.

Oh God, Marie, get me out of this. I'm begging you.

Marie:
James and his Uncle

The next day, I came into work a half hour early and went to the furnace room to give James the photocopied bank statements. I opened the door to quiet and dark and almost left, thinking he was cleaning up some other bit of goop somewhere else in the building. Then I heard sobbing.

My heart jumped, but I walked down the stairs. I thought I was going to find Farley, to be honest. I figured he'd come back and was feeling down in the dumps.

I was about to whisper "Farley, is that you?" but something stopped me. Thank goodness, because it was James I found, sobbing behind the furnace.

He had his face in his hands, and it was obvious he didn't know I was there. When I realized I was dealing with one of the living, I tried to back out before he saw me.

Of course, I ran into the side of the furnace as I tried to back away, and then I tripped over something—probably my own feet—as the furnace rang like a deep throated bell. James turned around, eyes blood red.

"What are you doing?" he asked. "You're not supposed to be down here."

"The door was unlocked," I said. "Are you okay?" I wished with all my heart I'd been quieter. He wasn't okay. Not even close.

James wiped his eyes hastily and stood up, kicking the chair he had been crouched on against the furnace, causing it to ring out its sombre, funereal tone again. "I got some bad news."

"I—oh, I'm sorry." I glanced around, actually planning a quick escape, then shook myself. He needed a little help here. The least I could do was listen. "What happened?"

"My uncle." James took a swipe at his nose with his open hand, like a kid would. "He—died."

"Oh, James." Without knowing how it happened, I was standing beside him, with my hand on his arm. "Are you—what can I do?"

"Nothing," he said, pushing past me and playing with some buttons on the furnace. "It's okay. It just shook me up, you know?"

"What happened?"

"They think it was a heart attack." James tried to smile again. Didn't pull it off. "He died at a blackjack table in Las Vegas. That would've pleased him." He turned and rammed his hands deep into his pockets. "I have to make some arrangements. Get him home, and stuff. I'm the only family left, now."

It didn't seem like the best time to tell him about the information I'd gathered. I stared down at the papers in my hand, not knowing what to do with them. I didn't want to take them back up to the office, in case Mr. Latterson was there. I didn't want to leave them lying around here, either. I took a tentative step toward him, and he slowly focused on my face.

"I have that information you asked for. If you want."

I held out the photocopied pages, and he stared at them.

"Thanks," he finally said. "I appreciate this." He took them from me and rolled them in a tube, then stared at the furnace again, as though he wasn't sure what else to do.

"Maybe you should go home." I tried to speak softly, gently. He didn't look like he could take anything more. "You know, and make the arrangements."

"Yeah. Maybe I should." He stared down at his hands, turning over the tube of papers as though he didn't recognize them. "Can you do me a favour?"

"What?"

"Call Mr. Carruthers and let him know what happened? Tell him I'll be gone for the rest of the day."

"Sure."

He shuffled a few steps, then stopped. "He was the only family I had left," he muttered.

"I'm really sorry, James."

"So am I." He looked at me with those bloodshot eyes, and I wanted to scoop him into my arms and hold him, but I didn't. I stood there like some kind of an idiot until he walked slowly to the steps and up, like his shoes each weighed a ton. Then he was gone, and I was down in the furnace room, alone.

It was creepy down there, and I left, making sure I shut off the lights and locked the door. Then I went back up to Mr. Latterson's office, getting ready before he arrived for the day.

When he walked through the door, Mr. Latterson looked like crap. His jacket was wrinkled, and his shirt looked like he'd partied hard in it. I didn't say a word, simply handed him his coffee and watched as he downed it in two huge swallows. He handed me the cup, indicating another, please. Without the please. As I made it for him, he stood there, staring at the top of my desk.

"Can I get you anything else, Mr. Latterson?" I handed him the second coffee, and watched him slug half of it back.

"No," he said.

"Do you have Mr. Carruthers' number?" It seemed like an innocent question. However, he jumped as though I'd shocked him.

"What do you need that for?" he finally asked, trying to brush off the coffee he'd spilled on his lapel, and managing to work it into the material so he had a big brown spot on the grey.

"James Lavall, the caretaker, asked me to let him know he wouldn't be in today. There was a death in his family."

"Oh." Latterson stared at me for a long, calculating moment. "Oh." The first hint of a smile touched his lips. "Hmm." He turned to his office, some of the bounce back in his step. "You let me handle that."

"Are you sure? It'd only take me a minute."

"No, it's okay. It's absolutely all right." He smiled, possibly the first real smile I'd ever seen on that man's face, and walked into his inner sanctum. The door boomed shut, and I was alone.

Farley:
The Nightmare Won't Stop . . .

"That'll sell on EBay," flash. "That'll sell on EBay," flash. "That'll sell on EBay," flash.

Marie:
Helping James

James came to work the next day. I was surprised to see him, considering how broken up he'd been about his uncle, but when I walked through the front doors, he was cleaning out a garbage can. He smiled as I walked up to him.

"How are you?" I asked, and then felt instantly angry at myself for staying stuck in inane mode. However, he seemed better, much better, than he had the day before.

"I feel okay."

"I'm glad." I fumbled around, trying to think of exactly the right words to say, and came up with nothing. James let me off the hook and started the conversation.

"When I was making the arrangements to get my uncle's body back I found out I'm the executor of his estate."

"Really." Seemed like the right thing to say, because he acted like he wanted me to keep the conversation going. "Does your uncle have much?"

"No. Not as far as I know, anyhow." He looked sheepish. "We weren't as close as we could have been."

"Even though you worked for him?" The question popped out of my mouth before I could stop it. Luckily he didn't seem to mind.

"Yeah. Even though I worked for him. Could be because I

worked for him. I hadn't even seen his new office. For the last few months, we just talked on the phone." He shuffled his feet, staring down at them as though surprised they were moving. "I guess it's too late to think about that, now."

"Yeah, I guess." I tried to sound sympathetic, but all I felt was a teeny bit of jealousy. He didn't have to worry about ghosts showing up, causing trouble. He just had to deal with never seeing his uncle again.

"I have to go clean out his offices and stuff," he said. "Guess I have a month."

"A month?"

"Yeah. I have one month to finish any of his unfinished work, get his bills paid, stuff like that."

"Oh."

"Shouldn't take that long, though. He just had the one case, as far as I know."

"Mrs. Latterson?"

"Yeah." He looked disconcerted. "I don't know what to say to her. She thinks Uncle is dealing with this. The information you gave me was good, and I thank you for it, but now I have to put it in a report or something. You know, like he would." He shook his head. "I've never done any of that before."

"Do you want some help?" I had enough on the go with two jobs, Mom, and Farley, but the guy just lost his uncle. I couldn't leave him swinging in the wind like that. "I could type it up, if you show me how it should be formatted."

"That'd be great. I have to go to his office tonight. Want to come with me? He had files, I bet we can look them over and figure it out. While you're doing that, I can start doing some cleaning." He shook his head. "Uncle wasn't the best for cleaning."

I had the night off. I was planning on doing some laundry, because I was at the desperation section of my closet, but the thought of going back to that completely empty apartment didn't thrill me, so I thought, *What could it hurt?* I said yes, I could help him. The smile he gave me was worth it.

James pulled up to the front of the Palais in an older model Volvo, one of the higher end ones, I guessed.

"Wow, nice car." I got in and rubbed my hand appreciatively

over the leather seat. "I didn't think Carruthers paid that well."

"He doesn't," James said. "This was my uncle's." He looked uncomfortable. "Now it's mine."

"Oh. Cool." I leaned back in the seat, enjoying the luxury of the butter soft leather for a moment. "You get anything else besides the car?"

"His business."

"He left you—?"

"Yeah. My uncle left me his business." James shook his head. "I'm still trying to figure out what to do with it. Probably sell it, or something. If I can."

"Why couldn't you sell a business?"

"Because, well, he was it, really. Now that he's dead—" He sighed. "He made me the executor of his estate. So now, I am, temporarily, a licensed private investigator."

"Temporarily?"

"For a month." He shrugged. "It's so that I can finish up the Latterson case, and whatever else he had going on. If there was anything."

"I never knew a private dick before," I said. Weak joke, I know, but I hoped he'd smile.

"I'm not a private dick!"

"Okay." I grinned and he grinned back. That was close enough to a smile for me. "Where's the office?"

"Chinatown. Uncle moved there to cut down on costs, I think." We drove north for a few silent moments.

"Any idea why he left it all to you?" I asked. Then I looked over at him, and I swear he flinched.

"Because we have the same name," he said.

"You have the same name as your uncle, and that's the reason he left you his business?"

"Yeah. He said I wouldn't have to pay to have the sign changed. It could stay 'Jimmy Lavall, Private Investigator'." James' voice got tight and a little high. He was readying himself for ridicule.

"Go ahead, laugh," he said. "I know you want to."

"No. No." I shook my head vigourously. "Honestly. I'm not going to laugh. Really." Then I laughed, a little. "Sorry. It's just—"

"Yeah I know."

"He must've been doing okay," I said. "I mean, look at the car."

"You'd think so, but he was living in his office. Does a guy that's doing okay live in his office?"

"I don't know."

"I don't think so. All he had was this car and that ratty little office."

"And his name—your name—on the door."

"Yeah. My name on the door."

James ushered me into the darkened office with an apologetic grin on his face. "It doesn't look great in here," he said. "Uncle was always messy."

I felt the smile freeze on my face as he turned on the lights.

"Oh, it's not that bad," I muttered, but it was. Messy? The place was a wreck.

I suppose if you cleared away the newspapers and magazines—and the old clothes, the ironing board and iron, the cot in the corner behind the desk, the hot plate and the many dirty and decaying containers of food sitting on and around the desk, it was probably a nice office. But really. It was supposed to be a place of business.

"No, this is terrible," James said as he glanced around the office. "Maybe we should forget about this. I don't even see his file cabinets." He looked horrified. "How could he let it get this way? This is his business, for heaven's sake."

I was going to say something glib like "my words exactly" and then let him drive me home, but I didn't. As bad as this place was, I wasn't ready to face my empty apartment.

"If I give you a hand, it won't take long to clean this place, and then I'll type up the report for you. Really. Won't take any time at all."

"But—" he started, obviously trying to give me a way out. I ignored him, and after a few minutes, we were both hard at work.

Two hours later, we were still at it. James had found some decent scotch in the bottom drawer of the tiny desk, and we were sipping it as we cleaned, using two chipped glasses I found stuffed in the back of one of the other drawers. We'd packed away most of the garbage, leaving the myriad bags and boxes outside the door of the office, so we didn't have to look at them anymore.

I found cleaning supplies stuffed under the cot, and went to town on the place. In a little while, it started to smell better and look less like a hoarder had lived there.

To be honest, I was beginning to think there was hope for the room. It was actually starting to look like a place of business. Except for the complete lack of office equipment, of course. Since I was the one that had to type up that report, I was the one to notice.

"Where's the phone? And a computer? Or a typewriter? Or anything?"

"I don't know." James emerged from the pile of old man clothes he'd been trying to fit into a woefully inadequate box. "Maybe he sold everything. It doesn't look he was doing much work here." He rammed a couple more shirts into the box, and folded the lid shut. "What should I do with this stuff?"

"Put it outside with the rest of the junk." I spoke without glancing up from the legs of the desk, which I was scrubbing. It felt good to do something, and be able to see the difference I'd made. It was also easier than trying to figure out how I was going to type a report on a nonexistent computer.

"This is good stuff," James muttered. "I don't think we should throw it away."

"Hey, do what you want. Only, if it's outside, we don't have to look at it anymore."

"Well, yeah. How about if I put it in there?" He gestured at the only other door in the room. We'd both avoided even looking at it up to that point. I assumed it was a closet. I know about closets and how much they can hold, and didn't want to see what an old man, and a pack rat to boot, could do with one.

"Just put it outside."

"No." James shook his head. "It'll be a good place to put the stuff we're not going to throw away."

"Hey, if there's room, knock yourself out." I went back to work on the desk legs. "If you get buried under a pile of garbage, I'm not helping you. Swear to God."

He placed the box on the desk and walked over to the door. I nearly laughed when he squared his shoulders before putting his hand on the doorknob and giving it a quick turn. Nothing. "It's locked."

I lost interest. "Leave it alone then."

"Why would he lock a closet?"

"I dunno. Are you getting hungry? I'm getting hungry. Is there a store around here, maybe we can buy a bag of chips or something?"

James didn't say anything, and I could hear the jingle as he fished around in his pockets for the ring of keys that had come with the car.

"I'm going to check this out, and then we can order a pizza. I want more than chips."

"Sounds good. What do you like?"

"I'm partial to cheese with fresh tomatoes," he said. He held up the key ring triumphantly. I watched him choose the third key and place it gently in the lock. It was a perfect fit. He turned the key and gingerly pulled the door open.

"Oh my goodness," he breathed.

"What?"

"Come here. You gotta see this, Marie."

Obviously, the second door did not open onto a closet. Not even close to a closet. This was where James' uncle really worked. Not the pathetic display in the other room. The only thing I can say is, he hid himself very well.

It was hard to describe the room beyond the outer office, because I had this vision of Dead Uncle Jimmy in my head, and I couldn't reconcile that vision with anything I was seeing.

Book cases—not shelves, cases—that looked expensive and went floor to ceiling, held old books that soon had James the Living laughing with delight.

"He used to have all these in his apartment," he said. "I thought he'd thrown them all away."

There was an old fashioned looking desk, probably an actual antique, with a computer screen sitting on its glowing top. Seven file cabinets, gun metal grey, standing side by side against one wall. Three pictures on the walls, all abstracts, and they looked original. Nice colours, and though it's not the type of art I like, I could appreciate what I was seeing. In fact, I could appreciate everything I was seeing.

It was a beautiful office, well used, and well kept, and it didn't look like anything that the person who had lived in the other office would have had anything to do with.

I sat in the beautiful leather chair behind the desk, and played with every bit of office equipment there. James couldn't keep in one place, going back and forth between the paintings and the books.

"There's a message on voice mail," I said, running my hands over the buttery soft leather chair. The old man really liked leather. "Should we listen to it?"

"Yeah." James didn't even glance over at me. He was back at the book cases, and he looked like a kid in a candy shop. "All right."

I stood over the machine for a moment before I pressed anything, because it looked like it could send a man to the moon. Then I pressed a button, hoping for the best.

"Mr. Lavall, this is Helen Latterson. Can you give me a call? This *is* day two." The machine then spouted off the date and time of the phone message. She'd phoned at 12:05 A.M. the night before. James stared at the machine as though the disembodied voice of his client was a voice from beyond the grave.

"What am I going to tell her?"

"Well, it's only—" Then I glanced at the clock on the desk. "Oh, it's 10:00 p.m. Do you want to call her this late?"

"I don't know if I should." James looked around like he suddenly needed a place to sit. "I mean, what do I have for her?"

"Actually, you have most of the information she needs. Call her up and tell her the report will be completed by tomorrow morning." I shrugged. "It won't take any time to type that up, now that I know where the computer is. Then we can eat."

"All right." James nodded his head. "I'll do it." He put his hand on the receiver, but did not pick it up.

"What's wrong?"

"I don't have her phone number." He grinned sheepishly. "It's on my cell."

"Well then, use your cell." I was starting to feel impatient. Why was he acting so stupid? "What's the problem?"

"Well, I left it at work—"

"Oh for heaven's sake!" I snapped, and, using the call display, looked for her number. It was not there. "I'm out of ideas," I said.

Then he snapped his fingers. "Uncle's worked for her before. That's how she had his number. I'll go through the files and see what I can find."

"Good enough." Small sigh of relief from me. I didn't want to think of James as an idiot, and chalked my feelings up to being hungry. Actually, ravenous would be a better description. "While you're in there, see how much he normally charged for a job like this. I'll make her an invoice."

"Yeah, getting paid wouldn't hurt, would it?"

"Not at all."

He stepped over to the files, then stopped. "Hey, I'll split this one with you, okay? After all, you found everything, and you're actually typing the report, so it's only fair—"

I almost said no, but thought of my mom, and my rent, and my overdue bills.

"Sure," I said, and smiled. Every little bit helps. I didn't think there'd be much. Even with all the nice stuff in this office, I didn't think James' uncle was living the good life, but I wasn't about to turn down a little extra cash.

James nodded, then turned to the file cabinets and began to go through the newest looking one, closest to the door. After a short search, he pulled out three files, and handed two to me. One of them had a copy of a report for a client, and one had some billing information that I could use to calculate how much Mrs. Latterson owed. It looked like 1.5% of all monies recovered had been Uncle Jimmy's standard, so I decided to use that number to calculate what James—and I—would be making on this deal, after I'd typed up the report.

As I worked, I listened to James on the phone. First he talked to Mrs. Latterson, who was not impressed that it had taken him so long to get back, but who seemed mollified when he told her he had information pertinent to her case, and it would be ready for her the next day. Then he called a pizza place and ordered a large, with everything but fish, exactly the way I liked it. I couldn't remember telling him that, and wondered how he'd guessed. But I forgot about that, as I began calculating how much Helen Latterson would owe us for the information I had given James.

"Come and get it!" James caroled from the outer office twenty minutes later. I couldn't answer him, because I was glued to the screen, pressing the occasional number and staring, then scratching the same numbers on a pad of paper by my hand and shaking my head, then going back to staring at the screen. I couldn't believe what I was seeing.

"Are you coming?" His voice was muffled, probably because

his mouth was stuffed with pizza. "This is really good."

"Don Latterson has more than five million dollars hidden away," I whispered to the empty room. I hadn't figured out a way to find out what he has in his security deposit boxes, and there were three of those that I knew about for sure. Most of the money I'd counted was in four different off-shore accounts. The rest was in the account under the name Rochelle Martin.

I was willing to bet that Rochelle Martin and Don Latterson were the same person, and this was where he kept his day to day, walking around money. Over one hundred thousand in walking around money. He was loaded.

"Holy crow." I recalculated the numbers again. "James, get in here. You gotta see this."

According to my calculations, we were going to make around $75,000.00. Seventy-five thousand dollars. For a second I thought it was seventy-five hundred, which would have been great, but I had the decimal in the wrong place, and we were going to make seventy-five thousand dollars on this deal!

"What?" James called, his mouth still stuffed with pizza. "What's the matter, Marie?"

"Nothing! Nothing's wrong at all! James, you have to see this!" I started to giggle. I couldn't help myself. It was such a lot of money.

"So what's so important you can't feed yourself, first?" James asked, coming through the door. "What—?" Then he stopped talking, because he saw me whirling around in the executive style chair with its buttery soft leather and multitudes of controls, giggling like a stupid kid. "What's going on?"

"We are going to be okay, James." I kept whirling around, my eyes catching his with every rotation. "Latterson's loaded, and we're going to be okay."

It took me a little longer to convince James that we had actually made a huge amount of money on the deal. He redid my calculations twice, to make sure I hadn't made a mistake, which ticked me off a smidge, but not enough to count, not really. Nothing could get me down.

We danced around singing the "We're in the money" song until we realized neither of us knew any lines past the first one and stopped. We stood in each other's arms and I stared so deeply into his eyes, I could've drowned.

That's when he kissed me. Or almost kissed me. It was so light I could have been wrong. And I almost kissed him back.

I did. My head was screaming "don't do it!" as I stepped closer and his arms went around me and our hearts beat together through the thin layers of our clothing. The screaming in my head finally got my attention as I stared into his eyes and seriously thought about ripping his clothes off, right then and there.

I took a tiny step back.

He looked into my eyes for the longest moment of my life, then loosened his grip on me. His heart no longer felt like it beat in my chest.

I stepped out of his arms and shakily walked to the desk, even though my heart was beating like a drum, and I was pretty sure he could hear it. I typed up the bill and popped it and the report into a manila envelope, scrawling Helen Latterson's name across the front. Then I went to eat pizza.

James left me two pieces, and I ate them, occasionally yawning. It had been a busy day, and a busier night.

"I'll give you a ride home," he said, as I finished the last of the pizza and topped it off with another small glass of scotch. "It's getting late."

"Yeah, I guess it is." I poured more scotch in the glass and hoisted the glass in a small salute to him. "Maybe you should consider keeping this business open yourself. You seem to have a knack for making money. Only two days since Mrs. Latterson hired you, and you're $75,000.00 richer."

"Technically, I'm only $37,500.00 richer." He grinned. "However, it beats the heck out of wages plus benefits, doesn't it?"

"It does." I glanced over at his name on the door, glowing backwards in the light from the hallway. Maybe his uncle leaving James this business had been a good thing for him.

Then, James wrecked the moment.

"Maybe we should go into business together," he said. "You know. Like this."

I almost laughed, thinking he was joking. Then I looked at him, and the laughter died in my throat.

"I don't think so."

I felt badly having to be so blunt with him, especially after he'd been good enough to split the money with me, and after I'd almost kissed him the way I had. But there was no way I was jumping into a business with this man. I didn't need more drama, I needed a paycheque and benefits.

I could tell by the way he put down his glass, his smile disappearing, that I had hurt him.

"I know you're looking for stability," he said. "I am too. But this . . . This wasn't like working for Uncle." He smiled. "Hanging around here, with you. Cleaning. Eating pizza. Finding out we're going to be paid a heck of a lot of money." He shrugged. "It was fun. Didn't you have fun?"

It had been fun. Most of it, anyhow. And I liked being with him. However, I had responsibilities. Responsibilities he would never understand. One of them was a dead guy, still trapped in the Palais Offices. I had to move him on, which meant I needed time to myself.

"I have two jobs already," I said. I didn't want to talk about myself anymore. "I don't need another one."

"Oh, so you can't use the cash?" he asked.

Oh.

"If you don't want to split the money with me, I understand completely," I said. I had to say it, though I didn't want to. We didn't have a deal going in—not really. And I knew I hurt him by saying no to his job offer. "After all, it's a lot."

"Hey, I made a deal with you," he said, his easy smile back. "You earned it. No matter what you say, I think we should work together, at least until I can get this place shut down. So, you have to give me a couple of days to convince you."

He was just talking about me helping him close down his uncle's business. He wasn't offering me a real job. I felt a huge surge of relief, but still wasn't sure that I should do something like that. "I don't know."

He smiled. "Just help me clean out the office. That's all I'm asking."

"I still don't know." I smiled back, in spite of myself. "But I'll give you a couple of days to convince me. If you want."

"Excellent," he said. "After that, I'm taking you out for supper."

"Oh." I put the glass down as I felt the walls close in on me.

"Because I owe you. Remember, you saved my life." He

pointed down at the envelope lying on the desk. "Twice, it appears. Just let me do this for you."

"All right. All right. We'll go out for supper. To celebrate." I glanced down at the glass sitting on the little desk. "And that's all."

"Fine." He gestured toward the door. "Now, let me get you home. You must be tired."

I was, and appreciated the ride, though I made him drop me off at a bus stop a few blocks from my place. I wasn't ready to let him see where I lived, wasn't ready to let him into my life like that. So I walked the five blocks it took to get home, to clear my head.

There were three messages waiting for me on my cell when I plugged it in. All three were from Gerald the Tyrant. The first two were calls for me to come in immediately, because someone had quit and he needed me to fill in. The last call was the equivalent of my pink slip.

I stared at the phone and thought about how I would've handled this information the day before. Then I pressed delete, and erased Gerald's grating voice from my life, with some relief, I must say. I didn't need him and his stupid job any longer. And then, I slept better than I had in a while, because, even though I'd almost kissed James like some kind of fool, it looked like things were finally going my way.

Marie:
Farley Went to Hell and Back. Again

I should have been happy when Farley finally did blink back, but wouldn't you know it, I was on the phone when he reappeared. He landed right on top of my desk and I almost screamed when he appeared, a dark, dirty smudge lying face up, not a foot from my face, but, like I said, I was on the phone. A good receptionist can't scream just because a ghost shows up, now can she? No, she can't. Especially when she's talking to James about the stupid celebration dinner he wanted to have.

He wanted me to choose the restaurant.

"It's called Mon Ami," I said, as I stared at Farley. His eyes were closed, and he wasn't moving. What had happened to him?

James said something witty about going to a French restaurant, and I said, "Yeah, I suppose. Any chance I can call you back?"

I was hoping that my voice would wake Farley up, but he didn't move and I started to feel creeped out. Could he be dead? Can a ghost die twice?

James said something else that I didn't catch, so I asked him to repeat, and he asked me for the address. "The address to what?" I asked.

"The restaurant," he said. "Aren't you listening to me?"

Well, no, actually, I'm not. I have this ghost on my desk, see . . .

"Yes, I am," I said. I gave him the address to the restaurant where we would be celebrating me saving his butt and making us a whole bunch of money. I didn't want to, but I'd promised him. "Did you get that?" I asked.

Mr. Latterson walked in and threw a three inch pile of papers on the desk, right in the middle of Farley. Farley opened his eyes briefly, then sighed, and closed them again.

"Do I need to take that?" Mr. Latterson asked, pointing at the phone.

"No," I replied, covering the receiver. "I can handle this. It's James. James Lavall. The caretaker."

"Why the hell is he phoning you?" Mr. Latterson looked suspicious, and I felt my heart tighten. Did he suspect something? Did he know what James and I had done?

"It's about the air conditioning," I lied quickly. "I'll take care of it."

Mr. Latterson thought for a moment, then shrugged, disappearing back into his office. I heaved a huge sigh of relief as his door closed, and put the phone receiver back to my ear.

"James, I can't talk right now," I whispered over his frantic sounding voice. "Mr. Latterson doesn't allow personal calls."

"I just wanted to ask you if you are sure about the address?" James asked. "It doesn't sound right."

"Yes, I am," I said impatiently. Jasmine had gleefully given me both the name and address of that restaurant when I'd told her about James wanting to take me out for dinner. She'd made me write it down, and I'd read it off the scrap of paper. Of course it was right. "I gotta go, James."

I hung up on him, and stared at Farley. He was still motionless.

"Farley," I whispered. "Are you all right?"

"Do I look all right?" he asked, his lips barely moving.

His voice sounded as though his voice box had been rasped raw. Wherever he'd gone, he'd been screaming. He looked as terrible as his voice sounded, and a quick knot formed in my throat. He couldn't take much more of this. Whatever "this" was.

"No, you don't," I whispered.

"Well, that answers your question, now doesn't it?" He opened his eyes again, and it looked as though it took all his strength to do so. "I was gone a long time, wasn't I?"

"Three days, Farley."

"Hmm."

"I was afraid you'd disappeared for good."

"Nope." He rolled on his side, his legs scrabbling for purchase, then gave up, and lay still. "Gotta beer?"

"A what?"

"A beer. I could really use one." He tried to move again, only managing to flop his arms above his head so he was stretched out flat on my desk. It was disconcerting the way all the office equipment stuck out of his body. "I thought I wanted a beer," he whispered. "I don't think I do."

"What do you want?" I asked.

I hoped he'd say he wanted to move on—even though I knew he didn't have the strength for that. If he didn't decide something, soon, he would lose what little strength he still had, and then he'd disappear from even my sight. Then he'd truly be beyond help.

He thought for a minute, then shrugged. "Oh, nothing, I guess," he sighed.

All right, that was not what I wanted to hear. However, I wasn't going to badger him. I would let him talk, hoping that he'd gather a bit more strength. Hoping that him telling me where he'd gone and what he'd seen would make him decide that moving on was preferable to what he'd just endured. "How was it, Farley?"

"Bad."

"As bad as the last time?"

"Worse."

"How?"

"It was longer."

"Oh."

This wasn't going the way I'd hoped. His one word answers weren't making him glow any brighter, and they sure weren't giving me anything to work with. He struggled to sit up.

"Did you know that even ultimate terror can get boring?" he asked. "I bet you didn't."

"No, I didn't," I said. "Please tell me what happened."

"The voice was back. Didn't sound like anybody talking through water, this time, though. More like talking through a tube." He shrugged. "I think the voice was saying 'that would sell on Ebay', or something. Then white. And then it would start all again. Thirty-five to forty seconds, tops. Over and over, for three fucking days." He gasped as though he'd used every last bit of his strength.

I tried to think of something to say that would comfort him, but nothing came.

"I don't want to go back there," he said.

"I wish I could stop it, but I can't." I meant it. What if he got stuck in that nightmare place, without the strength to make it back? He'd truly be in hell. "I still think you're trying to figure something out."

"Something?"

"Yes. Something."

"Like who killed me?"

"Could be."

"What the hell else could it be?"

"Lots of things," I said. I knew I sounded way too eager, but he'd finally asked about the process. I wanted to give him as much information as I could before he shut me down again. For a second, I wondered if this was the way my mother felt, when she was trying to talk to me.

"Remembering what happened to you could give you some insight into the way you lived your life." I thought of Sally, and how quickly she moved on, once she realized how she'd died. It had been such a quick jump for her—maybe Farley would be the same.

"Maybe you'll remember somebody you hurt or helped, someone who you loved or hated. Lots of things."

"But it could be who killed me."

"Yes," I sighed. "It could."

"Once I figure it out, you'll help me get the bastards?"

Oh. He wasn't looking for the truth. He was looking for revenge. That explained so much.

"No," I said. He had to quit thinking about revenge. Revenge was dangerous.

"No?" He struggled to sit up. "No?"

"I can't do that."

"What do you mean, you can't do that?"

"I mean, this can't be about revenge. If someone did something illegal, I'll make sure the police get the information, all right? However, this can't be about revenge."

"Why not?" He had started whining, and, even though I was trying really hard to be sympathetic and all that, the tone was getting on my nerves.

"Because it has to be about you," I said through gritted teeth. "How you are with things from your life."

"I've heard this before," he snapped.

"I know." I sighed, my anger collapsing into despair. Why wasn't he getting it? "There isn't much else to say. Examine your life, figure out what's holding you here, and make peace with it. It's simple, in principle."

He sat even straighter, and through the ash of his face, I thought I saw a faint tinge of light. "If all of this can't be about revenge, then why the hell should I bother?"

"Because revenge takes your light away, Farley," I said. "Soon, not even I will be able to see you. You've lost so much light, I can barely see you now."

He stared at me like I'd stuck a knife into his gut. Then he growled wordlessly, and pulled himself to standing.

"If you won't help me, I'll do it myself," he said, wounded pride oozing through every word. The interesting thing was, he gained a little more light. Trust Farley to find a way to gain strength this way. "I gotta go."

"Those nightmares hold the answer, I think," I said. "There has to be a reason you keep going there. Think about it, Farley. Think hard."

He didn't answer me. He simply trudged to the door and oozed through, out of my sight.

So, I went back to work. I mean, what else could I do? Mr. Latterson was still in his office, after all, so I couldn't just wander off. But the bit of light Farley was emanating cheered me. Even if I couldn't follow him. I could wait until Mr. Latterson left. Farley would still be here. I was sure of it.

I was typing up another "I'll pay you when I can," letter for Mr. Latterson, when he buzzed me on the intercom. "Coffee," he demanded. "Now."

I glanced at the Bunn, quickly calculating how long the coffee had been sitting. Nearly two hours. I figured if I added a bit more sugar, he wouldn't notice.

I doped his coffee and knocked on his door. Before he

answered, I walked in. He didn't notice me, because he was on the phone, his face purple as he screeched, "If you don't get this done, I will kill you, you stunned son of a bitch!"

That stopped me in my tracks. It almost made me drop the coffee cup, to be honest. Mr. Latterson finally noticed me, gasped, and slammed his hand over the receiver.

"Put it down and get out," he said. He was breathing as though he'd run a hard mile, and I imagined his heart was straining in his chest like a horse ridden close to death.

"Yes, sir," I said. "Sorry."

I put down the cup, thankfully without spilling any coffee on his desk, and backed away. As I opened the door to the reception area he returned to his conversation, so he didn't notice me leave the door open, just a crack. I had to hear the end of this conversation. It could possibly have something to do with the information I'd gathered for James.

"I only have three more days, do you understand me?" Mr. Latterson said. "If this deal goes south, you aren't worth shit to me anymore. Am I making myself clear?"

There was total silence in his office for a moment, and I could hear his teeth grinding as he listened to whoever was trying to soothe him on the other end of the line. I wished I was back at my desk, and not frozen to the slightly open door. If he burst out of that office, I knew I'd die of fright. However, he was still on the phone, literally choking on his next words.

"I don't give a flying fuck, you incredible moron! This deal has to go through. Do! You! Understand! Me?!"

There was more quiet. All I could hear was Mr. Latterson's ragged breathing. I could almost see him clutching the phone to his ear with a fist so tight every knuckle looked like it would pop right out of the skin.

"Fine," he finally said. He sounded calmer, which meant slightly less crazy. "Just do it."

I headed back to my desk on tiptoe. He said something else I couldn't make out as I carefully settled in my chair, intent on not making a sound. And then he laughed.

It was that dirty schoolboy locker room laugh all men have laughed, usually when they are talking about women in a bad way. It made my skin crawl. What had he said, and who was he talking about?

I wished for about a second that I hadn't snuck away from the door. That wish turned to watery-stomached relief when the door slammed open and he was at my desk. I'd barely made it.

"Have you finished that letter yet?"

I blinked and gaped like a fish out of water, then managed to gasp, "No."

"Well, get it done," he said. He stood, staring at me.

"Now?" I whispered. I was afraid to put my hands on the keys of the typewriter, to be honest. My hands were shaking so badly, I knew they'd give me away.

He didn't move. "Yes," he said. "Get it done right now."

I willed my hands to calmness, and began typing. It went well, all things considered, and after just a few moments, it was done, and I handed it to him with a flourish. He ignored it.

"I have another letter for you to send," he said. "Take notes."

"Yes, sir," I said, and grabbed my dictation pad. I frantically scribbled down his rambling, this time to a lawyer. I wondered if the lawyer was his soon to be ex-wife's. When he pleaded insolvency, I was sure I was right.

Why was he talking about this in front of me? Maybe he was trying to have me be part of the fraud. "Oh yes," I'd have to say to his ex-wife's lawyer. "He couldn't pay anyone. He couldn't even pay me."

This thought ran roughshod over my fear, replacing it with anger. Son of a gun. I was going to get ripped off, too. The information I'd given James was going to help Mrs. Latterson and her kids, but it wasn't going to do a thing to help me.

"You got a problem?"

I looked up, and Mr. Latterson was staring at me as though he'd read my mind. Maybe I wasn't as good at hiding my feelings as I thought.

"Are—are you going to be able to pay me?" I asked.

"Why would you ask me that?" he glared. I wasn't backing down. The only reason I'd taken this stupid job was because he'd promised to pay me more than I was being paid at the cab company. If he was going to rip me off, he'd have to tell me to my face.

I pointed to the letter I had just finished typing, and then to my dictation pad. He frowned as though he didn't understand, then laughed.

"Oh, these?" he asked. "Nothing for you to worry about. Really. You will be paid."

"You guarantee it?" I asked.

"Absolutely." His face momentarily went to stone. "You'll get everything you deserve."

"Thank you," I whispered, and turned back to the pad.

He hadn't made me feel any more secure. As a matter of fact, the look on his face had frightened me more than I wanted to admit. It didn't help that Farley decided to return at exactly that moment.

My heart nearly jumped out of my chest as he burst through the closed door, ecto goo splashing everywhere.

"You are in danger!" he cried, then shambled to a stop in front of my desk, and stared at Mr. Latterson. "Huh," he said. "Took me longer to get here than I thought it would. He was in his office—"

I glanced at him for a second, hoping he'd get the hint and shut up. I was surprised at how much brighter he was. Something out there had given him strength—but I didn't have time to figure that out. Mr. Latterson was back to dictating his "I have no money" letter, and I had to keep up. It was hard though, because Farley walked up to Mr. Latterson and stopped, inches from him.

It looked like he was staring at Mr. Latterson's sweat stains. I kid you not.

Now, Mr. Latterson was sweating more than usual, that was true. I suspected that the phone call had stressed him out. A lot. Still, it was eerie the way Farley stared at Mr. Latterson's back. The sweat stain right in the middle of his off white shirt was growing. Even I could see that. It was so wet, I could see the skin and the hair of his back through the fabric.

I hadn't realized Mr. Latterson was so hairy.

As he droned on about thin profit margins and the exchange rate of the dollar, Farley began to sway. For a moment, I was afraid he was going to drop to the floor—or worse, disappear again—but he turned to me, and stared, whispering, "I have to save you."

I jumped when Mr. Latterson rapped his knuckles on my desk. "Did you get that?"

"Yes," I said, hoping I wasn't lying.

"Type it now, and put it with the others," he said, and then disappeared into his office. I heard the door click shut, but skittered over to it and made sure it was closed, anyhow. He didn't need to hear me talking to Farley.

"I'm glad you're back," I said. "I was afraid—"

"Marie, shut up for a minute," Farley said, staring right into my eyes. "I got something important to tell you. I heard Don, down in the furnace room. I heard Don."

"Mr. Latterson wasn't in the furnace room. He's been in his office all day. What are you talking about?"

"I heard him—I was down in the furnace room—I could hear him through the furnace vents. He was on the phone, talking to somebody. He's doing something . . . something." He fell silent, still staring at me as though he couldn't look away, and groaned. "God dammit, what's wrong with my mind? This is important!"

He was whimpering. He sounded so afraid that I did my best to calm him.

"Relax. This happens, happens sometimes." I stared into his eyes, giving him a way to connect. "You'll come back. Give yourself a second."

"All right," he said after a moment. "I feel better. Much better."

"I told you," I said.

Then he reacted in true Farley form. He got angry.

"How the hell am I supposed to get any work done if my fucking mind keeps fading in and out like that?" he yelled, then shook his head. "Forget it. This is more important. Macho Don is going to do something sinister."

I tried to keep the smile from my face, but I could tell by his look that I was unsuccessful. "Sinister?"

"Yes," he barked. "Sinister. He's got some big deal planned for three days from now, and he said that you're part of it."

"I'm part of—?" Then I stopped in mid-sentence as another thought hit me. "Tell me again how you heard this? Mr. Latterson never left his office."

"Through the furnace vents," he said, again. "Why?"

I started to feel excited, and a little bit hopeful. Like I was on the verge of connecting a couple of really big dots. "When you were alive, did you listen to people through the furnace vents?"

He had the good grace to look embarrassed. "Sometimes."

"Did Mr. Latterson's voice sound like the voice you heard in your nightmare?"

"What?" He glared at me as though I was suddenly speaking Greek. "What the hell are you talking about?"

"Mr. Latterson's voice through the furnace vent. Was that the voice you heard in your nightmare?"

"Oh." He frowned. "Huh." Then he shook his head. "Similar, maybe, but it wasn't Macho Don."

"Are you sure?" My disappointment cut through me so hard I almost checked to see if I was bleeding.

"It couldn't have been," Farley said. "Macho Don moved into this office after I died. That nightmare is my death." He shuddered. "Over and over, my death."

"So, it was someone else's voice you heard," I said. "Any idea whose?"

"No." Surprisingly, he smiled. "There are only a few offices that I can hear in the furnace room. So, it'd be one of them."

"Good," I said, putting a clean piece of paper in the typewriter and bashing out Mr. Latterson's letter to the lawyer. I was still massively disappointed that it wasn't Mr. Latterson that Farley was hearing in his nightmare. I was really starting to dislike Mr. Latterson.

"I'll go check them out," he said. "It shouldn't take me too long. Promise me you'll watch yourself, okay?"

"Watch myself?"

"Macho Don is trouble, Marie. Real trouble, I think." He shook his head. "You didn't hear him talking about you. Like you were meat or something."

I stopped typing the letter and stared at him. "Did he laugh?' I asked, my voice catching in my throat.

"Yeah," Farley said.

I stared down at the half-finished letter, and felt sick. He'd been talking about me. Laughing about me. I thought for a moment about leaving, then I gave my head a shake. A dirty laugh wasn't enough to force me out. I needed to stay.

It didn't have anything to do with the money he was supposed to pay me, anymore. It was about helping Farley move on.

He wasn't going to be able to do that if he thought he could protect me. He had to quit worrying about me, and concentrate on himself. I was certain he'd never do that if he thought that I was in danger. So, I tried to lighten things, and get his mind off what he'd heard about me.

"Men are pigs," I said, shrugging. "What can you do?"

"Kick him in the nuts," Farley said. "For a start."

I laughed a little. "Maybe I'll try that," I said. "I appreciate the fact that you're trying to look out for my best interests."

I smiled at him, and he smiled back.

"I wish—" He took a deep breath and blew it out. "I wish I could stick around and watch you finish growing up." He said it fast, bravado leaking out of him like summer sweat. "I think you're going to be amazing."

Oh my.

"You know you can't, right?" I asked.

"I know."

"I appreciate it, though. I really do." I turned away from him, pulling the plastic cover back over the typewriter, and trying to wrap my head around what he'd just said.

First, he'd tried to warn me about danger, and then he'd actually said he wanted to stick around. Watch me grow up, or whatever. It sounded like maybe he was beginning to attach to me. And that was bad.

I needed a game plan, some way to deal with this, but I couldn't do it with him staring at me with his worried face. I was glad I legitimately had somewhere else to be.

"Farley, I hate to do this, but I have to go." I pulled my sweater from the hanger and pulled it over my shoulders. "I have a lunch date."

"Oh." His face went from worried to snarky in a micro second. "Goin' out with that guy—Johnson, or whatever his name is?"

"His name is James, and no. I'm having lunch with Andrea Strickland, the woman who works in 310. Remember, you asked me to check out her boss, Ian Anderson? Apparently she has a favourite bar she goes to, around the corner from this place. She wants to 'do lunch'. I think she's lonely. Her boss is out of town for a few days."

"Know where he's gone?" Farley asked.

The snarky look disappeared the instant he found out I wasn't seeing James. Good grief. Men don't change, even when they're dead.

"Somewhere down south," I said. "Las Vegas, I think."

"Vegas," Farley breathed. Colour and light drained from him

as he wrapped his arms around his chest as though he was going to fly into pieces right in front of me.

"What's wrong?" I gasped.

"Nothing." I watched him, and was hugely relieved to see a bit of his colour return. "Go have your lunch. Enjoy. I'll wait for you."

I thought about staying, I really did, but eliminating Andrea's boss as a "suspect" was more important than metaphorically holding Farley's hand.

Maybe a job would help him. "I have an idea," I said. "While I'm gone you can go check voices."

"What voices?" He frowned, but more colour returned, and with it a bit more light.

"From the offices connected to the furnace room. The ones you could hear."

"Right." He nodded his head. "Right. That's something I can do. Excellent idea."

"Thanks," I said. "Glad to help. I'll see you in an hour."

I grabbed my sweater and purse, and walked out the door. As the door swung shut behind me, I thought I heard him say, "I'll try," but I couldn't be sure.

Farley:
Let's Keep from Going to Hell, Shall We?

The thinning settled in when Marie said, "Las Vegas." I grabbed myself, hung onto myself as though I was going to fly into tiny pieces around the room. Las Vegas. Las Vegas.

Marie didn't see how bad I had been affected. She was already halfway out the door, still blathering about me checking the air vents, to figure out whose voice I had heard. That was definitely the last thing on my mind, believe me.

As the door shut, I tried to hang onto myself, and not go back to Hell.

Marie:
The Margarita Lunch

I wished I hadn't had to leave Farley so soon after he'd finally come back, especially since he was so upset, but I had to eliminate Andrea's boss, Mr. Henderson, as a suspect. I was certain that if I didn't clear this up for Farley, he wasn't moving on. That man could sure grab hold of a thing and hang on to it. That quality probably made him an excellent handy man. I bet he could've been a good cop, or something, too. I pushed that thought away, because it wasn't productive. It didn't matter what he could've been. He was done, this time around. He had to move on.

Andrea was waiting on the sidewalk, stopping traffic. She was a beautiful bleached blonde, with that plucked and primped to within an inch of her life look that men find extremely appealing. I never seemed to have enough time to get a quarter of that look. On top of it all, she was about four inches taller than me, so I felt doubly insignificant as I walked up to her.

Her outfit looked really expensive. I glanced down at my skirt, which I thought was kind of pretty, and felt insignificant, times three. Dowdy, almost.

I hated feeling that way and tried to ignore it, as I crept up to her like a little grey mouse. Something she'd probably skewer with one of her incredibly thin spike heels. She flashed me a huge white smile, when she finally saw me.

"You ready, Mary?"

"Marie," I said. She ignored my words.

"I love the skirt!" she said. "A gypsy look, that was so the rage last year, I can't quite pull it off, my legs are too long, but you look darling!" She air kissed my cheek, and I tried hard not to pull away. I was regretting this outing now that I was actually on it, but I pulled a smile from somewhere, and air kissed back.

"Thanks. Where is Joey's Grille?"

"Just around the corner. Doesn't seem like much, but it has the best margaritas in the world. The known world." She tried to frown, but Botox or something held a number of her features frozen. It wasn't the look she was hoping for, I was willing to bet. Nastily, I felt a tiny bit better. "I think they have food, too. We'll have to check."

She sashayed away from the Palais, and my good feeling collapsed as I tottered after her, wishing I'd at least left my outsized grey sweater back at the office. I was sure it made me appear even more like a mouse.

Joey's Bar and Grille *was* just around the corner, and Andrea walked in like she owned the place. The bartender called her by name, and set up a pitcher and glasses before she even had to order. I glanced around the place, hoping for a quiet table somewhere. I quickly realized I wasn't going to get it.

The tables were crammed with Business Types, all doing business, and all trying desperately to keep the creases in their obscenely expensive pants intact. I inwardly groaned. I had no idea how I'd keep Andrea focused on a conversation about her boss when the pickings were, for her anyhow, so good.

She pointed to a small table near the front window that two men had just vacated, and maneuvered toward it, her perfume and the length of her legs causing small fits at every table she passed. She didn't seem to notice the effect she was having on the room.

She sat down and crossed her legs, which caused minor chaos, and signaled for the bartender to bring the pitcher of margaritas to her. I plopped down opposite her, and tried to smile.

"So, how did you find this place, Andrea?"

"I happened on it one afternoon. A girl needs sustenance, doesn't she? And Carlos is so cute, and mixes such a mean drink— well, I couldn't stay away from either, now could I?"

She flashed her smile and blinded me. How could she get her

teeth so incredibly white? I leaned forward, then backed up when her perfume hit me. Too much. Way too much. In fact, everything about Andrea was way too much. When cute Carlos set the pitcher in front of us, I grabbed one of the glasses, filling it to the brim and drinking deeply.

"My, you were thirsty, weren't you, Mary?" Andrea drawled.

"It's Marie, and yes. I was. Am."

"Marie. Right. Well, they *are* kind of the same name, aren't they?" She reached for a glass with her long-fingered, perfectly manicured hand, and I took another big swig from my glass, trying to figure out a way to surreptitiously wipe the foam from my upper lip. Couldn't come up with one, and ended up using my sleeve, which brought on another round of swigging, before I finally pulled myself together.

Luckily, Andrea wasn't paying attention to me. She scanned the room as she sipped her drink, occasionally waving her fingers at one or another of the men. They melted, of course. That's what men do when a woman like Andrea graces them with a look. They melt.

However, the closer I got to the bottom of my glass, the less this bothered me. I searched for a menu, didn't find one, and poured myself another drink. After half of it was gone, I smiled at Andrea.

"So, tell me about Mr. Henderson."

Those were the last words I needed to say. Oh, I said some other stuff, and I think I even mentioned how cute I thought James was, way near the bottom of the first pitcher, but really, it was Andrea's show after that. Wow, was she mad at Mr. Henderson.

The thing that did me the most good was, she didn't do mad very well at all. In fact, a couple of times, she looked positively average. Mousy little me was pretty happy to see that.

I stumbled back into the office, fifteen minutes late and half-cut from the stupid margaritas I'd been pounding back with Andrea. I saw Farley huddled in the corner. He looked like he was in pain. I didn't know if the information I'd gathered was going to help him or hurt him, but before I could talk to him, Mr. Latterson stomped out of his office, mightily pissed at me. Apparently he'd had to answer the phone—twice—all on his own.

I snapped to attention while he gave me heck. Well, I tried to, anyhow. The swaying didn't really sell the idea that I was completely sober and ready for another half-day of work, yessir, yessir. Through it all, I tried to keep an eye on Farley.

He really didn't look good.

Mr. Latterson finally gave up, and told me to make more coffee before he walked back into his office. I honestly didn't know whether he wanted it for himself, or for me. I hopped to, and soon the Bunn was burbling merrily. When I turned to Farley he'd managed to stand up, and was walking over to my desk.

"What happened to you?" I asked. I stood beside him, feeling absolutely useless as he tried to sit on the edge of the desk and missed. He slid back down to the floor.

"I don't know."

He tried to get up again, then gave it up as a bad job, and stayed where he was, so I plunked down beside him.

"It happened as you were leaving," he said. "You said Henderson was going to Las Vegas—" he shuddered as though the words he'd spoken had cut him—"I don't know why."

Las Vegas? I thought he had reacted so strongly because of Ian Anderson. He was so certain that Anderson was involved—somehow—in his death. But Las Vegas? Where did that come from?

"You're about half as bright as you were when I left," I said. "If it has to do with Las Vegas, we have to figure that out."

That appeared to surprise him, which surprised me. Hadn't I mentioned the brightness thing to him? I was sure I had. Then I realized he'd zoned out again, and waved at him.

"Farley, pay attention. This is important."

He slowly swung his head back and stared at me.

"Sorry," he whispered. "What did you say?"

"I said—" I started, then realized I had no idea what I'd said, important or otherwise. "Heck, I can't remember. Why did I have that many drinks?" I pushed myself to standing. "I need some coffee. I gotta get my head together, right now."

I slopped some coffee in a cup, downing half of it in a gulp. It burned, and that was about all.

"That won't work, you know," Farley said.

"I have to try something."

I gulped the rest of the coffee even though it made my eyes

tear up something fierce, and then sat back down beside Farley. "I need to think. I really need to think right now. None of this is right, you know. Not a bit of it."

"Not a bit of what?" he asked.

"Of what you're doing. The fading away and blinking out. All that."

I slumped against the desk, pulling my skirt down over my legs. "You should be gaining strength, not losing it. Know what I mean? You have to get brighter, not fade away. You need the strength for the next steps, otherwise, I don't know if you'll make it."

"Make it?"

"To the next stage. Stage two."

"Stage two?" He frowned. "Is this more of that moving on crap? I told you—"

"Farley, if you don't at least get to the next stage, you are going to disappear from my sight. Do you understand what that means?"

"What does it mean?"

"It means we will be done. I'll never see you again." I felt a lump form in my throat. "I think you'll be stuck here. Forever."

"Forever's a long time."

"Yes. Yes it is," I whispered. "So please, let me help you get to the next level. All right?"

"All right," he said.

He settled back, close to me, and I felt the cold of his arm against mine.

"You're leaving a cold spot," I said.

"Sorry," he replied, and pulled away.

"All right, so let's go over what we know for sure," I said. "You were killed, brutally. Somebody in this building rigged it, we hope, because if we have to start searching outside this building, I may shit and go blind, excuse my French. It might have something to do with the fact that Carruthers hasn't been making much money in this place."

"Why would you think that?"

"Because you said he hasn't spent money on maintenance in years," I replied. "Besides, more than half the offices are empty. Aren't they?"

"Yep," Farley said. "They are."

"Another thing I figured out," I said. "Did you know this building is being designated as a historical site?"

"No," Farley said, and frowned. "Why would that matter?"

"I don't know," I replied, and rubbed my eyes. "But that's what I've figured out, so far."

"It's not much, is it?"

"Nope," I said. "Not yet, anyhow. But I will get more. I promise." I tried to wink at him, but it didn't go well, and all I ended up doing was blinking like an owl. "Like, for example, did I tell you that my new best drinking buddy Andrea thinks that her boss, Mr. Henderson, is involved in your death?"

Farley sat up straight. "She told you that?"

"Yes, she did. We became best friends and she told me everything I wanted to hear. More, even." I yawned. "Why do I drink? I am so bad at it!" I rubbed my face, hoping that somehow that would help. "What do you think of her?"

"Who, Andrea?"

"Yeah."

"I don't know." Farley was quiet for a moment. "Henderson has her in a shitty situation as far as I can tell—but really, I don't know her." He glanced at me. "Why? What do you think of her?"

"I think she was handing me a line of crap." I grinned at him. "I think she's really pissed at Henderson for using her as the office blow-up doll. I think she's trying to cause him trouble. When I started talking about you and how you died—she jumped all over it. Said she wouldn't put it past him, doing something like that. She tried to talk me into calling the police and telling them that he was involved."

I yawned again, hugely. I knew that if I didn't get up soon, I was going to curl up on the floor and go to sleep.

"The police?" he prompted.

"Yes," I replied. "The police. I asked her why she wouldn't make the phone call, but all she said was it could screw something she had in the works." I snorted laughter. "Who the heck says, 'in the works' anymore?"

"I don't know," Farley said, faintly. I glanced at him, and could see he was thinking, hard.

"Anyhow, she didn't even mention anything about you before I did. All she did was complain about him. So I think she's lying."

"Maybe she's not," Farley said. "She's got it bad with that

126

asshole—maybe she's afraid to go to the police on her own."

I laughed. Couldn't help myself.

"Farley, you act like such a knight in shining armour, I can't believe it." I chortled. "Always trying to save the damsel in distress, aren't you?"

"A what?" Farley leaped to his feet and glared at me as though I'd spit on his shoes or something. I'd pushed a great big button. "What the hell do you mean by calling me that?"

"I mean that you look at the world like a knight," I said. "I bet you wouldn't have to dig back too far to figure out why. It colours your perceptions about people, especially women people, a lot. Heck, you did it with me, remember? When Mr. Latterson laughed?"

"I remember," he said gruffly. "He shouldn't have done that."

"I know, Farley. It's kind of endearing, but we don't all have to be saved, you know. We're not all victims."

"There's nothing wrong with being a—what the hell did you call me? A knight?" He sounded stiff. Angry. Defensive. "They were good guys, except for the wars, and some of that other shit they pulled. They treated women with respect—"

"You don't have to defend yourself to me," I said, cutting him off. "You know that, don't you?"

"My daughter didn't like it, when I acted like that around her." Farley's voice sounded like the words were being pulled from his mouth like rotten teeth.

"Your daughter," I said. "Rose?"

"Yeah," he sighed. "I used to drive her crazy."

"Maybe she didn't feel like a damsel in distress," I said.

"But that's what I do!" The whine was back in his voice, full force. "I'm the go-to guy, the guy you can turn to when you have a problem, the guy that will save you . . . " His voice faded, and he hung his head. "Son of a bitch," he continued. "Even if you don't need to be saved."

"I think you're getting it." I stood, shaking out my skirt and picking up my mug. I poured myself one more coffee, even though I knew it wouldn't help. Not really.

"So what you're telling me is, I was right." He sounded stronger, and when I turned around, he had regained some of his colour. The tips of the hair on his head were beginning to glow.

Oh my God. He was starting to glow.

"Right about what?" I asked, barely able to believe what I was seeing.

"All this time, people have been telling me I could change. My wife, before my marriage crashed and burned, and my daughter after that. All these years, trying to defend my position, protect my territory. And now you're saying I was right? That it's just the way I am?"

I think if I hadn't had quite so many margaritas, I would have explained to him that the reason he couldn't change now was because he was dead. He might have been able to before, if he'd found out why this "knighthood" thing had become his essence.

That's what my mom calls it. The essence of the soul. The one defining characteristic of a person. It's a good beginning, but isn't everything. He had to figure out how he came to be that way. He wasn't born acting like a knight in shining armour. Something or someone brought him to that state.

But I was so relieved to see him getting brighter, all I said was, "Yes." It was enough that he knew. We could get to the why of it, after he remembered how he died and I wasn't so drunk.

He smiled, and then began to glow more brightly than I'd ever seen him before. "Look at yourself, Farley," I said. He glanced down, and even his smile brightened.

"This is a good thing, isn't it?" he asked.

"You're absolutely right," I replied. "Congratulations. I think you made it to Stage Two."

Stage Two
Gaining Awareness

Farley:
Let the Fading Begin

Want to hear something weird? My tattoos are starting to fade. Marie assured me that it was all perfectly normal. We all go through a fading period toward "uniform luminosity." I asked her if she was going to write a book, and she laughed. Didn't think there would be much of a market, since the only people who would really give a shit enough to read the book would be dead.

I don't know about that, though. There are enough pop psychology life after death spiritual transformation books out there to bury a city the size of Edmonton, so why the hell shouldn't she try her hand at it? Write a book, make a million, then she wouldn't have to pull these kind of bullshit jobs she does now, to make ends meet. She wasn't interested, though. Maybe later, she said. Maybe when she knows more. Me, I thought she knew plenty all ready.

She explained a bit more about the Three Stages of Acceptance. I thought there were supposed to be more than that, but she said it's all she'd ever seen with the dead, anyhow. Maybe we don't have the time to go through all the rest of the stages, or maybe we got them all balled up into three main ones. I don't know. I knew that for some reason, this shit was beginning to make sense to me. And since I hit the second stage, I didn't feel as afraid, and I didn't feel thin or stretched as often, either. And I hadn't gone to hell again. So Stage Two, the Awareness Stage, suited me fine. I wasn't sure what else I was supposed to "gain an awareness of," though. Except figuring out who the hell killed me and why. I wouldn't have minded gaining some awareness around that.

Even thinking about that made me feel a little thin.

Shit.

Marie:
Score One for the Good Guys

Even with the hangover, I felt great. I'd helped Farley make it to Stage Two—I knew I had. He'd popped up a couple of luminosity degrees when I mentioned the knight thing. He thanked me, told me he had a plan for getting more information about whether Andrea was lying about her boss, and then left me alone for the rest of the day.

Mr. Latterson had a pile of paperwork a mile high for me to type, and I finished it, though I made a lot more mistakes than usual with the margaritas still floating around in my system. At the end of the day, I went home and fell across my bed, and slept. In spite of the hangover, I felt great.

I woke up two hours later, still a bit hung over, and starving. I searched through my fridge, though I knew there was nothing whatever to eat. The single orange, collapsing in on itself in its mould-covered skin scowled at me from the middle shelf, so I turned to the phone instead.

The first person I thought about calling was James. Almost of their own doing, my fingers danced through the ancient phone book that had been in the apartment when I moved in. Soon I was staring at the name "James Lavall," with a number beside it.

"Probably not him," I muttered. I closed the book, keeping my finger at the page holding his name. Then I flipped it open again, and stared at it for a moment more, before mentally giving myself a good shake, and slamming the book shut.

"I do not need to get involved with another man. Not now." So, I phoned Jasmine instead.

"Jazz," I said, when she picked up the phone. "It's me. I need some company. You still up for some TV watching?"

She was free, her kids were in bed, and she was happy to hear from me. Ecstatic, in fact. She thought I was going to dump her as a friend after getting pink-slipped.

"Not a chance, Jasmine," I replied, laughing a little more heartily than I felt. "You can't get rid of me that easily."

After we said our good-byes, I grabbed my coat, and headed out of my quiet, dark apartment. I even sang a little as I waited for the bus.

Jasmine grabbed me in a hug before I made it into the door of her overstuffed bungalow. She smelled of baby powder and incense, and I leaned into her, because it felt like being hugged by a mom—even if it wasn't my own.

"So how you been keeping?" she asked me when she finally let me go. She peered at me hard, then a smile brightened her face. "My God," she said, shaking her head. "You started dating that James guy. Didn't you?"

"No." I said, throwing my jacket on the pile of coats by the overstuffed closet. "He and I are friends. Nothing more."

"I don't think so. Not by the look on your face." She pulled me into her kitchen, which was filled with a table overflowing with book bags and homework, and surrounded by mismatched chairs. She pointed to one, and turned to the stove, putting the heat on under the kettle. "Tea?"

"Sure." I plopped myself down, and thumbed through her daughter Ella's math homework, closing the book when I couldn't figure out what Ella had been working on. She was in Grade Six, and I felt like an idiot. "How are things?"

"They're good. Good." Jasmine kept her back to me as she fiddled with the teapot and tea, so I knew she was lying. She always looked at me when she talked, unless she was telling a lie.

"So, what happened?"

"Oh, it's that damned Gerald!" she cried, then glanced over at the hallway, as if to see if her swearword had careened down it and into the innocent ears of her children sleeping in the bedrooms hidden from view. "He's making life difficult, since you left."

"I didn't leave," I replied, shaking my head. "I was fired. By voicemail."

"That man," she sighed, shaking her head.

"So what's he doing?"

"Oh, the usual. Can't find good help, so he's given me three more hours a day to cover until he does. So now I need a babysitter for those hours." She slammed the top on the teapot, hard, then quickly checked for cracks. "I can't find one close to here. There's my next door neighbour—but he's old. My little sweeties would tear him apart. And my dear daughter Ella—" She sighed melodramatically as she set the teapot and two cups on the table in front of me. "Ella doesn't seem to have the ovaries for babysitting. I don't know what to do."

I made some sympathetic noises and poured myself a cup of tea. There was nothing I could do to help her, because there was no way I was offering to babysit her crew. I'd done it once, and still had the scars to prove it. Apparently I didn't have the ovaries for babysitting, either.

"Oh, I'll come up with something," she said, settling into a chair across from me with a small sigh. "Now, tell me about this man you've fallen for."

"I haven't fallen for anyone, Jasmine." I stared down into my tea cup. "I haven't."

"You're lying. I can feel it." She grinned. "If I feed you something, will you tell me?"

"There's nothing to tell," I said. "And I'm not hungry." My stomach growled, and I glanced back down into my cup. Jasmine laughed out loud.

"I have some leftover chicken and mashed potatoes."

I'd tasted her chicken before. It was to die for, and I was willing to take a little ribbing about the nonexistent man in my life if it meant I got to eat some of it.

"I'd love some," I said. "But you're going to be disappointed."

"Oh, I don't think so," she said, walking to her cupboard and pulling out a plate. "I think this is going to be terrifically interesting."

The chicken was amazing, and I ended up telling Jasmine all about James, all the while trying to give the impression I wasn't interested in him in the least. She wasn't buying it.

"I think you got it bad." She offered me more chicken, then put everything away when I shook my head and moaned. "So, when are you going out with him?"

"I'm not doing that, you know I'm not," I said, taking a sip of my lukewarm tea. "It's not in the cards for me."

"Are you still worried about that idiot Arnie finding you and giving you grief?" she asked, and poured me more tea. "Or are you going to use your mother as your excuse?"

I stared at her for a moment, resisting the urge to stare down into my cup again. Who to blame. My sick mother or my crazy ex-boyfriend. I decided on Arnie, who hadn't bothered me since I'd moved into Sally's apartment. My mother would probably be thrilled herself if I finally found "a good man." Actually, it was better to blame either than for the real reason. I wasn't about to lose Jasmine as a friend because I have a problem with ghosts.

"It's Arnie," I finally said. "I can't be sure he won't show up again. Start harassing me again. You know what he said to me, the last time."

"Yeah, I do. 'If I can't have you, no-one can.' He doesn't have much imagination, does he?"

I shrugged. When I was trying to get away from him, it seemed he'd had many ways to make my life a living hell. However, it had been a while since he'd bothered me. Since I got the restraining order. I hadn't really believed that a piece of paper would stop someone like Arnie, but it appeared to. More or less.

There was what happened just after I'd moved to Edmonton. That had been ugly and scary and all the rest. The police had actually helped that time, and I believed that he'd been scared off by the threats of jail time if he did anything like that again. He hadn't bothered me, anyhow. It appeared he was out of my life.

However . . .

"Maybe we shouldn't talk about him anymore," I said. "With my luck, he'll feel the vibe, and find me again."

"He's taken enough of your life," Jasmine said. "Don't let him take anymore. He's gone. He won't find you again. So I say you say, 'Adiós Asshole', and move on. You're allowed to be happy, you know."

"You said that before." I looked into my cup, so she couldn't see how close to tears I was.

"Because it's the truth," she said, reaching over and patting my hand. "Don't let it get you down. When I dumped the bane of *my* existence—and you know who I'm talking about, don't you?"

I nodded. "Albert."

"That's right. Albert. The father of my babies, and the biggest loser you would ever want to meet. When I dumped him I figured I'd never be involved with anyone again."

I waited for her to continue, but she simply sat, staring into the living room.

"But you're still by yourself," I finally said. "This feels like a pot and kettle situation, Jasmine."

"I'm alone because that's the way I want it," she replied, a smile playing around her mouth. "I'm happy. If I wanted a man, I'd have one. There's a difference."

"I guess."

"Yes, absolutely. Don't let that peckerwood hold you hostage any longer. Get out there. Have some fun." She grinned at me. "You're a normal girl with normal urges. Enjoy! That James sounds like a real catch. Get out of the friend zone, before you lose him."

"I'll think about it."

"That's a start." She glanced at the clock shaped like a chicken, hanging above her stove, and gasped. "My show starts in ten minutes, and we need popcorn. I can't afford to miss a second, I can't believe where they left me last week. On a cliff! An absolute cliff! If I miss the beginning, I simply may die!"

As we watched another episode of the night time soap opera Jasmine was addicted to, and ate popcorn and far too much chocolate, it was easy to let all thoughts of James and Jerk Arnie fall away. I lost myself in the fake lives of the fake people on the screen, giggling like a kid every time Jasmine felt the need to punctuate a scene with a small scream and much discussion. I had a good time, and when I packed up to leave after the show was over, I let her know.

She smiled, wrapping my sweater around me and pulling into her arms again. "Come back next week. We gotta find out how this ends!"

I promised I'd try, and left. I could feel her watching me through a small chink in the armour that is her front window drapes as I walked to the bus stop, and it comforted me. A three quarter ton truck drove by, all decked out, and for a second I was afraid, as though thinking about Jerk Arnie had brought him back into my life, but when I heard rap music beating through the truck and into the street, I knew it wasn't him, and relaxed.

I thought I saw the truck again, following my bus, but put it out of my mind. So what if some idiot was following the bus? It didn't concern me. I didn't know who he was, and didn't care, now that I was sure it wasn't Arnie.

When I got home, I crawled into bed and dreamily thought of the next day's work. Farley had some big scheme cooked up, and had assured me it would get me all the information we needed about Andrea's boss. As I drifted off to sleep, I hoped this would be the thing that gave him the push he needed, so he could move on. It was time for me to get on with my life.

Farley:
My Plan

All I can say in my defence is—it should have worked.

Marie:
Farley's Plan

The next day, Farley's plan didn't seem so good. In fact, it sounded stupid.

He wanted me to break into Mr. Henderson's office while Andrea was off buying herself a latte or whatever. She left every day at 10:30, and when Henderson wasn't in town, she was always gone at least an hour.

Or so Farley claimed.

He'd done as I had requested, and had listened to the voice of every occupant through the furnace pipes. He'd found no match, and had decided that since Ian Henderson was gone, it must be him.

"It's that process of elimination thing," he said. "Remember? All you have to do is break in, find proof that he's involved, and then go to the police."

That had been the day before, when too many margaritas were still floating through my system, and everything sounded like a fantastic idea.

"I've got a master key," he'd continued. "You can use it to get into the office."

Even though I was feeling serious reservations the next morning, it seemed that everything was lining up to make the big plan work. Mr. Latterson left the office very early, and said he'd be gone most of the day. The key was right where Farley said it would be, and I didn't run into James as I was sneaking around in the furnace room collecting it. And then, Andrea left at exactly 10:30, the time she always left. So, I went along with it.

The reason? I needed to prove to Farley that Ian Henderson wasn't involved in his death. I was positive Andrea was lying, but Farley had fixated on saving her. More of the knight in shining armour crap, I was positive, but nothing I said swerved him from his decision.

"We have to help her. I have to," he kept saying.

So, I broke into Henderson's office. You know what I found? I found out what Henderson was doing in Las Vegas. He'd gone to a convention for "Entrepreneurial Spirited Men." It looked like he'd originally booked a flight for Andrea too, and that one had been canceled. I made sure I photocopied that bit of information.

Other than the canceled flight, I couldn't find anything incriminating Henderson of any wrongdoing. His finances seemed in order, and there was nothing anywhere that indicated that he'd even known Farley was alive. When he was alive, I mean. And there was nothing—absolutely nothing—that showed he was involved in Farley's death in any way at all.

Andrea? Not so much.

Once I'd convinced myself that Henderson hadn't done anything to Farley, I went through Andrea's desk. Specifically, through her day timer. To be honest, even finding a day timer for her surprised me, because she seemed like a "keep my life on my phone" kind of person. But she'd carefully hidden it in the bottom drawer of her desk. Under her feminine protection, which told me she wanted to make absolutely certain that Henderson never touched it. I leafed through the leather bound journal, and saw that she wrote down every bit of her financial life in the thing. Henderson was paying her well, and she apparently paid off her credit card every month. When I saw that, I felt a twinge of envy.

Then I turned the page, and saw she'd deposited $30,000. No clue where the money had come from. Just the great big number, with five exclamation points behind it.

"Hmm," I muttered. "That's a lot of money, Andrea." I flipped the pages, looking for more. I was rewarded fifteen pages later, with another $30,000 entry. No exclamation points this time, and still no name.

I quickly flipped through the rest of the pages, but there was nothing more.

"Now, what were you doing for that money, Andrea?" I asked.

Didn't have time to figure it out, though, because Farley picked that moment to burst into the office, screaming like a banshee. Whatever that is.

"She's back!" he screamed, ecto goo flying absolutely everywhere. "Get out!"

"Where is she?" I asked, ramming the day timer back in its hiding place and slamming the desk drawer shut.

"Here!" he screamed, at exactly the moment the doorknob started to jiggle. Someone was fitting a key into the lock.

"Son of a bitch," I breathed.

"The fire escape." Farley pointed at the back room, and I flew—literally flew—into the cluttered little room, pushed open the window, and managed to get out before Andrea entered the office.

All I can say is, thank goodness for fire escapes.

I skittered down the rickety metal stairs to the back alley, then through the back alley to the front door of the Palais, only stopping long enough to wipe the fear sweat from my face and try to get my breathing to something like normal before I went back to Mr. Latterson's office. I honestly thought I was going to make it.

I ran up the stairs to the second floor, and unlocked the door to Latterson's office. I was almost home free. Even though the information I'd gathered wasn't going to make Farley happy, you could say it looked like the break-in was successful. Until I opened that door. Then I saw just how truly in the crapper I was.

You see, Mr. Latterson hadn't stayed away most of the day, the way he usually did. He hadn't even stayed away an hour. He was busy tearing apart my desk when I burst in.

"Jenner, where the hell were you?" he yelled. I stared at him. I had no idea how long he'd been back. By the look of my desk, a long time.

"I'm really sorry, Mr. Latterson, but—" I started. This is when Farley burst in, apologizing all over the place and throwing me right off my game.

"I'm sorry, Marie," he said. "I let you down."

I glared at him, to shut him up. A stupid, stupid thing to do. I should have ignored him and kept my eyes on Mr. Latterson, but I hadn't. That set Mr. Latterson off like illegal fireworks.

"What the hell is going on with you, Jenner? Don't you give a shit about this job at all?"

The moment I started to apologize, Farley decided to get involved. He jumped in front of me, anger rolling off him in waves.

"Tell him to go to hell, Marie!" he yelled. "He treats you like shit!"

I guess my face betrayed my anger. I was mad at Farley. Furious, in fact. Mr. Latterson thought my angry look for was for him, and blew an absolute gasket.

"I've had enough, Jenner!" he thundered. He drew himself up, and pointed imperiously at the door. "Pack up. You are done."

That got my attention. He was firing me.

I couldn't believe it. My second firing in almost as many days. I wanted to turn and scream "See what you've done!" at Farley, but I couldn't. I had to figure out a way to keep this job.

"Oh God, say something, Marie," Farley said. He'd gone from angry to terrified, much as I had. "Make him keep you on. Please."

For a microsecond, I thought about just leaving. Walking out. Leaving Mr. Latterson and Farley and finding anything else as a job to pay the bills. Maybe be a waitress. They make tips, right? That might be all right.

The look on Farley's face stopped me. I needed to stay for him. I'd promised.

So, I decided to use "Operation Teardrop."

All right, sounds silly, but when I came up with it, I was going through my World War II phase. Everything I did had "Operation" before it. "Operation Dishcloth" when I was doing the dishes. "Operation Find the Floor" when I had to clean my room. Stuff like that.

I invented "Operation Teardrop" just before my father decided to leave. Between the fights with my mother, he'd try to, you know, parent or something. It took me no time at all to figure out that if I turned on the waterworks, he'd give in. Every time.

I wasn't sure if it would work on Mr. Latterson, but I decided what the heck. I was so close to tears anyhow, it wouldn't take much.

So, I thought about my dog, Bear. He'd died when I was twelve. I felt my lips quiver, and thought about my Granny Jenner. I'd loved her, and she'd died too. Cancer. They'd both died of cancer.

I whimpered, and sniveled, and then I thought, for the briefest second, about my mother. Dying. Of cancer.

That's when the waterworks really started. They weren't all fake.

"I'm really sorry, Mr. Latterson," I boohooed. He turned around—he was at his office door—and his face contorted. Tears obviously made him uncomfortable, so I decided to see how he dealt with a whole bunch more.

"Really!" I screeched, and then wailed, hitting registers too high for the human ear, I was sure. I boohooed again, and felt tears and snot running down my face. "I am SO sorry! It's just my Mom is sick and I need to work to take care of her and—" For a second, I almost lost it. I was too close to the truth, but I hitched in a couple of breaths and decided on the big finish. "If I lose this job, I don't know what will happen to her!"

I threw myself on my desk, pounding it with my fists, spraying snot and tears all over my day timer. "Please don't fire me, Mr. Latterson. I'll be a better employee! Really I will!"

I hitched a couple more hiccupping breaths, and then sat up and dug in my sweater pockets for tissue.

"Here, take this," Mr. Latterson said. I looked up. He looked like he wished he was anywhere but there, and he handed me a tissue without making eye contact.

"Sorry to hear about your mother," he said. "Just pull yourself together."

I nodded, and started mopping up. I made sure to hiccup a couple more times, like another outbreak of hysteria was just around the corner.

"Now, now," he said. "Maybe I was a hard on you—you missed a bit, right up on your cheek there. Do you promise to stay at your desk and do your job?"

I nodded meekly, and held the tissue out to him. He pulled his hand away as though I was trying to hand him a bag full of crap.

"No, no, it's okay," he said, backing toward his office, one hand out behind him, clawing for the doorknob. "Keep it. Let's put all this nastiness behind us, shall we? You do your job as well as you can, and we'll forget this ever happened, all right?"

"All right." I wiped my nose again, and smiled tragically at Mr. Latterson as he clawed open his door and escaped to his inner sanctum. "Are you sure you don't want this back?" I cried, holding out the sodden lump of tissue.

"It's okay, you can keep it!"

His office door boomed shut. I took a deep breath, and blew it out. Worked every time. Then I turned on Farley, who looked nearly as shattered as Mr. Latterson had.

"If you ever do anything like that to me again, so help me, I will walk out of this place and you will never see me again," I said.

He blinked a couple of times, then took a hesitant step toward me, a stupid half-smile on his translucent face. "What exactly was it that I did?" he asked. "Just let me know. A pile of stuff happened, and I want to make sure—"

"Shut up," I said. He clapped his mouth shut and skittered back to the door, like he was ready to make a run for it. "I don't need this job, Farley. There are lots of jobs out there. The only reason I did all that—" and I pointed back at Mr. Latterson's office door, "—was so I can help you. Do you understand?"

He nodded slowly, his eyes pinwheeling as though he was still trying to figure a way out of that room.

"Now go," I said. I needed to pull myself together, before I really started crying.

"All right." He shuffled another step toward the door, then looked back at me. "When can I come back?"

"I don't want you back in this office again," I snapped.

"Oh." He looked horrified. "I'm really sorry—"

"Shut up." I felt real tears, very close. He had to leave. "I've got the master key you gave me. Tell me what office is empty. We can talk there."

"Carruthers' old office, on the main floor."

The main floor sounded like a bad idea. James was on the main floor, a lot.

"Won't people see me go in there? I don't want any more trouble in this building."

"There's a restroom down that hallway. If you act like you're going to use it, no one will notice. Just go past it, and around the corner is Carruthers' office, and a boardroom. Either would be a good place to meet. We won't be bothered. No-one is allowed in there."

I was almost ready to tell him to shut up again, when something he said hit me.

"Why isn't anyone allowed in there?"

"I don't know." He shrugged. "Carruthers told me to leave it alone when he moved out. So I did." Then he frowned. "Think there might be something in there that he doesn't want anybody to see?"

"Could be." I took another deep, shaky breath, then pointed at the door. "Now go. I have to work."

I tried to put some order to the chaos that was my desk until I was certain Farley was gone, then collapsed. My hands were shaking badly and I felt like I was going to throw up. I had to pull myself together.

Why had I agreed with Farley's stupid idea? I'm a levelheaded, down-to-earth girl—well, except for the whole seeing the ghosts thing—how did I ever let him talk me into that? Way in the back of my mind, another voice, the one that works hard at keeping me on the right track, whispered that Farley hadn't talked me into anything. I'd been a willing participant.

Man, two jobs in two days. I stared at my hands, willing the tremors to stop. The money I was getting for helping James was a Godsend, but it wasn't going to be enough. I needed to hang onto this job, at least until it looked good on my resume.

Yeah, right. The little voice squeaked in outrage when I tried the "it'll look good on a resume" gambit. That wasn't it, and I knew it. I shook my hands vigourously, until they were calm. Then I resumed cleaning my desk.

What was I going to do? I had actually let a ghost talk me into breaking into an office, which was a bit worse than letting James talk me into stealing from Mr. Latterson. But only a bit. I felt like maybe I was losing my mind.

As I tidied, I wondered if James had delivered the report about all the bank accounts to Mrs. Latterson. I hoped so. And I hoped that things would move quickly after that. No matter what I'd said to Farley, I didn't want to stay here. The little voice whispered that it was a good bet Mr. Latterson was going to rip me off, too. *That* little voice sounded like Farley, and I growled. I literally growled out loud. Because I knew that stupid voice was right.

So, why was I hanging around? Why was I coming to work at a job that was probably going to give me nothing in the way of wages at the end of it all? Was it all for Farley?

Or was it because of James?

James was cute, true, and interesting, and polite, and his eyes had this way of catching mine and holding them until I felt like I was drowning—but a good drowning, not like Mr. Peppercorn up in McMurray, it had taken Mom months to straighten him around enough to move him on—was it James?

Why wasn't I going to take the job James had offered me?

I poured myself a coffee, then sat back down and pulled a piece of paper from the middle drawer. Perhaps a "Pro and Con" list was in order.

I started drawing cat faces, because I wasn't ready for pros and cons. I needed to think about what working with James really meant.

It seemed that the money was good, and relatively easy to come by. I mean, it took me a grand total of six hours to find the information, plus type it up, and that included most of the cleaning time in his dead uncle's office. Imagine how much we could make in a month.

Was it just the money? Or was it his eyes? And if it was, did I really need James' eyes, right now? Not really. Because that led nowhere. I knew that. Because, the little voice reminded me, ever so gently, what happens when a man, even a man who says he will love you forever, finds out you have a gift, like seeing ghosts. They leave. Now the voice was my mom's. And she was crying over my father leaving. Again.

All right, so the nice eyes thing was out. Until I had completely eradicated all ghosts from my life, I wasn't going down that road. That was the reason I left Fort McMurray, for heaven's sake. Okay, so it wasn't the only reason. I'd also left because of Jerk Arnie. Arnie had been a pig and had made my life a living hell. So, on top of everything, I was a bad judge of character, especially when it came to men, so James' eyes and the fact that I was attracted to them—to him—didn't really put him in the best possible light, date-wise.

I glanced down at the cat faces, and started drawing curly whiskers with a freshly sharpened pencil, still thinking about James and his eyes and muscles and everything. Why couldn't this be easy? Why couldn't I say to myself, "Self, you're going to take the job with James, but it's going to be a business relationship and nothing more," or something like that? I needed a good job. One that could pay my bills and help me take care of my mother. This one wasn't going to do it. Since I'd lost the other one—and I cursed Gerald again, feeling fully justified—I should not look a gift horse in the mouth. I needed to take the job James had offered me.

However, Farley had to move on. I didn't want to see him do what the ghost in the telephone booth had done. Or worse. I felt an obligation to him—and maybe something more.

True, he was an exasperating old guy, and watching him pull his stomach in every time he got around me was starting to drive me crazy, I mean come on, you're dead Farley! Get over it! But there was something about him. Something that made me want to help him. However, he had to be put in his place. He too had to understand that it could only be a business arrangement. I was there to help him move on, and that was all. I'd made that commitment to him. I had an obligation. But that was all.

I set the pencil down and picked up the paper to throw it in the garbage, and saw what I'd written in the curlicues I'd made with the cat whiskers. "Call Mom."

I crushed the paper and tossed it. Why couldn't I come up with a better plan than that?

Farley:
My Lunch Date With Marie

I have to tell you, I didn't want to piss off Marie again so soon
after the mess up in Henderson's office, and then the mess up in
Latterson's office, and then her melt down. So, I went and
checked Carruthers' old boardroom out before she came, to make
sure I hadn't been bullshitting her. It looked exactly the same as
the day I'd locked the door.

There wasn't much dust. The small board room table in the
large outer office was covered by a big tarp, with the chairs
nestled under it, their backs leaving humps down the cloth like a
double backbone.

I stared out the window while I waited for her. Well, really, I
stared through a small opening left by an ill-fitting shade that
covered the window and toned the bright midday sun down to
dusk in the room. Outside, once my eye adjusted, I could see the
kid—what the hell was his name? Jack? No. James—I could see
James out cleaning clutter from around the tall pines in front of
the building.

I could tell he was whistling, even though I couldn't hear him
through the glass. He sure was a neat freak. Unless they'd hired
him to do that kind of shit work, too. I'd only been hired to keep
the building running properly. As I watched him dig under the
old pines, pulling out newspaper so weathered it crumbled to

dust in his hands, I wondered what had happened to the old guy they'd hired to come in twice a week and do the yard work.

"Maybe he died too." I said the words out loud without thinking, then shivered. "More than likely Carruthers fired his ass. If he can get this goon to do all the work for what he was paying me—probably less—then why the hell not?"

I turned away from the window, and waited for Marie to arrive.

Marie:
My Lunch Date with Farley

After I'd told Mr. Latterson I was leaving for lunch—to his face, because I seriously did not need to be fired again—I used the master key Farley had given me to open the door to Mr. Carruthers' old office on the main floor. Well, I tried, anyhow. The key went into the lock, which was all good, and it started to turn, but then the lock started to grind, horribly. Finally, finally, the door opened—but only a hair, and then it jammed.

"Son of a gun." I put my shoulder to the door and it finally popped open.

Farley was waiting inside. I knew it before I saw him. He was glowing even more brightly than he had up in Mr. Latterson's office.

"When was the last time you opened that door?" I asked, stepping inside and quickly shutting the door behind me. It closed more easily than it had opened, but I hoped it wouldn't jam again. That door was the only way out of the room.

Farley didn't answer me. He stood, staring, as though waiting for another outburst from me. Good.

The reception area was empty, except for a table and chairs, covered by a tarp. Two offices backed onto to this area. Both doors were open, and I glanced inside both. One was empty, but the other one still had a desk, a chair, and a computer. I frowned.

153

That was odd, leaving a computer in an abandoned office.

I walked back to the reception area, and grabbed a chair under the tarp. It was leather. Felt good under my fingers as I pulled it out and then sat on it. I left the tarp on the table, though. I didn't need the table. I wasn't sticking around.

"Are you going to stay mad at me forever?" Farley finally asked. He sounded so afraid, my anger crumbled. However, I had to be strong.

"I made a mistake with you, Farley."

"A mistake?" he asked. He sounded even more afraid. "Jesus, you sound like you're going to give me the 'it isn't you, it's me' speech. What, are you actually going to break up with me?"

I couldn't look at him. If he thought we had some kind of relationship past me moving him on, I had waited too long for this conversation. "I should have treated you more like a ghost and less like a person from the very beginning," I said. "But I found you—"

"Intriguing. Yeah, I remember." He walked a couple of paces closer to me, his hands clutched together like he was praying. He tried to speak, then stopped and sighed, waiting for me.

"Yes. You were intriguing. And when you were having those dreams or whatever they were—well, that was weird. Death is much more straight forward. A person dies, they gain some understanding about themselves, make a few decisions, bing-bang-boom, and they leave. But you! Man! You just keep sticking around."

"I don't want to leave," he said. "I told you that."

"I know," I replied. "That was wrong of me. I let you think that you could. That we could be like Sherlock Holmes and Dr. Watson or something, and figure out how you had died when we probably won't. Even though I was positive Ian Henderson had nothing to do with your death, I let you talk me into breaking into his office—I mean, what is wrong with me?"

My throat tightened. What *was* wrong with me? I felt one tear after another slip down my face, and I brushed them away impatiently. Now was not the time to cry.

"I was giving you hope when there shouldn't be hope," I whispered. "Hope's not what this last bit of time is about. It has nothing to do with that at all, and I'm sorry, Farley. I shouldn't have done any of that to you. You didn't need an adventure. You needed to move on. I held you back. It was probably all my fault, the blinking out and the fading, and everything. I really let you down."

"No, you didn't," he said. "I think you're helping me, you know, gain some understanding, or whatever it is that you said I needed to do. Really."

"No, I'm not," I said, shaking my head. "I know that much, anyhow. I *have* to talk to my mother. I really don't know how to handle this at all."

"Your mother?" Farley's tone changed, became more clipped.

"Yeah. My mother," I said. I was surprised at his sudden anger. I'd talked to him about my mother. Hadn't I?

"Why are you going to talk to your mother about me?"

"She has the same gift I have, plus loads more experience." I frowned. "I'm sure I told you about her. I'll just find out what I should do next from her. She'll know."

"Oh." He stared down at the floor for a long moment, then up at my face. I hadn't told him about my mother before. I hadn't mentioned a word. "Oh."

"I'm sorry," I said quickly. "I thought I could handle this, but it has gotten too weird. You know?"

"Yeah, I guess, but why didn't you, oh I don't know, touch base with your mother before this?"

His hands started to tremble. He stared at them for a moment, then looked back up at me. He wasn't just angry. He was furious.

"You're right, Farley," I said, hoping I could fix this mistake before it too backfired on me. "I should have. I'll call her tonight, and get this whole thing cleared up. I promise."

"Yeah, well, okay. We'll see." He stood up and paced. I could see he was getting angrier by the moment. "So, how much do you really know about this gift of yours, anyhow? Seemed like a lot of what went on was a surprise to you, know what I mean?"

"Well, I watched Mom when I was growing up and I thought—"

"You thought what? You'd wing it? What the hell, it's just Farley—"

"No! No, that's not what I meant," I said. "I meant—"

"You thought you could handle it."

"Well, yeah."

Farley turned on me, fury leaping from his eyes and stopping my words in my throat. "Jesus Marie, it was my eternal soul or some damned thing you were playing around with! Why didn't you tell me? Warn me?"

Now, maybe he was right, but darn it, I'd been trying my best. He was doing strange stuff. It couldn't be all my fault. I wouldn't let it.

"Warn you about what?" I asked, suddenly as angry as Farley looked. "My ineptitude?"

"Why don't we call it your amateur status?" he snapped back.

I was ready for a good fight, and so was he, I think. That's when another key pushed into the door, and another shoulder popped it open. A large shadow hung in the doorway and I recognized it. James.

My anger collapsed into abject fear. My God, James was going to catch me in an office that had been locked. What was I going to say?

James strode into the room, stopping when he saw me, a confused look on his face. "Marie," he said. "What are you doing in here?"

Before I could give him a story, a line, something that would explain why I was in a room that was supposed to have been closed off to everyone for a long time, Farley hissed, "We are not finished with this conversation yet."

Then, he looked distraught, and blinked away. Disappeared, before my very eyes. Again.

I guess I looked fairly stricken, because James walked up to me and took one of my hands. "What's wrong?"

With all my heart I wanted to say, "I'm trying to move a ghost on, but all I keep doing is making him disappear, and one of these times, he's not going to make it back and it will all be my fault," but I couldn't.

"I almost lost my job," I said, instead. "I managed to talk Mr. Latterson into keeping me on, but man, I can't lose this job. Not yet."

I was hoping for a little bit of sympathy, but I didn't get it. Not even close.

"Why not?" he asked. "I know you have a better offer—why do you have to hang on to this job?"

Oops. I'd forgotten about his job offer.

"Your offer is just for a month, James. You know that."

He said, "All right. All right." However, he didn't sound all right with it. Not at all.

"I thought I had until tomorrow to make my decision," I said, a little more snippily than I should have if I was till trying for the sympathy bid.

"I know," he replied. "It just feels likes a no-brainer to me. Latterson's a jerk who's trying to rip absolutely everybody off—including you, I might add—and I'm a nice guy who will treat you better than you've ever been treated." He shrugged. "Like I said, a no-brainer." He looked suspicious. "Are we even still on for tonight?"

"Of course we are." I tried to smile. "I picked the restaurant. Remember? The brand new place my friend recommended. Why? Is there something wrong with it?"

"You gave me the wrong address," he said, and laughed, sounding uncomfortable.

"I what?" I gasped. My shock was real. I'd given him the exact address Jasmine had given me. Hadn't I?

"You transposed the street and avenue." He laughed again, less uncomfortably this time. "I thought maybe you didn't really want to go with me."

"I must've written it down wrong," I muttered. "I'm sorry."

"Instead of you meeting me there, how about if I pick you up?" he asked. "Then if we get lost, at least we'll be together."

Yay, I thought. What I said out loud was, "All right."

I walked toward the door, hoping I could get out and away from James before he asked me the big question, which was—

"How did you get into this room?" he asked. Darn it. "I was told it's been locked up for a long time."

I stood with my hand on the door knob. So close. "The door was unlocked," I finally said. "I needed a quiet place to think, and figured no-one would mind."

"It was unlocked?"

"Yes. Why?"

He hmmed a bit before he answered. "I thought I'd checked it . . . Next time, if you want to come in here, let me know. I'll let you in."

"All right." I turned back to the door, then stopped again.

"How did you know I was in the room?" I asked.

"I heard you speaking."

This surprised me. These offices were quite soundproofed.

"Where were you?"

"Down in the furnace room, putting away my tools. I could hear you clear as a bell. Who were you talking to?"

I looked at him, and for the second time in as many minutes, wished I could just tell him the truth. Instead, I lied. What else is new?

"I was talking to my mother."

"Oh." James looked uncomfortable, the way most people do when a dying person is mentioned. "Well, next time, ask me and I'll find you a private place to talk to her. Okay?"

"Okay."

I snuck a glance back into Carruthers' old office, just before James herded me out and closed the door. I needed to check out that computer. There might be something there that would help Farley.

If he came back. If he still trusted me enough to listen to me.

God, he was right. I was definitely an amateur. I was wrecking everything.

Farley:
Back to Hell, with a Twist

"Mr. Samosa, Edmonton could be Las Vegas north, Las Vegas north, Las Vegas north . . ."

Oh my God. I'm back.

Marie:
Setting Up the Non-Date

The door to Mr. Latterson's inner office was ajar and I could hear him speaking to someone on the phone as I snuck to my desk and pulled out some paperwork that needed finishing. Mr. Latterson did not sound happy. Not at all.

"I don't understand what I'm reading here," he said. The papers crackled and swished as they were moved around on his desk by his angry, and I imagine, sweaty hand. "I'm an honest business man, I've fallen on some hard times here, I can't believe she thinks—that you think—that any of these are anything more than harassment, a joke, a bad joke on Good Old Don, and do you have any confirmation, I mean real confirmation, and how dare that bitch— Yes, I'm sorry. How could your client assume I had this much money hidden from her? I wouldn't do that, we had a life together, she's the one who wants to leave me—I *know* I started the proceedings, but for the love of God, the writing was on the wall, she's been treating me like crap for years and—"

I heard his hand slam down on the top of the desk, and couldn't stop myself from flinching. He was talking to his soon-to-be-ex-wife's lawyer.

Being the one who had supplied the information to that lawyer, I felt justified in being flinchy and jumpy. Mr. Latterson wasn't a person to cross. Not when he was signing my more than likely nonexistent paycheques. Not when I needed to remain in this office for a few more days, at least, to figure out Farley's deal.

I stared down at the top of the desk, and reminded myself that I was making some real money by helping James, money that could help my mom, and help me. It didn't make me feel any better. I'd actually broken into Mr. Latterson's office and stolen those documents. Thinking about that made me feel unclean, on top of everything else.

I listened to Mr. Latterson hammer the receiver down on the phone, and storm toward his door, and tried to put an expression on my face that did not radiate my culpability so completely.

"Mr. Latterson!" I said, sounding like I was gushing. I toned down and tried again. "Anything I can help you with? I'm finishing these reports. Maybe fifteen more minutes."

Mr. Latterson didn't act like he was really hearing me, which was good for me, I thought. He was staring at the far wall as he walked for the door out to the hallway. "I don't know if I'll be back today. Lock up, will you?"

"Yes. Happy to."

He stopped when he got to the door, and stood, with his hand on the knob, for some time. "Jenner, has anyone been here in the past couple of days? You know, snooping around?"

"Snooping around?" I tried to keep my voice normal, but it was getting more difficult, what with my voice box tightening up like I'd swallowed a mouthful full of lemon juice, or something. "What do you mean?"

"When I wasn't here. Has there been anybody? Maybe a guy, mid-forties, blond hair, losing it in the back, good dresser—nobody like that?"

I guessed he was describing Helen's lawyer, and my throat loosened. "No sir. There hasn't been anybody but you—and Raymond, of course."

"Of course." Latterson continued to stare at the glass in the door as though he wasn't seeing it at all. "Do me a favour, and keep track, all right? If there is anybody?"

"I will, sir."

I breathed a huge sigh of relief when he finally left. It looked like he didn't suspect me of anything, which was surprising, since he hadn't trusted me at all to this point, so I decided not to go to the paranoid place yet, and turned back to my work. My boring, legitimate work, for which I would probably never be paid.

I glanced over at the door to his inner office, hoping that he didn't check for fingerprints or anything. I belatedly thought of giving it all a wipe down, but threw that thought out when it surfaced. I wasn't going back in his office again. Not a chance. I'd done my nasty little bit for James, and now I was going to be only Mr. Latterson's secretary until I could move Farley on and find another job.

As I finished the report, I decided I'd pick up a newspaper on the way home, to start looking for that new job. No matter what I'd said to James down in the board room, I wasn't working with him. I had to start fresh, once more, with feeling.

Mr. Latterson didn't come back to the office before I left, and I hoped that was a good sign. I locked the door, and left the building, making sure I didn't run into James.

Now that I'd decided not to take James up on his job offer, I was having serious second thoughts about this non-date thing we had planned. I thought about phoning him and canceling when I got home. Maybe even text cancel.

All right, so it was weak, but I was feeling weak. Tired and weak, and all I wanted was my mom to tuck me into bed with chicken noodle soup and tell me everything was going to be all right. That wasn't going to happen, of course. It had been a long time since my mom had tucked me in. Or given me chicken noodle soup.

As I took the bus home, I gave myself a good dressing down. I was a grown woman, darn it, and could handle what life handed me. I didn't feel much better, but my attitude did go up a couple of degrees when I looked through the want ads and found four jobs to apply for.

"Good. I don't have to lie to James about the other job thing, anyhow. I legitimately have prospects. He can find somebody else to close up the office for him. He'll be fine. As soon as Farley moves on, I can get away from Mr. Latterson, and I'll be fine, too."

After I made some tea, I stared out the window, watching the traffic blast past my apartment as everyone tried to get home to their loved ones or wherever they were going and trying to feel really good about the way my life was going. Because my mom wasn't bringing me chicken noodle soup.

She was, however, going to give me some advice about how to deal with Farley. All I had to do was call her, and she'd have what I needed. What I really needed.

I dug my cell phone out of my pocket, almost dropping it when it rang. I didn't recognize the number, so I put the phone down. It could go to voicemail. I didn't feel like dealing with anyone I didn't know. At least I hoped it was someone I didn't know. I definitely didn't want it to be bad news about my mother.

It was James.

"Hi there!" he said cheerily as I momentarily reeled away from my phone as though his voice had somehow burned the skin on my face.

"Just touching base," he continued. "I'll be there at seven. Hope you don't mind, but I've decided to change our plans. I made reservations for supper, and then I've decided we're going to go dancing." He rattled off my address, said again he'd see me at seven, and hung up.

Dancing. Good grief. This was sounding more and more like a date. I looked longingly at his phone number, thought briefly about calling him back and canceling everything, but didn't do it. I glanced at the clock on the stove, instead. I had an hour and a half to get ready. More than enough time to call my mom and get ready for the increasingly date-like non-date.

With fingers that trembled ever so slightly, I punched in my mother's phone number. She answered on the third ring.

She sounded good. Chipper, like the old days. I knew it was an illusion, but I hung onto it, because I needed her to be well, even if it was only in my mind.

I hunched over the phone as I listened to her well-intentioned lies about feeling much, much better, maybe getting back out into the garden later this week, and formulated my request. This would have to be handled with kid gloves, and I wasn't that good in kid glove situations. I didn't want to get her yelling at me again, because sometimes when she yelled, she started coughing, and I was afraid one of these times would be the last time. So I listened to her talk about the condition of the garden, how she'd been neglecting it, adding the occasional "uh huh," to prove I was listening. Then she stopped. I don't think it was because she'd run out of things to say. I think she ran out of breath. But I dove into my problems, pretending she was just my mom, for a minute.

"I have a bit of a situation, and I need to ask you about it. And no, it's not a man," I said before she had a chance to ask. "I have a problem with a ghost. A guy in the building where I work.

"He died there less than a month ago. He acted like he was going through the stages, you know, but nothing since Stage Two. Interesting bit, he's trapped. He said it's like a membrane holding him inside the building. And he keeps disappearing. Like he's blinking out."

I held my breath, hoping she'd have the answer that would clear everything up for me. That she'd have my chicken soup. But she didn't. Not really.

The blinking out had to do with his memory loss, she thought. If I helped him regain his memory, the blinking would stop. Probably.

"Probably?" I asked. "You're not positive?"

Simple answer—she didn't know. And she'd never seen a ghost trapped behind a membrane before. Ever.

She promised to think about it, to see if she could come up with something that would explain what was happening with Farley, but her voice turned into a soothing blur that did nothing to soothe me. Mom didn't have the answer. I really was on my own.

I put down the phone, and slowly began to get ready for my date with James. I had to mop up once, when I started crying and ruined my mascara, but when he drove up to my building, I was looking great if I do say so myself.

I was ready to put on the best performance of my life. That everything was perfectly normal, and this was nothing more than a regular date.

Marie:
Going on the Non-Date

"I don't understand."

My jaw was set. I could feel it, like iron, my teeth grinding together and everything, but could do nothing to ease the tension. James noticed, and gripped the steering wheel of his dead uncle's car, hard.

"I don't understand," I said again. "We aren't going out for supper?"

"No. At least, not right away." James tried to keep the happy-go-lucky, everything's peaches and cream sound in his voice, but I could tell it was getting difficult for him. This was the third time around in this conversation, and I was no closer to understanding why we were changing plans. Mainly because I didn't want to understand.

To be perfectly honest, I saw this as a way out of this sticky non-date situation, and was hoping, with that nasty part of my mind, that if I picked a fight with him, the date would be over before it started.

"It'll only take a minute," he said. "Mrs. Latterson'll be waiting for us. Then we can go for supper and dancing."

"No. Do not put this car into drive until I understand what the heck's going on."

I did not want to meet Helen Latterson face to face. I didn't want her, under any circumstances, to associate me with James' detective agency, or whatever the heck he was calling it. All she had to do was mention to Don Latterson that she'd seen me with James, representing his detective agency, for God's sake, and he'd connect the dots and have me arrested for going through his personal stuff.

"At least let me pull around the corner. I'm going get a ticket here," James said.

I could hear the traffic piling up around us as we bottlenecked a really congested bit of 124th, and knew he was speaking the truth. I didn't care.

"No. Don't move until—"

A big truck, glowering about being caught in the bottle neck, pulled up behind James' car, blatting its horn impatiently.

"I'm moving around the corner, he's going to run us over!"

"Fine. Fine." I ground the words between my teeth as James put the car into gear and lurched forward into the traffic. This caused more blats from the horns of angry motorists as vehicles swerved to get out of his way.

"See, we almost had an accident, you happy now?" James glanced at me and I was pretty sure he saw my face had whitened appreciably. Sheer terror will do that to a person, no matter how carefully she applies her makeup. "I'm sorry I scared you, I just—"

"Had to get the car out of the way." I could mimic his whine pretty well, I thought, meanly.

"Mrs. Latterson requested this meeting and I have to be there. After all, she's going to give us a sizable amount of money. Let's hear her out."

"Please tell me you didn't mention my name," I said.

"I was going to do it at the meeting."

"Under no circumstances do that," I said.

He frowned. "Why not? After all, we were going to discuss the idea of you being on the team tonight, anyhow, so why shouldn't you be introduced to our first official client?"

I tried not to roll my eyes. He couldn't be that thick.

He caught my eye roll, and his voice iced.

"Do you want to know why I want to introduce you? Because I owe you. You're the reason she's getting this information. I wanted to make sure you got the recognition you deserved. That's why." His voice was so quiet I could barely hear him.

"Oh."

I almost felt bad that I was using this as a way to get out of going on a date with him. Then he absolutely creeped me out by turning toward me with a serious expression on his face.

"Are you trying to use this as a way to get out of going out on this date with me?"

"No!" As I tried to act appalled that he'd think that of me, I was reeling. What, could this guy read minds? "No, of course not."

"Then why are you acting like this?"

I decided part of the truth was better than an outright lie.

"What I did was illegal, James. I broke into her ex-husband's office and stole personal papers. And photocopied them. I don't want to end up in jail, because you're proud of the 'work' I did for you."

"Oh." It was his turn to whiten. He had obviously not thought of that. "Oh."

He thought hard, tapping his fingers on the steering wheel of the car.

"So, stay in the vehicle," he said. "I didn't mention your name to her or anything, so if you're out of sight, you can remain anonymous. This is just something about the bill, I think, and I want to get things straightened out. Does that sound okay?"

"Maybe." I saw my opportunity to break and run disappearing as he came up with a rational way around the situation.

"Good. That's great. After, we can go for supper. Discuss the case, stuff like that." He glanced over at me and tried to smile. He almost pulled it off. "Does that sound okay?"

"All right." My jaw unclenched. I would agree with this, but it was only for the money. Really. "So, where are we supposed to meet her?"

"Tim's, on 104th Avenue."

"A coffee shop?"

He had to good grace to look embarrassed. "She said she wouldn't be caught dead in Chinatown."

I started laughing, and didn't stop until we pulled into the coffee shop's parking lot, five minutes later. It sounded hysterical, but I didn't care. It felt good to laugh.

Helen Latterson was easy to spot through the window of the crowded coffee shop. She was a tall, stick thin, blonde woman, well dressed, and supremely angry. I could see the rage coming off her in waves, a dull red heat that kept people away from her table. James strode up to her and held out his hand.

She looked surprised and stared at his face for a long calculating moment. She had probably been expecting Jimmy the Elder. Jimmy the Dead. She glanced down at her hands clenched on the top of the table, then back up at James, and spoke.

James' face contorted, his hand hanging in the air like a dead fish. He finally dropped it to his side, and then started swaggering around, speaking very rapidly as he did so, and I was afraid he was actually trying to act like a private detective, like James Cagney or something. The problem was, from my vantage point, he came across a lot more like Clouseau than Cagney—or maybe it was Cagney, if he didn't know what the hell he was doing.

Helen spoke again, rather sharply, her lips thinning to nonexistence, and James collapsed onto the chair opposite her, a red-faced, sweating ball of confusion. I was ready to get out of the car and help him out, because the man really looked like he could use saving about that time, but he pulled himself together, and began talking earnestly to the furious woman sitting across from him.

I could tell the moment he told her Jimmy the Elder was dead. The absolute second. There is always that slack-jawed look, as though death is incomprehensible. She glanced down at her hands again, but James kept talking until she pulled herself together. I realized that now that he was no longer trying for the Cagney thing, he had her attention. She started to look relieved, and about ten years had dropped from her face by the time they shook hands, the meeting obviously over.

James didn't move from his spot at the table until her car disappeared down the busy street. Then he straggled out, looking as though he'd been through a war.

"I need a drink." He glanced around as though he expected something stronger than coffee to magically appear. Hoped it would appear.

"So do I." I pointed to across the street. "Come on. Let's go to Lucretia's."

We crossed the street to the little lounge that had been Gothic until Gothic didn't sell anymore. I think the only thing the new owners kept was the original name. As we parked, I heard James sigh, a bunch of times. It was going to be a long night.

We stayed longer than I wanted to. James nursed a beer, but I made a bit of a mistake and pounded back three scotches in quick succession and got bleary-eyed until James finally ordered food. He would not answer any of my questions about Helen Latterson. Then I guess you could say we had our non-date.

James seemed happy enough, once the food was served, but I wasn't. I felt really uncomfortable, especially since he wouldn't talk about how the meeting with Mrs. Latterson had gone. I tried to bring it up a couple of times, but he put it off, saying we could discuss it the next day, that this was a nice evening out, let's not wreck it with business talk.

That meant there was a problem, of course. I felt even worse, and barely picked at my food.

Finally, in the midst of one of his long winded-stories about his short-lived football career—I think he was talking about junior high—I told him I didn't feel well, and wanted to go home.

He was actually a real gentleman about everything. He didn't mention the fact that we were supposed to go dancing, and that this was supposed to be a celebration. He didn't mention that I'd told him I'd give him my answer about the job offer.

All he did was gallantly hold my chair for me, and offer to pay. I didn't let him, so I guess you could say I won that round, though it cut into my slender reserves. A lot.

The drive back to my place was dead silent until the traffic started to congest.

"What's going on?" I glanced down at my wrist as if I expected a watch to magically materialize. "Are the movies letting out?"

"I don't think so." James twisted his hands on the steering wheel as the traffic ebbed and flowed around us. "Maybe there's an accident up ahead."

I peered out the front window. "Isn't that smoke? I think it's a fire. Man, that's close to my place—"

My voice faded to nothing as the traffic stalled again. An ambulance, siren wailing, pulled to the wrong side of the road and parked.

"It *is* your place, Marie." James' voice raised an octave, and he gripped the steering wheel so hard I could hear his knuckles cracking, pop, pop, pop. "At least I think it's yours—"

"Jesus." I threw open the door of the Volvo, nearly nailing the car beside me as it tried to make a third lane on a two lane street. The motorist blatted his horn angrily, but I didn't care. I jumped out and ran between the vehicles, waving my hands as if to ward off the evil that seemed to surround me with the acrid smoke and grey ash.

"Marie!" James called. "Marie! Get in the car!"

"My place is on fire!"

I could hear the craziness in my voice as I took another lazy, shambling step toward my fully engulfed apartment building, feeling like I was running through glue. I stopped in the street, and the traffic lurched around me. I smacked the side of one car as it swept by me, close enough to brush the edge of my coat with its side mirror, then turned back to my building, and watched it burn.

"Marie, get in the car!" James yelled, edging up to me. "Now!"

He stopped, but all I could do was stare, unable to move. "Somebody burned it down."

I could feel the tears, the useless, useless tears, and could think of nothing to stop them. Everything I owned was going up in smoke, and I'd been out on a stupid date.

"Please get in the car."

"It's all gone—" A stupid, stupid date.

"Please, get in the car."

"It's all burned—" And I had no-one to blame but myself.

I couldn't move. Couldn't move a muscle until James barked, "Get in the damned car!"

It was like he slapped me, and I finally responded, flailing ineffectually with the door handle until he reached across and pushed it open for me.

"I have to stay," I said.

He started to say something, but the look on my face shut his mouth, and he simply nodded.

"I'll park the car."

He took off as I walked to the sidewalk, to the fire. To watch my life burn to the ground.

The firefighters were having trouble keeping idiots like me away from the building, which was still fully engulfed in towering, bellowing flames. I stood behind a hastily erected barricade, and stared. My coat was spotted with soot and tiny burns as the ash, still white hot, touched down. I didn't care.

James touched me on the arm, as though he was going to hug me or something.

"Don't," I said, without turning around. I couldn't take my eyes from my burning apartment building.

"Please folks." An older fireman, with a pot belly and a bull horn, acted like he was in charge. "You gotta move back. This is a dangerous place to be right now."

"This is our home!" Penelope Simpson, one of my neighbors, her hair still in curlers, fuzzy slippers black and sodden from the fire and the water, pointed at the burning building with one hand as she frantically clutched Harry, her fat, pissed off cat in the other. "It's—we—" And then she burst into tears, braying out her grief until the cat scratched frantically, trying to get away.

"Penelope!"

When I called her name, she whirled around, curlers flopping around her face like small dead fish, the cat's butt flying out away from her as she turned. I thought the cat was going to escape, until I saw how tightly Penelope was clutching him, and then I feared for his life. Cat's eyes shouldn't bug out like that.

"Marie!" Penelope cried, and stumbled toward me, over the hoses and debris and mud that had been, until a short time ago, our front yard. "Marie! My God girl, you're all right! We were so worried! We couldn't find you and—" She began braying again, tears falling in warm rain on her struggling cat's head. "It's burning."

"Come here, Penelope. It's safer over here." I reached across the barricade and grabbed her by the belt of her housecoat, pulling her further from the fire. "Come stand with me."

I took the cat away from the old woman, and tucked it into the crook of my arm, where it immediately calmed down and began preening. I put my other arm around the old woman.

"Where were you? We were scared to death."

"I went out for a drink."

"Oh, isn't that nice." The old woman turned toward James, with a half-smile on her smoke darkened face. "Were you out with this young gentleman?"

"Yes," I sighed. I didn't need this right now. I really didn't.

"Oh, how very nice. A date. You don't go—"

"It wasn't a date," I said hastily. "It wasn't a date."

"Oh. That's too bad." The old woman patted my arm, and turned back toward the fire. I turned, and James was beside me, looking heartbroken. I'd crushed him. I could tell.

"I'm sorry, James. It wasn't a date. Not really."

"I understand." He sounded angry, but I didn't have time to soothe his ruffled feathers right then, because Penelope clutched me frantically as something inside the building whined, then screamed, then exploded like a roman candle, spewing sparks and ash everywhere. Through it all, the cat sat in the crook of my arm and watched the melee with steady green eyes. And he purred.

Farley:
Las Vegas North

"Las Vegas north, Las Vegas north, Las Vegas north . . ."
Why can't I just die?
"Las Vegas north, Las Vegas north, Las Vegas north . . ."
Oh yeah. Too late.

Marie:
Couch Surfing, at the Office

The flames weren't completely out until three in the morning. The Red Cross helped everybody find a place to stay—even Penelope and her cranky cat. I turned them down, unwilling to leave until the last ember had been put out. James stayed with me. That was good of him.

When the fire was finally, truly out, he offered me his couch, which was also good of him, but even though I'd used half of my cash to pay for dinner and couldn't have afforded a room anywhere, I wasn't ready to camp at his place. Not after our non-date. I couldn't give him the impression I was relying on him. That I needed him—even though I did.

If I was going to be absolutely honest about the whole thing, I couldn't think of anything I wanted more than to have him take me back to his place and hug me, whispering to me that this was all a bad dream, and that we'd live happily ever after, when we got the smoke smell out of our clothes. That wasn't going to happen, so I watched the firemen wrap up the last of the hoses as daylight started to touch the sky with grey, and tried not to lean on him, even accidentally.

"Well, you have to stay someplace. What about the office? There's that cot, and we cleaned it all up the last time we were there. How about that?" He touched my arm tentatively, and seemed encouraged when I didn't shrug him off, this time. "You can sleep there and we'll figure out something more permanent tomorrow."

I didn't answer him, though it was the best suggestion I'd heard all night. I was starting to ache everywhere, as though I'd been through a disaster—which I guess I had, though I hadn't had to do anything except watch—and I wanted a cup of tea badly.

"Come on. You need some sleep." He tugged on the sleeve of my soot covered coat, and I followed. He was right. I needed sleep.

I glanced at the street as he led me to the Volvo. It was nearly empty now that the fire was out. A couple of cabs taking drunks home, a few cars, and a truck. The bass from its stereo pounded so deeply it made the material of my blouse jump on my chest. I couldn't see into the darkly tinted windows as it slowly slid past us, heading north.

"I think I recognize that truck," I said. James glanced at it, and shrugged. Then he took me firmly by the elbow and let me around the corner to his car, and I forgot about it.

I forgot about everything but the fact that I was homeless. Officially homeless. Finally, the tears came. James, ever the gentleman, lent me his handkerchief again.

Jimmy the Dead's office smelled clean, fresh, like good linen that had been hung on the line to dry. I felt bad for bringing the smell of smoke in with me. It hung off me like a shroud, even when I took off my coat.

"I stink." I tried to smile as I announced that fact, and almost pulled it off. James tried to smile back, and reached for the electric kettle, shaking it to see if there was any water in it. He'd promised me tea.

"The bathroom's down the hall. You can clean up there." He pulled out a towel and some hand soap. "This is all I've got here, sorry, it's not great soap."

I sniffed it appreciably. "Smells better than me." I headed for the door. "I'll be back in a minute."

It took me a bit more than a minute to sluice the smell off myself in that woefully inadequate sink, but I did feel better as I headed back to the office.

The herbal tea James had brewed smelled great too.

Strawberries and lemon wafted from the cup he handed me after I sank gratefully onto the cot James had opened up, and wrapped myself in a blanket.

"Thank you." I buried my nose in the cup, taking in the sweet smell of spring time. "This is good."

"You're welcome." He looked like he was going to start talking. I was afraid he would start quizzing me about my plans for the future or something, and I didn't want to think about those kind of questions, much less formulate an answer that would be close to coherent, and so I buried my face in my cup. He must have understood, because he didn't say anything. He simply sipped his own cup of tea, grimacing and putting it aside after the first taste.

"You don't like it?" I took another appreciative sip. "I think it tastes great."

"Well, this isn't the kind of thing I normally drink." He tried desperately not to act flustered, and failed. "I bought this—for you."

"For me?"

"Yeah. You mentioned you liked this kind. I thought it would be nice, you know, around the office." He stood, his face reddening ever so slightly. If I hadn't been so amazingly tired, I would have laughed—or smiled. I did neither.

"Thanks. That was kind of you."

"Yeah, well. You know." He stared out the window absently, then with more intensity. "What colour was that truck?"

"What truck?" My mind was starting to fuzz, and I searched for a place to set down the cup.

"That one near your place. That one you pointed out."

"It was a black Ram. Why?" I finally ended up setting the cup on the floor, and was wrestling with the blanket. I was so tired, it was positively oozing from every one of my pores.

"I think it's parked on the street."

"What?" The tiredness disappeared immediately, replaced by the adrenaline pop of fear. "Are you sure?"

"No. Well, maybe." He stared harder, nose to the glass. I pushed the blanket aside and walked over to stand beside him.

"Hurry," he said. "It's leaving."

By the time I got to the window, the truck had turned the corner. All I saw was the tail lights as it disappeared.

"Was it the one?" he asked.

"No idea." I walked back to the cot and plopped down, the tiny burst of adrenaline gone, replaced by more exhaustion. "No idea at all."

"I couldn't see the licence plate, the light was burned out." He stared out the window for another moment, then went back to the chair behind the desk. "Don't worry about it. You can tell the police tomorrow."

"The police?" I could barely keep my eyes open, and his words were flitting around me like so many butterflies, impossible to catch.

"Yeah. The police. Let them know about the truck."

One of my eyes slid shut, and after a brief struggle, so did the other one. I settled further into the blankets on the cot, thinking I could lie there and carry on the conversation with my eyes closed. It would be fine. And then, I was asleep.

Marie:
Off to Work

"I don't think you should go to work today."

James had spent the night curled up in the massively uncomfortable chair behind the little secretarial desk in the front office, while I slept on the cot. He was a bit cranky because of it.

I didn't say anything, because I was trying to rub the wrinkles out of my clothes with my hands and it was going badly.

"Wasn't there an iron here somewhere?" I glanced around the room, but there was nothing out of place. Even the tea pot and cups we had used the night before had been cleaned and put away. "I think I remember an iron—"

"I'll get it for you. I still don't think—"

"I know. I need to go to work. At least for the morning. Mr. Latterson needs an explanation, and—"

"Fine. I'll get the iron." James sounded exasperated, but I didn't care. I stripped off my wrinkled blouse and skirt, thankful that I'd decided to wear a slip the night before. And full bum underwear. No sneaking a peek for James.

He hauled out the iron and an ironing board, which I hadn't remembered seeing, from the inner office, and set it up for me, carefully averting his eyes when he realized I was as close to naked as he was probably ever going to see.

"Thanks." I set to work on the blouse, horrified when the smell of smoke wafted up from the warmed cotton.

"I don't understand why you won't give yourself one day. It's only one day. Latterson will understand."

I kept my head down, unwilling to catch his eye. It wasn't Mr. Latterson I was worried about, of course. It was Farley. He was going to come back soon, and I had to be there for him.

James flapped around as I smoothed the wrinkles from my clothes and got dressed, then tried to do something with my hair. I finally settled on a pony tail, pretending it was my version of an up do, until I caught sight of myself in the bathroom mirror as I brushed my teeth with baking soda, which was the only thing in the tiny fridge in the office, and my finger. My updo looked exactly like a pony tail trying to hide unwashed hair. I sighed and rinsed the gloppy, horrible tasting mess out of my mouth, hoping it would at least make my breath better.

"Promise me you'll talk to the police today." He was standing right by the door with a cup of coffee in his hands, which he handed to me as I walked by. I sipped it. It was exactly the way I liked it.

"I promise."

I meant it. I was starting to think hard about some of the things I'd found out about the Palais. I wanted to run some ideas past the police—after I'd talked about the fire, of course. Plus my homeless status. Thinking about that gave me a bit of headache. I took another sip of my perfect coffee, and sighed. It was going to be another long day. I could tell.

The police came to me before I could go to them. Sergeant Sylvia Worth and her side-kick Constable Williams were waiting at the front door of the building when James and I walked in, and I had a brief conversation with them. I couldn't talk about much really, not about Farley and the Palais, anyhow, because James was hovering around. After a few rather fruitless minutes of me saying things like "I don't know," and "I have no recollection," Sergeant Worth gave up.

"Thanks for your cooperation," she said, and waved at Constable Williams. "He'll finish the interview."

Constable Williams, a weak chinned individual who wouldn't make eye contact and treated me like I had somehow caused the fire myself, handed me a business card, telling me to call if I remembered anything else, and scurried out the door after the sergeant. I was free.

I dashed for the stairs, unwilling to wait for the elevator, waving good-bye to James, and trying not to think about the fact that it was in my best interests to keep on his good side, because he had a free place for me to sleep, at least for a while. I wanted to see if Farley had come back yet.

He wasn't in the office, but Mr. Latterson was. He was destroying a perfectly good pot of coffee, and jumped a foot when I charged through the door.

"Here, let me do that for you," I said, trying to act all fresh as morning dew, but he stared at me as though he couldn't believe his eyes.

"I saw you on the news this morning." He finished sprinkling coffee grounds near the vicinity of the filter and rammed the pot under the spout to catch the water that was already flowing freely over everything. "That was your place?"

"Yes. It was." I tried to move him out of the way so I could clean up the mess, because I really needed to do something with my hands at that moment, and cleaning up coffee seemed like the best bet. I hadn't seen the news crew. My mom watched the news, every morning, without fail.

"Well, that was a bit of bad luck." He finally moved aside, and I set to work cleaning up the mess he'd made. "Any idea what happened?"

"No. I don't think the police have a clue, either."

"The police?" I turned and watched his face turn absolutely green. "You've been talking to the police?"

"Just now, down in the lobby. They were waiting for me." I tried to laugh, and set out two cups. "I didn't have much to tell them. I got there after it was burning."

"Oh." He flapped around, getting in my way as I tried to make his coffee the way he liked it, which, I assumed, did not involve a large number of grounds. "I'm surprised you're here. I thought you would've taken the day off."

"Oh well, there isn't really anything I can do," I laughed, hoping it sounded real, and handing him his coffee. "It's not like I need to deal with insurance people or anything. No, I could use the day's pay. So, here I am!"

"No insurance." He stared down into the cup for a minute.

"Well, that's a bitch, isn't it?"

"Yeah." It took me a minute to get myself back under control, because the no insurance thing made the whole homeless thing more real, and I wished, for a second, that I still had James' handkerchief. By the time I pulled myself together, Mr. Latterson had retreated into his office, muttering about an afternoon meeting he had to prepare for.

I took one sip of Mr. Latterson's terrible coffee and pushed the cup as far from me as I could. Then I pulled out the flash drive on which I'd been compiling information about the Palais. I had so little real information, I felt embarrassed. Then, I thought of the computer, down in Mr. Carruthers' old office. What if there was information there that would help?

Without thinking too much, I hammered on Mr. Latterson's door, bellowing, "Going out for a donut, Boss. Want one?"

I didn't wait for him to answer, hoping that the post-fire sympathy was still running through his veins. I grabbed the key Farley had given me, and headed down to the main floor, to Mr. Carruthers' old office. I hoped that the computer had something—anything—on it, because going through old files was a lot better than trying to figure out what I was going to do with the rest of my week—or the rest of my life. This was something I could actually do something about. If there were any files.

James phoned me on my cell at quarter to twelve, giving me quite a start.

"Want to do lunch?" he asked.

"Give me twenty minutes," I said, staring at the files I had left to copy from the abandoned computer in Carruthers' old office to the flash drive. Fifteen more. That computer had a ton of files that someone had tried to delete. They hadn't done a good enough job though, and I'd recovered almost all of them. I'd started reading one, called "Biography" but the writing was so pathetic, I didn't check any more. I decided to simply copy the rest and check them out later.

"I'll pick up some sandwiches from the deli," he said.

"Sounds great," I said, because it did. First, because I love the sandwiches from that deli, and second because then James would be out of the building, and I wouldn't have to watch for him while I snuck out of Carruthers' office.

"We can eat on the bench at the front of the Palais again," he said. "You know, like a picnic."

The idea sounded almost heavenly, but I wasn't calling what we were about to do a picnic. I was calling it having a small talk about Helen Latterson and the conversation James had with her the night before.

Getting information for Farley was important, but it had become imperative that I get my hands on some of the money that Helen Latterson owed us, and quickly. I was pretty sure she and James had talked about it, before our non-date, and before the fire. So, I was going to make him tell me what was going on.

This was probably going to bring up the question about whether I would work with him at his dead uncle's detective agency, but I wasn't ready to answer that question anymore. I had been sure the day before, but one day can make a real difference.

I finished downloading the files and was safely sitting on the bench outside the Palais, enjoying the scent of the nearby pines when James walked up, loaded with bags and styrofoam coffee cups.

Soon we were munching on excellent sandwiches and drinking equally excellent coffee, made the way I like it. It was so nice, I almost didn't want to wreck the mood by bringing up Helen Latterson. Before I could bring her up, James did.

"I hate to have to talk to you about this right now, but Mrs. Latterson was concerned. I think that's probably the best way to describe her mood." James stared over his sandwich at me. "I knew you wanted to know. Because the money would come in handy now, wouldn't it?"

"Well, yes, it would." I blurted out that rather obvious confession as though I was being dragged over broken glass. "What did she say?"

"She felt, given my lack of expertise, we were asking for far too much money. And that she needed the originals of the bank statements, not copies."

"What?" I put down my sandwich, my appetite suddenly gone. "Too much money? Originals?"

"Yeah. To both." He took another bite of his sandwich, and stared past me to one of the huge old pines glowering over us. "I think I talked her into one percent, which is all right. However, the original bank statements are a real problem."

When he glanced at me, I saw that other James again, and wondered, for the first time, if I was being played. The cold little part of my heart suddenly got a whole lot bigger. Fresh handkerchief, indeed.

"There is no way I'm going to take those for you, James. Not a chance. No matter how much it's worth." I wrapped my sandwich and stuffed it in my purse, feeling exhausted. "Thanks for the lunch. I have to go back to work."

"No, don't leave, you misunderstood. I'm not asking you to get that information. Really. You've done more than enough." He held up his hands entreatingly. "Please sit down and enjoy your lunch. I wasn't trying to upset you. Not after everything you've been through. Really. I felt you needed to know what was happening with her, to keep you up to date. You know?"

I stared at him for a moment, trying to read his eyes, but they'd gone back to their nice, gentle, harmless blue and I wondered if maybe I was being paranoid. Having your place burned to the ground could do it.

"Yeah, I understand," I finally said, and took another sip of the perfect coffee. "Do me a favour though, and don't tell me how you plan on getting those documents. I really don't want to know."

"No problem." He grinned, and in spite of myself, I smiled back at him. "Do you want to stay at the office a few more days? Until you get settled somewhere else? I know it's not very comfortable, but the price is right."

I'd been thinking about calling Jasmine and seeing if I could go to her place, but liked the idea of Jimmy the Dead's office better. At least there were no rug rats roaming around, grinding chewed gum into your hair while you slept.

"Yeah, it sure is. Thanks, James." And then I said, "I'll think about it."

I needed a place to stay, the office was free, which fit into my complete lack of money very nicely, and he had treated me decently since the fire. Why the hesitation?

Because I was afraid he'd read more into me saying yes than just yes. That's why.

"I'll let you know this afternoon, all right?"

"All right." He finished the last of his sandwich and flicked the crumbs from the wax paper on the grass for the birds, a couple of which hopped right up to his feet to grab them in their greedy little beaks. "I should get back to work. You okay?"

"Yes," I lied, keeping my eyes from his, so he couldn't catch me. I didn't feel okay. I didn't know if I'd ever feel okay again, to be honest. "Thanks for lunch."

"You're welcome." He reached over and touched my hand for a moment, his warmth making my skin come alive. "Talk to you this afternoon." And then I was alone. Completely alone. Even the birds made a dash for freedom when James disappeared into the Palais.

When I went back into Mr. Latterson's office, he still had his door shut, so I had time to organize the information I'd gathered from Andrea's office. In the aftermath of almost getting caught and fired and things, I hadn't had time to write down what I'd learned.

As I typed out as much as I could remember—including the two thirty-thousand dollar payoffs Andrea had received—I knew that Farley wasn't going to be happy. He'd been so sure that Henderson was the one. But he wasn't. He was an A-hole, for sure, but he hadn't been involved in Farley's death.

However, it looked like beautiful blonde Andrea just might be. Who was paying her? And for what?

No answers to that, yet. I hoped I wouldn't have to "do lunch" with her again, in an effort to find out. I didn't think my liver could stand it.

After I typed out everything I remembered from Henderson's office, I went through a couple more of the files from Carruthers' old computer, in an attempt to get as much information organized for Farley that I could. If he came back.

Even as I thought the word "if," I knew it was not true. Mom had said as much. Farley needed to know more, before he could move on. I hoped that the information I was gathering was what he needed.

Farley:
Back Hanging Around with the Living

I came back sprawled on the floor between the restroom and the hallway going to the Latterson's old office. I felt old, used up. Like I had nothing left. I couldn't even move, so I lay on the threadbare carpet, listening as people left work for the day.

I could hear them chirping good-bye to each other as they left the building. They sounded relaxed—alive. I hated them for it.

Then I wondered—had I been gone hours, or days? Didn't have a clue.

I didn't want to move, but I knew I had to. I had to get to Marie, to tell her what I'd remembered. It was important.

Instead, I sank a few inches into the floor and stared at the layers of materials covering the wooden joists. A thin skin of cement, enough to get someone, probably an inspector, off somebody's back, then underlay, then the carpet. I was imbedded in underlay. How odd.

I pulled myself up to standing, barely able to keep my feet under me. I didn't feel substantial. Okay, realistically, I hadn't been substantial for some time, but this was definitely different. This time I felt like a ghost. Not of this world. Not even close.

I went to find Marie.

Marie:
Farley's Back

Farley oozed through the door, looking like a ghost.

All right, so he'd been a ghost for a while, but this time, he looked like it. He still had a little of his colour and glow, but he moved uncertainly, waving like a sapling in a strong breeze, as if he didn't belong in the land of the living.

In other words, he looked like I felt.

"I know you don't want me in here anymore, but I have news," he said. I barely recognized his voice. It sounded as ghostlike as he looked. And then he said, "News from beyond," and "oohed" a couple of times.

Gooseflesh popped up on my arms. "Stop that, Farley," I said. "It's creeping me out."

"Sorry," he muttered. "Trying for a joke."

He looked even more miserable, if that was possible, and for the briefest of moments, I wished I could give him a hug.

"So I guess this means you *are* done with me," he said, his ash dark eyes boring into mine so all I wanted to do was turn away. "You've had enough of stupid old Farley. Right?"

"No," I said. I'd lost enough. I wasn't losing him, too. "I said that stuff before because I was scared, you know, because I almost got caught and almost lost my job. Farley, I can't be what you want me to be." My throat tightened. "I can't be your friend, but I want to help you. When you're ready."

"I feel ready." His mouth worked. "I don't belong here anymore. This stuff—all this stuff, doesn't matter anymore. Does it?"

"Maybe it does." I stood up and clenched my hands together on my chest. I realized it looked like I was praying, so I released them. "I know you don't want to talk about moving on to the next plane of existence, but trust me, the alternative is much worse."

"You're talking about fading away, right?"

I thought about the ghost in the phone booth who had gone to her own form of hell. "Yeah, fading away is one," I said carefully. "And there's other things that can happen. If you aren't clear about everything."

"Clear?" He frowned. "Is this something your mother told you?"

"Yeah," I said. "Mostly. So, please, take my mother's advice. You need to regain your memory."

"Regaining my memory will help catch the guys who did it?"

"Maybe," I said. I tried not to roll my eyes. He had to get off this "catch the bad guys" track. He just had to. "But—"

"Good," he said. "So let me tell you about my last dream. It wasn't the same as the other ones. This happened a couple of days before I died."

"Oh." I couldn't decide whether that was good or not, and decided to be absolutely neutral. "What did you remember?"

"I remembered listening to Carruthers. In the vents."

"The voice you heard was Mr. Carruthers? You're sure?"

"Yep," Farley said. "He was trying to talk somebody—I think the name was Samosa, but I could be wrong—into investing in a plan he had for the downtown core of the city. Once the new hockey arena was in place, he figured they'd need a bunch more hotels and stuff, and he wanted to develop as much as he could. He told the guy that he could use the extensive underground malls and walkways already in place to connect all the hotels. Plus he wanted to turn the old Hudson's Bay building into a great big casino. 'We'll be able to bring in the big Vegas acts,' he said. 'We can call it Las Vegas north.'"

"Las Vegas," I whispered. "So that's where that came from."

"Yep," he said again. "He really was giving the hard sell to this Samosa guy. How easy it would be to turn this city into Las Vegas north."

"All right," I said, and held up the flash drive. "That ties into what I found in his old computer. He's been buying up buildings all over the downtown core. So, what you heard was him trying to get someone else to invest. It all ties together."

"Yeah. It seems to," Farley said. "But here's the thing. Remember when you found out about that society trying to get the Palais designated as historical? That apparently was the fly in the ointment. The Palais was like ground zero. If they couldn't tear it down and build the first hotel, the rest of the plan would fall like a house of cards. Samosa even asked about it."

"What did Carruthers say?"

"He told Samosa not to worry about it. That he had it handled. What he said was, 'I got a guy who deals with these kinds of problems all the time. The Palais is as good as gone.'"

Oh.

"That's what I heard, down in that furnace room two days before I died." Farley looked at me, his eyes two black holes in the translucent grey of his face. "My boss hired somebody to get rid of the Palais. Somehow, whoever he hired fucked up, and the place is still here. And I'm dead."

"Son of a bitch," I whispered. If this wasn't just a dream—if this really was a memory—Farley had just implicated Carruthers in Farley's death.

"Yep," Farley replied. "Exactly."

"I think I'm going to go back into Carruthers' computer files and see if I can find confirmation."

"Confirmation?" He quirked a half-smile, and I felt a bit better, until he glanced over at me and I could feel the deadness of his gaze. "Don't trust me?"

"I have to be able to show the police something, Farley. I can't tell them I got the information from a dead guy. Know what I mean?"

"Yeah. I know what you mean." He got up and walked a few steps away from the desk. Actually, he shuffled, as though he didn't have the strength to lift his feet.

"Stick with me for a while longer, Farley," I said. "We'll get this all figured out."

"Yeah," he said again, without turning around. "You probably will."

And then he left.

There was nothing more I could do for him, past proving that what he'd remembered had been the truth, so I went back into Carruthers' files to see if I could find anything that confirmed what Farley had said.

The good thing? I found some. Mr. Carruthers had money invested in properties all over the downtown core. Even in the old Hudson's Bay Building. He had everything set out in a complicated spreadsheet, including money invested, and what could be made if the investments were sold. The numbers were from months before, which had to have been the last time Carruthers had entered anything into the computer.

I couldn't find any emails, or anything that gave me a hint who this "'Samosa" person was, or who Carruthers had hired to destroy the Palais. However, I thought that the spreadsheet and his badly written biography would be enough.

I would take this information to the police, and let them deal with it. Maybe if they reopened the case, that would be enough to help Farley.

I hoped so, anyhow. I really didn't know what else I could do.

Farley:
Dying for a Bad Cause

I left Marie alone while she worked, and went down to the entranceway. I pressed my face against the barrier, staring out at the tree and the buildings, and the sky. I had died because of a money scheme. And, according to Marie, a bad one at that. The whole idea made me wince. Really.

I'd managed to convince myself that if it had been for a good cause, you know, a noble cause, then maybe it was all right that I was dead. But a shitty—really shitty—scheme to make that clown some cash? That was more than I could take. So I watched the sky, and the trees, and the buildings, and tried not to think about it. At least for a while.

Marie:
Taking It Under Advisement

I carefully saved the information I'd gathered, shut down my computer, and put a call into Constable Williams, the weak-chinned cop who had talked to me about the fire in my apartment building. I decided he was going to help me catch the bad guys.

I figured—actually, I hoped—this was one way to get Farley the closure he needed so he could move on, and I could begin pulling the shards of my life back together. I really needed a checkmark in the win column. It had been a tough couple of days.

So, I was thrilled when the cop answered the phone himself, his nasally voice droning, "Constable Williams, how can I help you?"

The thrill factor receded appreciably when he reacted coolly to my request for a follow-up talk. His day was full, he whined, any chance we could put this over until the next week? I persevered. Well, really, I got massively pushy and wouldn't take next week for an answer. He reluctantly agreed to meet me at his office in a half hour.

I slammed the phone down and pelted out of the office, barely taking the time to check the door to make certain it was locked. I practically ran all the way to the downtown police station, to make it on time.

Then, I cooled my heels for what felt like an hour as Williams took some calls, had coffee, played a video game, and wasted my time. Now, I don't know if he was actually doing any those things, because I was waiting for him to come and escort me to his office, but it sure felt like it.

By the time he did come down to talk to me, I wasn't in the mood for any foolishness. But that's what I was going to get.

"What information do you have for me, Miss Jenner?" He stared at me with his flat eyes, thumbs hooked into his utility belt, the fingers of one hand rubbing the edge of his flashlight like he could already feel it smacking me on the top of the head for wasting his time. I tried to put some semblance of a smile on my face as I gestured to the locked door that kept the rabble separated from the police.

"Can we go up to your office? I'll only take a minute of your time, I really would rather not talk to you about this down here."

I wished for a moment that my hair didn't look like a bad ponytail, or that I was wearing something more revealing, anything to break through the big wall of "I don't give a rat's butt" between him and me. He thought he already had all the information he needed to close the case, and nothing I was going to say was going to change his mind.

I tried anyway. I told him everything I'd found out about Carruthers. I told him about Las Vegas north, about the name of the potential investor sounding like Samosa, and about Carruthers hiring someone to destroy the Palais. I even explained why the Palais was going to be destroyed. Because of the historical designation, which would be decided in the next week. When I finally stopped talking, he stared at me with his flat blue eyes, thumbs still stuck in his belt.

"I don't see how this relates to the fire in your apartment building, Miss Jenner."

I stared at him, open-mouthed. I'd honestly forgotten that he was the one investigating the fire. "I'm—I'm sure it's all connected," I finally said, choking on the words. "I'm sure if you check, you'll find out Carruthers had something to do with it, as well. There's something going on, Constable! Please check this stuff out!"

He stared at me for a few moments more, then thanked me for coming down and giving him the information. He would take it under advisement, and get back to me. Next week.

I tried to hand him the flash drive with the information I'd gathered on it. He pulled his hand back as though I'd tried to burn him with it.

"I can't take that," he said. "Viruses and such. You know. Maybe you can print it all off and send it to me, next week."

I stared at him. "Aren't you at least going to write down what I said?" I finally asked. "I thought you were supposed to write everything down."

"I've got it all up here." He disengaged one thumb from his belt and tapped his forehead, twice.

"So that's it, then?"

"I'll get back to you next week."

That's when it hit me. It was the Friday of a long weekend. Constable Williams didn't care one way or another what information I had. He was trying to get out early, to start his long weekend early. I saw red.

"Who is your supervisor?" I didn't think I'd spoken very loudly, but everyone in the entrance turned and stared at me.

"You should calm down." Williams had obviously seen the looks, and took a step toward me, lowering his own voice to get me to lower mine. "You've had a bad couple of days, and—"

"I don't think you have any idea how bad my last couple of days have been, Constable Williams!" Yep, my voice was definitely loudish. The cops staffing the desk gave us a "do we have a problem here" glance, prompting Williams to give a quick head shake. No problem here. Absolutely not.

"Tell me who your supervisor is," I yelled, "and we are done here."

"Fine. You want my supervisor's name, fine. Her name is Sergeant Sylvia Worth."

Sergeant Worth was the other officer who had come to speak to me about the fire. If I could get hold of her right away, I could maybe put a kink in good old Constable Williams' long weekend plans.

"Great," I said. "I'll go and talk to her right now."

"She's not here," Constable Williams said, and had the gall to sneer a half-smile at me. "The boys at the desk can give you her number so you can leave her a message. She'll probably get back to you next week. Now, I have to go."

He turned without another word, disappearing through the

door that separated the inner from the outer—with me still standing, fuming, on the outer.

I stormed into the Palais, stormed up the stairs, and would have stormed down the hallway to Latterson's office except Farley popped up in front of me.

His colour was good. Surprisingly so. He had a pink tinge to his face I'd never seen in the dead before.

All that did was piss me off even more. Of course he'd be doing something else I'd never seen before. If I didn't move him on soon, I was pretty sure I was going to go stark raving mad.

"Did I ever tell you that cops are idiots?" I asked, before he could even open his mouth. "I tried to explain to that cop, Williams, or whatever his name is, what I thought was going on in the building, and he told me he would take it under advisement."

It took me three tries to get the key in the lock, my hands were shaking so badly. "What the hell does that even mean?" I yelled, as I fought with the lock. "I'll take it under advisement. Jesus!"

"I don't think you should go in there," Farley said.

"Why not?" The lock finally clicked open, and I walked into the office. Mr. Latterson's door was shut. "Any idea whether he's in there or not?" I asked.

"I don't know," he said. "You have to leave. Now."

"I can't leave. You know that," I said, glancing up at the clock above the door. It read 4:25. I still had time before the building was locked up for the weekend. I slapped my computer to life and pulled the flash drive from my pocket. At the very least I could go through some more of the files.

"So just check and see if he's in there," I said. "If he catches me doing this, I'm dead."

"That's why you have to leave," Farley said. "I think you might be in danger."

"Danger? I'm not in danger," I said, still staring at the computer screen. "What I meant was, I'll be fired, really this time, and I won't be able to help you. Know what I—"

"Shut up!" Farley yelled. "Listen to me. You are in danger!"

Shut up? He had the gall to tell me to shut up? I glanced up at him, ready to give him what for—and saw that he was even pinker than he had been in the hallway.

"Why are you pink?" I asked. "Any idea at all?"

"What?" Farley stared at me as though he couldn't understand what I was saying. Then he looked down at his hands, which were glowing as pink as his face. "I don't know," he finally said. "Why *am* I pink?"

"Of course you don't know," I snorted. This was so ridiculous. "Why would you?"

His colour deepened, turning quite neon.

"It's actually getting hard to take you seriously," I laughed.

"Because I'm pink?"

"Well, yes."

"Get over it. You have to get out of here, now."

"Why?"

"Because Jimmy boy caught that kid who's always visiting your boss—"

"Are you talking about Raymond?" I asked.

"Yes," Farley snapped. "Now shut up and listen!"

I snapped my mouth shut. That was the second time he told me to shut up in as many minutes. I didn't think I liked it.

"Jimmy caught him coming out of the furnace room with a bunch of tools. The idiot tried to convince Jimmy that he was doing work down there, but when he didn't have a work order, Jimmy roughed him up, and then called the cops."

"What?" I gasped. Raymond, down in the furnace room? Why would he be down there, unless—

I turned and stared at Mr. Latterson's door. "Is he in there?" I asked again. "Please check. If he's not, I need to get in there, right now, because if Raymond broke into the furnace room, then Mr. Latterson has to be involved. I need proof." I tore the flash drive out of my computer. "It will be in there. Please."

Farley shook his head. "You gotta get out of here, Marie."

I shook my head. "I have to do this, so you can move on, Farley. I think if I do this, you won't be tied here anymore." My throat tightened, and I put my hands to my eyes, just for a moment, to try to stop the stupid tears before they started. "It's all I can think to do."

"You don't have to do anything more for me," Farley said. He looked frantic. "Please, get out of here. I don't want you to get hurt."

"Always the gentleman, aren't you, Farley?"

"No, not always," he said. "Now please, go."

I didn't have a chance to go. I didn't have a chance to do much of anything past ram the flash drive back in my pocket, because Mr. Latterson came out of his office at that moment, with his arms full of papers.

"Ah, Jenner," he said. He looked absolutely frazzled. "Glad you're here. I have to leave, but I've got a job for you."

"A job?" I asked.

It was hard to hear him over Farley, who started yelling, "Get out, get out, get out!" at the top of his lungs.

"Yes," Latterson said. He sounded calm, but his hair, which was standing on end all over his head, quivered in time with his pulse. "I'm expecting a phone call." He glanced at the clock. "In about fifteen minutes. I need you to handle it." He smiled, and I noticed his right eye was twitching in time with his hair. "You don't mind, do you?"

I looked at the clock. If I stayed, it would be after five. "Who's calling?" I asked.

"It'll be my lawyer," he said. The topmost sheets on the pile of paper he was holding began to shift, and he attempted to slide them back into his arms. "Papers to sign and whatnot."

He overcompensated, and the sheets slid to the floor. "Son of a bitch," he muttered and reached down to gather them back into his arms. The rest of the sheets of paper slid from his grasp and landed on the floor at his feet, like the petals from a huge white flower. Without thinking I reached over to pick them up for him.

"Get away from those!" Latterson screamed, pushing me back. Which made me wonder what was in those sheets of paper that he did not want me to see. More bank accounts with even more money hidden from his wife and kids? Real honest to goodness proof that he was actually working for Mr. Carruthers, the owner of the building?

I needed to see what he was trying to hide.

"It's okay," I said, doing a little shoving of my own as I dove for the pile of papers. "I can get them."

He pushed at me, still screaming at me to get the hell away from his private papers, but I managed to grab the topmost sheet. That's when I saw that it was an insurance policy, and that my name was on it. He had taken out a life insurance policy on me.

Holy crap. His reason for hiring me, his only reason for hiring me, was so he could make money off my death.

He tried to push me away from the pile of paper, but I brushed his hand aside, tiredly.

"Is that why you want me to stay?" I asked, pointing at the policy.

"What?" Latterson asked, like he was going to try to bluff his way out of that room. Then he shook his head, and his face changed. Turned cold. "It's common practice," he said. "After all, I don't know what I'd do without you."

Yeah, right. "And the rest of these?" I asked, pointing at the pile. "All insurance policies?"

"Ah, it's one way of making a little extra cash off this deal," Latterson said.

"You have to get out of here NOW!" Farley cried. "I think it's gas!"

I turned to him. He was screaming pink, and as he moved an aura of hot fuchsia surrounded him. Quite pretty in a Barbie sort of way.

"You were right," I said.

Latterson glanced over in Farley's direction, then back at me as though I'd lost my mind.

"I know. But you have to go," Farley said.

"Not quite yet," I replied, and turned on Latterson. "You have got to be the stupidest man alive," I hissed. "The cops will be all over this building in a few minutes, and I'm going to tell them everything—everything I know!"

I pushed away from him, my rage all consuming. Which made me a little bit stupid, too. You see, I should have been running, but I wasn't. I was sitting on the floor, mouthing off to a man who'd taken a life insurance policy out on me.

"What do you know?" Latterson asked.

"I think you killed Farley," I said. "And I think you burned my place down, and now you're going to blow up this building. Aren't you!"

I couldn't shut my mouth and run, even though that was what Farley kept screaming. Latterson had to pay for what he did. The son of a bitch had to pay.

"You crazy bitch!" Latterson growled and lunged for me.

Farley yelled, "Run!"

I dodged Latterson's outstretched hands and ran out of the

office, heading for the stairwell, screaming my head off for help in an empty building,

Even though Latterson was right behind me, I honestly thought I was going to make it. I was fast, and fear made me faster. I fairly flew down the stairs. However, Don was angry as well as scared, and that seemed to tip the scales in his favour. He caught me as I reached for the big decorative doors down in the deserted foyer.

I fought him with every fiber of my being. His grasp loosened briefly when I kicked at him, but he grabbed me by the hair, and pulled me, screaming, down to the door of Carruthers' old office.

He used me as a battering ram. My head hit the door. I tasted blood and saw stars. He backed up and ran me at the door again, and I screamed in agony when I felt my shoulder pop. Thank God, the door finally gave way, and he threw me into the deserted room.

I landed in the reception area by the little board room table, on my hands and knees, stunned and spitting up blood. My shoulder hurt so badly I thought I was going to puke. But I had to get out of that room before he killed me.

I pulled myself upright, my eyesight darkening, but I had to keep moving, so I stumbled toward the door, hoping to get there before Latterson attacked me again. I could hear him gasping for breath and knocking things off a table behind me, and then Farley starting screaming.

"Move!" he cried. "For the love of God he's going to kill you!"

I lunged for the door, and almost made it.

Almost.

Latterson grabbed me and wrapped something—a wire, it was a wire—around my neck and pulled it tight. He tried to anyhow, but I'd managed to get a hand in the way, it was saving my life as I kicked back at him, trying to hurt him so he'd stop killing me, oh my God he was killing me, and through it all I could hear Farley screaming. And screaming. And screaming.

He was screaming about the wire. I gasped and choked and tried to pull the wire from my neck, but I couldn't. Latterson was too strong, and it cut into my fingers, and then into my neck, cutting off the air.

Farley screamed, "I see it all! Oh God, I see it all!"

I couldn't breathe. I kicked again, connecting with some part of Latterson and I felt him gasp, but the wire didn't loosen and my eyes were going dark.

Farley sobbed. "It was me. I killed myself, to stop them from hurting the Palais, and no-one even noticed."

I tried to kick again, my strength gone. I reached back and scratched his face. All he did was grunt. I scratched at his hands, but the pressure on the wire did not abate. I was going to die. He was going to kill me.

Farley cried. "I sacrificed myself to save the Palais, and Don's going to burn it down, anyhow. I did nothing."

He started to wail, and my eyesight dimmed even more. For the briefest of moments, I wondered if I would be able to finally touch Farley, when I died.

Then something smashed through the window of Carruthers' office, and the pressure from the wire was gone. I grabbed the wire and threw it away from me, sucking in a greedy lungful of air. My eyesight cleared enough for me to see what was happening.

James had Latterson by the shirt front, and was pounding the absolute crap out of him.

James was saving my life.

It had become strangely quiet in the room, in spite of the gasps and grunts and slaps and sickening meaty thunks as the two men pounded on each other. I didn't hear Farley wailing anymore.

I pushed myself up to my knees—possibly the hardest thing I've ever had to do—and saw Farley standing by the smashed-in window. He was glowing a bright, lethal red, and he was crying.

I reached out a hand to him—the one that had been caught under the wire and had saved my life before James—then watched as blood dripped from it to the floor.

"Marie!" James yelled. I swung my head in his direction. It felt like it weighed about a thousand pounds.

"Tell him to get you out," Farley said. I have never heard him sound so sorrowful. "She's gonna blow."

I swung my head back to James, and watched as he struck Latterson one last time. I heard a snap, possibly a rib, and Latterson finally was still. He wasn't quiet. He moaned like a spirit moving on to hell, even though he wasn't even half-dead. At least he couldn't hurt me anymore.

"James," I said. At least I tried. My throat hurt so badly, all that came out was a croak, but James seemed to understand me, and leaped over Latterson's prone body to my side.

"Just be still," he said. "The ambulance will be here in a second."

"You have to get out," Farley repeated. "The building's going to blow."

'There's gas," I whispered. "We have to get out."

James blinked at me. "Gas?" he finally asked. Then he sniffed. "Oh my God," he gasped. "There's gas!"

He scooped me up, grabbed Latterson by the scruff of the neck, and ran out of the office and to the decorative front doors of the Palais. Over James' shoulder, I watched Farley run, too.

We were through the double doors. The air smelled sweet, alive. James dropped Latterson, pointing at him and commanding someone, "Don't let him go."

Then he laid me gently on the grass. "We're safe," he said.

I looked past him, to Farley, who could not get through the membrane that was still holding him in the building.

His eyes locked on mine and he smiled.

Then, the Palais blew to kingdom come.

Farley:
Caught in an Explosion When You're Dead

I've never been in an explosion before. I wouldn't recommend it to anyone living.

For me it was the sound more than anything else. For those of the living persuasion, it probably would have been the flying debris, or the huge plumes of flame that towered above the building for a full fifteen seconds before cascading back down to earth again, to eat was left of the building. Or it could have been the building crashing in on itself—those bits of the building that were left after the initial explosion, that is. Any of those would have been distressing to be in the middle of, if you were living. I was not.

I really didn't know what was going to happen. I was, after all, trapped inside that building by that barrier—whatever the hell that was—so I thought maybe it would blow around me and then I'd be stuck—dead—in a ruin. It didn't work out that way.

I'd made it to the door when the explosion occurred, and watched it bellow its rage and blow the shit out of that building, tearing my pinkness away in shreds and tatters. The explosion hit me and those beautiful front doors, and I felt myself being lifted up and away.

The doors went through me on their way to their date with a powder blue Sunfire parked on the street, and then the rest of the building started raining through me like a putrid thunderstorm of death. It was a good thing I was already dead.

I stood up and tried to brush myself off. Of course, there was nothing there. Even the membrane that had trapped me in the building was gone. I was free. So, I did what any ghost in my situation would do. I went to find Marie.

Marie:
Almost Caught in an Explosion
When You're Alive

James tried to protect me from the explosion, but the heat and the sound slapped me half-senseless anyhow. I covered my eyes with my one good hand to protect my face as the windows blew out—boom boom boom boom—raining shards of glass everywhere. The front doors blew through a car parked on the street right in front of the building. I almost laughed when I noticed Mr. Latterson's Selectric II slam into the car's front windshield. It ended up balancing precariously on the front dash like one of those little Madonna figurines. For some reason, I wondered if it would still work.

Smoke spewed from the windows as the flame proceeded to eat was left of the building. I relaxed, thinking the worst was over, when the big explosion hit. Deep, deep in that building I heard noises that sounded like huge wild animals stampeding or something, and then I watched as the Palais literally lifted off its moorings.

"Holy shit," I whispered. It was almost like the building was levitating, but when it fell back to earth, it fell back in chunks. Burning chunks.

Flying debris fell around us, and though I felt half-deaf from the initial explosion, I could faintly hear the screams of other people who weren't as lucky as us.

James said something, and carefully picked me up, moving me farther away from the building. He gently set me down, and ran over to grab Mr. Latterson, who'd been trying to crawl away from the mess he'd made.

I saw Farley. He was free. He waved, then walked over and crouched beside me. I tried smiling, but my face was getting puffy from the beating, and it was hard to know how it appeared.

"You're pretty," I whispered. He was clear, like glass, with only a faint touch of aura showing. He wasn't ready to move on. I could tell, but at that moment, I didn't care. I was glad to see him—to see anything.

"At least I'm not pink anymore." He leaned over me, acting like he wanted to comfort me or something. "How are you?"

"Surprisingly well." I smiled, then when it hurt, stopped. Everything was starting to hurt like crazy. "Looks like I'll have to find a new job."

"Looks like."

"You're out of the Palais."

He shrugged. "But I'm still here."

"I see that."

"I kind of thought I'd move on. You know, once I got out of there."

"So did I."

"I'm sorry," he said, and my throat tightened dangerously. Here Farley was, still trapped, if not in the Palais, on this plane of existence, and he was apologizing to me. I didn't know if I could stand it.

"It's not your fault, Farley. It's not your fault."

Now I probably would have ended up crying like an idiot if the first of the fire trucks hadn't arrived.

It slewed up to the building, right behind the mangled little car, its siren still whooping and wailing. A few moments later, a Mercedes Benz careened to a halt in the middle of the street. A middle aged woman threw open the door and levered herself out of the driver's seat before stopping, one leg still in the idling vehicle. She stared at the burning building, with that old familiar blank stare of utter shock on her face.

"Who's that?" I asked.

Farley glanced at the woman and shrugged. "No clue."

I think I would have stopped paying any attention to her at all, if she hadn't slapped the fireman who came up to talk to her. Slapped him right across the face and screamed, "Do you know who I am?"

That caught my attention, I must say. I struggled to sit upright. "Find out who she is," I said. "I bet she's involved. Somehow."

I think he was going to say no, but at that moment the driver's door of the little blue car that had been hit by the front doors of the Palais—and Mr. Latterson's stupid typewriter—creaked open, and a thin blonde figure fell out, flailing around on the debris covered pavement.

"Holy shit!" Farley cried. "That's Andrea!"

The middle aged woman pulled free from the fireman—who didn't try very hard to stop her, I noticed—and threw herself at Andrea.

"You!" the older woman cried. "You owe me 60,000 dollars, you bitch!"

Oh.

Andrea didn't respond. She was still on her hands and knees and didn't look like she could even hear the woman screaming at her. But I could. In spite of the ringing in my ears, I could hear her just fine.

So, that's who had given Andrea all that money.

The older woman screamed some more, incoherently. Then the fireman finally caught her again, and she kicked out with her oh so practical flat shoes, and then spit at Andrea, who'd finally managed to get to her feet.

"It's not my fault," Andrea said. At least, I think that's what she said. She wasn't yelling, so it was hard for me to hear.

Whatever her words, though, they enraged the middle aged woman still being held by the fireman. She managed, somehow, to break away again, and threw herself at Andrea. Then they both started fighting in earnest.

"Find out who that is," I said. Farley nodded once, and flew to Andrea's side.

They only had a moment before the police showed up and the older woman was finally subdued and bundled, not too ceremoniously, into the back of a cop car.

Farley came back, shaking his head. "That was June Henderson," he said. "Asshole Ian Henderson's wife. Looks like she paid Andrea to screw around with him, and get it all on tape. Guess she wanted to divorce him, but there was a pre-nup she had to break, first. Apparently that didn't happen, which is why June wants her money back." He sniffed. "This is why I never amassed a fortune," he said. "You should marry for love."

"Sorry, Farley," I whispered. "Looks like Andrea wasn't as nice as you thought."

"No-one is," he replied.

For some reason, his forlorn words struck me as funny. I laughed until it hurt too much, and then stopped and lay back down. I was getting so tired . . .

James appeared, gently pulling me into his arms. "Ready to go to the hospital?" he asked. "The ambulance will be here right away."

"What about Mr. Latterson?" James' arms felt so warm, so good, around me, I didn't even mind, much, that I hurt absolutely everywhere.

"The police have him," James said, and I relaxed, finally feeling safe for the first time in that very long day.

As an ambulance howled its way to us, Farley turned toward the gutted building. "Look," he said, and pointed at the old iron fire escape, the one I'd used to flee Henderson's office, just the day before. It bowed tiredly in on itself and settled at the base of the hole that had been the Palais.

Farley was now as homeless as I was.

"I don't know what to do," Farley said. At least, I thought that's what he said.

"Come with me," I whispered. "We can talk at the hospital."

"Okay," James said, and he smiled that great big goofy grin of his as the EMs put me on the gurney and wheeled me to the ambulance.

"Okay," Farley said, and I could see he was grinning, too.

Marie:
Explosion Aftermath

I hurt everywhere. My face, and my arms, and legs, and everything else that was still attached to my body, which was, luckily, pretty much everything. Even my hair hurt. James was staring down at me, with that befuddled look he wore sometimes that drove me crazy. His mouth moved. He was talking to me, but I couldn't hear what he was saying.

"What?" I asked, then stopped talking when I felt how much my throat hurt.

"I'm glad you're awake," he whispered.

"What?" I was sure I'd heard him, but the explosion had caused a ringing in my ears, and he could have said, "I want to bring you a piece of cake," or something.

"I'm glad you're awake," he said again, louder, concern creasing his brow. "You *are* awake, aren't you?"

"Yes. My ears. The explosion." I hoped it was enough. It was all I had. Or so I thought, until he opened his mouth again.

"I'm calling your mother, and letting her know what happened to you, Marie."

Oh. That was bad. Very, very bad.

"I don't think so." I scrabbled around, trying to sit up. I managed to claw my way to upright in spite of the pain. "Leave my mother out of this."

Farley wandered in from somewhere, appearing brighter than he had in a long while. I ignored him and crossed my arms over my chest, though it hurt like heck to do so, and shook my head.

James had to be dealt with, immediately.

"Do not call my mother, James. Do not."

"She should know—"

"Give him hell," Farley suggested. I glared briefly at him before turning back to James.

"My mother does not need to be worried. Not when I'm going to be fine. I'll call her and tell her what happened when they let me out."

"But—"

"No buts. Leave it alone. She doesn't need this kind of stress. You know that."

"Yeah." He sat down with a small thump on a chair crammed next to my bed. "Yeah, I guess you're right."

"And you don't have to stay with me, you know." He'd really pissed me off, suggesting he call my mom. "They'll let me out soon, I'm sure of it. I'll go to Jasmine's or something."

"Oh, come on Marie, don't get that way." He acted absolutely crestfallen. "I thought—"

"No. You didn't think. If you had, you wouldn't have suggested calling her."

"I'm sorry, okay? I'll sit here quietly, and when they let you out, I'll take you to your friend's place, or wherever you want. All right?"

I stared at him, trying to decide whether he was telling the truth. "All right," I whispered, but then I was at the end of my strength, and flopped back down on the pillow. "Could you find me some water?"

He dove through the curtains as though he wanted to get away before I changed my mind and made him leave the hospital.

"How can you stand it?" Farley asked.

I put my hands up to my face to block the overhead light, which was suddenly hurting my eyes. "How *am* I going to tell my mother what happened?"

My throat constricted painfully, and I could feel the tears trembling at the edges of my lashes. When I took in a quick breath, the tears cascaded down my bruises to the pillow.

"Ah, come on, don't cry." Farley sounded like he wanted to give me a hug or something, and that threw me over the edge. I was supposed to be comforting him, dammit! "Gloss it over. Maybe don't tell her about Macho Don. Tell her the building blew up and you got a bit hurt, but not bad."

His suggestion sounded lame, but it helped. My throat suddenly didn't feel so tight and my tears stopped.

"I guess I could. I have to tell her something, after all, the building blowing up will make it on the news for sure, but I don't need to tell her everything. That might work. Thanks, Farley."

"Glad to help."

I tried a smile. It must have worked, because he smiled back.

We were finished talking though, because James came in with water and a couple of glasses. Then a nurse came in with news that they'd decided to keep me overnight for observation. That's when I started to cry again, because I'd convinced myself that a case of attempted murder, plus getting caught in an explosion, wasn't actually going to interfere with my life—or what was left of it—much at all.

As I tried to get myself under control, I could hear James flailing around until the nurse turned on him, all patience gone.

"Go wait out there," she ordered, pointing through the curtain. "When we have her settled in a room, you can see her. If she wants." The last she said to me. I was still trying to get myself under control, and not admit that wave after wave of exhaustion was finishing me.

James put the water down and left the room with a few backward glances at me. Farley followed him out. I was glad. I wanted to be left alone, so I could cry in peace.

I was stuck in Emergency for a couple more hours, until they found me a room. I had my eyes closed, enjoying the quiet of that room—a private room, lucky me—when I felt more than heard the door sigh open. It was James, with Farley on his heels.

I tried to sit up, and realized I couldn't move.

"Help me with these stupid blankets," I growled. "They've got them too tight."

"Maybe you should stay still," James said hesitantly. I realized he was speaking that way because he thought everything he said upset me. That upset me.

"I don't want to stay still." I glowered at him until he untucked the blankets, freeing my arms, then loosening my legs.

"Thank you." I pulled my hands up and ran them through my incredibly filthy hair. "That feels better." Then I glanced at him. "Hear any news on the TV? About the explosion?" I was concerned that my mother had already seen something. James had been right. Someone did need to call my mom, even if only to tell her half the truth.

"No. I was watching the news, but it was CNN. Why?"

I struggled to sit up so I could look him in the eyes. It was harder than I thought, because it felt like every muscle had seized up on me. Finally, I made it.

"I want you to do something for me, James, and you have to promise—promise on the eyes of your own mother, that you will do as I ask. Nothing more. Okay?"

"What do you want me to do?"

"No. Swear, first."

"Okay, I swear."

"On your mother's eyes."

"Good grief, Marie . . . "

"I'm not kidding. The eyes of your sainted mother."

"You're getting melodramatic."

"Don't care. Swear."

"Fine. I swear. On—what you said." I stared into his eyes, then, after a brief, uncomfortable moment for James, nodded and leaned back. I believed him.

"I want you to call my Mom, and let her know what happened. But only about the explosion, and that I'm okay."

"All right."

"That's all. Nothing more. Nothing about Mr. Latterson, or any of the other stuff."

"Okay."

"You understand?"

"Marie, I get it." James spoke sharply, and when I glanced at him, I realized the other James was back. I was glad. I was feeling weak and wanted someone to take care of me. The other, sharp-eyed James could do that.

"Well, that gives me hope that the boy has a pair," Farley snorted. I ignored him and touched James' hand.

"Thank you."

"I'm happy to do it, Marie. And don't worry. I won't say anything you don't want your mom to know about."

"Thanks." I automatically reached for my purse, which was not with me, then looked around the room for a pen. "I need to give you the number."

James found a pen and wrote my mom's number on his hand. "I'll go downstairs and give her a call and then—"

"And then nothing." It was the nurse. She was really quiet when she wanted to be. "It's time for you to go. There are tests to be run, and this young woman needs her rest."

James opened his mouth, then closed it with a snap. He could tell he was done.

"I'll be back tomorrow, Marie."

"Okay—and James?"

"Yeah?"

"Thanks for—you know, everything."

"I'm glad I was there." He smiled.

"So am I." There was so much more I could have said, but all I could do was wave at him like some kind of teenager in love as the door sighed shut behind him.

"What tests do you have to run?" I asked the nurse, hoping they wouldn't hurt much. I didn't think I could stand much more.

"Oh, there are no tests, but I didn't think the young man would go too far if I didn't tell him something like that," the nurse said, and smiled. "However, you need some quiet. Don't you?"

"Yes." I closed my eyes, enjoying the darkness. "I think quiet would be a very good thing."

"Does that mean me too?"

I nearly jumped out of my skin. I'd forgotten Farley was there. I held up one hand like a stop sign and glanced at the nurse. He nodded and leaned against the wall, and we both waited for her to leave. After she re-tucked the stupid blankets, she did just that.

I kicked my feet to loosen them again, then patted the edge of the bed. Farley glanced at me, then sat down. I couldn't read his face.

"You okay?"

"I don't know." He stared down at his hands, then out the window, which overlooked a parking lot. "I'm glad to be out of the Palais."

"But?" There was a but. I could see it on his face—and didn't need to hear what it was, because I was asking the same thing.

"Why didn't I move on?"

"I don't know."

He walked to the window, and stared out. "I figured out everything, I thought." He shuddered. "It wasn't Henderson who killed me. Or Latterson, even though that son of a bitch got somebody to blow up the Palais. I killed myself." He shook his head as though he still couldn't quite believe was he was saying. "I killed myself," he said again. "I know why I died. So, what the hell is keeping me here?"

"I'm not sure," I said.

"I can't tell you how tired I am of hearing that." He sounded lost, nothing like the Farley I knew, and my throat tightened.

"I'm sorry," I said, then willed myself to quiet. I was not crying again, even though I wanted to. There had been far too much of that, lately. "There is one thing I could do. It might help."

"What's that?" He didn't turn his head. I figured he'd probably decided that most of my ideas were crap, and he wasn't going to get too worked up about this one, either.

"Well, I could get hold of your daughter, Rose. Maybe meet with her."

"What?" He swung around and stared at me. I definitely had his attention.

"I could get hold of your—"

"I heard you," he said, anger in his voice. I'd definitely touched a nerve. "Why would you do that?"

"Because maybe you have something to clear up with her. Maybe she's the reason you're still here. A meeting might be—"

"No. You're not doing that." He turned back to the window. "I don't need to see her again. She's knows I'm an asshole. There's nothing more to say."

"There might be more *she* wants to say to you, Farley." I tried to speak softly, to mimic that tone my mother used, but all I did was get Farley flustered. He whirled around and stared at me, shaking his head frantically.

"I told you! I don't want to see her. Don't want to hear those words out of her mouth again. You got me?"

"What words?"

"What an asshole I am! Jesus, don't you listen? She let me know exactly how she felt about me." He clapped his hands together angrily, and walked toward the door, then whirled back toward me again. "Leave her alone! I'm not kidding."

He freaked me out a bit, and I cowered back in the bed. I guess being almost killed and then caught in an explosion had frayed my nerves, but seeing him so worked up really got to me. I hadn't realized how big the daughter button was.

"Fine. Fine! I won't call her, yet. But Farley, I think you're going to have to examine this part of—"

"NO! I told you!" he bellowed. "Leave her alone! Leave me alone!" He walked through the door, ecto ooze flicking away from him in long green strands, like a spider's web.

I put my head down on the pillow and tried to relax, tried to come up with the next thing I could do for Farley, but nothing came. I would need to call my mom, and get some more advice. Great. After everything that went on, I needed to get more advice from my mom.

I closed my eyes, feeling overwhelmingly tired. Someone entered the room, but I kept my eyes closed, hoping they would go away. They didn't. I opened my eyes, though it felt like two ton boulders were attached to each of them.

A police officer stood by the bed, looking tired and pissed off. I recognized her. She was Sergeant Worth, the other officer who had come to talk to me about the fire at my apartment building. It felt like the fire had happened years ago.

"You Jenner? Marie Jenner?" she asked, obviously not recognizing me. I nodded. "I'm here to take your statement."

I figured she'd listened to the rather nasty voicemail message I'd left her about Constable Williams. Finally. Then I frowned. She didn't remember me. That couldn't be it. "My statement about what?" I asked cautiously.

"About the incident that put you in the hospital." Worth went from looking slightly tired to looking slightly puzzled. "You *do* remember what happened to you, don't you?"

"Yes, of course I do."

I unsuccessfully tried to pull myself upright on the bed. The cop reached over, flicked a switch, and the back of the bed rose until I was sitting comfortably upright.

"Thanks," I said. "That's better."

"No problem." She smiled. Almost. "We got backed up at the crime scene. However, we're here now. You feeling up to giving a statement?"

"Sure."

The cop reached into her jacket pocket and pulled out a small note pad and a pen. She scratched something—I was guessing the date and time—on the top of the pad, then glanced at me.

"Now, in your own words, tell me what happened."

It took me only five minutes to go over the events of the day, which surprised me a bit, considering how eventful the day had been. The cop diligently wrote down every word I said without any questions until she was sure I was finished.

"Did you notice anything unusual happening before today?"

"I talked to another police officer about some suspicions I had, this afternoon," I said. "He took it under advisement."

Worth glanced up, her eyebrows quirking. "Who did you speak to?"

"His name was Constable Williams." I quirked my eyebrows back at her. "He told me you are his superior. I phoned you about him, just before the explosion."

"Williams has your statement?"

"He didn't write down a darned thing." I sighed. "Even the odd stuff."

"Odd?"

"Weird." I leaned back, my head spinning. "I don't know. I tried to tell him about Carruthers, but he wouldn't listen." My words stopped the cop cold, and she stared at me intensely.

"The owner of the building?"

I nodded, carefully.

"Why do you think he should have done something about the owner of the building?"

"Because he hired Don Latterson to blow it up," I said. "That's why."

The cop's eyes narrowed. "Why would you think that?"

"Didn't Mr. Latterson tell you Carruthers was involved?" I asked, struggling to sit further upright. They'd arrested him. She had to get the connection. She had to.

"No. He said he planned it himself, and hired Raymond Jackson to set off the bomb. He never mentioned Carruthers." She blurted the words out, then rolled her eyes. "Jesus," she muttered, "I need to get some sleep."

"Well, Mr. Latterson's covering for Carruthers. Carruthers paid him off, or something." I looked around the room for my clothes. "Can you open that closet, please?"

"Why?"

"Because I have the information on a flash drive in the pocket of my sweater that proves Carruthers is involved, and I don't know what the doctors did with my clothes."

She opened the closet, but it was empty. "They probably had to cut your clothes off."

"But—but the information—" I glanced around, frantically, hoping it was sitting on a counter top somewhere, but there was nothing there. Nothing at all. "I have to find that flash drive."

"Do you really think it will explain everything?"

"Yes. It will."

"I'll see if I can find it."

"Thank you."

"Why do you have information like that?" She peered at me with her sharp cop eyes, and realized I'd trapped myself. The only reason I'd collected what I'd found was because of Farley, and there was no way in the world I was telling this cop that a ghost had pointed me in Carruthers' direction. No way at all.

I could mention Farley being killed, though, couldn't I?

"There was the death—Farley's death—"

"Who? Oh, wait a minute, the guy who was electrocuted. I don't have the paperwork on that yet."

"Well, you should get it. Carruthers and Mr. Latterson are involved in his death, too. I'd bet my life on it."

All right, so technically Farley had killed himself, but those two were involved in blowing up the Palais, which was what Farley had been trying to stop. In my books, they were involved, and deserved to pay with lots and lots of time in jail.

The cop stared at me for a long moment, until I turned away. I listened as she tucked the pad of paper back into her jacket pocket. "I'll check with Emerg to see if I can find your clothes, and that flash drive. And then you and I will be talking again."

"Well, I don't think I'll be here much longer," I said, trying for a bright smile. I didn't pull it off. "At least, I hope not."

"If I need to, I'll find you." The cop turned toward the door, and without another word, was gone.

I pressed the button, sending the bed slowly back to flat. I was exhausted. Tomorrow I would deal with my missing clothes and the flash drive, and everything. Including Farley. I needed to make him understand why I felt it was so important that he reconnect with his daughter.

"Tomorrow," I whispered, and closed my eyes. "I'll deal with all of that tomorrow."

Farley:
Lucky Marie Meets the Rat

I stood outside Marie's room, watching the action. First the lady cop went in, and though I dearly wanted to know what the hell those two talked about, I stayed outside. I was still sizzling from Marie's suggestion that she connect with my daughter, Rose. There was no way on God's green earth I was letting that happen. That was a closed topic. No way in hell I was going back there.

When the cop left at nine, the ladies in white were getting everybody tucked in for the night. The occasional alarm sounded, but even those seemed sleepy. No-one got too excited, or did the "Code Blue" thing or anything. Just nice, efficient tucking in and putting to bed.

Until Carruthers, looking rich, powerful, and not about to take any crap, walked out of the elevators and up to the nurse's station at close to 10:30.

"I'm here to see Marie Jenner." His voice sounded like gravel, as though he'd smoked a couple dozen cigars in quick succession.

"It's after visiting hours." The nurse behind the desk didn't glance up. "Come back tomorrow between nine and nine."

"I don't think you understand me. I am here to see Marie Jenner. Now."

The nurse looked up, her eyes sparkling dangerously. I know

she thought this was her domain and that she wasn't about to be pushed around by an asshole in a suit, but I didn't stick around to see what Carruthers did to her. I needed to warn Marie.

I walked into her room, but she was asleep. Before I could wake her up the door swung open, and Carruthers entered the darkened room.

Marie:
Meeting the Rat

It was harder to fall asleep in that hospital than I thought it would be. They kept my door open, so all the noise from the ward kept floating in. Cries of pain, alarms beeping, plus occasionally, laughter.

Finally, the noise outside the room started to calm. Someone pulled my door almost shut, and even that noise was tamped down to a drone. Then I was finally able to fall asleep.

It was a bit bumpy, to be honest. Meaning a series of nightmares filled with flashes and smoke, and then Don Latterson grabbing my throat, looking more and more like a demon, until I wanted to scream, and I couldn't.

I couldn't scream. The wire was back around my throat and I couldn't scream . . .

I lurched awake, grabbing the top sheet that had tightened over my neck and flinging it away from me. I gasped in air like I'd actually been strangled again, and felt the pulse in my throat pound like a drum.

Farley was standing just inside the door, glowing softly. He put his finger to his mouth in a "shh," gesture when someone else standing in the dark asked, "Are you all right?"

I did not recognize the voice and screeched as I tried to fling myself to the floor, only managing to get myself even more tangled in the bedclothes. I couldn't move, and claustrophobia mixed with a resurgence of the terror I'd felt at the Palais. I honestly thought I was going to die. Again.

"Don't hurt me!" I cried. "Please don't hurt me!"

"I'm not here to hurt you," the man's voice said.

"You're a liar, you son of a bitch," Farley snarled. "A lying liar!"

"Who are you?" I asked, scrabbling with the stupid bedclothes which had me tied down so tightly I had another paralyzing moment of claustrophobia. "Who is that?" I asked Farley, but before he could answer, the stranger spoke.

"Let me turn on a light while you compose yourself, that's a good girl," he said. He walked toward the door and threw the light switch. "Is that better?"

A tall middle aged man in a power suit stood by the light switch. I didn't recognize him, which did nothing to make me feel calmer.

"It's George Carruthers," Farley finally said. "He's the son of a bitch who ordered Macho Don to blow up the Palais." He spat. The glowing spittle flew through the air and struck George Carruthers on the cheek. It hung there, glowing and quivering, unnoticed.

"I'll get help!" he yelled.

"Don't leave me!" I cried.

"Don't worry, I won't," Carruthers said as Farley disappeared through the closed door. I was alone with Carruthers. That was not good.

I groped in the bedclothes for the call button, and felt the air around me turn to glue when I couldn't find the stupid thing. Carruthers walked up to my bed and I licked my lips. I needed to calm myself, because if he tried anything, I only had my wits. My strength was gone, blown away when the Palais exploded all over me.

If this guy was going to do me harm, I needed to get someone else—someone corporeal—in the room with us. Since I couldn't find the stupid call button, I decided to play the "I don't know you," gambit, to buy some time.

"I think you have the wrong room," I said.

"Oh no," Carruthers said. "I'm in exactly the right room."

"No, I don't think you are," I said, and tried to smile. That did not go well. "If you go out and find the nurse—"

"The nurse told me exactly where you were, Miss Jenner."

As I tried to comprehend what he had just said, Carruthers pulled a chair up to the side of my bed and sat, crossing one leg over the other. He pointed at a bouquet of flowers on my bedside stand. "You like daisies?" he asked.

I quit staring at him, and instead stared at the bouquet, which had been placed in an empty water jug and leaned haphazardly. The flowers were wilting. There had been no flowers in my room when I'd fallen asleep.

"Why did you bring me flowers?" I asked.

"Oh, they aren't from me," he said.

I filed the flowers under "who cares right now" and focused on the man sitting way too close to me.

"Who are you?"

"George Carruthers," he said, and smiled. "No doubt you've heard of me."

"You're the owner of the Palais," I whispered. "How can I help you?"

"Oh, it's not how you can help me," Carruthers said. He glanced down at his beautifully manicured hands. "No, I'm here to find out how I can help you."

I blinked. "Help me?"

"Yes, dear. Help you." He stopped admiring his fingernails and glanced over at me. His eyes were like brown ice. "After all, you were one of my tenants, and—"

"I wasn't technically a tenant," I replied, still clutching the top of the sheet protectively to my throat. "I worked for one."

"Ah, yes, well, that is true. However, I want to take care of everyone who was in my building. Especially one who was damaged." Carruthers spoke the last word softly, delicately, and pointed at my face. "You *were* damaged, weren't you?"

"Well, yes," I said. "But I still don't see—"

"You're out of a job, and I'm going to make sure you're comfortable until you can find another one." Carruthers spoke abruptly, as if suddenly tired at the amount of his precious time our conversation was wasting.

"Comfortable?" What was he talking about?

"I'm going to look after you," he said. His eyes thinned, and he glared at me.

"Look after me?" Oh God, that sounded bad. "What do you

mean by that?"

"I'm going to take care of you."

That sounded even worse. God, he was going to kill me right here.

I grappled under the blankets, looking for the stupid call button again even as I knew I wasn't going to find it. Here he was, in my room, ready to kill me, and I was all on my own. Where were the nurses, and security, and the police? Why wasn't anyone saving me?

"Are you all right?" he asked, and the tone of his voice stopped my frantic scramble under the bedclothes. He didn't sound—or look—like he was about to pull a gun out and shoot me. He looked more confused than anything else, if I was going to be honest.

"You were hurt in my building, Miss Jenner," he said. "Since you were the employee of a trusted tenant, you should be taken care of, until you're back on your feet."

"Oh."

He wasn't talking about killing me. He was talking about actually taking care of me. Then the "trusted tenant" reference sunk in, and I frowned.

"Are you talking about Mr. Latterson?" I asked. "He blew up the building. You know that, don't you?"

Carruthers shuffled, looking uncomfortable.

"Yes, well, mistakes were made all the way around," he finally replied. "Up to the point where he blew up the building, he was a good tenant. And you, my dear, are out of a job. I want to make things easier for you. Maybe give you a chance to—oh I don't know, move back home, take care of your mother. She'd like that, wouldn't she?"

My mind literally froze. "How do you know about my mother?" I finally asked, my lips feeling as icy as my brain.

"You're not hard to track," Carruthers said, smiling, his eyes still like brown ice. "It took five minutes to find your mother in Fort McMurray. She lives in a mobile home up there, does she not?"

I nodded stiffly. My God, he knew where my mother lived. What else did he know about her?

"$50,000.00 would make things much better for her, and for you," Carruthers continued. "Wouldn't it?"

He was bribing me, obviously. But why? What did he think I

knew? Bigger question, what else did he know about my mother?

"Are you offering me money to move back home and look after her?" I asked.

"You don't need to move back home," Carruthers said. "You can go anywhere you want with the money. Anywhere. Personally, I don't care if you look after your mother or not." He shrugged. "You seem—attached to her. That's why I even mentioned her. Understand?"

There was the not-so-veiled warning.

"Yes. I think I do." I took a deep breath, and let it out slowly. "Can I think about it?"

"What is there to think about?" Carruthers said, a frown creasing his forehead. "I'm offering you free money. Take it and go anywhere you want that isn't Edmonton."

"I appreciate it, I really do, but —"

"But nothing, Miss Jenner. This is a take it or leave it proposition. You have to tell me right now."

The door to my room swung open. The nurse from the front desk stormed in, followed by two security guards and Farley.

"The cavalry," he said. He frowned. "Are you all right?"

Not even close, Farley.

"Ah, Nurse Penderghast," Carruthers said. "Good to see you again."

"I gave you your five minutes," the nurse replied, acidly. "Now, it is time for you to go."

She signaled to the security guards, who reached for Carruthers' arms. He nonchalantly shrugged them off.

"We're almost done here, aren't we, Miss Jenner?" He smiled. "All I need it your answer."

I stared at him. This guy believed, truly believed, that money could buy anything—or anybody. He'd paid people to do things—horrible things—and was now trying to pay me to keep my mouth shut about it.

If I turned down his bribe, he'd just use that money to have me—and possibly my mother—killed. His ice brown eyes let me know he'd have absolutely no problem with that.

"What is going on?" Farley asked. "The cavalry's here. Kick him out."

He knew where my mother lived.

"He had the Palais blown up," Farley said. "And he's the

reason I'm dead. Don't forget that."

"Yes," I whispered.

"Excellent," Carruthers said. "Will a cheque suffice?"

"What?!?" Farley roared. "What are you doing?"

"Make it certified," I said, wishing my head—and heart—would stop pounding so hard, and that Farley would quit screaming.

"Smart girl," Carruthers said, his eyes cold, like a shark's. "I'll get a certified cheque to you, ASAP."

"Thank you," I said. "My mother will appreciate it."

"I'm sure she will," Carruthers said, dropping his business card on my bed. "Call me if you have any questions, or concerns. You know. Anything."

Before I could answer him, he turned on his heel and walked through the door, the security guards wandering after him like they couldn't remember why they'd been called to the room.

"What the fuck have you done?" Farley asked.

I ignored him, staring instead at the nurse. I had to take my fury out on someone, and it was going to be her.

"Why did you let him in?" I yelled. Well, I tried to yell. It sounded more like a sob.

"Sorry," she said shortly. "He said he knew you."

I could tell by the look on her face that she was lying. I felt sick. There was no safe place for me, anywhere.

"Just get out," I whispered. "Get out."

She backed away from the door, making apologetic noises, but I ignored her until the door finally sighed shut and I was left alone with Farley.

"Nice work." The words sounded like acid dripping from Farley's mouth. "You sold out."

"I didn't sell out," I whispered. "He threatened my mother."

"Bullshit," he said. "You sold out."

He wouldn't look at me. Like he was afraid if he looked, he'd see greed on my face instead of fear. I had to make him understand.

"He threatened my mother," I said again. "My dying mother."

Farley snorted humorlessly. "Don't play the death card with me, Marie. Remember, you're talking to a ghost over here. I'm sorry your mother is dying, but—"

"I have to take care of her, Farley." I stared straight ahead, and felt my throat tighten. Shit, not now. But the stupid tears cascaded down my face, and I sobbed.

"You can cry all you want," Farley said, coldly. "You sold out. Son of a bitch."

"Well, wouldn't you?" I cried. "When you were alive, wouldn't you have taken the money to save your daughter's life?"

"Yeah, probably."

I sniffed, and wiped my tears on the bed sheet. "Then you understand."

"Don't take his money, Marie. Run away if you want, but don't take the money. He's an evil son of a bitch, and the evil will stick to you."

"If I don't take it, he'll think I'm going to turn him in," I said. "I can't not take it, Farley. Don't you understand?"

He backed away from me until he was just a light smudge in front of my door.

"You have to figure something else out," he said. "Or you'll be like me. Make bad choices when you're alive, and you'll be trying to figure out a way to stay out of hell when you're dead."

Oh.

"I'll try," I whispered. "All right?"

He didn't answer me. Just stared with his bright, unforgiving eyes until I finally turned my back on him, and pulled the covers over my head. I'd had enough. Enough.

Farley could go to hell, if that's what he thought was going to happen to him. I wasn't letting anyone hurt my mother. Not ever again.

Marie:
The Cop Comes Back, and I Am Sprung

Sergeant Worth was back first thing in the morning. She caught me picking at my breakfast, which I don't think I could have eaten even if it had been anything close to edible.

Farley was camped out by the window, completely and absolutely ignoring me, which was more uncomfortable than you'd think. He didn't turn when she came in. He didn't even act like he realized she was in the room.

"Two things," Worth said, before I had a chance to open my mouth. "First, that flash drive was not in your clothing." She dropped a plastic bag on my bed. I thought I saw the sleeve of my grey sweater peeking out of the top. She'd found my clothes. "You must have dropped it, getting out of the building. We're checking the debris. So far, nothing."

"Oh."

I pushed my tray away, suddenly feeling sick to my stomach. The flash drive. With it, Sergeant Worth would have proof that Carruthers was involved. Carruthers would think I turned him in, and come after me and my mother. But only if the police found it. They hadn't yet. Maybe we were safe.

Farley turned and glared at me, his eerie, glowing eyes cutting through me. "You gonna tell her about Carruthers coming here?" he asked.

Sergeant Worth did not need to hear anything about my late night visitor. I turned away from him, and looked at the cop.

"What's the other thing?" I asked.

"They're letting you out of here soon," she said. "So, I was wondering if you wanted me to give you a ride."

"You?" I asked before I could stop myself. "Why?"

"Hey, just trying to do a good turn," she said. "Unless you have an extra forty bucks to blow on a cab ride. Where are you going?"

"Home, I guess." Then I remembered. My place was gone, burned up in a fire. "I don't know."

"If you want to talk to Victim Services, give them a call." The Sergeant pulled a card from her pocket and handed it to me. "They're pretty good. Unless you got a friend you can stay with?"

Where could I stay? There was Jasmine, with all her kids. She didn't need me there. Maybe James—

"You want me to call James Lavall?"

I stared at her in shock as she flipped through her little booklet. Had I actually said his name out loud?

"You know his number?" she asked.

"No, but I've got it," I said, automatically grabbing for my purse. Then I stopped. My purse had been blown to kingdom come. My God. I really had lost everything.

"My purse," I said, inanely. "And my ID. Gone."

Worth waved her hand dismissively. "Yeah, well, let's get you settled first. You wanna go to James' place, right?"

Before she gave me a chance to answer, she pulled out a cell phone and flipped it open, punching numbers.

"Yeah, Jules," she said. "I'm over at the hospital talking to Marie Jenner, from the Palais explosion. Do me a favour, and get me James Lavall's phone number. Yes. Lavall. Two a's and three l's. It'll be in the file."

"It's really all right," I said, frantically. I didn't want to go to James' place with her. I didn't want to go anywhere with her. "I'll give him a call—"

"No problem," she said. "Got it."

She quickly dialed James' number.

"James Lavall? Yeah, this is Sergeant Worth. I'm here with Marie Jenner—she wants to know if she can come over to your place for a couple of days. I can bring her over, no problem at all, right on my way." She listened, and then laughed. "Coffee sounds great. Put it on, we'll see you in about a half hour." She flipped the phone shut, but when she looked at me, all trace of humor was gone.

"All set up," she said. "Get dressed while I get the paperwork."

Cops don't give people rides. Not unless they suspect them of doing something wrong. And if Carruthers saw me leave with her . . .

"Are you jealous, Marie?" I nearly jumped out of my skin when Farley whispered in my ear, cold air wafting around me. "Maybe the cop's got a thing for good old James?"

I did my best to shrug him away. What an idiotic thing for him to say.

"Stay away from my ears," I snapped. "That was disgusting."

"Yeah, whatever," he said, turning his back on me. "Why don't you get the cops involved? Just tell her what Carruthers is trying to do. She can protect you and your mom."

"No, she can't," I said. "And she won't. Cops don't do stuff like that for people like us. You know that as well as I do. If Carruthers even suspects that I'm friendly with the cops, I'm in real trouble."

"I'd say you're in real trouble now," Farley said, very unhelpfully. "She's already suspicious. After all, you were squealing at her about arresting Carruthers, and now—you got nothing for her? Man, I'd check you out myself. And, I don't care what you think, she does seem to be cozy with Lavall—"

"That has nothing to do with anything!"

"Yeah, right. Hang on to that thought, Marie."

I thought, desperately. There had to be a way out of this. Somehow. I could think of nothing, until Farley came to my rescue.

Yeah, great, right? Here I was, supposed to be the big ghost mover onner or whatever, and I needed him to help me. Again.

"What about this?" he said. "You go to Lavall's place, and I'll follow the cop around. If I get anything, I'll figure out a way to get back to you, and then you'll know what she knows."

I was going to say, "You don't have to do this for me, Farley," but I couldn't. If he had eyes on the police, then all I would have to worry about was Carruthers. It wasn't much, but it was something.

"Sounds good," I whispered. "Thanks."

"You're welcome," he said. "Now, maybe you should get dressed."

I nodded. "That sounds good, too."

All right, none of it was good. I just couldn't think of anything else to do. So, Farley left, and I pulled on what was left of my clothes. Then I walked out of my room, and up to Sergeant Worth.

"I'm all ready," I said, trying to smile bravely. Then my head started to whirl, and I staggered a half-step to the right and ran into the wall. One of the nurses grabbed me, and helped me stay upright.

"Sit down, Dearie, and we'll get you out to the parking lot," the nurse said, gently leading me to a nearby wheelchair.

I sank into it gratefully, my head still whirling. "I thought I felt all right," I whispered.

"James is making breakfast," Sergeant Worth said. She grabbed my wheelchair and pushed me toward the elevator doors. "You'll feel better when you have something to eat."

"Do you want your flowers?" The nurse who had helped her to the chair held up the half-dead bouquet of daisies from my room. "You forgot them."

"Oh," I said. Those stupid flowers. "Throw them away."

"You didn't even open the card," the ever-so-helpful nurse said. She pulled the envelope from the bouquet. "Do you want me to—?"

"No," I said. I grabbed it, and attempted to stuff it in my sweater pocket. The good sergeant didn't need to see who was sending me flowers.

"You should open it," Sergeant Worth said. "Getting flowers is always nice."

"I'll do it later," I said.

"No," Sergeant Worth said. "I think you should open it now."

Well, there was another not-so-veiled threat. I reluctantly pulled the small card free.

I was only going to glance at the signature and then ram it back into the envelope before she had a chance to read it over my shoulder. And after that, I was going to lie my head off about who the bouquet was from. I was fairly certain it wasn't from Carruthers, but even if it was, she didn't need to know. I hated the way cops dug into my life—even when I didn't want them to.

Then I read the inscription and I could do nothing more than stare at it, as my head swirled and I felt like I was going to puke.

It said: "I'll be seeing you soon." No name, but then, he never did write his name. He knew I'd know who the card was from. Who the card was always from.

My ex-boyfriend, Arnie Stillwell, had found me. Somehow.

"Who were they from?" Sargent Worth asked, and I could tell by the tone of her voice, I was going to have to tell her something. For once, I was okay with telling the truth.

"They're from my ex-boyfriend," I said.

Sergeant Worth said nothing. Farley opened his mouth to speak, but I shut him down. "I don't want to talk about it." Then I looked right at Sergeant Worth. "Can we please go?"

"Absolutely," Sergeant Worth replied, pushing the wheelchair to the elevator. "Do you want to buy a change of clothes or something? I know a good place—"

"No, it's okay." My eyesight momentarily greyed, and I leaned forward, holding my head in my hands. "I need to lie down."

"All right. I'll get you in the car, and we're outta here." The elevator doors opened, and the cop pushed me inside facing the back. She punched the button and impatiently waited for the doors to shut.

"Don't worry, Marie," Farley whispered. "I'll take care of you."

"That's a comfort," I mumbled, staring at the back of the elevator, without really seeing it.

Arnie had found me again. He was probably watching me, right now. I closed my eyes, and hoped that the Sergeant was driving a cop car, with the lights on the top and the whole bit. If Arnie saw me get into it, maybe he'd leave me alone.

Even as I made the wish, I knew it wasn't going to happen. I just hoped he wasn't going to do even more, this time.

"What's a comfort?" Worth asked. I grimaced.

"Just being able to get out of this place," I hastily improvised. "I don't like hospitals much, know what I mean?"

"Yeah." The cop leaned against the back wall beside me, and stared straight ahead. A look—could've been sadness, it was hard to read her face past the impatience and the exhaustion and the ever present suspicion, but it could have been sadness—touched her face. "Yeah. I know what you mean."

I was so bound up in my own misery, I didn't even notice hers.

Farley:
So Marie Has an Ex. Who Knew?

The look on Marie's face when she opened that card reminded me of the look on my ex's face whenever I dropped in uninvited, just to see how Rosie was doing. And that was not good. Not good at all.

Whoever this guy was, she didn't want flowers from him. Or anything else, was my guess.

Huh.

Marie:
Casa del James

"Well, we're here," Sergeant Worth said as we finally pulled to a stop in front of a fairly upscale apartment complex.

"Isn't that good," I muttered.

Those were the first words spoken in the silent forty minute ride from the hospital. Even Farley kept his mouth shut, which was a bit surprising.

James, who had been waiting by the front door, burst out into the bright sunlight, squinting as he energetically waved at us both.

"Looks like he got rested up." Worth spoke sourly, as though she was jealous of James' capacity for recuperation.

"He always looks like that." I could hear the same sourness curdling my voice and couldn't do a thing to stop it. Worse than that, I couldn't get a smile to form until James puppy bounced over to my side of the car and threw open the door.

"Welcome to Casa del James!" he cried. I tried to laugh at his weak attempt at a joke, I really did, but it didn't sound like much, so I stopped, and simply held my hand out so he could help me from the vehicle. When he held my hand a second longer than he needed to, Farley moaned, loud and long. I ignored him.

"How are you feeling?" James gingerly helped me to the sidewalk.

241

"Not great."

"Of course not," he said hastily, as though he'd asked something truly stupid, which, I guess it was. "Let's get you inside, I've made breakfast, I hope you like bacon and eggs. Sergeant, the coffee's on."

"That sounds great, James." Sergeant Worth put on her happy face, which wasn't too terribly happy, and got out of the car. She pulled out a plastic bag with my last name written across the front, and a sheaf of papers that the nurse had handed her as we'd made good our escape from the hospital, and followed us as we inched our way to the front door and into the cool shadows of the entryway. The few steps felt like miles.

As James pulled out his key, the Sergeant's cell phone beeped and she snapped it open. "What?"

She stared down at her feet as someone on the other end talked for a long time. I felt like falling over, but got a nasty rush of adrenaline when she glanced up at me once, with an incredulous look on her face. Then her eyes went back to her highly polished boots. When the one-sided conversation was finally over, she snapped the cell phone shut and handed everything in her hands to James.

"This is her stuff," Worth said, acting like I wasn't even there. "There's a prescription for pain meds in there, somewhere. You should get that filled. She looks like she's going to need them."

Then, she turned on her heel, back toward her car.

"Aren't you going to stay?" James seemed disappointed, but the news made me feel considerably better. I didn't want her around anymore.

"Sorry, duty calls." She threw a small smile over her shoulder as she got in the car.

"I'll find out what that phone call was about," Farley said. "Plus whatever else I can." He waved and followed her back into the car. My knight in shining armour.

I turned to Sergeant Worth. "Thanks for the ride," I said, trying to sound grateful. "It was very kind of you."

"You're welcome," she said. "I might drop by later. See how you're doing, you know, stuff like that."

The look on her face let me know that she wasn't just going to make sure we were all right. In fact, I didn't think the visit would be nice at all, and tried to keep my teeth from grinding. "That's great. However, I don't know how long I'll be staying here—"

"Oh, come back any time," James said, with a big grin and aw shucks look that put my teeth back on edge. Worth smiled back, and it seemed genuine.

"I'll do my best." Then she and Farley were gone, a small spurt of dust from her rear tires as she headed back out to battle evil. Plus all the appropriate paperwork, of course.

"Let's get you inside," James said, and tightened his grip on my arm.

"Yeah, I think so," I whispered. Getting out of the car had taken what little strength I had left, and I needed to lie down, desperately.

Without another word, James scooped me up and carried me through the various hallways to his apartment. He impressed me when he only fumbled a little while getting out his key and opening the door, all without letting my feet touch the ground.

He placed me gently on the couch, and touched my hair, such a light touch it could have been accidental, before he walked into the kitchenette.

"Want something to eat?"

I leaned against the brightly coloured pillows that graced the end of the armless, nondescript couch and sighed. It sounded and felt like it was coming from the lowest place in my soul.

"Can I sit here for a minute? I need to rest."

"Of course." He poured a cup of coffee into a mug. "How about a cup of—"

"No, nothing. I need to rest." As I spoke I closed my eyes, partly so that I could block out the sun, which was making my head pound, but mostly so I didn't have to see the disappointment on his face. I listened to him pour the coffee into the sink and set the cup down on the counter.

"Yeah, no problem."

"Thanks."

I was nearly asleep when Farley came back fifteen minutes later. He oozed through the door, looking furious, and I struggled to sit up.

"I got ten frigging blocks. Ten blocks!" He threw his arms up, and ecto goo flew everywhere. "Then BAM! I was back in front of this apartment building." He threw himself down beside me on the couch. "What the hell is going on?"

I felt sick. The only reason he would bounce back here that I could think of was, he'd attached to me.

Was it because I'd asked him to help me? Probably. I wanted to cry. I couldn't even get help without screwing things up.

"We need to talk," Farley said. "Get him out of here."

Now, I couldn't exactly ask James to leave his own apartment, but I could go hide somewhere.

"Did you call my Mom?" I asked James.

He nodded. "I told her you were okay."

"Did she believe you?"

"I don't know," he said, and shrugged. "She's a lot like you."

"Oh."

I didn't quite know how to take that.

"Maybe I should give her a call," I said.

He pointed at the telephone sitting on the counter, but I shook my head.

"A little privacy." I struggled to pull myself out of the couch which felt like it had half-eaten me.

"Oh," he said. "Sure. You can use the phone in my bedroom."

"That would be good." I struggled against gravity for a moment more, then fell back into the couch. "A little help?"

"Oh, yeah, sure." James scurried over and gently helped me to my feet, then hovered around as I inched my way to the hallway. Even with the pain killers the nurses had been pumping into me, I've never hurt so much in my whole life.

"It's on the right. Bathroom's on the left and there's a closet, but—" His voice faded as I shot him a withering glance. It was taking all my energy to get to the hallway. I didn't need him jabbering at me. "It's on the right."

He went back to his safe spot behind the counter, and I could feel him watching me as I walked into the hallway, using the wall for support.

It took me forever to walk those few steps. Farley followed me; I could hear him huffing and puffing his impatience behind me. I didn't care, though, and kept going, until he decided to go through me so he could get into the room first.

The anger in that man almost flattened me. Tendrils of anger wrapped around every part of his being. It was horrible, and I tried to get away from him, and nearly pitched myself face forward on the really beautiful hardwood floor, which would have hurt like anything.

"Jesus!" we both yelped at the same time, and I scowled at him as I tried to regain my balance.

"Everything okay?" helpful James bellowed from his position of safety by the coffee pot.

"Yeah. Took a bad step." I stared Farley out of the way until I finally got to the door of James' room. He did have the decency to look chagrined. And scared. I wondered what it had been like for him, inside me. Probably not great.

I opened the door and walked into James' room. I think a monk would've had more in his cell than James had in that room. A single bed, carefully made, if we'd tried the bouncing the quarter trick I'm sure it would've worked, and a small wooden crate as a bedside table. On it was a light, a book, old, heavy looking, with the title *Sherlock Holmes* emblazoned in gold across the front, and the phone.

I hobbled over to the bed and sank down, gratefully. Then, I turned to Farley.

"You have to leave. I'm not calling my mom in front of you."

"Oh. Okay, sorry." Farley pulled back. "Thought maybe you needed some moral support, you know. I'll go stand in the—" He glanced around the room. There were two doors, the one we had entered, and one for the closet. "How about if I stand in the closet?"

"Go out in the living room."

"What if you need—"

"You are not listening to this conversation."

"Oh."

"I mean it, Farley. Go out with James. I'll be there in a minute. You're not going to miss a thing. Really."

"Okay." He tried looking humble, but came across as sneaky. And he didn't move. I was too tired to fight with him anymore, so I waved him away. "I'm sorry," he said. "I'll leave you alone."

"Thank you."

When he finally disappeared, with many a forlorn glance back at me, I picked up the phone and called my mom.

The call started off okay. All that, "Oh yes, I'm fine, no it wasn't as bad as it looked on TV, yes it was scary" stuff a person says when she is trying to keep someone who couldn't help anyhow out of fear. Then, I did a truly stupid thing. I asked about Dad.

I don't know why I did that. Maybe it was the flowers in my room, and the lie I'd told. Maybe it was the explosion. Maybe I wanted to pretend that in spite of how screwed up my life was, things would be close to normal back home. I should have known better.

"What do you mean, you haven't heard from him in a month?" I heard myself getting loud, wondered whether Farley and James could hear me through the door, and tried to lower my voice. "I thought you told me he was helping out."

I listened as Mom explained that she hadn't mentioned it because she didn't want to worry me. This cut a bit. I didn't like the idea of her pulling the same trick as me. She tried to appease me by telling me that Ramona was helping out.

"Isn't that nice of her," I said. That set my mom off a bit, because I'm not so good with hiding sarcasm—not that I was trying so hard.

"I'm sorry," I said. "I'm glad she's helping. It must be hard."

I managed to sneak around that potential bombshell, and straight into another one. I knew it was there, of course. A girl can't talk to her mother about either a living or a dead man without some questions. I got them—both barrels.

"I need to talk to you about Farley." I whispered the ghost's name in case James had finally become unglued from his safe spot in the kitchen and was listening at the door. Of course, Mom didn't hear me, so I had to repeat his name. Twice.

"Yes," I finally said, when she got it. "The dead guy. He's with me now." I glanced around the room, to make sure he wasn't actually with me at that very moment. "He followed me out of the Palais to here."

Mom asked me where I was.

"At James' place." Then I hunkered down and waited for the interrogation to begin. It didn't take long. I went through James' stats as though I was talking about a second string catcher for the Mets, and got her back to the topic at hand. Farley.

As I told her what had happened, and listened to what she had to say, I felt my heart drop into the basement of my soul. I thought it had already found bottom, but apparently attempted murder and an explosion isn't enough. Apparently, hitting bottom involved my mother confirming what I already knew. The reason Farley was able to follow me everywhere but couldn't leave my side was because he'd attached to me.

So I did what I do when I get to that black place. I blamed my mom and picked a fight with her.

"Good grief, can't you help me at all with this?" I cried. "I thought you were supposed to be the professional. Now you're telling me that he's attached to me—and it's what, my fault or something?" My voice broke for a second. It *was* my fault. "I can't do this alone. I can't."

I heard her voice go cold, the way it always did when I struck out at her like that, and I felt like a jerk, as she gave me more information about what I could do about Farley. She talked about the attachment and about conflict, and that she felt that it was possibly unfinished business with his family that was still holding him here.

"Like his daughter?" I asked, then listened to dead air for a full fifteen seconds before she sighed, and said maybe. Children can be a factor.

"So, I should push for him to see her?" I hoped, I hoped, but Mom said it wasn't a good idea. He had to want to see her, to make amends or whatever, if this is what needed to happen. Didn't help with my mood one little bit, but I tried to sound appreciative when she told me to keep talking about her, keep working at finding out what had gone on between the two of them, to make sure this was really the thing holding him here. Yeah, just what I want to do. Dig around in Farley's memories, to find out why he believes his daughter thinks he's an asshole. Thanks Mom.

All I said was, "That makes a lot of sense." I did remember to thank her before I hung up the phone. Then I sat on James' neat as a pin bed, and gnashed my teeth. She hadn't helped, and all I'd done was pick another fight with her.

I thought about stretching out for a minute—or an hour—but knew Farley was dying to know what she'd said. So I got up, muscles screaming mightily, and hobbled back out to the living room.

James was gone and Farley was on the balcony, staring at the skyline. I thought it was funny when he nearly jumped out of his skin as I pushed the patio door open to join him.

"Finally got you back, did I?" I joked. He didn't laugh. He just stood, staring out at the sky.

"So where's James?" I asked.

"I don't know."

"When did he leave?"

"I don't know."

He'd listened to my phone call. I could tell. "You listened, didn't you?"

He stared out at the sky, looking absolutely devastated.

"You're not talking to my daughter," he said. "Understand?"

I didn't answer. There was no point. He'd listened to me piss and moan to my mother about him. I should have realized he'd do that. That he'd hear me.

"You didn't tell her about Carruthers," he said. "Why didn't you?"

And again, I didn't answer. I didn't want to think about Carruthers, because Carruthers wasn't the biggest problem in my life. There was also my stupid ex-boyfriend who had somehow found me at the hospital. He was higher on my "crap to be dealt with list" than Carruthers. However, Farley didn't need to know about any of that, not if I wanted him to detach from me.

If he thought he needed to continue to save me, he would never leave. And that would be on me.

I wished, for a second, I could put an arm around his shoulder and comfort him, but I couldn't do anything like that. So, I offered him stupid platitudes instead.

"Don't worry about me, Farley. Mom and I will both be fine."

He didn't respond. Just stared out at the skyline.

"Mom will work out what's going on with you," I said, a little bit desperately. "She's been at this a long time. You'll get where you need to go."

"But you're still in danger."

I sighed. "Right now, yeah."

"So I guess we're both stuck."

We stood and stared out at the blue of the sky until James came back from putting on a load of laundry. I left Farley there, wishing I could do more, and knowing I couldn't. He was as alone as I was.

Marie:
Time to Go

James looked after me like a nursemaid, never leaving my side unless I told him to. I didn't tell him to leave too often. My nightmares were horrible, and I wanted someone living around me. He was good, and never mentioned me working for him, or anything. It was like he knew I needed to heal before I made any decisions like that. And I appreciated it. I really did.

However, I could tell by Monday that I was pushing the limits of his niceness. I thought I was being good, but Farley dourly kept pointing out to me when I slid over into bitch mode. Apparently it was a lot.

It was whenever Farley mentioned me taking Carruthers' money, and he mentioned it all the time.

I didn't tell him he was right, but I realized I couldn't take that money and live with myself. I was going to fix it when I got away from James. I didn't want James to know I'd almost done something like that. I couldn't. It was too horrible to contemplate.

Hence the bitch mode.

James had washed and patched my explosion clothes. When I put them on, they fit perfectly, and you could barely tell I'd been in an explosion. Except for the bruises and cuts all over my face and arms, of course.

"Thank you," I said, twirling like a crippled ballerina so he could see his handiwork. "They look great."

"Glad I could help," he replied. "You don't have to go, you know."

"I know, but you know what they say about house guests. They don't know when the heck to leave, or something."

"So you're going to Jasmine's?"

"Yes."

"She's okay with that?"

"Oh yeah, she's great. She has an extra bed for me to use and everything." That was a lie. I was couch surfing again, but he didn't need to know that. "I'll be fine."

"Good." He glanced down at his hands, then back up at me. "If it doesn't work out, you can always come back here. You know?"

"I know. Thank you."

He really was being sweet about the whole thing, but I needed to get away from him. I wanted to deal with Carruthers and the money issue, but it was more than that. In all honesty, I was afraid that if I didn't move soon, I never would.

Yes, I had gotten to that stage. He was a good man. A genuinely good man, and it would have been so easy. I was glad Farley was still hanging around with that woebegone look on his face. If he hadn't been there, I don't know what I would have done. Probably something stupid like trying to live happily ever after.

I didn't have my bus pass anymore, so James offered to drive me.

I leaned back in the leather seat, tired by the short walk to the car. Farley curled up in the back seat, looking surprised at how nice the car was. I could feel the questions percolating, but I ignored him. I didn't have the energy for him, either.

"Want to warm the seat?" James asked. "It might make you feel better."

That sounded wonderful, so I said sure, and he touched a button, and I was in heaven, the ache in my bones slowly easing. He drove to Jasmine's place without another word.

I'd given him the address when we left his building, then sat and soaked in the warmth radiating from the seat. I jumped a bit when he shifted, impatiently, and asked, "Are we close to your friend's place yet?"

I glanced out the window. "Just down the street."

Farley glanced out the window. "Your friend sure picked a shit hole of a neighbourhood to live in, didn't she?"

I looked around. I thought it was nice enough. Maybe it was a bit rundown and close to some of the seedier parts of town, but most of the houses in the area had been "gentrified", and Jasmine's place fit right in. I decided to ignore him again, wishing he'd go back with James, even though I knew that wasn't going to happen. I was the one he was attached to.

Lucky me.

"That's her place," I said, pointing at Jasmine's neat little bungalow. The drapes were still pulled tight, and I wondered if she ever let any natural light in at all. I didn't think she did. She only had silk plants, and she did worry about her couch fading.

"Looks fine," James said. He stopped the car in front of the house, and turned to me. "You going to be okay?"

"Yes. It'll be fine."

"You got a key?"

I smiled. "The next door neighbour is keeping it for me."

"Do you know the guy?" James frowned. "Maybe I should come with you. Just to make sure."

"No, it'll be okay. He's a nice old guy. Don't worry about it."

I turned to the door, and worked at getting it open. I still felt as weak as a kitten, in spite of the warmth of the seat and everything, but I knew if I didn't open that door on my own, he'd end up staying here and helping me until Jasmine got home—and the last thing in the world I wanted was Jasmine meeting him, and maybe mentioning some of the truly embarrassing things I'd said to her about him, the last time I was here. I didn't need that at all, and finally, desperately, managed to open the door.

"See, no problem at all!" I tried for gaiety, but sounded hysterical. Farley shook his head.

"Tone it down a notch or you'll never get rid of him."

"I'm fine," I said, more sedately this time. "Thanks for everything, James."

"I'll call you later. See how you're doing," he said.

"That would be great." I meant it. I stepped away from the car, trying for a breezy smile that probably didn't fit my bruised face. "See you."

Then I turned toward Mr. Beaverton's house next to

Jasmine's, hoping James would drive away, hoping he wouldn't watch me navigate those four steps to the front door. I was afraid I'd end up crawling. He didn't move, so I bounced up the steps, cursing under my breath with every jolt to my ribs, or my neck, or every other place that hurt, and knocked at the door.

Old Man Beaverton took a few minutes to get there, and I leaned against the jamb, trying to get back my strength. I managed to smile as he opened the door, staring suspiciously at me over his glasses until he finally recognized me.

"Ah, Jasmine's friend," he said. "I was waiting for you." Then he frowned. "Are you all right?"

"Had a bit of an accident, Mr. Beaverton, but I'm okay," I said, clinging to the door jamb for dear life. "Just tired."

"Oh. Oh! Well, that explains the flowers, doesn't it?" he said.

"Flowers?"

"The delivery truck was here about two hours ago. Dropped off some flowers." He smiled. "There were so many, I was afraid there'd been a death."

"Flowers?" I still didn't have a clue what he was talking about, and it must have showed.

"Don't worry, I let him put them in Jasmine's house. You must have a lot of friends, my dear. They seem to care very much. They're expensive, I think."

"Flowers?" I was beginning to feel positively stupid, because I still didn't understand what Beaverton was talking about.

"Yes. Expensive." He reached in his pocket and pulled out a set of keys. "Here you are, my dear." Then he frowned again. "Are you sure you're all right?"

"Fine," I muttered, and took the keys.

"Enjoy the bouquets," he said.

"I will."

I walked across the grass to Jasmine's house, with Farley on my heels.

"Nice place," Farley said.

"Shut up."

I didn't turn around because I had to concentrate on working the key into the lock. I felt like I was ready to keel over, and didn't need any of Farley's sarcasm.

"No, I'm not kidding," he said. "I shouldn't have made the 'Shit hole' comment. This doesn't seem too bad."

He turned and counted the bikes littering the front yard. "Three," he said. "She's got three kids. Two boys and a girl. Right?"

"Right." The stupid key chattered around the lock. Why wouldn't it go in?

"That's nice," Farley said. He sounded different, and when I glanced over at him, he looked sad.

"Anything wrong?" I asked.

"Just feeling a little homesick," he said. "I hope Sylvia kept up the yard. I liked that yard."

"Sylvia's your wife?"

"Ex-wife, yeah." He looked at the ground, and frowned. "Get that door open, all right? Otherwise Jimmy boy is going to want to know what the hell's going on."

"Oh. Okay." Finally, the key slipped into the lock, and I managed to get the door open. I turned to wave at James, and Farley walked past me into the house.

"Oh wow," he said. "Marie, you gotta see this."

I slammed the door shut on James' wave, and walked into the living room, then stood stock still, staring. It was jam packed with bouquets of flowers. The splashes of colour were jarring against Jasmine's silk plants and boring beige, wrapped-in-plastic furniture.

It was the creepiest thing I've ever seen. Me, who can see ghosts, was saying that.

"Jasmine wouldn't have ordered these—her youngest has allergies." I reached out a hand, almost touching the flowers in the closest bouquet. There was no card.

"That's weird."

"Maybe they all came from the same person," Farley said. "The old man said there was one delivery, didn't he?"

"I can't remember," I muttered, staring at the rest of the bouquets that littered the entryway and wishing Farley would shut his mouth for just one minute. The last bouquet of flowers I'd received had come from my ex-boyfriend.

My heart started to pound, hard. Had he somehow known I was going to come here and sent all these?

Farley glanced around. "They're too bright for my taste, but what the hell," he said. "I didn't know you were so popular."

"Shut up, Farley," I whispered. I walked into the living room, horrified. "Shut up."

The big vases and baskets full of flowers were everywhere. Every available counter and table, plus a big bunch of the floor was taken up with the garish displays.

I inched into the room, creeping around the huge bouquets balanced precariously on the floor. On the biggest, most brightly coloured one I saw an envelope. I plucked it free, and ripped it open with hands that were shaking so badly, I could barely control them.

The card was more brightly coloured than the flowers, if that was possible. "Hope You're Feeling Better" was printed on the outside.

Oh my God, I thought. *He found me.*

I opened the card, and a piece of paper fell to the floor. I looked at the inside of the card, but there was nothing written there.

Arnie always made sure I knew he'd sent his gifts. What was going on?

I bent and picked up the piece of paper between two fingers, as though it was dirty. It was the cheque from Carruthers, made out to me, and certified, as I had demanded.

Arnie hadn't found me. Carruthers had.

"You can't accept that," Farley said.

"I know," I whispered, staring at the cheque. For about a second, I thought about how many zeroes were on that cheque. How far that many zeroes would go to solve my problems.

Here was the big kick to the head. I knew that it wouldn't. You can't get rid of someone who wants to control you by playing nice. You couldn't take their apologies for all the times they hurt you, and you sure couldn't take their money.

Because they'd be back, and they'd demand more. And more and more, until the only way they could be satisfied was if you were dead.

I dropped the cheque on the floor, and turned to Farley.

"How did he know I was going to be here?" I asked. My voice was high pitched and scary sounding. I barely recognized it.

"I—I don't know," Farley said.

"Neither do I," I said. And then I guess you could say I lost my mind.

I started tearing apart the bouquets of flowers, one by one.

"What the hell are you doing?" Farley flittered around me like a—well, a lot like a hugely useless ghost—as flowers and bits of greenery flew in all directions.

"That son of a bitch thinks he can buy me off with stupid flowers!" I cried. "Stupid, stupid flowers!" Another vase hit the floor and begonias, baby's breath, and shards of glass flew everywhere. "Son of a bitch!" I grabbed another bouquet and began to dismember it, my breath catching in my throat in small sobs.

"Jesus, Marie, have you lost your mind?" Farley cried.

I stopped, momentarily, and stared at him.

"I don't think so," I finally said, and threw another handful of flowers against the wall. "Maybe. I don't know." More flowers flew, piling in a multi-coloured riot around the room.

"Why are you doing this?" he asked.

I stopped, and considered the question before carrying on.

"It's because of what he did to you. He can't buy me off after what he did to you." The rain of flowers resumed.

"That's nice," Farley said. "I mean, thank you and all that, but . . ."

"But what?" I reached for the next vase—nope, not a vase this time, but a basket. It wasn't going to shatter when I dropped it—and began taking it apart, flower by flower.

"This isn't really helping. Is it?" he asked.

"No," I said. "Probably not."

"Then why don't you stop?"

"Because, Farley, I'm not done yet." I grabbed the last arrangement, threw the whole thing at the far wall, and watched with some satisfaction as it smashed into a thousand pieces. "Now I'll stop." Then I burst into tears.

"He blew up the Palais, and he was the reason you killed yourself, Farley. And he threatened my mother. He thinks I can be bought—I was almost bought . . . "

"Yeah," he said. "But you weren't."

I took a deep hitching breath and blew it out in small puffs as I tried to get myself under control. "Yeah. I wasn't."

"Let's figure out how to get him," Farley said.

So, we sat down in Jasmine's living room, littered with the remains of the most expensive bouquets I'd ever seen, and we planned our revenge.

The plan we came up with was pretty simple, which was good, and legal, which was better. I would send the cheque back to Carruthers, and then go to Sergeant Worth and tell her how he'd tried to bribe me, and how he'd implied that my mother was going to be in danger if I didn't comply. Neither of us were sure what would happen after that, but it felt like the right place to start.

First I had to find the cheque. After some digging it popped into view, worse for wear but still legible. I stuffed it into an envelope and scribbled down the address from the business card he'd given me. There was a mailbox at the far end of Jasmine's street, and I gimped my way to it, feeling much better when it was out of my sight. Then I started to clean up the mess.

"Don't you think you should rest a minute or something?" Farley asked.

"Actually," I said, and smiled at him, "I feel pretty good. And I have to clean this up. Jasmine won't like this mess one bit."

James called to see how I was doing as I stuffed the last of those stupid flowers in the stupid garbage bags. I thought he felt like a jerk for not being the hero and coming in with me, but I was wrong. He told me he had news from Helen Latterson and suggested we have a quick meal so he could tell me about it, if I felt up to it. I said yes, I'd be happy to.

All right, so maybe I was missing him a bit.

He was smart and didn't say a darned thing about a date, which could have set me off, if I hadn't been in such a good mood. He suggested Thai food, which sounded great, and said he'd pick me up at sevenish. Which, if I knew that man at all, meant seven on the dot, but it was okay. It was all right. Everything felt all right.

I was so glad that cheque was out of my sight and on its way back its rightful owner that I sang as I scrubbed the last of the green marks off Jasmine's living room rug, thanking whatever interior decorating Gods there were that she'd gone with something with actual flecks of green in it so I didn't have to try that hard. The money would have been a Godsend, especially for a person in my situation, no doubt about it. It was a lot easier, now that the cheque was not in my hands.

"What time does your friend come home from work?" Farley asked. I glanced up from a particularly stubborn patch of something I'd thought was plant goo until I figured out it was Play Doh, and frowned.

"I don't know. Maybe four-thirty, or five-ish?"

"Well, it's three thirty-ish now." He pointed to the small clock adorning the top of Jasmine's fake fireplace. "Isn't it?"

"Good grief!" I looked around at the six bags of plant remains, and for a moment it felt like the scene of a crime. Which, to plant lovers, it probably was. "I have to get these out of here!"

Luckily they weren't heavy, and it didn't take me long to get them to the back yard, by her garbage bins. However, I felt light headed by the time I got back into the house.

"I need to lie down for a minute," I said, wiping a sheen of sweat that had gathered on my brow. It felt cold and clammy, and suddenly things got dark.

"Sit down, now!" Farley barked, and I did so gratefully. My eyesight came back immediately, thank goodness, but I had obviously overdone.

"Go have a nap," Farley said. "You can call Sergeant Worth after you've rested."

I nodded my head, and groped my way down the back hallway to Jasmine's room. The bed was soft and I'd nearly fallen asleep when Farley came into the room a few moments later. His soft glow made everything seem pretty, though Jasmine likes Sopranos style furniture, which is not to my taste in the bedroom. Or anywhere for that matter.

"I wanted to tell you," he said, staring down at me. "How proud I am of you."

"For what?" I asked, trying, barely, to pull myself back from the brink of sleep.

"For doing the right thing."

"Thanks," I whispered, and in that instant before I fell asleep, I felt proud of me too.

Farley forgot to wake me up. In fact, no-one woke me up. I was shocked when I opened my eyes and it was nearly six o'clock. I moved one arm, and the pain of my bruised muscles brought me fully awake.

"God," I muttered, waving my appendages pathetically, like a turtle on its back. "I feel like crap."

"She's awake!" one of Jasmine's kids bellowed, outside the now opened bedroom door. I was pretty sure it was Billy. "Can we turn on the TV now?"

"All right." That was Jasmine, but she didn't sound like herself. As I swung my feet over the edge of her bed, gingerly, she walked into the room, and I noticed she was moving gingerly too. We both jumped when the TV blared on.

"Turn it down!" she yelled, then turned back to me. "How do you feel?"

"Not bad." I was lying, and didn't try to hide it. "How do I look?"

"You look like absolute crap." She breathed out the words as though awed by my bruises. I glanced at the mirror, and was momentarily awed myself.

"Wow, you're not kidding. I look terrible." I tried to laugh, and almost pulled it off. "I have to go out tonight. I don't think there's enough make up in the world to hide this."

"You and I have to talk, Marie."

I could tell by the look on her face, and the fact that she hadn't jumped at the mention of me going out that something had happened. Something not good.

"What's wrong?" I couldn't read her face past "not good", and it made me afraid.

"I found something, when I got home." She frowned, and shook her head. "What's going on, Marie?"

I thought she'd found the flowers. I honestly thought that's what she'd found. I knew it wasn't Farley, wherever he was. She was good with the living, but had no clue about the dead.

"What do you mean?"

"There was a message left on my answering machine." She frowned again, ferociously this time. "My kids listened to it. What's going on, Marie?"

"What message?" I asked, my mouth drying with fear. If it was Carruthers—and I kicked myself for not thinking about the fact he knew I was there. What had he said? Had he threatened the children?

"I think you better hear it," she said. "Can you get up?"

"Yes." Now, I was very afraid. If I'd brought that man down on her and her family, I would never forgive myself. I pushed myself to standing, and hobbled over to the bedroom door.

"The police just got here," she said. "I called them when I heard it. They want to talk to you."

"The police?" It was as bad as I thought. "We need the police?" She nodded.

Well, at least I didn't have to make the trip to the police station the way Farley and I had planned. They'd come to me.

"Thank you," I said.

"You're welcome." She walked ahead of me, down the hallway and to the living room.

The police officers were both sitting on the plastic covered couch, untouched coffees in front of them on the mock antique coffee table, acting supremely uncomfortable. Farley was on the floor between Amber and Billy, two of Jasmine's kids, appearing happier than I'd ever seen him. He didn't look up when I came into the room, so I decided to ignore him, and focus on the police.

"What's going on?" I asked, trying for breezy, but sounding like a crotchety old woman. I took a tottering step into the living room, and grabbed for the wall to steady myself. "Is there a problem here, officers?"

Jasmine didn't crack a smile. "This is Officer Landsdown and Officer Regal," she said. Then she walked into the kitchen.

"Come here!" she called. "All of you!"

We all jumped to, the police acting embarrassed that Jasmine's mother voice had pulled them to attention. Officer Landsdown obviously decided to assert his authority by the time we were all assembled around the phone.

"What can you tell us about this voicemail message?" he asked, pointing to the machine as if I could tell him purely by osmosis.

"I don't know what you're talking about," I said. I looked to Jasmine for help. She merely stared at the machine as though she wished it was no longer in her house.

"I don't want you turning that thing on when my kids can hear it," she said, grabbing Landsdown's sleeve as he reached for the button that would start the message. "Please."

I'd never heard that pleading tone in Jasmine's voice before.

"What's on there?" I asked, fear trickling down my spine like ice water.

"It's nasty. Really nasty." Farley had snuck up on me, and I jumped about a foot and a half. "You won't want to hear it," he continued, and I groped for a chair, to sit down.

"Who is it?"

"I don't know," Farley said.

Not Carruthers, then.

"We would like you to listen to it and tell us," Officer Landsdown said, then looked at Jasmine. "Please send your children to their rooms. She has to hear this."

"Fine." Jasmine's voice was cold, and she did not look at me as she went into the other room and herded her complaining children into one room, and slammed the door. She stayed with them. For a minute, I wanted to join them. But I couldn't. I had to identify the voice on that tape.

Farley glanced at me sympathetically, then went down to the room where the children and Jasmine were hiding. He gave me one more look that I couldn't read, then disappeared through the door. I was alone with the police.

"How bad is this?" I asked, hearing the quake of fear in my voice, and unable, unwilling to stop it.

"Bad enough," Landsdown replied. "You ready?"

"Okay."

He pressed the button, and the voice started. I knew who it was, of course. After the first three words. After that sing-songy "I see you!" I knew exactly who it was. Jerk Arnie. My ex-boyfriend. Unfortunately, it sounded like he'd made the quantum leap from stalkery jerk to full-fledged psycho.

"I know who it is," I whispered, my mouth so dry I could barely speak. Landsdown made a move to shut off the voice, but I stopped him. I had to hear the whole thing. After all, he'd left it for me.

Jasmine had an old fashioned machine, one that didn't stop after a few minutes. This one ran and ran and ran—and Arnie had used the whole thing to tell me in great detail exactly what he'd do to me if I didn't come back to him. Not only what he'd do to me, but to anyone who helped me. I closed my eyes through that bit, thinking about Jasmine hiding in the other room, with her kids. What had I brought down on them?

After the voice finally stopped, Landsdown turned to me. "Who is that, Miss Jenner?"

"It's Arnie Stillwell. We used to date, up in McMurray."

"Have you had any contact with him lately?"

"I haven't spoken to him since I got the restraining order," I whispered. "But two days ago, he sent me flowers at the hospital."

The officer's eyebrow quirked. "Why were you in the hospital?"

"I was in that explosion. The Palais."

"Hmm." He jotted something down. "You've had a busy week."

"You don't know the half of it," I replied. I ran my fingers through my hair, wishing I could have a shower. I suddenly felt filthy, as though his words were all over my skin.

"He found me twice after I came to Edmonton. The last time, I got the restraining order. I thought he understood."

"Understood what?"

"That I don't want to see him again."

Landsdown snorted. "Doesn't sound like he got it," he said.

Understatement of the year.

"So what do I do now?"

"We'd like you to come down to headquarters with us and answer a few more questions."

I was about to say all right when the front door rang, and I jumped about a foot and a half straight up instead. As the other officer went to answer the door, I shakily glanced at the clock hanging on the wall above Jasmine's fridge. It was seven o'clock. On the dot.

"That's James Lavall," I said. Landsdown stared at me. "We work together. We're supposed to be going out for dinner."

"You're not going," Landsdown replied.

I turned my head and watched James handle having a big, pissed off cop glower at him through the suddenly opened door. He did well, all things considered.

Marie:
Bringing James Up to Speed, Sort Of

"What is going on here?" James asked.

"Nothing," I replied.

I don't think he believed me. We were in the kitchen, where I'd dragged him after the police had finally decided to believe that he was, in actuality, James Lavall.

"Tell me right now," he said, and grabbed both my hands in his. I knew without looking at him that the other James was back. The hard-eyed James who got things done.

You wouldn't believe how much I wanted to tell him everything and let him look after me. So, of course, I acted like an ass.

"I'm not telling you anything, James. This has nothing to do with you." I slapped his hands away from mine, and turned.

Jasmine was standing at the kitchen door, staring at us.

"Another of your men, Marie?" she asked. Her tone sounded sour, and I didn't blame her. "Am I safe?"

"This is James Lavall," I said. "You remember, I told you about him."

"Oh." Jasmine's voice warmed appreciably. "So, this is James." She held out her hand to him. "So nice to finally meet you. I was beginning to think she'd never take the plunge."

James took her hand, and shook it. "The plunge?"

Before Jasmine could speak, or I could clap my hands over her mouth to keep her from speaking, he frowned. "What did you mean 'am I safe'? What happened here?"

And then Jasmine spilled the beans.

"Please don't," I whispered.

"He needs to know this," Jasmine said. "Why would you keep it a secret?"

Because it made me look like the biggest victim in the world, that's why.

She wouldn't stop, and James didn't even look at me again as she told him everything she knew about Arnie Stillwell. Which was pretty much everything.

"I tried to get her to take one of those self-defence classes after the last time he messed with her, but she wouldn't, would you?" she said. She looked at me and smiled brightly.

All I could do was stare at her, because I didn't want to look at James. And for sure, I didn't want to look at Farley. He'd wandered in halfway through Jasmine's explanation of my absolutely dismal love life, and had leaned against the kitchen counter, his arms crossed and a bemused expression on his face.

He was going to be an ass about this. I could just tell.

"And then he called here," Jasmine said. "He was very threatening, wasn't he, Marie?"

I grunted something close to affirmative. Why wouldn't this stop?

Because Jasmine wasn't finished. That's why.

"So we called the police, didn't we, Marie?"

I grunted again, wishing with all my might that all of this was over and I could go crawl in a hole in the back yard and become a hermit, or something.

"Now we're going to give the little bastard what for, aren't we, Marie?"

"Your kids are in the house," I said weakly. Jasmine didn't allow swearing in the house, even if the kids were not there. All she did was laugh.

"They're still in my bedroom," she replied. "And sometimes, it is important to use the proper word, even if it is a little bit naughty. Isn't that right?"

"Fuckin' eh," Farley said, sourly. Though I desperately wanted to glare him into the ground, I couldn't. No one was standing close to him, and I didn't want either Jasmine or James to think I'd suddenly lost my mind on top of everything else, so I did the only thing I could do and I ignored the heck out of him.

"Because he is a bastard for what he's done to you," Jasmine continued, her smile disappearing. "This can't continue. Something must be done."

"Well, the police are here now," I said, still sounding weak and victimy, but not knowing how to stop. "They'll look after everything, so let's just let it all go. Okay?"

"Nope," James said. "That's just not going to happen."

Fantastic. Now he was going into knight in shining armour mode. I desperately tried to think of something—anything—I could say that would calm him down, but came up with nothing.

Luckily, or maybe not so luckily, James' cell phone rang, and he had something else to think about.

"Yes?" he snarled. Then I watched the blood literally drain from his face as he listened to the reply. He didn't say another word until whoever was on the line stopped speaking.

"I'll be right there," he said, and rammed his finger on the screen of his phone to end the call. I was pretty sure I heard something break, but didn't point it out to him. He was angry enough already. "That was Sergeant Worth. She wants to see us both. Right now."

"Why?"

"Because someone firebombed my place, Marie." His face was stone. Absolute stone. "Worth thinks it's connected to your place and the Palais. We gotta go in. Now."

"Oh my God, James," I said. "How bad was it?"

"I don't know." His face was still stone, and I took my hand from his sleeve. He didn't want me touching me. I didn't think he even wanted me near him. I didn't blame him. He'd had a nice life, before he met me, but now?

Now, everything had changed.

Officer Landsdown offered to give us a ride downtown. James brushed him off, saying, tersely, that he'd drive because we had things to discuss. I was kind of hoping Landsdown would push, but he didn't, so I ended up in the passenger seat of James' Volvo, on one of the most uncomfortable rides of my life.

Landsdown followed us downtown in his cruiser, leaving the

other officer with Jasmine and her kids until something more permanent could be arranged. I hated hearing that. Permanent sounds so—permanent. Like this was never going to go away.

Farley settled into the back seat of the car moments before James took off.

"I like that house," he said. "You need to take me back there, when you're finished with all this foolishness."

Before I could figure out a way to answer him, he sprawled out and appeared to go to sleep. At least he wasn't harassing me. I had enough on my plate.

"So, when were you going to tell me about Arnie Stillwell?" James' voice sounded tight, and I knew, without looking at him, that I'd have to find more room on that plate, somewhere.

"I don't know," I said. "I don't want to talk about this anymore."

"Yeah, well, tough," James said. "You need to tell me everything about this character, right now."

I glanced over at him, and shook my head. I was not going to let the tough guy act work. Not a chance.

"Let it go. I'm not telling you anything more about him."

"Why not?"

"Because he's none of your concern," I replied. Farley snorted in the back seat, and I glanced at him, but he seemed to still be sleeping. "That's why."

"Marie, I don't know what your problem is, but I think it's time you start telling me. You have a stalker and you need to be protected."

I couldn't keep up the ignoring pretense any longer. "I need to be protected?" I cried, doing a little glaring of my own. "*I* need to be protected? I don't think so. I've done all right so far, without—"

"Are you kidding me?" he yelled, and I knew, without looking, that the other James was back, with a vengeance. "You have been strangled, and blown up, and your apartment has been burned to the ground! I would say that you need a bunch of protecting! If you aren't smart enough to understand that, you're not as smart as I thought you were!"

"What?" I snarled. "What the hell are you trying to say? That last bit made no sense whatsoever! Talk about being smart—"

"You know what I mean!" he roared, startling Farley out of his dream.

"Tell him to shut the fuck up," he muttered, and rolled over. "I'm sleeping here."

"Quit yelling," I said. "People are staring."

"What people?" James glanced around, but did lower his voice. I was glad. I didn't need both Farley and him on my back.

"Never mind," I said, trying for a more reasonable tone myself. It was time to put a stop to all this "I'll protect you," crap. "You have to understand, James, that this has nothing to do with you. We have—more of a business relationship. This is my personal life. And—"

"You don't want me involved in your personal life." He snarled out the last bit. "I imagine that includes dating. Wouldn't want me to be involved in anything as personal as dating—would you."

His last statement was just that—a statement, so I didn't answer. Didn't see the point. He was too mad to talk to. I glanced out the window, relieved to see we were at the downtown station. He wheeled into the underground parking lot, taking up three parking slots, and pulling the hand brake as hard as he could.

"Even if you don't want to talk to me about your personal life, you are going to have to tell Sergeant Worth. Know what I mean?"

"Yes. I know exactly what you mean," I said softly, and without another word, followed him into the elevator and up to the Sergeant's office.

Marie:
Good Cop, Bad Cop, All Rolled into One

"All right you two, what the hell's going on?" Sergeant Worth scowled at both of us as we stood in front of her excruciatingly neat desk in the cramped cubbyhole she called her office. There was a picture on the desk. When I tried to sneak a peek, the Sergeant slammed it face down with a growl. "I asked you a question. What is going on?"

"Tell me what happened to my place, Sergeant." The other James was still there, dangerous sparks flying from his eyes. Sergeant Worth ignored the sparks, and stared us both down.

"Someone firebombed it," she said.

"How bad?"

"There was some damage."

"Can I go home?" he asked.

"No. The investigators are still working. I'm sorry." For about a second, she actually looked sorry. Until her cop mask snapped back into place. "Now, tell me exactly what you two are involved in. From the beginning."

"*We* are involved in nothing. There is absolutely nothing going on with us," James snapped. "Is there, Marie?"

"What?" Sergeant Worth looked confused, then angry. "What the hell are you talking about, Lavall?"

"Maybe Marie would like to answer that. She's the brains of

269

this operation, aren't you, Marie? I mean, you're the one who decides everything, aren't you? Where we go, what we eat—and what we're going to call it once we're done? Right?"

James stared at me, his face paper white, his eyes like crazy pinwheels. I was doing a little staring of my own. His place had been firebombed, for God's sake, and he was worried about whether we were dating? I couldn't believe it, and laughed out loud.

"Get over yourself, James. We've got more to worry about here, don't you think? Okay, so I'm not going to call going out for supper a date. It was fine, we had good food, good conversation, we don't have to start labeling—"

"Both of you shut up!" Sergeant Worth yelled.

I jumped about a foot and a half. So did James, and I was happy about that. I didn't want to be the only one.

"In case it hadn't come to your attention, someone tried to burn down both of your apartment buildings. Both of them. Within days of each other. Doesn't that strike you as odd? Especially when you consider the fact that you were both caught in an explosion under a week ago. Both of you. Same explosion. Isn't this all a bit peculiar?"

"Well, maybe you want to talk to El Capitán here, she seems to have all the answers," James started, pointing his thumb in my direction.

I was certain, for a moment, that the Sergeant was going to literally explode right in front of us. With shaking fingers, she signaled for James to shut his mouth. He did so with an audible snap, her anger seeming to pull him out of whatever insane fugue he'd been in.

"I don't know what games you two are playing, and really, I don't give a shit," she said. "You tell me what the hell is up with you two right now, or I'm throwing you both in jail. I swear to God. Jail. And I can leave you there as long as I want."

I almost told her I thought that was against the law, but the Sergeant cut me short with a look. "As long as I want," she repeated, her tone absolutely chilling.

There was a short silence while we all collected our thoughts. I was trying to work out how James and I could simultaneously answer her and keep quiet, and I think pretty much the same thing was going through James' head, too.

"Well?" Worth finally asked. "Who's going to start?"

"I will." I tried to keep my voice soft, and watched for any signs of the cop snapping again. "I think this all has to do with Ian Carruthers, the owner of the Palais."

"Ian Carruthers?" James asked, and I inwardly cringed. I hadn't mentioned my recent interactions with Carruthers yet. A little too busy trying to explain the crazy ex-boyfriend.

"So, we're back to him, are we?" Sergeant Worth asked. "You got a love hate thing going for this guy, don't you?"

"Yeah," I looked down at the tops of my shoes. They were still covered in muck and ash. I was surprised. I hadn't noticed it before. "I guess I do. But he tried to pay me off."

That finally got the look of surprise back on her face.

"He what?"

"He came to see me at the hospital and offered me $50,000.00 to disappear." I shuffled uncomfortably. "And then he had the cheque delivered to my friend's house. It was waiting for me when I got there."

Worth frowned. "So he knew you were going to your friend's house?"

"Yes."

"How? Did you tell him?"

"No." It was my turn to frown. "I didn't tell anybody." I turned to James. "Did you tell anybody?"

"No," he said. James looked like he'd been poleaxed. "No, I didn't tell anyone."

"Interesting," Worth said, and made a note. "Give me the cheque."

"I can't."

"Why? You planning on keeping the money?"

I flushed. "No, I'm not keeping it. I already mailed it back to him. I was going to call him—but thought I'd talk to you first."

"Marie." James sighed out the words, like he couldn't believe what he was hearing. "Why didn't you tell me?"

"Because it didn't have anything to do with you, James." I spoke more sharply than I intended, and worked hard at softening my tone. "I had to decide how I was going to handle the whole thing." I turned to the Sergeant. "I know. I should've told you at the hospital."

"Damned straight you should have," Worth snapped. "Why

was he trying to pay you off? Did it have to do with the flash drive you talked about?"

The shrewd look was back on her face, so when James sucked wind, I didn't look at him. I kept my eyes on her.

"No. He didn't know about that. Maybe he thought I knew about Don Latterson's involvement with him."

"Did you?"

"Not really."

"Why didn't you tell me about this before?" Sergeant Worth asked.

"Because I—because—" My bit of bravado leaked out of me like helium out of a balloon. "I don't know. It was the money or something. I really don't know."

"Keeping information from me isn't the right way to go, Marie." Surprisingly, the Sergeant's face had softened. "I know you didn't have the easiest time up north, but we are the good guys."

"Do you mean Arnie Stillwell?" That was James. I couldn't say anything. I felt like a deer that found itself having a staring contest with the headlights of a Mac truck. Sergeant Worth was the Mac truck.

"The other cop is handling that, James." I said it quietly, I thought. Obviously not quietly enough.

"Handling what?"

The sergeant pulled a file from her drawer. I could see Arnie's picture—and it was not flattering at all—pinned to the top of thick file. He had quite the rap sheet, no doubt about it. I suspected a fair bit of it had to do with our messy little relationship.

"What's he done now?" she asked.

"He called my friend's place." I glanced around and grabbed a chair, throwing myself into it. My legs had started shaking so badly, I knew I couldn't stand another second. "He made some threats. It scared my—"

"When?"

"Earlier today. We already called the police. Officer Landsdown is handling it." I stared at her. "Really. It's being handled and it has nothing to do with the other. I'm sure it doesn't."

Actually, I didn't know any of that, I was just sick of everyone knowing my business. Seeing how out of control every aspect of my life was.

"How can you be so sure?" James asked.

"Because Carruthers—" I started.

"Forget Carruthers," he said. "I don't think he had anything to do with the fires at our apartments."

"Why do you think that?" I asked.

"The explosion at the Palais was caused by the furnace. Latterson's nephew, Raymond, did it, on orders from Latterson. Correct?'

The sergeant nodded.

"But Marie's place," James continued. "That was a firebomb or something. Wasn't it?"

"That's true," the sergeant said. "The fire marshals just finished investigating. The fire started in Marie's apartment. An accelerant was used. However, Raymond—"

"Who caused the explosion in the Palais," James said.

"Had not yet been arrested," the sergeant continued. "He could have set the fire."

"But he couldn't have set the fire in my building," James replied. "Because he's still in custody. Isn't he?"

"Absolutely," Worth said. A smile touched her face. "And the information I received from the preliminary investigation confirms that the fire was started, not just in your building, but in your apartment."

"Just like Marie's," James said. "Was Arnold Stillwell ever arrested for arson?"

"No," I said.

"Yes," said the sergeant.

"What?" I gasped.

She flipped open Arnie's file. "He was accused of starting a fire in an outbuilding at the Rogers Forest trailer park in Fort McMurray."

My mother lived in that trailer park.

"Looks like it happened a month or so after you moved," she said, and looked up at me. "He used a Molotov cocktail. Didn't your mother tell you about the fire?"

"I guess she must have forgotten," I mumbled. "She's been sick."

"Tell me about your mother, Marie."

There was something in Worth's face that made my mouth go

bone dry. Why was she asking anything about my mother?

"She has nothing to do with this."

"I think she does. I've heard interesting things about her from my compatriots up in McMurray."

Oh God, what did she know? I desperately tried to remember if my mother had ever worked with the police, but nothing came.

"You're wrong," I whispered. We played the staring game for a few seconds until Worth smiled, and threw her pen down on her desk. I could have crumpled into a heap right there, and touched the edge of the desk to keep myself upright. Quicksand was everywhere in that room.

Sergeant Worth slapped the file shut. "Looks like you aren't the only one in your family to keep secrets," she said. She gave me another measured stare, and I willed myself quiet. I was nearly out of danger.

"However," she continued, "this does put firebombing a couple of apartments right in Arnold Stillwell's wheelhouse." She turned to James. "Excellent deducing, there, Lavall."

"Thanks," he said, putting on his "aw shucks" face.

"We'll put out an APB on Arnold Stillwell. He should be off the streets soon."

"And Carruthers?" I asked.

"We'll do what we can," Worth said. "Latterson still hasn't linked him to anything to do with the Palais, and the explosion destroyed—well, nearly everything. If you'd kept the cheque, we could have used that, but the way it sits, it's your word against his. We'll keep digging."

"The cheque was from his business account," I said. "C&R Holdings."

Worth looked at me dourly. "Well, that's something."

But it wasn't enough. Even I could tell that. Without the cheque, it was my word against his. He was a rich businessman. Me? I was nothing.

"I guess we're done here," Worth finally said. "You two need some place to stay or something? Need to talk to Victim Services?" She started fishing in the top drawer of her desk. I shook my head.

"You already gave me their card," I said.

"Fine." She looked past me to James. "If anything more comes to you, give me a call."

"I will." James held his hand out to the woman. "Talk to you soon."

"Yes, you will." Solemnly, she shook his hand, then turned away from us, pointedly. Interview was over. Time to go.

Thank God.

Farley:
The Drive to the Office

"So, are we going to talk now?"

It was Jimmy boy's voice, pulling me out of a great dream. Funny thing, I didn't feel pissed at him. As I stretched, I realized I was still in the back of his car, and looked with some amusement at my legs, which were hanging out through the left side of the vehicle. Bet the kids would have laughed their asses off if they could have seen that.

The dream had been about Jasmine's kids—and about Rose. My daughter Rose, miraculously the same age as Jasmine's daughter, playing innocent games with her, by a river, under a tall tree. I'd been leaning against that tree, watching them. We were all laughing, and having such a good time. It had been so beautiful, I felt like I still held the sunshine from that dream on my skin.

However, the look on Marie's face told me I'd missed something big.

What had I missed?

Marie:
The Drive to the Office

I ignored Farley as James dug in his pocket for his car keys. He hadn't said a word since we'd left Sergeant Worth's office, and I couldn't read his face.

"So, what's going on?" Farley asked. He looked around the underground parking garage. "Are we still at the cop shop?"

"Do you want to talk, James?" I asked.

James pulled the keys from his pocket, and shrugged. "I thought none of it was my business," he replied. "Isn't that what you said?"

I didn't know whether to laugh or cry. "I guess since Arnie tried to burn down your place, some of my business is now your business. Know what I mean?"

"Yeah, I do," he said, and unlocked my door, even holding it open for me. "So where do you want to go to have this talk?"

"I don't know." I unlocked his door. As he climbed in, my throat tightened dangerously, but I pulled myself together. Crying time was definitely over. "I'm not going back to Jasmine's until they catch Arnie, and I don't have a penny to my name. So I don't know."

"Well, we can't go to my place," he said, rather unhelpfully. "What about a restaurant?"

"You could go to Jimmy Boy's office." Farley said. "Because I

279

don't want to spend the next nine hours or whatever down here while you two try to make up your minds."

I glanced back at him, surprised. That was a good idea. We needed a quiet place to talk, and the office was definitely quiet. I looked at James.

"Do you want to—" I started.

"Well, you know," he said at the same time, then we both stopped and then did the politeness stammer.

"You go first," James said.

"No, *you* go first," I replied, keeping my voice even. "Please."

"What the hell is up with you two?" Farley barked. "Make up your frigging minds!"

"I was going to say maybe we could go to my uncle's office," James said. "We can talk there. What were you going to say?"

"The same thing," I admitted, and felt the heat of a blush touch my cheeks.

"All right, we'll go there, then."

But he didn't start the car. He glanced at me, and he looked like he had more to say. I looked down at my hands, waiting for the yelling to start again.

I wouldn't have blamed him. If he'd known about Arnie, he could have gotten away from me. Protected himself. Then his place wouldn't have been burned down.

"Look," he finally stammered, "I'm sorry about everything I said in the Sergeant's office. I shouldn't have acted like that."

Oh. That was definitely not what I had expected. "Don't worry about it," I said cautiously.

I felt Farley's eyes boring into the back of my head. "What the hell went on?"

"You don't have to tell me anything you don't want to," James said. "I understand that. I just want to make sure you're safe."

"Thanks, James," I said. "I appreciate it. The police will catch Arnie, and they'll figure out the rest of it. I think we'll both be all right."

"I wasn't really talking about your ex-boyfriend or Carruthers," he said. "There's more you're not telling me, but I can wait."

I sighed. Even if he hadn't run away when he found out about Arnie, I knew he'd run away when he learned the rest. I wanted to put this off until I felt stronger.

"You know most of my dirty little secrets now, James. Can that be enough for a while? Please?"

I tried to keep my voice light, but the pleading was there. Even James sensed it. And he left it alone, gentleman that he was.

He nodded and started the car, pulling carefully out to 98th Street. We were only about three blocks from the office.

"Do me a favour," he said, as he waited for the traffic to give him sufficient room to make the turn. "Get my parking pass out of the glove box, would you? It's an orange tag."

I flipped open the glove box and started digging through the paper and bits of crap that always seem to collect in glove boxes everywhere. "I don't see it," I finally said.

James maneuvered the turn, then glanced at me. "Keep searching. It's in there somewhere. I don't want to get a ticket."

I dove back into the junk-filled glove box one more time, and James watched me do it. Wasn't the best thing for him to do, focussing on the inside of the vehicle like that.

"Son of a gun!" he cried, and slammed on the brakes, nearly driving me into the glove box. I looked up. He'd nearly rear-ended the vehicle ahead of him that had stopped for a pedestrian. A truck following us squealed its tires mightily, and I braced for impact.

Somehow the truck missed us and pulled into the lane adjacent. I scrambled back into the seat and looked out at the vehicle that had almost hit us. I was honestly going to wave apologetically or something, but what I saw froze me. Absolutely froze me.

"Oh my God," I whispered. "It's Arnie."

Arnie was not pleased at being spotted. He began cursing a blue streak, and digging around under his seat for something that had evidently fallen to the floor.

"That's Arnie?" James asked. "What's he doing here?"

"What do you think he's doing? He's following me," I gasped. I couldn't stop staring at Arnie, who stopped digging under his seat when he felt my eyes on him. He looked up, with his crazy, crazy eyes, and I shuddered. He had definitely gone from stalker to psycho.

"We have to get away from him!" I cried.

James shut his mouth, and nodded once, glancing around for some place to go.

Arnie was back digging under his seat, and hadn't been paying attention to an old guy toddling across the street, so when traffic began to move again, James took advantage, pulling in front of him with shrieking tires.

I did some shrieking of my own, then quieted down when it became apparent that we weren't going to die in the first few seconds. I started again when James managed to almost get the Volvo up on two wheels going around the corner onto Jasper Avenue, and then again when he made an illegal left hand turn in front of about two tons of traffic down the hill by the MacDonald Hotel.

"Where are you going?" I yelled, clutching the dash for dear life as we weaved through the traffic on their way down the hill.

"I don't know!" he yelled back, lurching into the right lane, and cutting off a number of vehicles in the process. "I'm trying to get away!"

He blasted down and around, looping back and forth in the maze that is the river valley. I always hated trying to get anywhere down there, but he seemed to have a good handle on where he was going.

"Is he still following us?" he bellowed.

I chanced a backward glance. "Yes."

"Son of a gun!" He found another gear, and blew down Victoria Trail, weaving through traffic like it was standing still.

We went past the Royal Mayfair Golf Club and caused the first accident as a Jaguar that was leaving the parking lot lurched to a stop in order not to be crushed by us, and was promptly rear-ended by the Lexus behind it. Horns started to blow, which caused gawkers driving in the other lane to slow down and stare. This caused the second accident.

James didn't falter, didn't stop and do what was right. He kept blasting hell bent for leather, toward the Groat Road exit, with Arnie rapidly gaining on us.

We got pulled over just past the golf course proper, at a Check Stop. A cop jumped out in front of the car to direct it into the parking lot.

"Son of a gun!" James yelled. The car slewed side to side as he fought to bring it under control. The cop leaped out of the way even though we weren't that close, just seemed that way, the speed we were going—and glared mightily as we pulled to a sliding stop near the other cop cars. It didn't take the police long to pull James out of the car and throw him face down on the ground.

"We were being chased!" I yelled as the cops helped me, a lot more gently, from my seat. I tried to pull loose, so I could point at the big black Ram three quarter ton flying down the street.

"Get him! It's him!" I screamed. I kept screaming and pointing as we all watched the black truck as it slowed down and toddled past the parking lot as though out for a leisurely stroll.

"Son of a gun," James moaned into the gravel as the cops again turned their unwanted attention back to him. "Son of a gun."

Marie:
The Drive to the Office, Part Two

It took us a long time to talk our way out of that one. Actually, it was Sergeant Worth who saved us.

"Talk to Sergeant Sylvia Worth," James kept saying, as the police roughed him up. "She knows us. She knows what's going on."

One of the officers got her on his radio phone, and after that, a couple of the officers who had been lounging around watching us get beat up sped off in their vehicles to see if maybe, maybe, they could track down Arnie's truck that we had all watched scoot merrily away.

James got the ticket, of course, but the police quit threatening him with hauling him downtown to charge him with trying to run down a police officer. One of them even helped him brush the gravel dust off his clothes before they let him back into his car and out on the road again. I for one was glad Sergeant Worth pulled so much weight.

We didn't speak until we were back on the road again.

"Are you all right?" I asked. I was afraid to ask it. He had not been treated kindly, and it was because of me. "I guess we were kind of lucky the police were there. Kind of."

"I knew they were there." James' jaw worked as he maneuvered through the traffic heading back downtown. "I heard it on the radio earlier this evening. I was hoping they'd stayed."

"I'm impressed." And I was. That was quick thinking on his part. "That could've gotten messy."

"Yeah." James sighed the word, and I could tell that as far as he was concerned, that had been messy enough. "I don't know about you, but I'm starving. Want something?"

"Sure."

He pulled into a convenience store parking lot and stopped the car. Gravel rained out of the turned-up cuff of his pants as he got out.

"What would you like to drink? Pop or something?"

"Something stronger." I pointed to the liquor store next door, and tried to smile.

"Scotch, right?"

"Yes." I watched as he entered the convenience store, then turned to Farley.

"Jesus, Farley, he almost caught us. I was so scared . . ."

"He didn't, though. Jimmy boy really came through."

"He did, didn't he?"

"You know he's going to want an explanation, Marie. That freak wasn't after him. He was after you. Now you got him in the middle of this."

"He's already in the middle of this, Farley. I think Arnie caused the fire at his place." I leaned back, and felt truly miserable. I'd brought nothing but trouble down on James, and he was still buying me treats. Why couldn't I be nice to him, at least?

"And he still doesn't know what the hell's going on with me?"

"No. What can I tell him?"

"Tell him as much as you trust him to know."

That was the last thing in the world I wanted to hear. I covered my face with my hands, as though that would block the thought from my head. It did no good, of course. Thoughts like that can leak through lead.

"I don't know if I trust him enough to tell him anything."

"He keeps saving your life, Marie. Hasn't he earned a bit of trust?"

"It's not that. Yeah, he's a good, honourable guy, but that doesn't mean much in the long haul."

"I don't understand."

"Well, they always leave, don't they?" My voice had taken on a shiny, bitter tone, like the ring of a coin that had been polished in acid. I could hear it. It always sounded that way when I talked about my dad.

"They don't always leave."

"Sure they do. You did." I could still hear the bitter tone, and knew, in my heart I knew I was attacking Farley so I didn't have to think about my dad, but couldn't stop myself. "You left your family, didn't you Farley?"

"It was mutual. A different thing." I'd stung him. I could hear it in his voice, and I wished there was a way to take it back, to really explain to him what I meant, but it was not in his best interests—and I didn't want to talk about it with anyone.

"You're not talking about me, I know you're not," he barked. "So who the fuck is it?"

"No-one." I sighed, as I realized I never should have started this conversation with him. "Never mind."

He lost it.

"Jesus, you remind me so much of Rose, I could kick you square in the ass!" he bellowed, throwing around ecto goo as he waved his arms angrily. "You give me some vague or impossible trail to follow in the ups and downs of the emotional roller coaster you all seem to love to live on, and then, when I don't get the hint, you shrug, or sigh, and say, 'Never mind!' What is it with you?"

I didn't have a chance to answer him, because James came back, laden with supplies. As he got into the car, Farley yelled, "That was horse shit, Marie and you know it!" as loudly as he could, and I know he enjoyed it when I flinched away from the noise. Luckily, he settled back, still looking pissed, as we drove back to the office.

I found the parking pass, and watched everywhere for Arnie's truck, but saw nothing out of the ordinary. Farley left as we parked and unloaded the car. I was staggering, I was so tired, but James didn't seem to notice, just walked ahead of me up the stairs and to his dead uncle's office.

"I have to call Jasmine," I said when we were inside. James nodded without looking at me, and wolfed down a sandwich as I sat down in the small secretarial chair that felt like a bit of heaven to my overtaxed muscles, and dialed Jasmine's number.

I'm lucky to have a friend like her. She wasn't mad anymore. She kept asking me how I was, and how sorry things had gone the way they had. The police officer was still there, and was watching TV with her.

"He's cute," she whispered into the phone. "And he likes kids."

I promised to talk to her the next day, to see how things were going, and put the phone down. Farley oozed out of the wall in a very disconcerting manner, and stared at me as I tried to get the strength up to get out of the chair.

"Are the kids all right?" he asked.

I nodded, glancing over at James to make sure he wasn't watching me. He wasn't, and I felt a pang of something close to dismay. Man, I had to get a grip—or at least some sleep.

"I want to see them again. Soon."

I looked back at Farley again, surprised. I hadn't noticed how attached he'd become to Jasmine's kids, but things had been a bit topsy-turvy for me.

"I'm not kidding."

I nodded, not knowing if that was the right thing to do, but unable to think of anything else to do at that point. I'd screwed up everything so royally with him, what could one more mess up matter? I'd think it through in the morning. After I'd slept.

"Good." He faded back against the wall, only his eyes showing where he was.

I hoisted myself out of the chair, imagining this was how it would feel when I was fifty or something. I didn't like the thought of it. I hurt everywhere, and all I wanted was sleep. James had poured me a small shot of scotch.

"How's your friend?" he asked, handing me the glass and scooting over on the rollaway cot that he'd pulled from the other room and opened by the window. "She okay?"

"Yes. She sounds all right, anyhow." I sat down on the cot, and leaned back against the window. "She's entertaining the police officer that stayed with her." I tried to smile. "I think she's in love."

"Good. That's good."

He glanced over at me, and I was certain he was going to start cross-examining me, so I took a big gulp of the scotch, enjoying the burn it made all the way down to my stomach.

"You know that flash drive Sergeant Worth asked you about?"

he asked.

I nearly choked on my scotch as I tried to change mental gears. The flash drive holding all the information I'd gathered about Latterson and Carruthers was the last thing I thought he'd mention.

"Yes."

"I found it in the ambulance after they took you into the hospital. I loaded it on the computer. In case you needed it."

"Thank you." Then I glanced at him. "Why didn't you say something to Sergeant Worth?"

"Because I looked at some of the files, and I don't think you want her to have all the information you have on that thing. Do you?"

"Not really," I muttered.

"I get Carruthers' files. You were trying to link him to Latterson, right? But what was all that stuff about Farley Hewitt?"

It felt like my blood was literally freezing in my veins. I knocked back the last of the scotch. It didn't help.

"I was trying to figure out whether he'd done the deed himself," I said. "You know, whether he'd committed suicide."

"So what about the Three Stages of Acceptance thing?" he asked.

Oh God, he'd looked at a lot more than just a couple of the files. Why had I started that file on Farley? Why oh why?

"Just research," I said, feeling desperate. "I just wanted to figure it out, James."

When I glanced at him, he'd pulled one of the blankets up to his chin and was staring off into space.

"And about your mother?" He spoke nonchalantly, as though the words had no meaning. "Sergeant Worth really acted like there was something going on with her."

"I don't know," I whispered. I grabbed the bottle of scotch and poured myself another shot.

"Or you do know, and you don't want to talk about that, either. Right?"

"Right. I really don't." I turned toward him, trying to sound courageous and sorry, but sounding as tired as I'd ever sounded. "I know. Lots of secrets. I wish—"

"What do you wish?"

"I wish I was like everybody else," I whispered. "No secrets. Everything out in the open."

He frowned. "Do you really think you're the only one with secrets?" he asked.

"No," I said. "I'm sure others do too. Just not so many." I pointed at him. "You, for example. Do you have any secrets?"

I honestly expected him to say no. Not one. My life is an open book.

"Of course I do," he said.

"Stuff you haven't told me about?" I asked, rather stupidly, but I was beginning to feel pretty stupid, I must admit.

"Yes." He wasn't smiling anymore. In fact, his face looked strained. Holy crap, he wasn't kidding. He'd actually been keeping things from me.

"You mean to tell me you've been harassing me—"

"Well, I wouldn't say harassing," he mumbled. I held up my hand for quiet, and he shut his mouth.

"Harassing me," I continued, "and here you are, with secrets of your own?"

"Yes," he said, and had the good grace to look embarrassed.

"So, are you going to tell me?" I asked.

"Tell you my secrets?" he replied. I nodded my head. "No," he said. "I can't. Not now."

"Oh," I said. "Interesting."

"You're right. We're both keeping secrets." James stared at the far wall of the office. I could see sunlight beginning to crawl up that wall. It was almost morning. "How about this? When you're ready, you will talk to me, right?"

"Right. And when you're ready, you'll tell me."

He grunted something that could have been a yes, and pulled the blanket further up around him, closing his eyes.

I put down my glass, and did the same. The last thing I saw, before sleep finally took me, was Farley's eyes, glowing in the early morning sun.

Farley:
Paying a Visit to the Good Sergeant

I decided to let the living sleep, because the dead had things to do. I was going to see what good old Sergeant Worth was doing with her day. That woman knew something about Marie that she wasn't letting on, and I thought maybe I could figure it out.

The good thing was, the cop shop was only five blocks from James' office, so I could actually get there. The bad thing? The cop shop first thing in the morning is not the most pleasant place to be.

They're letting the drunks out—mostly young, mostly male, what is it with young men and drinking until you make a complete ass of yourself and get arrested for drunk and disorderly? Did it myself a time or two, and I still don't know. I hope to God it's not our version of a rite of passage.

Anyhow, I hustled through the maze of corridors and rabbit cage offices, finally finding Worth.

She was sitting hunched over her desk and talking urgently on the phone.

"What's your big news, Lamont? I've had a couple of really shitty days, don't even think about toying with me."

She leaned back in her chair and stared at the ceiling as she listened to Lamont, whoever he was, spouting on. I was ready to leave, because it didn't look like I was going to get anything good, past a quick glance at the framed photograph on her desk. A good looking guy in a uniform, probably the husband, isn't that nice, crime fighting is the family business, with a couple of kids' school pictures tucked into the edges, a boy and a girl, both at the gawky, awkward, just stepping into junior high stage. I realized Sergeant Worth—tough as nails Sergeant Worth—was silently crying. Whoever Lamont was, he wasn't giving her good news.

"Really. That's nice. Good for you. On with your life." She threw open a desk drawer and brought out tissue, grabbing one and pressing it to her face. "Wish Sherrie good luck for me, will you? She's going to need it."

She glanced up at the ceiling again, probably to keep the tears from coming back, and nodded as Lamont—the ex-husband, see it doesn't take me long—kept talking.

"We can talk about this tomorrow. Tomorrow. Come on, Lamont, keep the days straight, will you? It's my weekend with the kids. I'll pick them up around four. Four. Well, change the plans. I haven't seen them in a month. I *know* the last time it was my fault . . . we can't keep going over this pile of shit. Have the kids ready. Yeah. I mean it this time."

She hung up the phone, then picked up the picture sitting on her desk. She carefully plucked the two kids' pictures from the frame, then flung the picture at the wall as hard as she could. Way to go, Lamont. You pissed the woman off.

"Rory, you bastard, what have you done to my life?" she cried as the picture shattered, thin glass and cheap frame spraying all over the wall next to the door.

Rory? Who the hell was Rory?

The door opened slowly, as the bits of glass still rained down to the industrial type carpet on the floor. A fat, red-faced cop stepped into the room, nervously crunching shards of the glass with his well-polished boots.

"Bit of a mess there, Boss. Want me to pick that up for you?"

Worth stared at him wordlessly until he did an anxious little dance, crunching more of the glass as he did so. "Yeah, we got something on the DB in the tree. Want to look it over?"

"Leave it on my desk." Worth's eyes, which had gone flat and dead, never left the fat cop's face.

"Yeah, sure, right boss."

The cop barely took another step into the office, glass

crunching under his feet, before he tossed the file at her. I was surprised he hadn't tried an overhand throw, he was far enough away. The file splayed open in front of her, and I got to see the dead guy the cop had been talking about.

He hadn't been hung in the tree, or set by the tree, or shot under the tree, or anything like that. He'd been crucified. The tree had been his fucking cross. Who the hell would do something like that to another human being? I felt myself go thin, first time in a while, and I turned away as the fat cop made good his escape, slamming the door so hard he almost knocked a commendation award Worth had hung on the wall down to the carpet, too. Then Worth's phone rang behind me, and I jumped about a foot, thinning a little more. Wow, the photo of the dead guy had really spooked me.

I tried to centre my chi, or some such meditation shit, so I could listen to the telephone conversation Worth was having. I didn't need to be blinking out, now that I was finally striking pay dirt. This one was about Marie.

Marie:
Looks Like Business Is Picking Up

The phone started ringing at 7:30. Just two hours after James and I had finally managed to go to sleep.

I lurched to wakefulness—well, more or less to wakefulness— my latest and greatest nightmare trudging back to my subconscious while I flailed around, trying to get up with a body that felt even older than the day before. Man, would I never feel good again?

My flailing woke James. He blinked awake, frowning when the phone rang again.

"What is that?" he asked.

"It's the phone," I said. "Get it."

I could have kicked him when he leaped up, looking completely awake and completely without any aches or pains of any kind. I didn't kick him, though. I was still fighting with the blanket.

He answered the phone cheerfully. Then all cheer fell from him.

"Who is this?" he asked.

"What's going on?" I felt a flutter of fear. "Is it about Arnie?"

He shook his head, still concentrating on the call.

"Yes," he finally said. "Yes. He died two weeks ago. He was on holiday."

Oh. Someone was calling about James' uncle. He'd need coffee to handle this phone call. I finally kicked free of the blanket, and set to work.

As I poured water into the coffee maker, I glanced around, but didn't see Farley anywhere. Went to the inner office. It was empty, too. He appeared to be gone. I wasn't going to worry about him, though, because James was starting to sound a little panicky.

"What's the problem?" I asked as I hobbled back into the reception area.

James slapped his hand over the receiver, looking distraught. "He wants to know when we're having the memorial service."

"For your uncle?" I asked. "Hasn't he been buried?"

"Well, yes," he replied. "But there was no service."

I shrugged. "Tell them that, then."

He spoke quietly into the phone as I poured coffee for both of us, and then hung up. "That was unnerving," he said.

"I guess your uncle had at least one friend," I said, handing him the coffee. "That's nice."

The phone started ringing again. We both stared at it as though it had suddenly been possessed. That phone had only rung once since Jimmy the Dead had died.

"What the heck is going on?" James asked.

"I'll get it," I sighed, and picked up the receiver. "Jimmy Lavall's Detective Agency," I said. "How can I help you?"

Three hours later, the phone was still ringing off the hook. James had hidden in his dead uncle's inner office while I answered the phone, trying to put off all the people who were calling to find out what had happened to his uncle.

"Yes, I know, it came as a shock to all of us," I said. My coffee cup was empty, and I stared wistfully at the coffee machine just out of reach. "No, I'm sorry, I'll have to get back to you about that. Thank you. You're very kind."

Farley stepped through the closed outer door as I hung up the phone.

"Where have you been?" I whispered.

"Cop shop," he said. "I told you I'd check the good sergeant out, so I did."

I was going to drill him about what he'd learned, but James

wandered in, carrying one of the old books from his uncle's bookcase.

"Another one?" he asked.

I nodded.

"So, how many is that?"

"That makes fifteen."

"He had a lot of friends."

"What's going on?" Farley asked. I glanced at him, half-shrugged, and turned back to James.

"All these old friends of your uncle. They want to know when the service is. Where they can send flowers, donations, stuff like that."

"Huh," Farley said. "People checking up on the old fart. Too late, I'd say."

"What are we going to do?" James asked. He held the book like it was a shield. "He's buried."

"I know that, and you know that, but his friends don't," I replied. "Obviously."

"Yeah," James said. "Maybe we *should* have a memorial service. What do you think?"

"'We.' That sounds a bit domestic, doesn't it?" Farley said. Then he shook his head. "Forget that. I have information. Come out into the hallway. We have to talk."

I didn't bat an eye, though my blood pressure rose with the "domestic" comment. He wasn't funny.

I pushed my chair back from the desk, and stretched.

"We can talk about what to do for your uncle later. I have to freshen up. Can you hold the fort for a minute?"

"Yeah, yeah." James barely glanced up from the book he was devouring. I opened the door, and the phone rang again. James didn't move, so I headed back in to take the call.

"He can get it," Farley said shortly. "We need to talk."

"Answer the phone, James," I said. "I'll be back in a minute."

"Righteo!"

I watched him set the book aside, and approach the phone like it was some kind of WMD or something. "Just answer it," I hissed. "It won't bite you."

He trudged to the phone and picked up the receiver. "Jimmy Lavall Detective Agency," he said. "How can I help you?"

"Get out here!" Farley cried. I quickly stepped into the hallway

297

and closed the door.

"You were actually listening to his telephone reception skills, weren't you?" Farley asked incredulously. "Are they up to snuff?"

"Oh, leave me alone." I laughed, that embarrassed "you caught me at stupid shit" laugh people always try when they get caught at something stupid. "What news do you have for me?"

"Like I said, I was over at the cop shop. Looks like they picked up your old boyfriend."

"They what?" I must have heard him wrong.

"Arnie was arrested." Farley sniggered. "Sounds like they put him in the hospital. He deserved that, at the very least."

"What?"

"Arnie Stillwell's in jail."

To be honest, it didn't feel real. I kept waiting for Farley to say, "Just kidding" or something, but he didn't.

I was free.

"And catch this," Farley said, grinning. "The idiot is trying to convince anyone who will listen that our boy Jimmy is the big mastermind behind everything," He snickered again. "Imagine that. Jimmy as a mastermind."

I felt a spike of fear jolt through my heart. "They don't believe him, do they?"

"No," Farley said. "The good sergeant is convinced Jimmy is clean as new fallen snow. Right now, the sergeant is checking to see if Arnie has any connection to Carruthers."

Huh. Well, stranger things have happened. "Have they picked up Carruthers yet?"

"No, but it's just a matter of time, I think. All they need is proof that he would profit if the Palais disappeared. Then he'll be gone, too."

I thought of the information on James' dead uncle's computer. That just might do it. After I removed all evidence of Farley moving through the Three Phases of Acceptance, of course.

My stomach loosened, for the first time in what felt like forever.

"Good," I whispered. "Maybe this will all be done soon."

Farley looked taken aback. "Yeah," he said. "I guess it will. Too bad. It was fun."

"Fun?" I asked. "Getting blown up and threatened and being homeless is fun?"

"Well, maybe not so much fun for you," he said. "But when this is all over, you get to go back to your life. Me? I just go back to being dead."

He was right. I felt like the pressure was off, and I could actually start to live again. James and I were still going to split Helen Latterson's fee when it came in, so money wasn't even going to be a problem anymore. I could look around, figure out what I wanted to do. Heck, maybe I'd go back to school or something. It felt like, for once in my life, all options were open.

Once Farley moved on.

The last time I'd spoken to my mother, she'd suggested that Farley's daughter, Rose, could be the key. And since Farley had actually had a dream about her, maybe he was ready to listen to reason.

"I've been ignoring you, Farley, and I'm sorry," I said. "I think I've figured out how to help you, if you're willing."

"Oh?" He didn't look as excited as I thought he would. Hoped he would.

"I think the reason you haven't moved on yet has to do with your daughter," I said.

"I told you to leave her alone," he growled.

"But she was in your dream," I said, as gently as I could.

"Yeah," he said. "So?"

"There's a reason you're thinking about her, Farley. You have unfinished business, even if you don't think you have. Let me call her. Talk to her. Maybe then—"

He held up his hand, stopping my words. "I said no."

"All right," I replied, trying not to grind my teeth. "But Farley, this could be your last chance to move on. You have to move on. You understand that, don't you?"

"I know!" he cried, and for the first time, he sounded afraid. "Let me think about it, all right?"

"All right."

I hoped he wouldn't take too long deciding, because I was certain all I had to do was get him to reconcile with her, and he'd be able to move on.

"Was there anything else?" I asked, pointing at the closed door. "We're waiting for a call from Helen Latterson. James left her a message about her information, asked her to call back." I touched the door knob, then turned back to him. "Don't worry,

Farley. You won't be stuck here much longer."

As he opened his mouth to say something, I heard the phone ring.

"I gotta go," I said. I left him standing by himself in the hallway, as I went to help James take the phone call that was going to change both our lives for the better.

Farley:
Unwanted and Unloved

I was going to say more to Marie, but the door slammed shut in my face. Yeah, I know, I can ooze through doors like nobody's business, but it hurt, you know? She didn't ask me if I wanted to come in. Like I was finished business, too.

All right, I admit it, I was whining. But I didn't know if I could do what she was asking me to do. I didn't want to face my daughter, because I didn't think it would make a difference, no matter how much it hurt. My daughter was the wrong track. I was sure of it.

However, something was holding me here. I had the sneaking suspicion that I was responsible. I was afraid I was clinging to the land of the living through my connection to Marie, and yeah, even to Jimmy. I was watching them live their lives, and I was content to do so. Like this was enough. My own personal soap opera, live 24/7.

Except—and this was a big except, the biggest except—Marie didn't want me around. I knew that.

If I wasn't here, hanging on to her coat tails, then she could go to school or date Jimmy or get married and have kids, or whatever the hell she wanted. But she couldn't, or wouldn't, if I was still around. Still stuck here. I was her responsibility. Still a big "unfinished" on her to-do list.

I don't know how much longer I would've hung out in the hallway feeling unwanted and unloved if I hadn't heard Jimmy boy yelling at someone in the office. So, I had to go find out what was going on. Hey, my soap's on.

Marie:
Things Go from Decent to—What a Surprise—Worse

"You can't do this, Helen! All right, Mrs. Latterson! We had a deal. We shook on it and everything!"

James was sitting bolt upright in the big comfy executive chair behind the desk in his dead uncle's office, and I was doing nothing more than dancing ineffectively from one foot to the other beside him. I wanted so desperately to tear the phone from him and handle the rest of the conversation, but I couldn't do anything that he wasn't already doing. So all I could do was listen in horror as she reneged on our deal.

"No, that was never part of the deal!" he yelled, pounding his fist on the desk top. "It was one percent plus expenses when we found your money for you. *That* was the deal. No. NO! You can't do that! But—but . . ." He sat straighter in the chair, and his eyes blazed lightning bolts.

"Fine. Fine. Yes, I'll have the expense claim ready with your information. Yes. I understand completely."

He slammed the phone down without saying good bye. Telephone manners out the window, but I wasn't about to say anything. Not when he was as angry as he was. Not when I could smell disaster in the air.

"What happened?"

"She says she's not going to pay us until she has the money in her hands. Just our expenses for the seven hours we were on the job."

"She can't do that!" I yelled, feeling as shocked and angry as James looked. "We did what we said we were going to do. You shook on it and everything. I saw you."

"She says that's not what she meant. She says she meant she'd pay us when she receives the money."

James pushed himself away from the desk and stood up. "That could be years. She has to go through the courts to get her cash, and her ex-husband is in jail. He has other court cases to worry about before this one. And she said if we push it, or hold back the information we have for her, she'll take *us* to court. Son of a bitch!"

"Well, she can't expect us to give her the original bank statements," I said. "After all, those blew up in the—"

"No, they didn't," James replied. "I recovered them, just before the explosion."

"You did? When—how— "I stared, then glared. "You broke into my office?"

"Technically, it was Latterson's office," he replied, and wouldn't look at me. "This has to do with my dirty little secret. I don't think you're going to like it, much."

My mouth dried. "What?" I whispered.

He ran his fingers through his hair, distractedly. "Later, all right? Mrs. Latterson is sending someone over to pick up the envelope. We better get the expense claim ready, or we won't get that money either."

"Well, you had pizza," Farley said, obviously trying to be helpful. "And the tip. And . . ."

I stared at James for a moment, then decided to let his confession go. After all, we had a deal, and I wasn't going to push him. I couldn't really, could I? Not with all the secrets I had.

"How much did your uncle charge? Do you know?"

"No." He looked absolutely miserable. I had the feeling I looked about the same. "He handled all the paperwork."

"Check his files," I suggested. "See what he charged for a day."

James opened the cabinet and pulled out a file at random.

"This is from 1976," he said. "He charged $50.00 per day for his time." He glanced up, caught my ferocious frown, and rammed the file back in the cabinet. "Let me find something else."

James had to go to the bottom file, at the very back, to find the cases his uncle had worked on recently. The last one had been filed one week before he left for his holiday. One month before his death.

"Just tell me how much he was charging so I can write this up." I had found the expense form on the computer, and had it sitting on the screen waiting for input.

"$200 a day. That's what this invoice says, anyhow."

"Good enough." I hammered away at the keys, typing in $230.00. "She can pay for the pizza on top of that."

"Two hundred dollars isn't too bad," James mumbled, still poring over the old case file.

"Yes, it is," I said. "Compared to $75,000.00, it is."

"I know." James put the file back. "But it will have to do, until we figure out another way to get what's owed us."

I printed off the invoice and rammed it into an envelope, then glanced over at James, who had pulled another file and was reading intently. "What's that?" I asked.

He jumped as though I'd used a cattle prod on his delicate parts, and nearly dropped the file. "Just seeing what Uncle Jimmy was up to."

He spoke apologetically, as though I'd caught him at something he shouldn't have been doing. I felt bad. He could read whatever he wanted. This was, after all, his place. I tried to make my voice sound softer. It wasn't his fault Helen Latterson had done what she'd done.

"Sorry, James. What did you find?"

"Looks like he was investigating whether a woman was cheating on her husband."

"Oh. Was she?" I lost interest, and went back to the computer, trying to figure out where to file the teeny tiny invoice we'd made.

"Yeah. Yeah, she was. Wanna know who he was tailing?"

"Will I care?"

"Maybe. It was Sergeant Worth."

"What?" Oh, James had my attention with that one. Even Farley perked up a bit.

"Yeah. Uncle was following her for a couple of weeks. She was fooling around with another cop."

"Rory," Farley breathed. I glanced over at him, then back to James.

"Who was it?"

"Callahan, Rory Callahan. Uncle took pictures and—whoops!" He closed the file abruptly, his face flushed deep red. "He has pictures."

"Oh." I didn't want to see the photos, though Farley scurried over to check them out, old goat. James rammed the file back into the cabinet and slammed it shut.

"Do you think she knew about your uncle investigating her?" I asked.

"She couldn't have." James closed the file with a metallic thud. "If she had, she would've given us a much harder time. On general principle."

He stared at the closed cabinet as though he was still seeing the pictures. "Maybe her husband never used the information. Maybe she didn't know he'd suspected anything. Maybe they're still together."

"Nope, they're divorced," Farley piped up. "She talked to him this morning. Something about who gets the kids this weekend." He shook his head. "I don't think it was terrifically amicable."

I turned to James. "I think he probably did use the information," I said, before I really thought.

"Why?" James glanced at me suspiciously. It didn't take much for him to look at me that way. "What do you know?"

"It's a feeling I had. She acted like someone who was divorced. Sad. She has that sad thing going on." I backpedaled as hard as I could, and James almost seemed satisfied with the answer. Almost. "So, I don't know for sure that she's not still with her husband, it's just a feeling I have. Don't be so touchy!"

"All right." He frowned. "There's a lot you don't tell me, though. It puts me on edge."

"He's got you there." Farley leaned against the wall, obviously enjoying my discomfort. I hate getting caught like that.

"I thought we had a deal about the secrets," I said, stiffly. Why couldn't he just leave this all alone? After all, he had secrets. Why couldn't I?

"It's just, you have a lot of them. Your mother. And the dead guy. Farley. Right?" I could see Farley jump a bit, hearing his name coming out of James' mouth. It made me feel a bit better. Nasty I know, but it did.

"Please don't push, James." I wanted him to leave it all alone. I wanted him to just be the nice James who only wanted to date me—not the other James who wanted to know all about me.

"Are you ever going to tell me?"

"I don't know," I whispered. And that was the absolute truth.

"Oh."

I could tell that wasn't what James had wanted to hear. He wanted a full confession, and a real date, and to live happily ever after or something, but I couldn't give him any of that. I glanced over at Farley. Not with him hanging around. Not with any of them.

"I'm trying to be honest, James. You want me to be honest, don't you?"

"Well, yeah."

I had the feeling he would have taken a lie. He wanted me to say something that could give him some kind of hope that he was being invited into my life.

I couldn't do that. No matter how much it hurt him.

"So, that's what I'm being. Honest. Can you accept that?"

"I'll try." He didn't act like he was trying very hard. His jaw had set, and he turned back to the file cabinet without another word. He opened the lowest drawer and began to read through another of his uncle's old cases.

I turned back to the computer, and opened another document. The least I could do was help James figure out his dead uncle's online filing system, but all I got was another one of his stupid Solitaire games. The old man had them stuffed everywhere. It looked like he'd saved every game he'd lost, like he was going to go back and redo them, when he had the time. I sighed, and closed it. He'd run out of time for that, too.

"So, what're you going to do now?" Farley asked. He'd snuck up behind me, and I tried not to jump. "He isn't going to wait forever for you to decide you trust him, you know. The way you're going, he'd probably be happy if you disappeared off the face of the earth."

I pressed a button, and a blank screen popped into view.

"I don't need your help." I typed quickly, then glanced at him to make sure he read it, before pushing another button, deleting the page. He frowned as he read the words.

"Fine," he said. "I'll leave you alone. Watch me disappear, just like that page. Watch me."

I half expected him to vanish in a puff of smoke or something, even though he couldn't do that. All he does is ooze through doors and walls and things, and it looked like he was trudging toward the door to do just that when James set down the file he'd been examining.

"Marie?"

"Hmm?" I didn't look up from the screen. If he wanted to interrogate me some more, he could go ahead. I wasn't playing.

"The police called, while you were—indisposed. Just before Mrs. Latterson."

That caught my attention. "What did they want?"

"They wanted to let you know that Arnie Stillwell has been arrested."

I blinked, and felt my throat tighten. All right, so I already knew about Arnie—but somehow, hearing it from someone living seemed to make it all real.

"Wanna get some breakfast, to celebrate?"

From the set of his jaw before he'd turned back to the files, I would've thought food would be the last thing on his mind. I grabbed a tissue and touched it to my eyes, then tried to smile.

"That would be fantastic," I said. "If you want to."

"I do," he said.

"Are we okay?" I whispered.

James stared at me for what felt like forever, then nodded. "Yeah. I think so."

I could have danced for joy, but I didn't. "Then yes. I'd like some breakfast to celebrate."

"There's a place downstairs, maybe we can try it out after Helen picks up the invoice."

"Can we give her a hard time?" I asked hopefully. "After all, she is treating us horribly."

James shrugged. "Let's leave that until we get all our money," he said. "It'd be terrible if she didn't even pay us for this."

He had a point.

"Fine," I said. "But after she pays us out—"

"We verbally destroy her," he said.

I smiled. I liked that idea. A lot.

As we waited for Mrs. Latterson, James went back to his book, and I continued cleaning out all the garbage files on his dead uncle's computer. I dearly wanted to open the files I'd stolen from Ian Carruthers' computer, the ones James had loaded while I was in the hospital, but I did not want him to catch me deleting all references to Farley and moving on and all that stuff. The instant I was alone, I was doing it, but right at that moment, I didn't go near it.

I thought I had lots of time. I really did.

Marie:
Following the Money

Helen hadn't come to pick up the invoice herself, so I couldn't have harassed her even if I'd wanted to. She'd sent some big—and I'm talking really big—guy rammed into an expensive looking suit to get it for her. He tried the door handle, rattling it a couple of times so hard he set the glass ringing, then gave it a turn, and it popped open. He looked surprised that it had opened. Looked even more surprised to see me at the coffee station, getting the millionth cup of the day.

"Can I help you?" I asked.

"Are you Marie Jenner?" the big guy asked. To be honest, he was bigger than big. He was like a mountain dressed in a really expensive looking suit and Italian leather shoes. He made me nervous.

So nervous I said, "Yes," instead of telling him to go to hell.

"You got something for me?" he asked. His voice sounded like it was coming from the centre of the earth or something. He held out a hand that was as big as a foot, and waggled sausage fingers at me.

I handed him the envelope, and he rammed it into his inside breast pocket. "We'll be in touch," he said. "Soon."

James sauntered into the reception area, his nose still in the book he'd been reading.

"Look who Helen sent," I said.

James looked up, and shrugged. "Make sure your contract's iron clad," he said to the big guy. "She'll rip you off, just like she did us."

The big guy's forehead creased as he frowned. "Who are you talkin' about?" he asked.

"Helen Latterson," James said. "Don't let her rip you off."

He looked at me, smiling at his joke, then back at the big guy, who was staring at him, frowning hugely. Man, everything this guy did was huge.

When the big guy said, "Mrs. Latterson. Right," sounding like he'd never heard her name before in his life, I knew we had a problem.

James turned to me as the big guy left, slamming the door shut so hard I was certain the glass was going to shatter.

"I have a question," James asked.

"What?" I said, reaching for my sweater.

"Do you think that guy really works for Mrs. Latterson?"

I stopped, and turned to him. "No," I said. "I really don't."

"Neither do I," James said.

"That's why I've decided to follow him," I said.

James chuckled. "You?"

"Don't you think I can follow somebody?" I asked. "I can do it." I pulled on my sweater. "Watch me."

"Good grief," James said, taking me by the arm. "Nobody can take a joke today."

"Maybe because you're not funny," I said.

"Yes, I am," James said. "I'm hilarious."

"How about if I follow him," Farley said. "While you play the sexual tension game with Jimmy boy."

I wished for just a second that I could touch Farley, because I would have slapped him for the sexual tension comment, but then I realized that Farley had actually come up with a good idea. He'd have much better luck following the big guy than I would. I nodded, and Farley dove through the door.

"Fine," I said, to James. "You're hilarious. Now, what are we going to do about the mystery man?"

"I say we call Sergeant Worth and let her know," James said, pulling out his cell phone and pressing a button. He had Worth's number on speed dial. "And then we go for breakfast."

"Breakfast?" I'd forgotten the celebration breakfast.

"Aren't you hungry?" he asked.

"I'm starving," I replied. That was the honest truth.

James' smile faded as he obviously got the sergeant's voicemail. He left a brief message telling her to call him back, then grabbed my hand and pulled me to the door.

"Let's see what he's driving," he said. "My guess, a Lincoln Navigator."

I shrugged. I had no idea what one of those looked like.

We opened the door, and the hallway was empty. We ran down the three flights of stairs and out into the street. The big guy was gone. So was Farley.

"Son of a gun," James said. "He was fast."

"It's all right," I said. "Worth will figure out who he is. Let's go get breakfast."

"Okay," he said. But he didn't sound like he was all that hungry anymore.

I wished I could tell him that I had a tail on the big guy, but I couldn't.

More secrets.

As I followed James into the restaurant, I wished for the briefest of moments that I had no more secrets. None at all.

Farley:
Following the Mountain . . .

I'd never had the chance to ride in a Lincoln Navigator before. Nice ride, and the bruiser behind the wheel handled the car like a real pro. As he drove, he pulled out the envelope Marie had given him. Looked at the name scrawled across the front, snorted, and pulled his cell phone free.

"Yeah, hi," he said after a long wait. "Is he in? I got an issue here." Then he sat, a massive stone statue with a cell phone glued to its head, while he waited to be connected to whoever had sent him over.

So, Marie was right. This guy had not been sent by Helen Latterson. Who was the "he" this bruiser was waiting to talk to?

"Yeah, hi." The mountain finally moved, shifting the cell phone and sitting straighter as he spoke. "I went to talk to Jenner like you told me to—but she handed me an envelope." He glanced down at the envelope. "It's addressed to Helen Latterson. Yeah. Latterson. L-A-T—yeah, yeah, that's right. When I saw the name, I thought you'd want to see it. So, I booked."

He tore open the envelope, obviously at the command of whoever was his boss. He stared at the papers for a long moment, then shifted the cell back up to his ear.

"Looks like a bill. $230.00. For services rendered. Plus photocopies of some bank statements."

The big guy shifted uncomfortably. He had no idea what he was holding in his hand, and since there was no-one to beat up or squeeze the life out of, he obviously wanted to shift the thinking duties to someone else.

"You wanna see it? Yeah. I'm on my way." He clicked off the phone, and heaved a sigh as he kicked the Navigator to high gear, heading to the good end of down town.

I crossed my fingers, hoping wherever he was heading was within my stupid ten block radius, and for once, I was in luck. At nine and a half blocks, we stopped in front of a glass and steel tower, and the bruiser shoehorned himself out of the Navigator. He entered the building, heading for the elevators. It didn't take long before we were packed in that elevator with a lot of other people, and let me tell you, I was making many of them extremely nervous. We shot up to the twenty-first floor. It didn't surprise me at all when I saw the name on the door as the bruiser pushed his way into the office. "C&R Holdings." Coulda made money on a bet like that.

The bruiser barely glanced at the petite woman sitting behind the desk as he walked to a door to an interior office. As he reached out to put his hand on the door knob, the door flew open and Carruthers stepped through, acting a lot less cool, calm, and collected than usual. The big guy jumped back like a frightened girl.

Without a look up—way up—Carruthers hooked a finger at the guy and turned back into his office. The bruiser followed, as meek as a lamb. He shut the door behind him, then stood, quietly, before the desk.

"I told you to take care of Marie Jenner," he said.

"She's not going anywhere," the big guy replied, but he sounded nervous. Really nervous. "I think you want to see what she handed me."

"Give them to me," Carruthers said, and the big guy handed over the envelope, apologizing quietly for having ripped it. Carruthers paid him no heed, placing the sheets of paper before him on the desk and staring at them, going from one to the next very deliberately. If the vein on his forehead hadn't started to throb, you would've sworn he was reading the Sunday funnies.

"That idiot!" he finally growled. "I told him to treat his wife with more respect. Look at this!"

The big guy obediently stared down at the pages on the desk top. They were upside down, and he had no clue what they meant anyway, but he stared at them all the same. "Just look at what that idiot has done," Carruthers said again, his voice sounding strangled.

"Yeah boss." The big guy hung there, staring at the pages, waiting for his next instructions.

"I have had just about enough of Miss Marie Jenner," Carruthers said. "She has to go." He tapped the photocopies of the bank statements. "So does Helen Latterson, unfortunately. Make her disappear. Make them both disappear. Understand?"

"Yeah, sure thing, boss." He turned to leave, stopping when Carruthers rapped his knuckles, hard, on his desk. "This gets handled today. Both of them. Today! Understand?"

"Yeah. No problem."

"Try not to hurt the kids."

The big guy nodded, then his forehead knotted. "What about the guy the Jenner broad is hanging around with?"

"The caretaker? Eliminate him, too. He's nothing to me."

"Got it."

So did I. I got it in spades. I needed to get back to Marie before the big guy found them and killed them. Killed them all.

Marie:
Breakfast, and What Happened After That

Breakfast was great, until Farley came back. I was slopping a piece of brown toast in the last of the egg yolk left on my plate when he burst into the restaurant, screaming his head off.

"Helen!" he yelled, flying through a number of patrons, and putting about half the breakfast crowd off their eggs and bacon. "It's Helen!"

I was proud of myself. I didn't jump when he exploded into the room screaming like a banshee. I wanted to enjoy the last of my breakfast, and nipped off a piece of the yolk-soaked bread, and rolled my eyes at him. So the big guy actually had been sent by Mrs. Latterson. What could possibly be the problem with that?

"It's Helen!" he yelled again. Louder this time. As though he thought it would help.

"So, do you think Mrs. Latterson will pay that invoice?" I asked James. "Or will she try to stiff us for that, too?"

"Only if the big guy was really working for her," James said. "However, Sergeant Worth can deal with that." He turned back to his own piece of toast, which was generously slathered with strawberry jam.

I gave Farley my best "What's your problem" look, and turned back to my meal.

"The guy who picked up the envelope wasn't sent by Helen

Latterson," Farley said. "He was one of George Carruthers' goons. Carruthers sent him to talk to you about the $50,000 cheque. You remember that? He hadn't heard from you, and was making absolutely sure you were doing what you'd promised. "

I gasped. It was Tuesday. He'd been expecting a call from me, thanking him for the $50,000, and promising I would leave town, and stay out of his life forever. Instead, I'd sent him an invoice intended for Latterson's wife, with photocopies of the bank statements that showed Carruthers had paid Latterson two days before Farley had been killed.

"He took one look at the bank statements and went ballistic," Farley continued. "He said that you had just signed Latterson's wife's death warrant, and told the goon you both had to die. Jesus, Marie, the goon is going to Helen's house right now, because of what was in that envelope. And he's going to kill you next! So quit screwing around with the toast and call the fucking cops! Right now!"

I threw down my knife and fork and pushed my chair back so fast it slammed into the chair behind it.

"I have to go," I said to James, who was staring at me, openmouthed, strawberry jam dripping from his toast. "I have to make a phone call."

"Right now? You're not finished with your breakfast —" Then he really looked at me. "What's wrong?"

"Please pay the bill and come up to the office. I'll tell you as much as I can when you get there. God, I have to go!"

I dashed for the door, more frightened than I had been in a long time. I could feel James watching me, a thoughtful expression on his face, but I didn't have time for him. I had to phone the police.

I tried getting hold of Sergeant Worth, but her phone was still going to voicemail, so I dialed 911 instead. Explained everything as well as I could, and that Sergeant Worth should be informed. "Please send police to Helen Latterson's house right now. She's going to be killed, and it's because of me. Something I did. You've got to save her. Please!"

I was still on the phone when Farley came in. I was impatiently drumming on the desk with my fingernails, then really had a look at them. They were ragged. The past few days had done nothing for my manicure.

"You and Jimmy boy are in trouble, too," he said. "Did you mention that?"

No, I hadn't. In my haste to try to save Helen, I'd forgotten that James and I were next on Carruthers' kill list.

"I think I'm a target too," I said. Saying it out loud like that frightened me so much, I started to cry. "Please stop him. Please."

I grabbed an invoice sitting on the desk and read the address to the operator. "That's where I am. Please hurry. Yes. I will. Yes I'll stay on the line. Thank you. Thank you."

I covered the receiver with one hand, and leaned back in my seat, suddenly too exhausted to move.

"Everything I do turns to shit," I whispered. "I can't keep going on like this."

"Oh, come on, don't be so hard on yourself," Farley said, looking like he couldn't believe he was going to have to give me the "Come on, buck up speech," not when there was a hired thug coming to do major damage if the cops didn't catch him first.

I couldn't move. Couldn't even put the phone back up to my ear, even though I could hear the emergency operator calling my name. I sat in the chair like a rag doll, staring up at the ceiling.

"Not everything you do turns to shit," he said.

"Name something that hasn't."

He thought for a bit.

"Can't think of one thing, can you?" I knew he wouldn't be able to. It was all my fault.

"Well, not off the top of my head, but give me a minute." He thought a bit more, and then shrugged. "You've had an eventful couple of weeks."

He tried to keep his voice light, like I had all the time in the world. Like there wasn't a big, probably ugly guy coming to kill me. Still I couldn't move. It *was* all my fault.

"You can think all day," I said. "You won't come up with anything."

I put the phone back to my ear. "Yes, I'm still here," I said to the 911 operator, and then slapped my hand over the receiver again.

"What should I do now?"

"I would suggest getting the hell out of here," he said. "If you want to live."

"First I have to get rid of some of those files," I turned on the computer. "Before the cops get here."

I clicked on the Farley file, and deleted the document that James had read. The one about Farley moving through the Three Phases.

"What was wrong with me?" I asked. "Starting a file like that?"

"Maybe you wanted somebody to find it," Farley said. "Maybe you want somebody to know your secrets."

"No," I said, making absolutely sure the deleted document was gone, never to be retrieved. "If people knew everything about me, they'd think I was crazy or something. And then they'd leave."

"Not everybody leaves," Farley said. Then he glanced over at the half-closed door and frowned. "Where is Jimmy? It wouldn't take a monkey this long to pay a fucking restaurant bill."

"I don't know."

I opened the document I'd taken from Carruthers' computer called "my bio" and stared at it, wondering if I needed it, or if I should delete it too.

"Did I tell you that I finished reading Carruthers' biography? He met Don Latterson in college. They were best buds."

"Interesting," Farley said. "I guess."

I decided to keep it, and moved on to the next document. It was the spreadsheet Carruthers had put together, showing how he would turn downtown Edmonton into Las Vegas north, if he could just get rid of the Palais. That one needed to stay, too.

Farley looked back at the door. "I have a suggestion, since it looks like you're not going to leave this office. Instead of dicking around with the computer, why don't you come up with ways to protect yourself?"

"Why? We got them," I said, holding up the receiver. "It's all good."

"Just call it a feeling," he replied. "At least lock the fucking door. Something."

I shook my head. "I have to wait for James."

Farley frowned and pointed at the partially open door. "Maybe that's who I hear," he said. "I think he's listening to you, Marie."

"Jesus," I growled. "Just what I need."

If James was outside that door eavesdropping on me, after all our talk about being able to keep our own secrets until we were ready to divulge, then it was a good thing I'd called the police. I was going to kill him.

I dropped the telephone receiver on the desk and stormed over to the door.

"James," I said, flinging open the door. "You promised my secrets were my own."

That's when I found James lying unconscious in the doorway of the outer office, and George Carruthers standing outside the door, listening to every word I'd said.

See? I was right. Everything I touch does turn to shit.

Marie:
Looking Down the Barrel of a Gun

I always thought if I ever found myself face to face with a maniac with a gun that I'd keep my cool and figure out a way to disarm him, possibly with a neat karate move or something. It didn't happen quite that way.

I barely even saw Carruthers past the barrel of the gun. It looked huge, and deadly, and I knew at that instant that I was going to die. So, I screamed like a girl and tried to slam the door shut. It didn't work. Carruthers got his foot in the door, then muscled his way inside.

I made a move toward the desk, thinking that if I could get the desk between him and me, I'd be a teeny bit safe. "Stand perfectly still," Carruthers said, in a slow measured tone that did nothing to make me feel any better at all.

I stopped, and went back to staring at the black hole of the business end of the gun. It was starting to look a mile across.

"Where's your friend?" he asked.

"He's out there with his head kicked in, you bastard!" Farley yelled.

I didn't say a word. Just stared at the gun, and tried to keep from wetting myself.

Carruthers looked around. "I heard you talking to someone in here. Who was it?"

"I'm right here, you prick!" Farley screamed, which did no good whatsoever.

"There's no one here but me." I tried to make my eyes move, to look at Carruthers, but I couldn't. They were glued to the end of that gun. "I was talking to myself."

"Oh." Carruthers glanced around the room, then back at me. "You talk to yourself. Well, who knew." He brought the gun up a hair, so that is was pointing at my head. "Stand perfectly still. You and I need to have a talk."

I couldn't have moved if I wanted to. I felt absolutely frozen.

"Good girl." Carruthers took a deep quick breath in, and blew it out, as though steadying himself. "Very good. Now I want to be very clear about this next bit, because if I'm not and you screw it up and I end up killing you, I would feel bad. Understand?"

I nodded.

"Where have you put the originals?"

"The what?" I could barely breathe out the words.

"The original documents. Where are they?"

"I don't know what you're talking about." I hazarded a glance up at him, and wished I hadn't. Believe it or not, the look on that man's face was more frightening than the gun barrel. He looked like he was ready to pull that trigger. Like he didn't care whether he got the documents. Like he just wished I was dead.

"Quit playing with me, girl. I've had as much as I can stand. You have fucked up EVERYTHING—" and he suddenly screamed the words as fury overtook him—"EVERYTHING since the Palais. You stole my files from the computer in my old office, and you read my biography, which is in the first draft stage and you should never read the first draft of anything . . ."

He took another deep breath, trying to pull himself together, and then spoke in a monotone that scared me more than his screaming fit had. "Get me the bank statements you stole from Don Latterson's office right now, before I put a bullet between your eyes. Have I made myself clear yet?"

"Yes. You have. Please don't kill me, I know what you want now, I was scared, they're in the desk drawer, can I go back and get them?"

I had no idea where James had put the originals of the bank statements. I just needed to figure out a way to keep the maniac from pulling that trigger before the cops arrived. The emergency operator was still on the line, and if I could just get close enough to the receiver, she'd hear everything.

Finally, I'd have a witness who wasn't dead. If I could survive the next five minutes.

I was so afraid, I could barely control the shaking of my hands as I pointed at the desk. Carruthers took a menacing step toward me, and I cowered back.

"Please, please, please, don't hurt me," I begged. "I'll do whatever you want. I promise. Just don't pull the trigger. Please!"

"Jesus, shut up!" he barked. "Yes, go to the desk. Get them, right now."

I skittered over to the desk, trying not to look at the telephone receiver sitting next to the keyboard. "Do you want me to delete your biography from this computer?" I asked. My voice sounded so shaky, I almost didn't recognize it.

"That's a good idea," he said. "Delete all the files. You have three minutes."

"All the files off the computer? I'll need more time than that." The gun came up and aimed between my eyes again, and I nodded. "Okay."

Very carefully, I sat down at the keyboard. "I'll delete the files first, okay?" I said. I started clicking on the keyboard, my hands still shaking so badly, I couldn't make the stupid thing work properly, and all I brought up was one of James' dead uncle's Solitaire games. I deleted it, and Carruthers smiled. He obviously thought I'd deleted some of his stuff. So I clicked on one more of the Solitaire games, and deleted it, too. Just as long as he stayed on the other side of the desk, I didn't need to lose any of the proof I'd gathered. However, if he decided to watch what I was doing, and caught me deleting nothing more than Solitaire games, I was dead. Literally dead.

"Once I'm done here, I'll get the bank statements," I said. My voice sounded strangled. "Would that be all right?"

"Whatever." Carruthers acted bored, and the stubby nose of the gun pointed down, a little. "I have a meeting in half an hour, and it's across town."

"Oh."

I heard a faint noise from the reception area of the office. I glanced up at Carruthers' face, but he didn't look like he'd heard it. "What kind of meeting?" I asked.

"Have you lost your fucking mind?" Farley cried. He looked absolutely beside himself, but I wished he'd shut up. I needed to listen, hard. "He's a fucking looney, don't antagonize him . . . "

I chanced a glare at him, and he looked confused, but shut his mouth. Thank goodness. If James was waking up, we were still in lots of trouble. But if it was the police . . .

"It's none of your business, little girl," Carruthers said. He brought the gun barrel back up to level. "Get to work on those files. You have two minutes."

"No, a minute can't have passed yet," I said. "Are you sure a minute's gone by?"

I glanced past him to the half-open door, seeing a grand total of nothing in the darkened reception area. I hammered away at the keys, bringing up files and deleting, deleting. "It only felt like a half minute," I said. "Maybe even less than that. Maybe it's because you have a gun pointed at me that time feels like it's slowing down. Is that the way that works? If a gun is pointed at your face, time slows down, but if you're holding the gun, time seems to go by quicker?"

Movement. I saw movement in the darkened reception area. I prayed it wasn't James, and looked at Carruthers again. I could tell by the look on his face that he suspected nothing.

"I'm sure it was only half a minute," I said again, trying to fill the office with the sound of my voice so he wouldn't suspect anything until it was too late. "Did you look at your watch? Does it have a stopwatch feature? Maybe you can time me—"

"Shut up!" Carruthers yelled. I'd gone too far, because he'd pulled the gun up to eye level again, and all I could see was the big black hole, with his crazy eyes just above it, and movement behind him, dark movement behind him . . .

"Put the gun down." Sergeant Worth touched her gun to Carruthers' left ear. He screamed and inadvertently shot off a round, hitting the computer monitor right in front of me.

I screamed and threw myself to the floor under the desk, then watched as Sergeant Worth deftly knocked Carruthers on his ass and took the gun away from him, tossing it to the side before quickly handcuffing him.

"Clear!" Before the words were properly out of her mouth, a bunch of guys in uniform hut-hutted into the small office and swarmed over Carruthers. Then they hut-hutted out again, with

Carruthers in tow. He'd howled out his outrage once, but after he'd been tased to bring him under control, he got really meek really fast. Then he was gone.

"Are you all right?" Worth walked over to the desk, where I was still cowering and making little screechy noises. "Are you hurt?"

"I'm safe," I whispered. "I'm really safe." Then I bounded out from behind the desk like a demented gazelle and grabbed the flabbergasted cop in a bear hug.

"Oh my God, it was you, I thought it was you, but then I was afraid it was James and that if that guy heard him, he'd go back and kill him—and Oh! My! God! You saved my life!"

I kept pulling her around in circles, doing my version of a dance of joy until Worth none too gently pushed me away from her.

"Is James all right?" I asked. Then fear pierced my heard when she didn't answer immediately. "He isn't—"

Farley popped in from the reception area. "Quit screaming," he said. "He's alive."

"He'll need to go to the hospital," Worth said. "Nasty bump on the head, he'll need X-rays, but I think he'll be all right."

"Did you save Helen Latterson?"

"Yes," Worth said. "She'll be fine. We picked up Big Randy Ferguson, too. Thanks for the tip, Marie. You saved that woman's life." She stared at me oddly for a moment. "Some day, you'll have to tell me how you did that."

"But not today," I said. "All right?"

Worth laughed. "You know what, I'll give you that. But some day." She pointed to the telephone receiver still sitting next to the keyboard on the desk. "Who's on the line?" she asked.

"Emergency operator," I said. "Tell her thank you."

"Will do," she said.

As she quickly brought the operator up to speed, I grinned at Farley like a fool. I couldn't say anything to him, of course. But I could smile.

Worth and her cronies quickly emptied the office of anything that was remotely connected to Carruthers. They took the computer tower, and went through the desk drawers, taking the file that held all the original bank statements, which were in the drawer I'd pointed out to Carruthers when I thought he was going to kill me.

I guess I know James better than I thought.

Worth looked at the file cabinets, but didn't touch them. "If we need anything, we'll be back," she said. I nodded at her, wondering if James would want to remove the sergeant's file before that happened.

Some secrets are better kept.

Then, she turned to me.

"You really kept your head, Marie. Nice work. Now, we're moving James to the hospital. You want to go along? He'd probably like to see a friendly face when he wakes up."

"That would be great, Sergeant. Thank you." I followed the cop out of the inner office, and to the hallway. That's when I realized Farley hadn't followed me, so I went back.

He was standing in the reception area, staring out the window.

"What are you doing, Farley?" I whispered. "I'm going to the hospital. You have to come. Remember?"

"No," he said. When he turned, his eyes were glowing, and I felt a jolt of something close to fear. Was he going to move on? He wasn't ready yet. He hadn't figured out what he needed to figure out.

But then, they faded back to normal. "No," he said again. "I think I'll just stay here."

"The hospital's more than ten blocks away," I said. "You know you'll get yanked to wherever I am—"

"No," he said. "I don't think that's going to happen anymore. You have proved beyond a shadow of a doubt that you can take care of yourself. You don't need me. Do you?"

I stared at him, wondering if, just maybe, he was right. Had I been the one who had linked us? Was it really as simple as me letting him go?

"I'm sorry if I did that to you," I whispered.

"Go, look after Jimmy boy," he said. "I'll hold down the fort."

"And you'll be here when I get back?" I asked. I heard the doors to the ambulance slam shut, and knew if I was going to go, I had to go now. "Promise me you will be."

"I promise," he said.

Farley:
Meeting One of My Own

Marie and James were gone for hours, so I tried to take a nap. I hadn't gone to nothingness in a long time, and thought maybe I needed one, and besides I was bored, but it didn't happen. So, instead, I went for a walk.

I went over to the crucifixion church—the one I'd seen in the police photos on Sergeant Worth's desk. I don't know why I went, but I did.

There wasn't much going on. All the yellow tape was gone. There were a few people still milling around, staring at the tree, at the church front, talking quietly amongst themselves. If there hadn't been so much blood on the trunk of the tree—and on the lower branches, and the grass around it—it would have been a peaceful scene.

One guy sat on the church steps, staring out at nothing. He looked like a drug addict who needed another fix to get him through a very long day. He also looked like he'd taken a real shit kicking at some time in the recent past. I walked past him to get to the tree, and he stood up and wandered over. He ended up standing next to me.

"Got any change?" he asked. He was staring at the tree, which was pretty hacked up, probably from the emergency guys getting the body down. "I really need to get some food in me. I don't feel so good."

I didn't answer him. No reason to. Nobody can see me but Marie.

"Come on, just a couple of bucks."

I glanced around, but there was no-one near the guy. Just me.

"Are you talking to me?" I said, feeling like an idiot. Of course he wasn't talking to me. No-one talks to me except Marie.

"Well, yeah." The guy seemed confused. "I need a coupla bucks . . ."

I moved to the right, and sure as shit, his eyes followed me.

"Are you all right?" the guy asked, shuffling a couple of steps away from me as though it suddenly occurred to him that maybe he should be a bit afraid.

"How do I look to you?" I asked. "Do I look clear to you?"

"Clear?" The guy shuffled another step away, and I followed him. I wasn't letting him get away that easily.

"Yeah, clear, you know, like glass."

"Do you think you look like glass?"

Jesus, the idiot was talking to me like I was a retard or something. "Tell me how I look to you. I'll get you some money if you tell me."

I figured Marie would like to meet someone else who could see ghosts. All I had to do was persuade him to come back to the office with me. She had to see this!

The other guy shrugged. "All right, I'll go along. You look old, kinda fat, and you're wearing sandals with socks." He bent over, really had a look at my foot and shuddered. "Man, you shoot off your toe or something? That looks bad."

No worse than he looked. But why wasn't he seeing me as clear? That didn't make any sense.

"So I don't look like glass to you?"

"No, you don't." The guy looked impatient as well as sick. "I did what you asked. Gimme the money. I really don't feel good."

"I don't have any money on me," I said, and pointed down the street. "I gotta a friend though, lives couple of blocks over, if you come with me, I'll get you some."

"Son of a bitch." The guy turned away from me.

"Really," I said. I was hoping he'd come with me, so Marie could explain why he didn't see me the way she did. The way I saw myself. "I'll take you to my friend, she'll give you money."

"Fuck off." He sat down on the steps of the church, and looked like he was about to cry. "The first guy that acts like he sees me, and he's a fucking looney. Fuck off and leave me alone. I don't feel good."

He pulled his legs up to his chest, then flopped over in the fetal position. People walked around him as though he wasn't there. It wasn't until someone walked through him that I finally got it.

"Oh my God, you're dead," I said.

I wheeled away from him, and then left. Another ghost. As if Marie needed anything like that in her life. She was stuck with me. Wasn't that enough?

I guess not.

Funny how the world takes great delight in kicking a guy—or a girl—when she's down. I got back to the office just as Marie's mother was leaving a voicemail message, for Marie. It was about me.

The gist? I'm still not ready to move on. I had something more to learn about the way I lived my life. What I knew for sure was, I'd barely lived my life at all, but something about that pathetic attempt was still holding me here.

Isn't that sad? Isn't that just about the saddest thing you've ever heard in your life?

Poor Marie. And poor me.

Marie:
Back from the Hospital, Once More

By the time James and I got back to the office from the hospital, the sun was going down. I managed to manhandle him up the stairs and into the office, him weaving around like he'd had way too much to drink, and me weaving around just as bad, as I tried to keep him upright.

I had been surprised when they let him go, to be honest. It had looked like they were going to keep him overnight, so Sergeant Worth and the rest of the cops had left. That's when a doctor came in and said that it looked like he could go home. Luckily, James had some money, so we'd been able to take a cab instead of trying to make it by bus. By the time I got him to the office, I was ready to collapse.

I saw Farley standing by the window, watching the sun go down. He didn't turn. Didn't acknowledge our rather dramatic entrance or anything, and I realized I was going to have to find some more strength from somewhere to deal with him.

First, though, I had to deal with James.

"You're not going to throw up again, are you?" I asked.

He shook his head, gently. He still looked green.

"I must have the flu or something," he mumbled. "I never throw up like that."

"Don't worry about it." I sighed and maneuvered him closer to the door of the inner office. "I think if you lie down for a while, you'll feel better."

"Oh, I hope so," he muttered. "Are your shoes all right?"

"Fine. Don't worry about it." I didn't even want to look at my shoes. "Can you help a little bit? You just have to get through the door, then you can lie down."

He managed to put one foot in front of the other until we were in the office, and I got him on to the cot. Before I even got his coat off, his eyes were closed, and he was snoring. I left him lying in a heap, and went back out to Farley.

"I think he has a concussion or something," I said. "I don't think they should have let him out so soon."

Farley turned and stared at me, and I quit talking about James. I was right. Something had happened to him.

"You don't look so good," I said, cautiously.

"I don't feel so good."

"What's wrong?"

"I dunno," he said, and sighed. "Maybe that dumb fuck Jimmy gave me his stomach flu." He leaned against the desk, then sank to the floor. "What do ya think? Can Jimmy give a dead guy stomach flu?"

"I don't think he has the flu, I think he was reacting to the pain killers," I said. "What happened?"

"I went out for a walk," Farley said. "I met a dead guy."

"A dead guy? You mean a ghost?"

One ghost seeing another ghost didn't happen all the time, but often enough that I didn't have to tell Farley he was doing something else completely off the chart. It usually happened when they were both at the same Phase of Acceptance. I wondered who it was he saw.

Farley slid flat on the floor, staring at the ceiling. He glanced at me, saw I was staring at him, and he rolled over on his side, his face away from me.

"Yeah," he finally said. "A ghost. Just like me. I figured I should tell you."

"Thanks," I whispered.

Farley simply interacting with another ghost shouldn't have brought on feelings of sickness again.

"What else happened?"

"Your mom called," he said, and waved at the desk. I looked at the phone, red light flashing. "She left a message. You might want to listen to it before Jimmy boy wakes up. She has a bit to say about me."

Oh. Had my mother given Farley bad news? Could that be why he was looking as terrible as he was?

"What did she say?"

"I don't know, some shit about something," he mumbled. "I couldn't figure it out. She doesn't think I'm ready to move on yet, though."

"Oh."

"And you're supposed to be nice to me."

"Oh?" I felt my mouth quirk in a half-smile. Trust Farley to hear that.

"I'm not kidding. That's what she said. I'm delicate or something." He shuddered, as though the very thought of him being delicate was more than he could bear. "She says you're supposed to let me stay with you, until I do figure it out."

"Oh." I thought about pushing the button so I could hear the message. He'd obviously missed some important information— Then I realized Farley was staring at me, the look on his face intense.

"So?" he asked.

"So what?"

"You gonna let me stay?" The words rushed out of him as though he'd been holding them in forever. "I know this isn't what you want, it interferes with your plans and all, but . . . What do you think? You gonna stick with me to the end?"

He looked at me with such naked need, I realized what was making him weak. It was me. Again.

He didn't know if he could trust me to be there for him to the end and I didn't blame him. All I'd done since I'd met him was try to figure out ways to get rid of him. I'd tried shortcuts, and nastiness, and fighting with my mother. It was time for me to do the right thing by this guy, and actually start helping him. Really, this time.

"Yes," I said. "I'm going to stick with you to the end."

"Thank you," he said, and then hastily wiped his eyes on his sleeve.

"Every time I look out at the sun, I keep thinking about my wife," he whispered. "And my daughter, as she was growing up.

And my grandfather." He sniffled, and then wiped his nose. "Even that ornery son of a bitch."

His life. He was remembering his life. I was almost certain that was a very good sign, but decided to shut my mouth for once, and listen to my mother's message. I didn't want to hurt Farley any more than I already had.

I had to start doing the right thing for this guy.

"I'm going to listen to Mom's message," I said. "I'm not sure what to do next."

"That's a good idea," Farley replied. "Getting advice from you mother is a very good idea. Not like my grandfather." He shuddered. "He was mean. Did I tell you that?"

"No, you didn't," I said. I reached up and pressed the voicemail button, and the machine started.

"Marie," my mother's voice quavered. She sounded sicker than the last time I'd spoken to her. "You're really having a run of bad luck, aren't you? Maybe it's time for you to come home. I've always got room for you here." She sighed, then started coughing, and I wasn't sure she was going to be able to stop. Finally she did, and after she caught her breath, she continued.

"About your friend, Farley. I've been doing some thinking, and you know, you didn't do badly. I wanted to let you know that. Be gentle with him, dear, but help him see what he needs to see. It isn't the way he died, or who killed him. That's not what's holding him here. The manner of death never is, though it sometimes makes for a good book.

"No girl, it still comes down to him figuring out why he lived his life the way he did. From what you've said, he doesn't sound ready for that yet." She stopped speaking, and I reached for the button, certain she was done.

She wasn't. Not quite.

"I probably shouldn't have said that into this machine, should I?" she whispered. "Sorry dear. Give me a call. I'd love to hear from you." And then she was gone.

I deleted her message, then went back to Farley. "It still comes down to you figuring out why you lived your life the way you did," I said. "Once you understand that, you will be able to move on."

I couldn't tell if he was listening to me or not.

"Did you hear me, Farley?" I asked.

"Yeah," he said. "I heard you.'

He was staring at the floor as if mesmerized.

"The grain of this wood sure is nice," he said. "Nice, straight line to it. Good wood. A person can appreciate wood like that."

He tilted his head, caught my eye, and smiled.

"Know what I mean?" he asked.

I really didn't, but before I could ask him what he meant, he disappeared before my very eyes.

Stage Three
Seeing What He Needs To See

Farley:
This Wasn't Like Before

This wasn't like before, when I'd blinked away to that horrible nightmare place where I'd died.

This time I went back to my childhood, when I was six—

Marie:
Making the Phone Call

I stared where Farley had been, and tried to think. Exhaustion was overtaking me, because way too much had happened, but there had to be something I could do.

I struggled to my feet, and sat down at the desk. Mom said Farley had to figure out why he lived his life the way he did so he could move on. I was still convinced that his daughter Rose was the key. It had to do with the way he lived his life concerning her. He had to deal with this. I was convinced of it.

I called information, to see if I could get her number, half-onvinced that I wouldn't find her. She was probably happily married and listed under her husband's name. Maybe she was living on the other side of the world. Something to make this all very hard.

She wasn't. There was exactly one "R. Hewitt" in Edmonton, and when I dialed the number, I knew it was her, before she said hello.

She sounded remarkably good, for someone who had lost her father such a short time before. So good, I suddenly didn't want to bother her. But as I looked at the spot where Farley had disappeared, I knew I needed to finish this. For him.

"My name is Marie Jenner," I said, using my best receptionist voice, and hoping she wouldn't think I was calling about a survey or something and hang up before I had a chance to get the right words out. "I knew your father. I think we should talk."

She sighed, and when she answered again, she didn't sound as good.

"Are you with a paper?" she asked. "I already told you guys, I'm not giving interviews. My father's death was not news. You understand?"

"I'm not a reporter. I knew your father, and I have information for you. I think you should hear it."

She sat silently for a moment, and though she were trying to decide whether to hang up or not.

"Please," I said. "Hear me out."

"All right." Her voice was tight. Angry. "What do you want to tell me that's so important?"

"Your father—your father —"

"What about him?"

"He—loved you. Very much." I felt my face heat as I spoke the words, and wondered, for the briefest moment, what I was trying to prove.

"Who did you say you were?" Rose's voice had sharpened, and I could hear hints of Farley there.

"I'm Marie Jenner."

"How do you know my father?" Her voice faded. "Were you his girlfriend or something?"

"What?" *Me,* Farley's girlfriend? What a horrible thought.

"Well, well," she continued. "He got himself a girlfriend. And a young one, by the sound of your voice. Sounds like he finally found a life, at the end."

The conversation had severely derailed, so I tried to get it back on track. I needed to have her meet me, have her talk to Farley through me. I needed this more than I was willing to admit.

"I wasn't his girlfriend. *Really.* I think you and I should get together and talk about him. How he lived, how he died, stuff like that."

"I'm sure you mean well, but I'm not meeting you. And I'm not talking about my father to you. He and I parted ways a long time ago, and now he's dead. Going over it won't bring him back."

I glanced at the spot where Farley had been, half-expecting to see him reappear.

"You might be surprised," I murmured. "I think it's important that you understand how much that man loved you—"

"I do know," Rose replied. "I understand completely, Marie. I loved him too. But loving him wasn't enough, you know? He couldn't get past his compulsion to keep me safe, and for my own sake, I had to leave. He couldn't let me grow up, couldn't let me make my own mistakes, couldn't let me be. I've forgiven him, because he couldn't help it. I know that. I've moved on."

"He died thinking you thought he was an asshole," I whispered. "You can't have thought that of him. Did you?"

"Yes I did. Because he was." She chuckled. "I know he couldn't help it, but he was."

"But—" I wanted to stop her, wanted her to take the words back, because this wasn't the way I had this playing out in my mind. She was supposed to admit she had unfinished issues with him, we were supposed to meet over his grave, she was supposed to cry and say that she loved him, that she didn't think he was an asshole—and he had to hear her, so he could move on. But it wasn't going to happen. None of it.

"Let it go, Marie," Rose said. "I made my peace with my father years ago. It might not seem like it to you, but I have."

I thanked her for her time, and put the receiver down. Farley had been right. They really were done. He didn't need to see her again. I felt my throat close, and the tears come. Sometimes you don't get closure—not the way they do in the movies, anyhow. Sometimes all you get is what you have. No matter how much it hurts.

I sat down beside the place where Farley had disappeared, and waited for him to come back. I didn't have a clue what I was going to say to him, or how I was going to help him. Not a clue.

Farley:
Dreaming of Grandpa Harry

I am with Grandpa Harry and I'm helping him fix the fence. The horses broke it down, and then got out on the highway, and Grandpa's mad, again.

My gloves are too big and they keep getting caught on the barbs and slipping off and it's funny, kind of, so I laugh, but Grandpa Harry doesn't like that because we have to get the work done. It's important, more important than anything, so I make my hands big so the gloves stay on and I can hold the wire the way he wants but I can't and I wish for a minute they could be like Mickey Mouse's, nice and big like that with their own gloves painted on, then Black Jack, one of the horses, comes over for a visit and I look away from the wire for a second so I can breathe in Jack's warm grass breath, and the glove pops off.

The wire whizzed away from my hand and caught Grandpa Harry right under the eye. It flicks out a chunk of skin and flesh, and then there's blood, and I'm not laughing anymore, because the wire snarls around me as I try to grab it and get it away from him so he can fix his eye, and then, as I grab for it, my glove dances further away, speared through by the barb, and I feel the wire biting me, biting me, and Grandpa Harry looks at me and growls, blood slipping down his face like red tears and I've never seen him cry before, and he says, "I TOLD you to hold the wire, boy!"

I know I'm gonna get it, so I try to dance away, but the wire is holding me, and Grandpa Harry already has his belt out and I can't get away, but I know not to cry or say sorry or anything, because you have to take it like a man.

Grandpa Harry's hard hand clutches my arm, crushing the wire into my skin, and I close my eyes and wait because you never know where he will start—but the belt doesn't whistle through the air, and instead of more growls I hear him say, "Well, that's not right," very softly, as though he's really surprised at something. I open my eyes a crack and watch the belt fall from his hand, and I watch him go down to his knees slow, like he's tired, and then he says, "Help me, boy," before he falls face first into the fence.

It curls around him, and it curls around me, and I am bound to my grandfather by the biting, snarling wire.

It takes me a long time to get free and run back to the house to get help. Black Jack follows me all the way, dancing around me like he wants to play, his tail up like a black tattered flag.

It takes me too long, and Grandpa Harry dies. It's all my fault, but I don't cry. I take it like a man, and make the promise on his grave that I'll never let anyone close to me ever get hurt like that again.

Ever.

I didn't blink back the way I had before. I sobbed as the old man, lying broken and bleeding in the snarl of barbed wire, faded and faded, leaving me nothing but the sky blue of his shirt, and a faint whiff of his aftershave. Then that paled, and in its place was Marie, leaning over me, yelling into my face.

"What?" I said, my throat still so tight I could barely speak. "What do you want?"

"Oh, Farley!" she yelled, falling into me and bawling her fool head off. I was too tired to move, so I let her heart beat in my chest for a while, and let her warmth touch the coldness of my soul.

Marie:
Farley's Confession

I realized I was acting like a blubbering idiot, and tried to stop. Watching Farley slowly coalesce back to being, crying, "I'm sorry, I'm sorry, I'm sorry," as bloody scratches covered him, and then slowly faded. Where had he gone? Who was he apologizing to? What the heck had happened to him?

I pulled away from him, and saw, as the scratches faded away to nothing, that he was beginning to glow more brightly than I'd ever seen before. He groaned, and shifted, pulling at his shirt as though something had him bound.

I heard James moving around in the other room. "I'll be right back," I whispered, and tried to breathe warmth into Farley's cold face. Instead of responding, he flopped back and stopped moving. It frightened me. "I promise. I'll be right back."

I ran to the inner office, and caught James trying to get up.

"What's wrong?" I asked, trying to sound all calm so I could get him back in bed. He smiled at me, still zonked by the drugs he'd been given in the hospital.

"Nothing," he said. "It sounded like you were crying out there. You weren't crying, were you?"

"No," I whispered, feeling my throat tighten as I said the words. "But I have work to do. Lie back down. If you need anything, give me a holler."

"Give me a holler. That's cute." James stared up at me blearily. "You're really cute, you know that? Even with the visions and all, you're really cute."

"Visions?" I didn't need this. Not at all.

"Yeah. Visions. Like down in the restaurant. You had a vision, right? Don't worry, I think it's very attractive. Everything about you is pretty darned attractive . . . " He waved his hand in front of his face, and momentarily distracted himself with it, laughing like a loon. It was not a pretty sound, but I was glad to hear it. With any luck, he wouldn't remember a thing when he finally did wake up.

"He's tanked." It was Farley's voice, and even though I knew he was still in the other room I could hear him as though he was standing right next to me. Almost like he'd spoken in my head. As I wrestled James back into bed, I wondered how he'd done that. Spoken in my head, without moving.

"You go to sleep now," I said to James. "You'll feel better when you wake up."

"I hope so. My head really hurts." He opened one eye, and then the other. "I have something to tell you, Marie. A secret."

Not now.

"Just go to sleep, James—"

"I was working for my uncle, you know. When I took that job at the Palais. The handyman job was a cover. So I could get the information about Latterson, and then get out. But then, I met you."

"Oh." I didn't know what else to say. I honestly felt frozen.

"Yeah, I met you, and everything changed. I'm sorry I lied. Not a good way to start a relationship, is it?" His smile faded as he fell asleep.

I stared down at him and tried to digest what he'd just said. He'd lied to me about his job and his uncle. And he'd used me to gather the information he'd needed for his case. He'd lied to me.

And I'd lied to him. He was right. That was no way to start a relationship. I gently closed the door and settled down on the floor beside Farley again.

"Can you hear me, Farley?" I was afraid he couldn't, and that I'd lose him, that he'd end up wandering around, trying to find someone else like me, who could do a better job. Stuck, for all time.

"Cut Jimmy boy some slack," he whispered.

"What?"

"The big hero." He turned his head and stared at me, his eyes glowing intensely. "He was doing a job. And he finally did come clean."

"Oh, so you heard that?" I looked over at the closed door. "I don't know. He lied, Farley. How can I trust him?"

"Figure out a way. He's going to do that for you, when you finally come clean." He smiled. "He cares for you. A lot."

"He does, doesn't he?" I asked, a shiver running down my spine. "All right. I'll try, Farley. I'll try."

"Good." He closed his eyes briefly, then opened them again, staring at me. "Did I tell you about the dead guy?"

This time I could barely hear his voice, though I was right beside him. "Yes, you did."

"I think you should help him. He was crucified. Down by a church. Should be easy to find him."

I almost laughed. "Yeah, probably, but I honestly don't know how much help I am to the dead, Farley. Look at what I put you through."

"It wasn't that bad," he said, then laughed. "Well, maybe it was, but promise me you'll help that guy out. He really looked like he could use a hand."

"I promise I'll try," I said. And I meant it.

"Thank you." He leaned back, looking exhausted.

"Can I ask you something?" I asked, afraid he'd say no.

"Yes," he said, his voice sounding like wind over water.

"What did you see? When you disappeared?"

He stared up at me, his mouth working. Then he closed his eyes, and tears clung like glowing embers to his lashes.

"I saw my grandfather. He looked after me, when my mom took off. He was a mean old man—and he was all I had." He opened his eyes, and the pain in them was so real, I felt like I was suffocating.

"I let him die," he sobbed. "I couldn't save him."

"When did this happen?"

"I was six."

"Oh Farley. You were a baby." I could feel my heart breaking—literally breaking—for this man. "His death was not your fault."

"That sure as shit determined the way I lived the rest of my life," he whispered. "Didn't it?"

He glowed more brightly, and tiny flecks of red and orange began to whirl in his aura. "I decided then and there I would never let anyone get hurt on my watch. I would save everyone."

"Even if they didn't need to be saved," I whispered.

Rose had been right. He didn't need closure with her. His grandfather was the key. I had been completely wrong.

"Yeah," he said, and closed his eyes, his aura gaining strength. "Even when they didn't need to be saved." He chuckled. "I guess I was a pretty shitty knight in shining armour, wasn't I?"

"Not all the time. You saved my butt, Farley. And Helen Latterson. You saved her too."

"Yeah. I did do that, didn't I?"

He nodded, and the colours flared as the white of his aura brightened and stretched. I could feel that he was ready. Finally, Farley was ready to move on. There was only one more question I had to ask him.

"What do you want to do now?"

He smiled, the most beautiful smile I'd ever seen on that old man's face.

"I want to start again," he said. "I missed a lot this time, I think. If I could, I'd start over."

"Then you probably will," I said as his aura ran over my hands and up my arms, like electrified silk.

"I feel good," he said, and his glow brightened even more.

"I know."

"I wish I'd had more time to—you know—get to know you."

"And I'm going to miss you, Farley." I meant that, with all my heart.

His aura had reached my face, and I bathed in its light for a moment, before pulling myself away. This was not for me, no matter how good it felt. This was for Farley alone.

"Promise me one more thing, will you?" he asked, his voice getting lighter, less substantial by the second. "Make sure you deal with your dad. Because I'd guess that no matter how much he fucked up, he still loves you. Just like I love my Rosey."

"My dad?" I stared at him, unable to move, unable to think past that point. "My issues with—"

"Your dad. Yeah." He smiled. "I know about that stuff. I can tell you're mad at him. Don't let his mistakes bind you so tightly you can't live. Rose didn't, and I'm proud of her for that. She's a good kid. You'd like her, I think."

"I probably would," I said, and touched my head to his one last time, letting my strength run to him so that he could finally move on. "Thank you, Farley. Thank you."

Then Farley saw the light. And it was beautiful.

Marie:
Life after Farley

I stayed on the floor as Farley's light flickered away to nothing. I knew there were things I had to do, but I couldn't convince myself to get up.

That changed fairly quickly when the outer door opened and a woman stepped into the room.

"I'm sorry, we're not open for business," I yelled as I scrambled to get up off the floor. The woman didn't move, just stood, framed in the doorway, until I was on my feet. I stared at her, and couldn't believe who I saw.

"Andrea Strickland?"

It was Ian Henderson's old secretary from the Palais, appearing perfect, as usual. I was wearing Salvation Army blue jeans and one of James' sweatshirts. "What are you doing here?"

"Mary?" she asked and she smiled at me, all cool perfection, as I tried to pull some semblance of order to my hair, then gave it all up. She wasn't noticing me, anyhow. She was trying to make certain the waning light from the window was catching her profile just so.

"It's Marie," I said. She shrugged.

"I didn't know you got a job here. How cool! Isn't Jimmy a sweetie?"

Andrea held her pose one more moment, to be sure I saw how

perfect she was, then walked over and gave me a quick hug.

"I heard you ended up in the hospital after the explosion. Wasn't that just terrible? Did you see that horrible woman attack me? I almost got killed and she attacked me!" She sighed theatrically and sat down in the chair in front of the desk.

"Is Jimmy in his office? I have to talk to him, I've got a situation brewing and I need his advice."

She posed dramatically for a moment more. When I didn't react appropriately, she frowned.

"So, can I talk to him or what?"

"Are you talking about Jimmy Lavall?" I sat down in the chair behind the receptionist desk. It was a good thing I did, too, because my legs began shaking. I needed to drink water, a lot of it, very soon. But first, I had to deal with Andrea.

"Well, yes. Who else would you think I'd want to talk to?"

"You can't talk to Jimmy."

"Why not? Is he out of town? God, that guy goes out of town more often than I change my underwear!" She got up and sashayed impatiently in front of the desk. "When's he coming back?"

"He's not coming back." I gestured to the chair she had so recently vacated. The water and everything else was going to have to wait. "Sit down, please. I have something I have to tell you."

After I told Andrea that Jimmy the Elder was dead, and Andrea had a cry, I persuaded her to tell me why she needed a private investigator.

"It's not really for me this time, it's for my cousin," Andrea sniffed, dabbing at her eyes. "She got herself into a bunch of trouble, and I needed Jimmy to help her out." That brought on a fresh round of tears, and I handed her the entire box of tissues instead of doling them out one at a time.

"What happened?"

Andrea dug around in her oversized purse and pulled out a newspaper with "Death by Crucifixion!" emblazoned across the front page. She opened up the paper, and placed it on the desk in front of me.

"The police think she's involved, somehow. In this." She pointed at the huge headline, and then at the picture of the victim. "They think she killed him. She's a nut bar, but she wouldn't kill anybody. I'm sure of it."

I stared at the picture of the tree, which was situated in front of Holy Trinity Church, not four blocks from here. I realized this was the place Farley had told me about, before he moved on. The ghost Farley had seen was the guy who'd been murdered. And Farley had told me exactly where he was.

"Andrea, I know the perfect person to take this case." I tried to smile as I spoke, though I felt like I was talking through cotton, like I was suddenly stretched as thin as spider web. I needed to hydrate desperately.

"Oh, who? Somebody good, I hope, because my cousin is in it deep."

"It's the guy who now owns this agency. It's Jimmy's nephew, James."

"Oh, isn't that cute!" Andrea's mouth quirked up. "He won't have to change the name on the door or anything. Is he any good?"

I thought of James lying in the other room, his head swaddled in bandages, trying to sleep off the smack to the head he received in his last case, and I snorted. It made me feel better. Closer to normal. Whatever that is.

"He's the best money can buy." I glanced down at the headline, and then over at her, trying for a sprightly smile. "And he has a good team."

"So, do you think he'll take the case?"

When he learns how to be a detective, he will, I thought.

"Yes, he probably will."

I glanced back at the closed door that separated James from us, and hoped he'd keep quiet a bit longer. "He'll be back later this evening. We'll get in touch with you, then."

"Wonderful!" She stood and hugged me again, before heading for the door. "I'm so glad to see you. We must do margaritas again, soon."

Then she was gone, a not-so faint whiff of her perfume hanging in the air.

I walked over and grabbed a glass, pouring myself some tepid water, and downing it as quickly as I could. As I poured myself a second glass, I glanced back at the newspaper article, and shrugged.

"This one will be easier than Farley. After all, I know where the dead guy is, and we know he's been murdered. All I have to do is go down to the church and talk to him. I mean, how hard can that be?"

I drank most of the next glass, and sloshed over to the desk. I was doing this because both James and I needed some money so we could pull our lives back together. Oh, and I had made that promise to Farley. I was determined to follow through on that. Those were the two big reasons I'd agreed to take this job.

After that, I'm done. After that, it's a normal life.

I mean it this time.

Acknowledgements

Wow. Where to start? I guess at the beginning. My thanks to the 3-Day Novel contest, where I met Farley Hewitt and Marie Jenner for the first time. (This was also where I learned how much I love caramel apples!) I didn't win, but I won. You know?

To Billie Milholland and Ryan McFadden. It feels like we've been friends forever. You two held my hand through the many iterations of this story (plus all that other crazy stuff we tried) and kept me more or less sane. More or less. I don't know what I'd do without you.

I have so many friends in the writing community, I barely know where to start. But some of you had a direct impact on this book, so... Aaron Humphrey, thanks for pointing out Marie needed a real voice in this story. You're the reason I ended up writing it this way! To the rest of the Cult of Pain, thanks for helping me beat the beginning into submission. Chad Ginther, thanks for telling me what genre this story was, for real. Best book whisperer, ever! Janice MacDonald and Randy Williams, you are both so giving of your time and your expertise, we in the genre writing scene in Edmonton are lucky to have you. (And my launch dress is going to look spectacular!) To Robert J Sawyer, thanks for your support for all these years. You're a good teacher and a good friend.

Now, to family. Jess, thank you for reading the very first raggedy ass version of this novel from beginning to end, even though you had finals and had to study. You helped me realize I just might have something worth keeping. (And your first cover idea is still hanging in my office, as inspiration.) Thank you Jon, for convincing all your friends that they just might like reading my stuff as much as you do. Thank you Mom, for listening to me ramble on, hour after hour, about my imaginary friends and all the trouble they cause. And thank you Harold, for giving me the space to actually be a writer, this time, for real. I love you guys!

Special thanks to Guillem Mari for the amazing cover art, to Lucia Starkey for the cover layout, and to Ryah Deines for the interior layout.

And finally to Margaret Curelas, publisher, and one of the bravest women I know. Thanks for wanting to see this story out in the world as much as I did.

Biography

E.C.Bell (also known as Eileen Bell) has had short fiction published in magazines and several anthologies, including the double Aurora Award winning Women of the Apocalypse and the Aurora winning "Bourbon and Eggnog." When she's not writing, she's in Edmonton, Alberta, living a fine life in her round house (that is in a perpetual state of renovation) with her husband, her two dogs, and her ever hungry goldfish.

ALSO FROM TYCHE BOOKS

One's Aspect to the Sun
by
Sherry D. Ramsey

Captain Luta Paixon of the far
trader Tane Ikai needs to know why
she looks like a woman in her
thirties—even though she's actually
eighty-four. She isn't the only one
desperate for that information.

With the ruthless PrimeCorp bent
on obtaining Luta's DNA at any cost,
her ninety-year-old husband asking
for one last favour, and her estranged
daughter locking horns with her at
every turn, Luta's search for answers
will take her to the furthest reaches
of space—and deep inside her own
heart.

Helix: Blight of Exiles
by
Pat Flewwelling

Perfected by nature. Twisted by
science. A miracle cure gone very, very
wrong.

An abandoned forest resort should
have been paradise for a creature like
Ishmael. Isolated from civilization, so
far removed from human eyes, Ishmael
could have reveled in his true nature
without threat of discovery.

But he had been abducted, drugged
and marooned there, sent into exile by
the cryptic Wyrd Council.

And he's no longer the apex predator.

WWW.TYCHEBOOKS.COM

CPSIA information can be obtained
at www.ICGtesting.com
Printed in the USA
BVHW030744280421
605987BV00001B/7